THE JADE STEPS

The Story of the Liberation of Mexico
by One of History's Most Heroic Women

Jack Wheeler

The Jade Steps
The Story of the Liberation of Mexico by One of History's Most Heroic Women

Published by Vervante
18685 Main Street #101-457
Huntington Beach, CA 92648
www.vervante.com

Design and Layout
Redshed Creative Co.
www.redshedcreative.com

Printed in the United States of America

ISBN 978-1-4507-0981-1

First Printing, 2010

To Rebel, Brandon, and Jackson

Prefatory Note

This story is true. It actually happened. Every named person is a real person with that name. There are no fictional characters – save for the story's interlocutors. Every event, every battle, every public speech actually took place, as chronicled by eyewitnesses.

Few stories of history are more extraordinary than the creation of Mexico by Cortez – and equally few are more distorted. Thus the real story remains unknown. It is the story of one of the most heroic women of all of human history.

This is her story. May it bring peace to the civil war waging within the soul of Mexico.

Table of Contents

Pronunciation Guide for Aztec Words and Names

A note on the spelling and pronunciation of Aztec words. Nahuatl, the Aztec language, was not a written lanuage until Spanish priests transcribed it with an often confusing orthography that has become traditional.

Unless the pronunciation for an English speaker is obvious, the first time a Nahuatl word or name is used, its phonetic spelling will be in parenthesis. Thereafter, please consult this Pronunciation Guide. One exception is *Mesheeka*, the original pronunciation for Mexican/s. It was the name the Aztecs exclusively applied to themselves and no one else in the land that was to become Mexico, and will therefore be used throughout.

Axayacatl – *ah-shah-yah-cottle*

Camaxtli – *kah-mashed-lee*

Chalchihuite (jade) – *chal-chee-wee-tay*

Chichimecatecle – *chee-chee-mek-a-tek-lay*

Cihuacoatl ("Snake Woman" – Royal Counselor) – *see-wa-ko-wattle*

Cimatl – *see-mottle*

Citlalpopocatzin – *seet-lal-popo-cot-zin*

Citlatepetl – *seet-la-tay-pettle*

Ciuacoatl – *si-wah-kwottle*

Cohuixin – *ko-week-shin*

Conacochtzin – *kona-kotch-zin*

Cuatzacualco – *kwats-a-kwahl-ko*

Cuitlahuac – *qweet-lah-wok*

Cuitlalpitoc – *qweet-lal-pee-tok*

Huexotzinco – *way-shot-sing-ko*

Huitzilopochtli – *weet-zil-o-poached-lee*

Ixkakuk – *eesh-ka-kuk*

Ixtlilxochitl – *ish-tleel-zoh-cheetle*

Iztaccihuatl – *ish-tox-see-wattle*

Izta Quimaxtitlan – *ish-ta qwee-mosh-teet-lan*

La Malinche – *la-ma-lin-chay*

Malinche – *ma-lin-chay*

Malcuitlapilco – *mal-qweet-lah-pilco* (end of the line of prisoners)

Maxixcatzin ("Ring of Cotton") – *mah-sheeks-cot-zin*

Mixquic – *mish-qweek*

Motelchiuh – *mo-tell-chee-you*

Nauhcampatepetl – *now-campa-tay-pettle*

Nezahualcoyotl – *nesha-wal-coy-yottle*

Olintecle – *oh-lin-tek-lay*

Popocatepetl – *po-po-kah-tay-pettle*

Quetzacoatl – *kwet-za-kwattle*

Quiahuitztlan – *qwee-ah-weets-tlan*

Techcatl (sacrificial stone) – *tetch-cottle*

Tecuichpotzin – *tay-qweech-pot-zin*

Teculehuatzin – *tay-coolie-wat-zin*

Teipitzani ('evil-blowers,' sorcerers who blow evil upon others) – *tay-pit-zah-nee*

Temilotecutl – *te-meelo-tay-cuttle*

Tendile – *ten-deal*

Tenochtitlan – *ten-osh-teet-lan*

Teocalhueycan – *tee-oh-kal-way-con*

Teocuitlatl (gold) – *tee-o-qweet-lottle*

Tetelpanquetzal – *teh-tul-pan-qwet-zul*

Teteotcingo – *te-tay-oat-singo*

Texcoco – *tesh-coco*

Tianquizlatoatzin – *tee-ahn-qweets-la-twat-zin*

Tizapacingo – *tiz-ah-pah-ching-go*

Tlacatecolotl ('owl-men,' wizards who cause magical illnesses) – *tlaka-tay-co-lottle*

Tlacaxipeualiztli (The Flaying of Men) – *tlah-kashee-pay-wal-eesh-tlee*

Tlacochcalcatl ("Spear House Chief" – Royal military commander) – *tla-coach-kal-cottle*

Tlatoani – *tla-tow-ah-nee*

Tlaquiach – *tlah-qwee-otch*

Toltequequetzaltzin – toll-tay-kway-kwayt-zalt-zin

Tzompachtepetl – *zom-potch-tay-pettle*

Xochicueyatl – *zo-chee-kway-yottle*

Xocotlan – *sho-coat-lan*

Chapter One

CASA COLORADA

Tim and Cindy Jorgenson were having a terrific honeymoon. After a week on the beach in Puerta Vallarta at the "rich and famous playground" of El Careyes Resort, they were spending a few days in Mexico City. They had found the famous canals of Xochimilco far too touristy, however. A ride in one of the *trajinera* boats had proved to be an experience to endure rather than enjoy, with its swarms of vendors shouting for them to buy their wares, and the floating *mariachi* bands coming alongside and wanting too many pesos to play.

Instead, the couple decided to take a break from tourist sites and spend the afternoon in an old part of the city called Coyoacan. In the Nahuatl language of the Aztecs, the term translated to 'the place of coyotes.' Coyoacan was far older than the Aztecs, having been founded by the Toltecs in the 7th century A.D. In modern times, Coyoacan's tree-lined, narrow streets were filled with cafés, boutiques, art studios, museums and colonial homes, splashed in a palette of pastels. There was no nicer place for a relaxing afternoon in all of Mexico City than Coyoacan.

Tim and Cindy marveled at the 16th-century frescoes lining the ceiling of San Juan Bautista church on the Plaza Hidalgo, then indulged in an overly-large piece of chocolate cake at La Mucca Espresso Café, behind the church.

Needing a stroll after such a caloric extravagance, they meandered along Calle Higuera, a street leading diagonally off the plaza. After about three blocks, they came to a small, shaded park, the Jardin de la Conchita. As they settled down on a park bench, they noticed a woman across the street.

She was standing on the sidewalk in front of a faded, rose-colored, two-story house with "57" on it: 57 Calle Higuera. She looked as if she were praying to the house, her arms stretched up and open in supplication. She then brought them down and clasped her hands together in the gesture of prayer.

When she reached out again in wide supplication, she began calling out in a loud voice, as if she were beseeching someone, but neither Tim nor Cindy could make out the words. The windows of the house were shuttered and remained so. No one came to the door. A policeman sauntered up, hesitated, and then began to shoo her away. Wiping tears off her cheeks, the woman walked across the street to the park, sat down on a bench and, oblivious to Tim and Cindy, began to softly sob.

She must have been at least in her fifties, judging by the gray streaks coursing through her dark hair, which was pulled back into a bun. She was dressed plainly, but not poorly, in a serviceable black skirt and white linen blouse. Her only jewelry consisted of a simple gold wedding band and a gold crucifix suspended on a thin chain. Her face was not deeply wrinkled, nor were her hands, so it seemed likely that she had not spent her life toiling in some farmer's field in the sun. Her nails were neat and clean, indicating that she probably lived and worked in the city.

Concerned and puzzled, Cindy approached the woman and asked gently, in her passable Spanish, *"Estas bién?"*

Not looking up, the woman nodded.

Cindy indicated the house across the street. *"Qué casa es?"*

"Casa Colorada," came the mumbled reply.

"The Red House?" Tim echoed doubtfully, glancing from it to Cindy and back again. "Doesn't look very red to me - sort of dusty pink. Ask her who she was praying to - somebody in the house?"

When Cindy did so, the lady's reply was barely audible.

"She says she was praying to someone named *La Malinche*," Tim's new bride informed him. "She calls this person *La Madre de Mexico* - the Mother of Mexico."

Tim pulled a fresh bottle of mineral water from his pack and offered it to the lady.

The woman accepted it with a gracious nod of her head and for the first time looked up. Her eyes were glistening and she gazed directly at them.

Tim and Cindy glanced at each other. "There's an old soul behind those eyes," Cindy observed softly. Nodding in agreement, Tim said, "This lady is no peasant. She has a real look of intelligence."

A bittersweet smile brightened the lady's face. "Thank you for the water," she said in English. "My name is Maria Consuelo de la Rodriguez, and I speak English. I am a document translator for a company that does much business with the United States."

"Wow!" Tim exclaimed, as Cindy asked, "Who is...?" With a smile, Tim deferred, and Cindy asked,. "Who is 'La ma-*lin*-chay'? Does she live in that old house?"

"She did almost five hundred years ago. Cortez built the home for her. It is the oldest home in Mexico City today," came Maria's reply.

"Cortez? Hernando Cortez?" asked Tim. "The conqueror of Mexico?"

Maria's eyes narrowed. "You mean the *liberator* of Mexico. It was Cortez who liberated the peoples of Mexico from the butchery of those Aztec cannibal bastards. But he could not have done so without" - Maria pointed at Casa Colorada - "La Malinche!"

"I was always taught in school that the Aztecs were the innocent good guys," Cindy mused, "while Cortez and the Spanish Conquistadors were the evil bad guys."

Maria's face contorted in contempt. "That's what those *cabezas del huevo*— "

"Egg heads," Cindy whispered to Tim.

" – in the universities, here and in *Los Estados Unidos,* tell you." She shook her head in wonder. "Why do the people who think they are so smart and educated make themselves so stupid? Maybe because they are so afraid of the truth."

"What *is* the truth?" Tim asked.

"The truth," Maria responded, her gaze smoldering, "is that I, like the majority of the people in this country, am *mestizo*. There are over a hundred million Mexicans, and some seventy million of us are not pure Indian and not pure Spanish, we are *both*, mixed together. And none of us would be here today if it were not for *her*." Again, she pointed to Casa Colorada. "We owe our very existence to La Malinche, and that is why we Mestizos call her our Mother." Maria's voice lowered. "The truth is the most amazing story ever told - but it is one that all of the professors and writers and poets are afraid to tell."

"Could you tell us?" asked Cindy, and Tim nodded his encouragement. "We have open minds – don't we, Tim? And we certainly don't believe everything our professors back in California told us."

"It is a long story…" Maria said warily.

"We've got all afternoon," Tim assured her. "We're on vacation. In fact, we're on our honeymoon."

"Yes," added Cindy, "you could look upon your story as a wedding present for us!"

That made Maria smile. "How can I resist the opportunity to tell two *Americanos* the truth about the history of Mexico? I have studied this history for many years in our libraries. It is my passion." She took a slow breath, and settled herself more comfortably on the bench. "Well, then, the story begins with a little girl. She is a princess, the only daughter of a powerful king who loves and adores her. Her name is Malinali…"

Chapter Two

PRINCESS

Malinali giggled. It was the kind of squeal and squeak that only a little girl who is deliriously happy can have. She was hiding behind a curtain in her father's palace.

"Ixkakuk! Ixkakuk! (*Eesh-ka-cook*)" her father called out, using his nickname for her, meaning Beautiful Goddess. "Where are you? I can't find you!" He crept up to the curtain. "But when I do, I'm going to" – he grabbed the bulge in the curtain – "tickle you to death!"

The little girl's shrieks of mirth rang through the palace. King Teteotcingo (*Te-tay-oat-singo*) released his grip, and Malinali raced away across the throne room, laughing and yelling, her father chasing after her.

The uproar reached the ears of Malinali's mother, Queen Cimatl (*See-mottle*), in an adjoining chamber attended by her courtiers. She sighed disapprovingly. "You would think the King would have more important matters of state to attend to than playing with little girls."

Malinali was on the verge of being captured by her father when an old, dignified woman entered the throne room. "Malinali," she called, "it is time for your lessons."

The King looked down at his child. "Go with Grandmother Ciuacoatl (*Si-wah-kwottle*), Ixkakuk. Mother, what will she be studying today?"

"What all young girls should be learning – cooking, sewing, learning to run a household," came Ciuacoatl's answer.

"A household?! Mother, Malinali is my only child. She must be raised to run not a household, but a kingdom! One day, she will be Queen of Paynala, the most powerful kingdom in Cuatzacualco (*Kwats-a-kwahl-ko*)!"

"Teaching her how to be a good queen is your job," Ciuacoatl smoothly informed her son. "My job is to teach her how to be a good wife and mother." With that remonstration, she took little Malinali by the hand and led her out of the room, as Queen Cimatl walked in.

"And just how do you think a woman is going rule Paynala, my King?" she inquired. "It's a man's job, isn't it? Especially when it comes to dealing with our Aztec masters."

"Don't you dare give me that innocent smirk, Cimatl," Teteotcingo riposted. "If you think you know a woman's place so well, then I would advise you to behave that way. You may run along now and focus on your queenly duties." The King nodded to an attendant, who courteously escorted Cimatl from the room.

* * * * *

As the years passed, Teteotcingo spent more and more time with Malinali, developing her speaking skills, as well as the arts of reasoned argument and persuasion. His favorite place to do so was underneath a large tree by a stream that ran near the palace. "A ruler must lead his people by the force of his words and his mind," he explained. "He cannot lead by his muscles alone." He flexed his arm. Malinali squeezed the huge bicep admiringly. "Well, it does help for a ruler to be strong," he said with a smile. "But to be strong in here" – he pointed to his chest – "and here" – he pointed to his head, "that is more important, especially for you."

"*Tahtli*[1], what can we do about the Aztecs?" she asked.

Her father stiffened. "The Aztecs are monsters from hell," he pronounced. "They were a tribe of savages from the northern deserts not long ago, a place they call Aztlan. They hired themselves out as mercenary soldiers for kingdoms around the Mesheeka Valley -- *mesheeka* is a weed that grows in the valley's Lake Texcoco (*Tesh-coco*), and is what the Aztecs call themselves now. They don't like to be called *Azteca* – people from Aztlan – anymore as it reminds them of their primitive origin. So we still call them Aztecs to insult them.

---

1   *Tahtli* means 'father.'

"When they got strong enough, they conquered those same kingdoms and began building an empire. Now their empire has grown far beyond the Mesheeka Valley. They conquered Paynala and all of Cuatzacualco when my father was young. Every month now, their tax-men come to collect our food, our riches - and our men for sacrifice. As I said, child, they have built a huge and wealthy empire, but one that is evil at its heart. Someday, if the gods permit, we will be rid of it."

"Do I have to learn Aztec Nahuatl, *Tahtli*?" she asked plaintively.

"Yes, you do, Little Miss Dry Grass" -- Malinali meant "dry grass," and was the name of the winter month in which she was born[2] -- was the answer. "Our dialect of Nahuatl is different from theirs. Few things will be more important for you as Queen than to be eloquent in the language of our oppressors. So let's get back to studying your pictograms[3]."

* * * * *

By the time Malinali was twelve, it was obvious she was going to become an exceedingly beautiful woman. Tall for her age, she stood erect with a royal bearing. She remained playful and unpretentious, however, teasing her grandmother and intentionally changing the ingredients during her lessons in herbal medicine to drug unsuspecting Ciuacoatl fast asleep so that she could run off and explore the forest unattended.

Teteotcingo was determined that his daughter know how to fight, so he gave her lessons in handling a copper-tipped lance and a wooden obsidian-edged sword, the latter so sharp it could slice off an opponent's head or arm in one swing. As Teteotcingo parried his daughter's thrusts during a practice session, he smiled proudly. "You are getting strong, Ixkakuk! That's right - harder, faster!"

Suddenly, the King dropped to his knees and grasped his chest. He looked up at his daughter, bewildered, and gasped for breath.

Malinali screamed, "*Tahtli! Tahtli!* What's happening??"

The King rasped, "Get your grandmother…"

---

2   December, 1500.
3   The Aztecs' form of written communication was a detailed form of picture-drawing.

They were the last words Malinali would hear her father speak. By the time she had brought Ciuacoatl, accompanied by the court physicians, to where her father lay, it was too late. The King was dead - and Malinali's childhood was over. Life for the Princess was about to take a very bad turn.

Chapter Three

SLAVE

After Teteotcingo's funeral, Queen Cimatl asked to see her daughter. "Malinali, there is something you must know," the Queen said. "A kingdom requires a king, and now Paynala no longer has one. So I have decided to marry the brother of my sister's husband, Cohuixin (*Ko-week-shin*). I must, you realize, always put the interests of Paynala and its people first."

Malinali was so stunned, she lost her composure and blurted, "The Lizard-Man[4]? You are going to marry the Lizard-Man!? Mother, how can you insult our people, insult me - insult yourself! - and insult the memory of King Teteotcingo in this way?" She obviously did not care for her mother's choice.

"It will soon be King Cohuixin," Queen Cimatl responded firmly, "and he will be your king, and your father. The decision is made."

Malinali exploded. "You are only fooling yourself, Mother, if you think I will ever regard the Lizard-Man as my King, much less my Father!" Suddenly, though, the young Princess saw the image of her father in her mind, and thought, *My father would not lose his temper in such a situation. Calm down and think clearly, Malinali - right now!*

She took a deep breath and spoke again before her mother could chastise her. "And yet, Mother, if this is your decision, I accept it. Tell the Lizard-Man to enjoy a few years of ruling Paynala. But, as you know, *I* am the legitimate heir to the throne - the *only* heir - and when I come of age, just six winters from now, *I* shall become Queen, and you and your Lizard-Man may enjoy a happy retirement without the cares of ruling. In the meantime, my only

---

4   *Cohuixin* means "lizard."

request is that you keep the Lizard-Man away from me. I want nothing to do with him."

Her mother stared emptily at her. Finally, she said, "As you wish... Ixkakuk," and glided out of the room. Queen Cimatl had never before called her by her father's nickname, and she pronounced it not affectionately but with a prolonged, icy sneer, leaving Malinali feeling as if her marrow was frozen.

* * * * *

Malinali spent as much time out of the palace as she could from then on, hunting deer with her spear in the forest, or gathering herbs and medicinal plants for her grandmother. What time she did spend in the palace was with Ciuacoatl, who consoled her grief and taught her all she knew about the healing arts.

One day, she returned from the forest to hear the noise of a celebration in the village adjoining the palace. Walking through the streets, disguised as always by a plain cotton cloak, she heard people shouting, "A son! A son! A Royal Prince! A son!" She had known for some time that her mother was pregnant, but had never dwelt on what that might mean for her, since she did her best never to think about her mother at all. *So,* she thought now, listening to the villagers rejoice, *I have a brother! It's not his fault who his parents are. It might be fun. I shall try to be a good sister to him...*

With these thoughts, she returned to the palace with a sense of expectation. Near the gate, she noticed a group of nomadic traders. There was nothing unusual about that; those kinds of folks were a common sight, wandering from town to town, selling their trinkets and handicrafts. When they approached her to regard their wares, she politely brushed them away, as she normally did. One of them, however - a short, stocky fellow with enormous forearms - stepped forward, grabbed her arm, and said, "Are you sure you don't want to buy something... Princess?"

She tried to pull away but the man was far too strong. "How do you know who I...?" Her words were cut short as the man and his followers threw a heavy blanket over her and carried her away. No one seemed to notice in the twilight, and her muffled protestations went unheard.

She was carried for a long time, then set down by a campfire. The blanket was removed, and she was bound tightly. She said nothing, inspecting her captors one by one until she could discern their leader, the man with the bulging forearms.

Her silent stare made the man uneasy. "Yes," he said, "there is no doubt. You are your father's daughter, the Princess Malinali. Unfortunately, you are also your mother's daughter, which means that you are a princess no longer."

"What am I then?" Malinali demanded, shocked by his words.

"Your mother intends for her new son to be king. You were in the way, and so… she has sold you to us."

"Sold me?" Her eyes flared. *"What do you mean, 'sold' me? I am Princess Malinali, the future Queen of Paynala, and you will release me immediately!"*

The man shrugged. "You are not even alive, much less a princess."

Malinali gasped. "What do you mean, 'not alive'? I may be tied up but I am not dead yet."

Forearms wagged a finger at her. "Oh, yes, you are. By chance, the daughter of one of the workers in the palace died yesterday from some fever. She was just about your age. Tomorrow, your death will be announced, and there will be a great grieving and burial ceremony. While it will be that girl's body that will be buried, not yours, you will still officially be dead."

For the first time in her life, Malinali felt real fear. Her insides clenched, as if she was going to throw up. Shaken, she stared blankly into the flames of the fire for a long minute. Then she looked up at Forearms. The firelight played across his wide face. He was looking at her with an expression that almost seemed like sympathy. She looked around at the others, sitting in a circle with the firelight dancing over them.

"We are not bad people, you should know that," said Forearms quietly. "We are not going to harm you. Your mother paid us a lot of money to take you, and you are now our *tlacotli*[5]. We own you, and you must do as we tell you. Your mother did what she thought she had to do. But she made us promise that we would not mistreat you or share you among the men - and we will keep that promise."

The only sounds were the crackling of the fire, and the word *tlacotli - tlacotli – tlacotli -* reverberating with a pounding force inside Malinali's brain.

---

5   *Tlacotli* – tlah-coat-lee -- means "slave."

She passed into unconsciousness.

* * * * *

"Malina! Malina, wake up! There is work to do!"

Malinali felt herself being rudely shaken. It was Forearm's wife, and Malinali looked up at her uncomprehendingly. Slowly, she realized that she was unbound, and that someone had put a blanket over her. The fire was in embers and dawn was breaking.

"We cannot call you Malinali. It would draw attention," the woman explained. "Your name is now Malina. Come, we need to get water for cooking, and quickly. We need to be off before the sun is over the treetops."

Following the woman to the stream, she asked, "Where are we going?"

The woman pointed to the right of the rising sun. "To Xicalanco (*Sheeka-lan-ko*). That is where we are from."

"Xicalanco? Isn't that in Yucatec[6]?"

The woman cast a wary glance over her shoulder at Malinali. "Yes. How do you know this?"

"My father taught me much about the world," Malinali replied, and sighed. "Xicalanco - it is far away from Cuatzacualco…"

The woman stopped and spun around. "Malina, don't you understand? You are dead there! If you ran away and went back to Paynala, you would be killed. Your home is now with us, for you have no other."

Malinali realized that the woman was right, and that she had better start thinking clearly. When they reached the stream and had filled their tightly-woven baskets, she asked, "Your accent, is that Yucatec?"

"Yes. We are Maya. But as traders and travelers, it is important for us to speak Nahuatl, as well."

"Could you teach me to speak Maya?"

Again, the woman eyed her. "Yes, I will teach you. My husband will approve. It will bring a higher price for you when we sell you in Pontochan. That's on the way to Xicalanco."

"I know where Pontochan is," Malinali hissed. "But I thought you said my home was with you."

---

6   Yucatan, land of the Mayas.

"Only until we sell you. My husband is sure that the King of Pontochan will pay a good price for you. From now on, Malina, your home is that of whoever owns you."

They walked back to the camp in silence.

Chapter Four

STRANGERS

And so Malinali trudged through the forest and swamps to Pontochan, where Forearms sold her to the King. She was living in a palace again, but now as a slave, not a princess.

Malinali soon became very appreciative of Ciuacuatl's lessons because, given her skills at sewing, cooking, and medicine, she was assigned to the household staff and not put out into the maize or cacao fields as a manual laborer.

Five winters passed. She became fluent in Maya, and learned how to do her work well and quietly, so as to be noticed as little as possible. She listened attentively, however, and began hearing talk of mysterious strangers who lived in gigantic war canoes. No one knew where they came from. Their skins were light, and they had hair on their faces. Some wore metal on their bodies. Their canoes had carried them across the salt water from the south. They had stopped at the mouth of the Pontochan River and tried to talk to a group of Mayas, but no one could understand what they were saying. The strangers had continued across the water to the north and had not been seen again.

The palace hummed with talk of who these strange people could be, and soon that talk turned into an uproar. Various sub-chiefs appeared before the King and demanded to know why these strangers had been allowed to land in Pontochan. "They should have been repulsed!" was the charge.

"But the strangers did us no harm," the King protested. "Why should we have done harm to them?"

"Because we know warriors when we see them," said a sub-chief. "These were men of war. They were dangerous, and yet we did not fight them. Now all of our neighbors are laughing at us and calling the Pontochans cowards. Should those strangers ever come back, we must attack them, kill them, and rescue our honor." All the other sub-chiefs loudly concurred.

"Very well," concluded the King. "If they return, we will be ready."

But the strangers didn't come back. The summer passed, then the winter. By springtime, Malinali and everyone else had forgotten about them. Then, one morning, the huge white cloths of the strangers' giant canoes were spotted on the horizon.

By the time the giant canoes came into the mouth of the river, hundreds of Pontochan warriors lined the banks. The giant canoes continued up the river to a small island across from the Pontochan capital. Malinali came out of the palace with everyone else to see. She was stunned at the size of the strangers' canoes. She heard one of the sub-chiefs say, "These are not the same men as were here before, but obviously they are the same kind of men, and we shall fight them anyway."

The next morning, all the women and children were taken out of town, to the edge of the forest. Malinali managed to place herself where she could see the strangers on the island. Over a thousand Pontochan warriors were awaiting the 200 or so strangers as they rowed in small canoes across the river towards them. When they got close, one of them stood up and started talking to the warriors in a loud voice. The warriors responded with a volley of spears, stones from slings, and arrows, accompanied by derisive yells and blasts from conch shell horns.

Immediately, fire and smoke burst from the giant canoes, and smaller bursts of fire from metal tubes the strangers were carrying. Suddenly, the Pontochan warriors were falling down, bleeding and wounded, by the dozens. The strangers poured out of their small canoes, struggled through the mud and mangrove trees on the bank, and began cutting down the warriors with metal swords. Then, from out of the forest to her right, Malinali saw another group of 100 strangers attack the warriors from the rear. "They prepared well for our attack," Malinali noted grimly, as she saw the Pontochans caught in the pincers of the strangers and cut to pieces. The remaining warriors fled into the woods.

The strangers then marched into the town, past the two big temples and a number of adobe houses to the town square. In the middle was a large ceiba tree. The man who had first stood up and spoken in the small canoe, thus prompting the Pontochan attack, seemed to be their leader. He took out his sword and, with powerful strokes, cut three deep gashes in the bark of the tree, then said something to his men. They responded with cheers.

Malinali was fascinated. She felt little sympathy for her Pontochan masters who, after all, had instigated the battle. But now she was hustled away with the others. They all marched inland for some distance, to a valley called Centla. All day long, Pontochan warriors from surrounding villages streamed into Centla. At night, the bonfires burned high as all the sub-chiefs rallied their men, urging them to annihilate the "white skins" who had come from nowhere.

By the next morning, 30,000 Pontochan warriors had formed into five divisions, all armed with bows and arrows, slings for throwing darts and stones, and charred-tipped wooden spears. They wore thick, quilted cotton armor, had painted their bodies as colorfully and as menacingly as possible, and were proudly donning their feather headdresses. Their chiefs positioned them cleverly on a slope of cleared ground called the Plains of Centla. They outnumbered the strangers by 100 to 1.

Again, Malinali managed to secure a good vantage point to watch the spectacle. Surely, said those around her, the strangers were about to be destroyed.

When the strangers appeared, they did not hesitate. Immediately, the few hundred men facing 30,000 warriors... attacked! They ran straight into the center of the mass of warriors and began hand-to-hand fighting. *These are the bravest men I have ever seen*, Malinali thought. Then she saw a detachment of strangers struggling to pull large metal tubes on round, rolling circles across the swampy mud of the field. As a swarm of warriors sent a cloud of arrows and darts at them, wounding several, the tubes flashed fire, and the swarm was swatted away.

Thousands came after them, yelling cries of vengeance. After almost an hour of incredibly fierce fighting on both sides, the warriors were finally beginning to push the strangers back into the swamps. Then Malinali heard something like thunder.

Another group of strangers had made its way around Centla, and began attacking the warriors from behind. Malinali screamed in terror, as did every-one with her, for this group of strangers weren't men - they had transformed themselves into huge, godlike animals with four legs and two arms, racing faster than any man could run, crushing warriors underneath them and slash-ing with swords from above.

All the others around her ran away into the trees, but Malinali was trans-fixed. She watched as, with wild shrieks of utter terror, the warriors broke and fled for their lives, leaving thousands of their fellows dead on the Plains of Centla.

Malinali found the King and his retinue where they had retreated to a nearby village. Nobody could say anything. Their minds had gone blank with awe and fear.

No one slept well that night. The next morning, however, two sub-chiefs appeared whom the King thought had been killed. Instead, they had been captured by the strangers, and they were now bringing a message.

"There is one among them who speaks our language," they said. "Through him, their chief says that this battle was our fault, and that we must blame ourselves for all of our dead. He says that he will do us no further harm if we remain peaceful. To show that we intend to be peaceful, he orders us to bring food and presents at once."

Thus forty sub-chiefs, dressed in their finest cotton robes and caparisoned with jeweled feathers, appeared at the strangers' camp in the town square, accompanied by several dozen slaves bearing turkeys, fish, maize, and honey.

Malinali was among them.

Chapter Five

THE LEADER

The leader of the strangers stood underneath the big ceiba tree he had slashed with his sword. He addressed the sub-chiefs assembled in front of him through the stranger who spoke Maya.

"I come to you from the greatest king in the world, His Majesty Don Carlos of Spain. The mighty country of Spain lies on the other side of the Great Ocean, and we have crossed it to trade peacefully with you and to instruct you in the religion of the One True God.

"His Majesty Dos Carlos commands us to come in peace, yet you attacked us and tried to kill us for no reason. We do not understand why you attacked us, but you must understand that, if you try to attack us again, we will kill you all. You saw yesterday the power of our lightning-bearers. The lightning-bearers are still angry with you, and it is hard for us to control the death-fire they carry in their bellies…"

Without warning, one of the huge metal tubes lined up on the edge of the square went off with an enormous explosion and a belch of fire. No one was hurt but, just the same, Malinali fell to the ground terrified like all the sub-chiefs, who proceeded to call out to the strangers' leader, asking his forgiveness for their aggression and disobedience.

The leader accepted their pleas. "His Majesty Don Carlos forgives you. He commands you now to return to your villages, to return to your homes in this town, and to work without fear. Go, therefore, to your people and tell them this, and tell them to be ready to trade with us when we come among them."

The sub-chiefs were amazed at the leniency of the strangers. They had fully expected that a number of them would be tortured, killed, and eaten - the normal way that captured enemies were dealt with by their victors. To show their appreciation, they presented the leader and other strangers with gifts of golden ornaments - a lizard, a duck, two dogs, earrings, and other objects.

The leader asked where the golden artifacts came from.

"They come from Mesheeka, the land of the Aztecs," he was told. "It is the richest land in the world, far to the west, whose armies shake the ground when they move."

The leader looked closely at the sub-chief who said this, but Malinali noticed that it was a look of interest, without fear.

Before they left, a sub-chief asked the stranger who spoke Mayan, "May we ask your leader his name?"

For the first time, the leader smiled. He answered, "I am Captain Hernando Cortez."

* * * * *

By the afternoon, the King of Pontochan, followed by his retinue and a horde of townspeople, entered the town. The King showed no fear, but he and all the rest expected a trap.

There was none. Some of the strangers were camped in the square, while others were back in their giant canoes. The King could not believe they had not taken over his palace. Indeed, the strangers had not even ransacked it to steal what they could.

"What kind of people are these 'Spaniards,' as they call themselves?" Malinali overheard the King ask one of his attendants. "What kind of gods do they believe in, that they would act this way?"

The King ordered that food and presents be delivered to the Spaniards, several of whom went through the town and traded for jewelry, feathers, and ornaments with small transparent stones of different colors. Their leader, Captain Cortez, was not to be seen. Malinali thought he must be back on his giant canoe.

The following morning, the Captain appeared at the palace and requested that the King accompany him to the battle-site at Centla. Assembling a large retinue of servants, including Malinali, the King walked in a long procession with the Captain and the Spaniard soldiers to the Plains of Centla. There, they found that another group of soldiers had placed a large cross of wood in the ground. The cross was painted white.

The Captain spoke to his men, and the man who spoke Mayan interpreted for the King.

"This Cross commemorates our great victory at this spot. To be victorious against such impossible odds means that Heaven fought on our side. Our own strength alone could never have prevailed over such a multitude of enemies. Let us give thanks to the One True God for this victory, and know that His purpose for us is to bring the word of Him to the people of this land."

With that, the Captain and all of his men, without exception, went down on one knee and bowed their heads for some moments.

Arising, the Captain addressed the King. "You are now the vassal of His Majesty Don Carlos of Spain. This Cross is the symbol of our religion and of the One True God. You are to make sure it stays here forever. Our King commands us to continue our journey, so we depart from you in peace. When we return, we expect that it shall be in peace, also. If you dare to attack us again, you will die."

The King could not believe his good fortune. He had tried to kill these strangers, they had fought back, conquered him instead, and now they were leaving! His cacao and maize fields weren't destroyed, his palace and capital were not burned down, his wives were not raped, and his men in the hundreds or thousands weren't killed and sacrificed to the strangers' gods!

Overwhelmed by relief and gratitude, the King ordered that twenty slave girls be presented to the Captain. "You will need women to cook and clean and care for you on your journey," he told the Captain. "Please accept these twenty slaves as a gift from the Pontochans, who are now your friends and vassals."

The Captain received the offer graciously from the King and expressed his appreciation. With that, the procession returned to the town, where the Spaniards collected their belongings and camp-gear, boarded the small canoes, and rowed across the river to the giant canoes at the river island. Twenty slave girls were sent with the Spaniards.

Again, Malinali was one of them.

Chapter Six

DOÑA MARINA

My third set of masters, Malinali thought to herself. These people, these 'Spaniards,' were different from any others she had known or even imagined. They seemed to her to almost be not of this earth. *Perhaps they are from the stars*, she thought.

Are you afraid of them, Little Miss Dry Grass? she asked herself, summoning her courage, her sense of humor, and the memory of her father all at once. Yes, a part of her was afraid, of course. Who wouldn't be? But then she heard her father's counsel: *"What reason do you have to be afraid? Have these strangers shown themselves to be cruel and unmerciful, or kind and forgiving? They are impossibly fierce in battle, yet impossibly generous in victory. Use your intelligence. Learn how to gain the respect of these Spaniards. Never forget, Malinali, that you are a still a Queen! Never show any fear!"*

Her thoughts were interrupted by the words of the stranger who spoke Mayan. He addressed them all, assembled on the floor of this great floating home.

"In the name of His Majesty Don Carlos and Captain Hernando Cortez, you are welcomed to our ship, the *Santa Elena*. My name is Señor Jeronimo Aguilar. Your king has given you to us as a gift, but we cannot accept this gift until you undergo a purification ceremony we call 'baptism.' In this ceremony, you will be asked to accept the One True God and His Son, Jesus Christ, and to renounce all false gods. We cannot force you to do this. You must do this by choice. But you will be returned to your king unless you do so. Do you understand my words, and do you agree?"

One of the women asked, "How much do you cut us with knives in your ceremony? How much blood does your god need from us?"

Aguilar's eyes widened in shock. "Jesus Christ does not want your blood. He wants your love. He loves you as he loves all children of God. All He asks is that you return this love."

Then he smiled. "I see. You think that the One True God is no different from your gods, who always want torture and sacrifice. No, the One True God is very different from any god of yours. You will see. We purify you not with blood, but with water."

The women all cast furtive, wondering glances at each other. Malinali spoke first. "I will accept," she announced.

The nineteen others quickly followed.

Another stranger stepped forward, dressed differently from the rest. He wore a dark brown hooded robe with a rope belt, and he carried a small black object. A cask of water was placed in front of him. He looked at the black object and spoke words in his language while waving a metal cross over the water. He then beckoned for Malinali.

Aguilar asked her, "Do you accept the One True God and His Son Jesus Christ as your savior, renouncing all false gods?" She nodded in assent. The robed man then took a ladle of water and poured it over her head while speaking in an odd tongue.

"What is your name?" Aguilar asked her.

"I am called Malina," Malinali said, not wanting to give her real name.

Mistaking the 'l' for an 'r' in her pronunciation, Aguilar announced, "You are now christened *Doña Marina*." Addressing her by her new name, Aguilar looked at her gravely and said, "Doña Marina, you are now a Christian."

Malinali still had very little idea of what he meant. Nevertheless, she had made the choice to stay with these Spaniards, rather than return to her Pontochan slave-masters, and she was glad she had made it.

A tall man stepped up to Malinali. "Doña Marina," Aguilar said to her, "this is Don Alonzo Hernandez Puertocarrero. He is of noble birth, and is the cousin of the Count of Medellin." Malinali wasn't sure what this meant, but she kept on listening intently. "Captain Cortez has assigned you to him. You are to prepare his meals, wash and mend his clothes, and look after his equipment. Do you accept this duty?"

Malinali glanced briefly at her latest master. She had become quite expert at discerning the signals given off by those who controlled her life, and how those signals revealed their personalities, thoughts, and desires. She quickly saw what Aguilar meant by "noble birth," for Don Puertocarrero carried himself with a natural dignity and elegance. The look in his eyes toward her was respectful, rather than crude and lustful. Although relieved that she had been given to this sort of man, she said nothing to Aguilar, merely nodding her head in assent.

* * * * *

Living in a floating village sailing on the Great Ocean soon became a thrilling experience for Malinali. She could not communicate with her new master except through gestures, but that enabled her to do her tasks quietly and stay unnoticed. She had the other Mayan women to talk to. Still, whenever she could, she focused on Aguilar, the one person through whom she could learn about these 'Spaniards.'

"Señor Aguilar, how is it that you speak Mayan?" was her first question to him. "You are the only Spaniard who does."

"Ah, you wish my story!" he said with a smile. "I, like all the others, come from Spain, in my case from a small village called Écija in the region of Andalusia. I heard of the discoveries of a New World across the ocean when I was a young boy, and I joined a crew to sail to a place called Panama. That was nine years ago[7]. The next spring, I was assigned to accompany a Captain Valdiva, who was carrying a report to our Governor in Santo Domingo on the island of Hispaniola.

"Our ship sank, hitting shoals off a group of small islands we call the Viboras[8], near the big island of Jamaica. About twenty of us, along with Captain Valdiva, made it into a small boat, and the currents carried us to Yucatan. There were only ten of us still alive, and Mayans called Calachiones captured us when we landed. They killed Captain Valdiva and four others, and ate their bodies in a fiesta. The rest of the survivors and I were put into cages to be fattened.

---

7   In 1510.
8   *Viboras* means "vipers."

"But we broke out and fled. Eventually, we came to another village. The chief there, Shamanzana, didn't kill us but he made us slaves. It was there that I spent the next eight years and learned to speak Mayan. Three more of us died, and only Gonzalo Guerrero and I were left. Gonzalo married the daughter of a powerful chief, Na Chan Can, and had three children. But I always dreamed of escaping, and every day read my Book of Hours[9].

"My prayers were finally answered when messengers came to tell Shamanzana that my countrymen had come to ransom me. I ran to tell Gonzalo, but his wife cursed at me and chased me away. So I left alone with the messengers – but when we reached the place where the ships were supposed to be, they had left. I threw myself down on the ground and cried in despair. The messengers then told me that the ships had sailed to *Cuzamil*, known as Swallow Island[10]. In a small canoe, we paddled across the dangerous waters to the island, only to learn that the ships had sailed the day before.

"I was ready to drown myself, but then, suddenly, I saw the ships returning! By a miracle, one of them had sprung a leak, so they were returning to *Cuzamil* to repair it. The two Mayans and I paddled fiercely up to the ship with the captain's banner flying, and I called out, 'Gentleman – are you Christians and Spaniards?' They answered, 'Yes.' Overcome with joy, I yelled, 'God and Saint Mary of Seville!'

"When I came on board, Captain Cortez asked, 'Where is the Spaniard?' – for I did not look like one. My skin was dark brown from the sun, and my hair was shaved like a slave's. I had an old sandal on one foot, with the other tied to my belt, and I was naked but for a ragged, torn cloak and a filthy loin cloth. I squatted on my haunches like an Indian and clutched my Book of Hours, old and worn, wrapped in leaves. I replied, 'I am he.'

"Cortez ordered clothes for me, a shirt and doublet, pants and sandals, and I told him my story. He embraced me and said God had brought us together."

Malinali was grateful to Aguilar for taking the time to tell his story to her, and she thanked him. "Your life in some ways has been like mine," she confided to him. "I, too, have been a slave for the past eight years. You were fortunate to have someone rescue you."

---

9   A Catholic prayer book from the monastic cycle of prayer, dividing the day into eight segments or 'hours': Matins, Lauds, Prime, Terce, Sext, Nones, Compline, and Vespers.
10   *Cuzamil* means "swallow" in Mayan. The island is known in English as Cozumel.

Aguilar saw the look of pained resignation in her eyes. "Ah, you wish for rescue yourself?" he said. "Doña Marina – you have been rescued, just like me!"

Her eyes widened with wonder.

"You must understand – you are now a Christian!" Aguilar informed her. "Your soul has been freed! You are with us now, and are no longer condemned to a barbaric life."

Malinali's temper flared. "Señor Aguilar, how can my soul be free when my body not? How can I be a Christian like you and still be a slave?"

Taken aback, Aguilar was silent for a moment. Finally, he replied. "Doña Marina, you have asked a very good question." He looked at her carefully, as if truly seeing her for the first time. "You are a very intelligent woman," he mused. "Someday, I will ask you to tell me your story, just as I have told you mine. For now, however, I expect Don Alonso needs attending to."

However politely, she had been dismissed. With a sigh, Malinali returned to preparing her master's evening meal.

Chapter Seven

QUETZACOATL

Malinali soon discovered that Don Alonso was unlike any of her previous masters. True, she had never been roughly abused or raped, either by her Xicalanca captors or the rulers of Pontochan. But Don Alonso exhibited a courtesy to her that the others had not, treating her with dignity. Was it because he recognized her royal birth, or did he and the other Spaniards all make it their practice to treat women differently?

In a way, to her Pontochan masters she had not really existed. She had been invisible to them - an invisibility that Malinali strove consciously to maintain. In particular, she had done all she could to hide her beauty. She hadn't walked straight, tall, and proud – instead, she had compressed herself and slunk around the palace when doing her chores.

She decided to abandon this shrunken invisibility with the Spaniards. She no longer wore her cloak over her head. Her bountiful black hair was now left free to glisten in the sun. She carried herself as her father had taught, regally, with her head high. But she was never insolent, and she obediently did as she was asked, without resentment. She could do this because Don Alonso always made requests of her, not dismissive demands. He treated her as an individual, not as an invisible non-entity.

Now that she was so clearly visible, Don Alonso could not help noticing Malinali's beauty. *Who is this slave-girl who carries herself like a queen? She is perhaps the most beautiful lady I have ever seen.* It was, of course, expected that Malinali stay beside him at night and satisfy him sexually. The same had been expected of her by her Pontochan masters - but for them it had been no more than the occasional relief of a physical need. Even then, she had remained essentially invisible to them. With Don Alonso, it was very different.

Through gestures and facial expression, he always asked her consent. His requests to have sex with her were delivered with a courtesy that made her feel invited, not commanded. This enabled her to willingly comply. She felt that Don Alonso was having sex with her personally, that she was not just some interchangeable, faceless slave. Malinali had never felt sexual desire before, at the hands of her masters, but now she felt it awakening.

* * * * *

As they sailed north along the coast, Don Alonso would stand with Captain Cortez and other men, pointing to various places of interest. It was as if Don Alonso had been there before. Curious, Malinali asked Aguilar if this were true.

"Yes," he told her. "There have been two expeditions of our people here before us. Well, only one, really, because the first one, led by Hernandez de Cordoba, two years ago[11], only reached to Champotan, which is well below Pontochan. He and his men were attacked there by the Mayans. After Cordoba returned to Cuba, he died of his wounds.

"Last year, the Governor of Cuba, Diego Velazquez, sent another expedition, led by his nephew Juan de Grijalva. Several of the gentlemen with us now were with Grijalva - Don Alonso, Pedro de Alvarado, Francisco de Montejo, Alonso de Avila, and others. There is even one man who was with Cordoba as well - Bernal Diaz del Castillo.

"When Grijalva reached Champotan, the Mayans pretended to be friendly, but he was prepared. The Mayans attacked but many were killed. After Champotan, the expedition sailed to Pontochan, where it was received in peace. That is why we did not understand why the Pontochans attacked us. We expected them to be friendly, as they were to Grijalva."

Malinali interjected, "It was because the Champotans ridiculed them and called them cowards for not attacking the strangers as they did."

Aguilar responded, "Perhaps both have learned their lesson now." He continued, "Captain Grijalva sailed where we are going now. Don Alonso

---

11   In 1517.

and Pedro de Alvarado have been telling Captain Cortez of the places they have seen on this coast, like Ayagualulco, which they call La Rambla, Tonolá which we call San Antonio, and this river we are passing now, for which we have no name."

Malinali gazed out at the estuary and its surrounding features, which she recognized with a jolt. "That river is the Cuatzacualco. Near that far hill with the two humps in the distance is where I was born."

"That is your home?" Aguilar asked.

"No," she responded. "It was once, but it is not any longer."

Aguilar noted the bitterness in her voice but chose not to inquire further.

"How far did your Captain Grijalva go?" Malinali asked, to change the subject. "Where does Captain Cortez intend to go?"

"We go to an island just off the coast, to the north of here. Grijalva called it San Juan de Ulua. Nearby, I am told, is another island, a terrible place that Grijalva called *Isla de Sacraficio*, the Island of Sacrifice, for there they came upon an evil temple with an altar to the Devil. Five Indians had been sacrificed there, the night before. Their chests had been cut open, their hearts ripped out, their arms and legs cut off, and the walls were all covered with blood. The people who did that must worship the Devil, and the men were both angry and afraid."

Malinali said, "It was the Mesheeka, the Aztecs. Their gods are always hungry for the blood of those they conquer."

* * * * *

It was a gorgeous morning. The Santa Elena anchored off San Juan de Ulua with the other ships. Malinali was weaving a mat on the deck when Aguilar greeted her. "It is Maundy Thursday, Holy Thursday, Doña Marina. An auspicious day[12]. The men are looking forward to going ashore and…"

He stopped and looked, along with everyone else at two large canoes approaching the ship. The Indians in the canoes were unlike any that the Spaniards had seen, wearing elegantly embroidered cotton robes and loin cloths,

---

12   The day before Good Friday. In 1519, that was April 20. Cortez departed Pontochan on Palm Sunday, April 16.

and resplendent in green feather headdresses and gold armbands. They were welcomed aboard the Santa Elena, which, with its banners and pennants waving from the masts, was obviously the lead ship. They began speaking in a language that Aguilar did not understand; he shook his head in frustration.

No one on the ship understood what these newcomers were saying, newcomers who carried themselves as dignified nobility. No one - except Malinali.

The newcomers kept repeating one word: *Tlatoani*. Malinali pointed to Cortez, whom the newcomers approached. They bowed graciously to Cortez and began addressing him, but to no avail. Cortez spoke quickly to Aguilar and asked him to bring Malinali to him.

"Doña Marina," Aguilar said to her, with Cortez watching closely, "the Captain wants to know why you pointed to him after these men spoke."

"These men call themselves Mesheeka," she answered. "They are also known as Aztecs. They asked who among you is Tlatoani, which means Speaker, the one who speaks for and leads you. Thus I pointed to Captain Cortez."

"You speak their language?"

"Yes. It is very similar to the language of my home."

"Then excuse me, Doña Marina. I must explain all of this to the Captain, who wishes to know who you are."

There followed exchanges in voluble Spanish between Aguilar, Cortez, and Don Alonso. It seemed that Cortez had never noticed Malinali before, so busy had he been with the expedition. He was certainly noticing her now.

"Doña Marina, Captain Cortez wishes you to explain what these 'Mesheeka' are saying to me in Mayan. Then I will explain it to him in Spanish."

When Malinali addressed the Aztec messengers, they drew back and looked at her in surprise. Women were not supposed to speak in public. For a woman to address any man other than her husband, or a close relative such as her brother or father, was an insult to the man. Yet here was a woman who appeared to be one of them, not of these strangers, and who spoke their language as well as they did, but who presumed to speak directly to them.

Moreover, if it was ever necessary for a woman to speak, perhaps to answer a question, she must always do so in a hushed, barely audible tone, with her eyes lowered, never daring to raise her eyes to a man's level and actually look at him. This woman, however, was both speaking to them in a normal tone of voice, looking right at them as a man would look at another man. The Mesheeka emissaries found it deeply unsettling.

The shock in their eyes passed quickly, but Malinali saw it, and knew exactly what had caused it. She had to glance away and stare out at the sea with the sunlight sparkling off it, in order to suppress the urge to burst out laughing. The look on their faces was the funniest thing she had seen in many years.

She felt a surge of happiness fill her soul, something she hadn't experienced for a very long time. Then she heard her father's voice of caution: *Be careful, Malinali. Do not make these Aztecs suspicious of you. Instead, be a mystery to them.*

Taking a calming breath, she turned back to the emissaries. However she might try, she could not resist standing tall, but she did avoid assuming the airs of the Queen of Paynala.

"The Tlatoani requests that you introduce yourselves and make your wishes known to him," she said flatly, and then relayed their response to Aguilar. "They say that they are messengers from the governor of this place, whose name is Tendile (*ten-deal*) and who gets his power from the Great Montezuma, Lord of all Mesheeka. They ask what kind of men you are, and why you are here. If you are in need of anything for your men or your vessels, they say they will supply it."

Cortez's answer, which he gave with smiles and flourishes, came back through Aguilar, then Malinali:

"Messengers of Tendile, we are servants of our Great Lord, Don Carlos of our land of Spain, on the other side of the Great Ocean. We come to trade in peace with you and to tell you many important things. We thank you for your welcome. In turn, we welcome you to our ship, and look forward to meeting your governor Tendile."

As Malinali finished, Cortez called out for cups of wine to be offered to the emissaries. There was considerable bowing and raising of cups in salutation between the Spanish officers and the Aztec messengers who, after three cups or so, began to seem quite pleased with everything. Cortez then ordered that transparent blue beads be given to the emissaries, who treated the beads as objects of great value.

As they happily departed, Malinali was asked to tell them, "Tomorrow, we shall come ashore, and wish to invite your governor Tendile to visit us in our camp."

They smiled and nodded in approval as they clambered back into their canoes and paddled off.

Aguilar turned to Malinali. "Doña Marina, Captain Cortez and Don Alonso wish to thank you," she was told. She looked at them briefly and nodded her appreciation. Don Alonso elegantly bowed his head ever so slightly. Cortez met her eyes with a glance as intense as it was quick, then returned to conversing with his officers.

"Aguilar," she said, "May I ask a question? What are the green and blue stones you can see through?"

"They are made of glass," he said with a shrug.

"What is 'glass'?" she wanted to know.

"You have no such thing? You have never seen it?" he responded incredulously.

"No. It looks like chalchihuite[13] (*chal-chee-wee-tay*), which is valuable to the Mesheeka. They were very happy that you had given it to them, as they think it is of a kind they had never seen before - a kind one could see through -- so that it must be quite rare."

"Colored glass beads - rare and valuable?!" Aguilar laughed with astonishment. "I must tell this to the Captain!"

Cortez burst out laughing at Aguilar's revelation, then suddenly became still. Malinali could almost see his thoughts. This 'glass,' evidently of little value to the Spaniards, had suddenly become something important with which to trade with the Aztecs.

* * * * *

The next day, which the Spaniards called "Good Friday," Cortez led his men ashore to set up a camp on a set of large sand hills. They built huts and shelters for themselves, and also for the horses. Malinali was just getting used to those huge animals, learning not to be so frightened of them.

The dogs were another matter. The only dogs she had ever seen were tiny little hairless creatures which were raised as food to eat. The Spaniards, by

---

13   *Chalchihuite* is jade.

contrast, had giant dogs they called "mastiffs," dogs that growled and barked and had large, sharp teeth. Aguilar explained that they were war dogs, used for hunting and to fight in battle. However, the Spaniards had two other dogs that she liked, sleek hunting dogs that ran like the wind. The Spaniards called them "greyhounds."

A large delegation of Mesheeka arrived the following day, led by a chief named Cuitlalpitoc (*qweet-lal-pee-tok*). They brought turkeys, maize cakes, and plums for the men to eat, and large cloths to cover the shelters from the blazing sun. Through Malinali and Aguilar, Cuitlalpitoc explained that the governor, Tendile, would be arriving the next day - whereupon Cortez gifted them with blue glass beads.

The following day, an even larger delegation of Mesheeka appeared, led by Governor Tendile himself. When he was brought to Cortez, Aguilar turned to Malinali with a request. "Doña Marina, please tell Lord Tendile that this day is, for us, a most holy day. It is Easter Sunday[14], the day of the resurrection of Jesus Christ, the Son of God. We are honored by Lord Tendile's visit, and we invite him to witness our ceremony of Easter Mass."

A large wooden cross was placed in the sand. All the Spaniards bowed and knelt before it. Wooden tables were brought, and white cloths placed over them. Burning sticks in holders were placed on the table, which Aguilar had told Malinali were called 'candles.' The man who had baptized her stepped forward, wearing his brown hooded robe. Malinali now knew him to be Friar Bartholomew de Olmedo. In a powerful and beautiful voice, he chanted a ceremonial song in a language Aguilar called 'Latin,' accompanied by his assistant, Padre Juan Diaz. A bell was rung, and all the men recited a prayer in Latin that Aguilar called the Angelus.

Malinali could tell that Tendile was both moved and puzzled. She knew what he was thinking: *Why are these strange men humbling themselves before two pieces of wood - and why does their ceremony consist of chanting and not sacrificing the hearts of human victims to their gods?*

After the Mass, Cortez took Tendile and Cuitlalpitoc aside, beckoning for Malinali and Aguilar. There were just the five of them - with Malinali, of course, the only woman. *I may still be a slave,* she thought, *but I am becoming a very important slave to the Spaniards. How else could they speak to the Aztecs,*

---

14   April 23, 1519.

except through me? She didn't know which was more satisfying, this status with the Spaniards or the knowledge that the Aztecs were scandalized at having to converse with her, a woman.

"Doña Marina," said Aguilar, "please inform Lord Tendile that Captain Cortez comes here at the request of his King, the great Don Carlos, who is the greatest King on earth and has many princes under his command. For many years, His Majesty Don Carlos has heard stories of your great country and of Lord Montezuma, and so he has sent Captain Cortez to tell Lord Montezuma that he, Don Carlos, wishes to be friends and trade in peace. Please tell Lord Tendile that we are Christians, and that our King has sent Captain Cortez to meet with Lord Montezuma, so that he can explain to him many things about the One True God which, once Lord Montezuma knows and understands them, will please him greatly."

Malinali spoke directly to Tendile, and however shocked he was at a woman talking right at him, he seemed far more startled to hear the request. She recognized the tone of haughty sarcasm in his voice, yet translated his reply unemotionally: "Lord Tendile says you have just arrived in our country and already ask to meet with the Great Montezuma. He will relay your request to him. For now, please accept these gifts in his name."

A chest was brought forth, full of gold ornaments like rings and amulets. Tendile's men also presented ten loads of beautiful white cotton cloth interwoven with feathers, as well as food for the Spaniards: turkeys, baked fish, and fruit.

Cortez, in turn, presented Tendile with a number of glass beads, an ornately-carved wooden chair inlaid with blue stones called 'lapis lazuli,' and a crimson cap adorned with a gold medallion. Pedro de Alvarado led his horsemen at a gallop across the sand, while the soldiers paraded to the music of drums and fifes. Malinali had by now learned that the 'lightning-bearers' were not living, but rather were machines called 'cannons' or 'lombard guns.' Tendile and his men, however, did not know it and so, when the lombards fired off in deafening explosions, the Mesheeka fell to the ground in fear.

Cortez held up a handful of the gold rings from the chest. He spoke to Aguilar, who said to Doña Marina, "We call this 'gold.' What do the Mesheeka call it?"

"They call it *teocuitlatl* (tee-o-qweet-lottle), which means 'the excrement of the gods," she replied, and noticed Aguilar and Cortez exchanging looks of amazed amusement. She was then told to ask Tendile if Lord Montezuma had much more of such holy waste, as it cured an 'illness of the heart' possessed by many Spaniards. Tendile answered, 'Yes, a great deal more.'

Tendile then pointed to one of the Spaniards, who was wearing an old, rusty yet gilded helmet. He explained that such a helmet resembled the one of pure *teocuitlatl* that the god Huitzilopochtli (*Weet-zil-o-poached-lee*) wore in the Great Temple of Tenochtitlan (*Ten-osh-teet-lan*), the capital city of the Mesheeka Empire. Would Captain Cortez consider letting Lord Montezuma examine this helmet? Malinali gave him Cortez's answer: "Yes, it is our pleasure - but we request that it be returned filled with gold powder or dust with which to treat the heart ailment of our men."

Malinali could tell that neither Tendile nor Cortez were speaking their true minds. There was some hidden complexity regarding gold for both of them, but she was at a loss to know what that could be. Then she overheard Tendile comment to Cuitlalpitoc, as they were soberly examining the crimson hat, "This gift to the Great Montezuma is red - the color worn by Quetzacoatl (*Qwet-za-kwattle*)," and she saw Tendile glancing at Cortez with a look of fear and wonder.

Then she understood, at least about the Mesheeka. Her father had told her the Aztecs believed in a god named Quetzacoatl, the 'Feathered Serpent.' In the remote past, Quetzacoatl had descended from heaven and taken human form as a priest who condemned human sacrifice. This infuriated another god, Tezcatlipoca (*Tez-cat-lee-po-ka*), the 'Smoking Mirror,' who defeated Quetzacoatl and forced him to leave. Quetzacoatl sailed away across the East Ocean on a magic raft to an unknown land, and promised to return in a One Reed year.

Malinali felt her legs give way at the shock of her thoughts. With her strongest effort of will, she managed not to faint. Aguilar gave her a look of concern, but she nodded, assuring him that she was all right. Soon thereafter, Tendile and his entourage bid their goodbyes, and Malinali could finally find a place to sit alone and reflect. Cautiously, she added up her thoughts:

The Aztec calendar was measured in cycles of 52 years, with each year having a name, like 'One Reed.' Three 'One Reed' years had passed, according to the legend, since Quetzacoatl had sailed away, and he had not come back[15]. This year[16] was the fourth 'One Reed' year… and Captain Cortez had arrived, sailing on a ship so huge that it seemed magical, from an unknown land across the East Ocean! Moreover, the legend described Quetzacoatl looking very unusual - as having white skin and a black beard, again just like Captain Cortez. And Quetzacoatl, in the pictograms of him that her father had showed to her, always wore a red hat!

Further, what had Captain Cortez preached to the Mesheeka and the Mayans: that they should abandon human sacrifices to the gods, just as Quetzacoatl had decreed! *Can it be?* she asked herself. The question was so awesome that it pounded and roared in her brain: *Could Captain Cortez be the human form of the god Quetzacoatl, returned as he promised to destroy the Aztecs for their sin of human sacrifice?*

---

15   The years 1363, 1415, 1467.
16   1519.

Chapter Eight

MALINCHE

Aguilar found Malinali cowering in the lee of a large sand dune. Perspiration was pouring off her, her chest was heaving with rapid breaths, and her eyes were glazed with panic and terror. "Doña Marina!" he cried, "What is wrong?!" He got a wet cloth and patted her brow.

Her eyes slowly focused on him. Finally, she stammered "I… must talk… to Captain Cortez…"

Aguilar was startled. Nonetheless, he said he would relay her request. A few moments later he returned and beckoned, then brought her to the Captain's tent.

Cortez, sitting in his chair, looked up at her when they entered. Malinali stood still, her legs quivering, desperately trying to subdue her breathing and her emotions. Cortez, seeing that the girl was abjectly terrified, motioned for Aguilar to bring her a drink of water.

"Doña Marina," said Aguilar, "what is it that you wish to speak of to the Captain?"

Malinali closed her eyes to listen to her father's voice. *Ixkakuk!* she heard her father say, *a true queen is always in command of her feelings and fears!*

As she opened her eyes, Cortez saw her transform into a different person. Instead of a shaking slave girl who was scared out of her wits, suddenly standing before him was a regally erect woman of extraordinary beauty, poise, and calm - a woman who looked directly into his eyes as she said to Aguilar, "I must ask Captain Cortez if he is a man or a god."

The briefest look of fear passed through Cortez's eyes, and he crossed himself. "There is only One True God," came his answer through Aguilar, "whose Son came to Earth to save mankind, many centuries ago. Please know that I am a sinner like every other mortal human being, and would never commit the sacrilege of pretending I was not."

Cortez and Malinali locked gazes. She realized that he was indeed a man - but a man unlike any she had ever imagined.

"Doña Marina…?" She heard Aguilar's voice as if it were coming from a great distance, so deeply had she fallen into Cortez's gaze. "Doña Marina, the Captain wishes to know why you would think him a god."

As she explained the Aztec legend of Quetzacoatl and how Cortez fit into it, Cortez's gaze never left her. When she finished, Cortez stood up and replied through Aguilar, "Your coming here with the fearful question you had took extreme courage. I wish to applaud your bravery. You have given me much to think about. For now, be assured that I am a man, a Spaniard from Spain, and not this… Quetzacoatl." He took her hand, raised it to his lips, and lightly kissed it. "Thank you… Doña Marina," Cortez said quietly as he looked into her eyes once more.

For the first time in her life, Malinali blushed.

As they turned to leave the Captain's tent, Cortez said, "Señor Aguilar, I have a request for you - I wish for you to teach Doña Marina to speak Spanish."

"It will be my pleasure, Captain," he replied.

* * * * *

Over the next several days, Aguilar found Malinali to be a quick learner. Hour after hour, they would walk on the beach or go through the camp, identifying objects and discussing the meanings of words. "Your brain is like a sponge, Doña Marina," he told her.

After a week had passed, Tendile returned, borne as usual on a litter held aloft by several slaves, and accompanied by a large entourage. With him was an Aztec noble named Quintalbor, who looked almost exactly like Cortez except for darker skin and no beard. Dozens of slaves came forth with food for the Spaniards - turkeys, eggs, and maize cakes. It was, however, sprinkled with what looked and smelled like blood.

Aguilar asked Malinali if this was true. "Yes," she replied, "the Mesheeka put the blood of people sacrificed to their gods on food to honor their guests."

Cortez and his men were nauseated. They spat on the food and angrily threw it back at the Mesheeka slaves. "How dare you insult us so?" he thundered to Tendile through Aguilar and Malinali. He grabbed the hilt of his sword. "I should kill you right where you stand!"

The Mesheeka were terrified. Tendile fell to the ground and begged Cortez to forgive him. Quickly, he ordered the slaves to bring other food, sweet potatoes, guavas, avocados, and cactus fruit. Then he had large cloths and mats spread on the ground, and had laid upon them gifts of treasure from Montezuma of such opulence that they left the Spaniards speechless: an enormous wooden disk, over six feet in diameter, covered in beaten gold to represent the sun, and an even larger disk, covered in silver to represent the moon, both elaborately engraved with astrological hieroglyphics; necklaces of jade and gold and turquoise; gold ducks, jaguars, deer, and monkeys; huge feather headdresses; cotton cloaks embroidered with quetzal plumes and gold…

On and on came the Treasure of Montezuma.

Cortez's anger vanished, and he accepted the gifts graciously. He bade Tendile and Quintalbor to sit beside him, while Aguilar and Doña Marina stood close by, to translate.

"Malinche (*Ma-lin-chay*)," Tendile began, addressing Cortez.

Malinali's head snapped back. Tendile was calling Captain Cortez not by name but as her master, for *Malinche* meant Master of Malina[17]. It signified that the only way the Aztecs had of talking to Cortez was through her. But she had no time to reflect on this, for Tendile was speaking rapidly, with fright in his voice.

"Malinche, I have returned from our city, Tenochtitlan, where I had the honor of telling the Great Montezuma about you. He asks me to inform you that he welcomes you to his land, and sends his most cordial greeting to your King Don Carlos. The Great Montezuma welcomes you with these gifts, and if there is anything more you need, such as more *teocuitlatl* to cure the heart sickness of your men, you need only to ask and it will be provided. The Great Montezuma, however, regrets to say that it will be impossible for you to meet with him. He cannot come here to the sea. He has sacred ceremonies to pre-

---

17   An 'r' sounded like 'l' to Nahuatl speakers. They thus transposed 'Marina' back to 'Malina.'

side over, and it is too dangerous for you to come to Tenochtitlan, as there are too many deserts, mountains and enemies along the way."

Malinali could tell that Cortez was completely unimpressed by Tendile's excuses. Nevertheless, he smiled graciously at Tendile and ordered wine for his guests. *Cortez can smell fear in others,* she thought, *but he is expert at disguising his knowledge.*

She translated his response: "Lord Tendile, I am overwhelmed by the generosity of Lord Montezuma. I deeply thank you, in the name of King Don Carlos. But please understand that my King would be very displeased with me, he will punish me, if I do not meet with Lord Montezuma in person."

Tendile blanched, and replied, "Malinche, we have one more gift for you from the Great Montezuma. Here are four *chalchihuite* stones, which are the most valuable thing we possess. They are worth far more than all the *teocuitlatl* we have. Please send them to your King, as recompense for the Great Montezuma being unable to see you."

The conversation was interrupted by the ringing of a bell. All of the Spaniards knelt before a large cross set upon a sand dune in the middle of the camp, and bowed their heads in prayer.

Tendile asked Cortez why his men humbled themselves before a tree cut to make a cross.

"It is exactly this that I wish to explain to your Lord Montezuma," came Cortez's answer. "This cross represents the True Cross upon which our Savior, Jesus Christ, died so that our souls might live and be blessed. Our Savior is the Son, the Only Son, of the One True God. We humble ourselves before the Cross to confess our sins and ask God's mercy and our salvation. We also ask for the salvation of you and Lord Montezuma. Your gods are false gods. They are evil, and for sacrificing the lives of human beings to them, your souls are damned. It is my moral duty as a Christian to explain this personally to your Lord Montezuma, so that he may understand the truth and abandon the evil beliefs which curse your land."

As Malinali translated Cortez's words, Tendile's eyes registered continual shock. When she finished, there was silence, as Tendile struggled to compose himself. Struck speechless by the audacity of Cortez, all he could do was bow and ask Malinali to say they were leaving.

She did so quickly. Then she moved towards the Mesheeka as Tendile was being lifted into his litter, and listened carefully as the Mesheeka nobles talked among themselves. The hundreds of Aztec slaves Tendile had brought with him, and who had been providing food for the Spaniards, were told to leave. As they did so, Tendile spoke with his entourage. Malinali, skilled at not being noticed, continued to listen. Finally, the entourage, together with the bearers carrying Tendile's litter, marched off -- and Malinali went to find Aguilar. She had something very interesting to tell Captain Cortez.

* * * * *

After Aguilar ushered her into Cortez's tent, Cortez said nothing, simply listening as her words came tumbling out in a mix of Spanish and Mayan. Soon, his glance told Aguilar to have her stop and to translate her Mayan into Spanish, as usual.

"Doña Marina wishes to inform you, my Captain," Aguilar said, "that as the Mesheeka were leaving, she overheard them talking about you and Montezuma."

Cortez's eyebrows arched. "And what did they say?"

"When Lord Tendile came to the Great Montezuma's palace in Tenochtitlan," came Malinali's tale, "to tell him about his meeting with you, it was late at night, yet a great ceremony was prepared. Tendile and his escorts were brought to the main hall, where there are captives kept in cages ready for a sacred sacrifice whenever needed. Montezuma ordered several of the captives selected and prepared, having them painted in the color of the earth. The captives were brought to Montezuma's private sacrificial chamber where, one by one, they were held down on the *techcatl*[18] by four priests, while a fifth held back each sacrifice's throat with a collar.

"Montezuma himself plunged the sacred knife into their chests and cut out their hearts, one by one. The god Huitzilopochtli will only accept live hearts that are still beating. The hearts were placed in a *chacmool*[19], and blood was taken from the captives' bodies and squirted onto Tendile and his escorts. This was done to purify them so that they could then be permitted to address the Great Montezuma.

18 *'tetch-cottle,'* a stone altar on which humans are sacrificed.
19 A sacred receptacle carved of stone.

"Tendile told Montezuma of the metal ball flying out of the cannon with thunder and a spray of sparks, and described how, when it hit a tree, the tree turned to dust. He told of the men dressed in iron who rode giant deer and refused to eat human hearts, and of their leader with his white skin and black beard, who sent Quetzacoatl's red hat as a gift to the Great Montezuma and insisted on coming to Tenochtitlan to see him.

"At this report, Montezuma seemed convinced that Captain Cortez could be Quetzacoatl returned to overthrow Tezcatlipoca and the other gods. Such warfare between the gods would mean the destruction of the Mesheeka and the entire cosmos. The sun would fall from the sky, and the Earth would be destroyed. But Montezuma hoped that Quetzacoatl, with sufficient persuasion, could be encouraged to leave, and return to his paradise across the East Ocean.

"Thus Montezuma ordered Tendile to return to the strangers' camp with as much treasure as could be quickly gathered, with blood-sprinkled food as a test (for it would be rejected by Quetzacoatl), and with many *tlacatecolotl*[20] and *teipitzani*[21], to curse the strangers and make them sick.

"This Tendile has done, yet now he is very afraid, for none of this worked. For some days now, the owl-men and evil-blowers have been here among the other Mesheeka, throwing their curses and spells upon you, and none of you has gotten sick. You rejected the food with the sacred blood. And all the treasure has done no good - you are more determined than ever to see the Great Montezuma and make war upon his gods. Tendile now returns to Tenochtitlan, where he knows that Montezuma will sacrifice him for his failure and will have his heart cut out to appease the angry gods."

---

20 *'tlaka-tay-co-lottle,' 'owl-men,'* wizards who cause magical illnesses.
21 *'tay-pit-zah-nee,' 'evil-blowers,'* sorcerers who blow evil upon others.

Chapter Nine

MALINALI'S PRAYER

When Malinali finished her story, Cortez spoke to her directly. She had learned enough Spanish to understand most of what he said.

"Doña Marina, you know now that I am a man, and not this Mesheeka god, yes?"

She nodded.

"Yet the Mesheeka king does not think I am a man just like him. He believes, instead, that I could actually be one of his gods?"

She nodded again.

Cortez crossed himself and looked at Aguilar. "These Mesheeka are stranger and more evil than I thought possible, Jeronimo. Their religion is the worship of Satan himself. The gods they worship are devils - except for one god, this Quetzacoatl, who preaches good, not evil. And it is him they are afraid of, it is him they have somehow confused with me. What is it that they fear?"

Aguilar shrugged. Cortez's dark eyes shifted to Malinali.

She heard her father's voice: *Ixkakuk - now is the time to talk of my dream!*.

"Captain Cortez, if my father were here, he could tell you what frightens the Mesheeka. He…" She had been trying to express herself in Spanish, and she glanced at Aguilar for help.

"Please continue, Doña Marina," Aguilar soothed her. "If you have trouble with your words, I will help."

Her eyes thanked him. "My father hated the Mesheeka" she continued. "They are in constant warfare with other kingdoms and peoples, in order to capture victims for sacrifice. The Mesheeka have so many warriors, their army is so enormous, that no one kingdom can oppose them. My father had a dream. He told me he dreamed that several kingdoms joined together to destroy the Mesheeka. If my father were here…" She closed her eyes and took a deep breath to calm herself. "If he were here, he would say that what the Mesheeka fear is that you can make that dream come true – that the Great Montezuma fears that Quetzacoatl has come to unite the other kingdoms against him."

Malinali stood still in front of Cortez, trying not to breathe too heavily, telling her heart to stop racing, while Cortez, looking up at her from his chair, seemed to be looking right into her soul.

"Your father was an interesting man, Doña Marina," observed Cortez.

"My father…" She faltered. She still missed her *Tahtli* so badly - and she had sworn never to reveal herself to her masters, whoever they might be, even these Spaniards. Yet she felt her soul leaping into Cortez's eyes.

"My father," she continued, rising straight and tall, "was a great man, a noble man. He was King of Paynala, the largest kingdom in Cuatzacualco. He knew much, and taught me much. He was teaching me how to be…to be…"

She stopped. Why was she revealing herself like this? She should stop and say nothing more! But Cortez's eyes compelled her to go on.

"My father was raising me to be Queen of Paynala," she said, looking straight at Cortez. "But in my twelfth winter, he…he died. At first, I thought I would become Queen as soon as I came of age. But then my mother married my uncle, and they had a son who they decided should be King. One day I was a Princess, destined to become a Queen, but then, quickly, it all changed. I became an obstacle." She heaved a sigh. "That is why my mother sold me."

"Sold you?!" both Aguilar and Cortez exclaimed.

"Yes. I was sold as a *tlacotli* - a slave - to the Pontochans."

"Your own mother sold you into slavery?" Cortez asked, incredulous.

All she could do was nod.

Cortez stood up and gently took Malinali's hands in his. "Doña Marina, you said your father was a noble man. I can see that you are a noble woman. There is nobility in your soul, not the servility of a slave."

She looked up at him, uncertain where his words were leading.

"You have also shown great loyalty to me," Cortez told her, "by revealing to me what is in the hearts of the Mesheeka. This loyalty must be rewarded." He released her hands and stepped back. "Señor Aguilar," he said firmly, "I announce in your presence that Doña Marina is no longer our servant or slave, but a free woman. If she chooses to remain with us, it must be of her own free will."

Aguilar stifled a gasp, while Malinali's eyes teared up in gratitude and widened with bewilderment. She wanted to say so much, but all that she could do was stammer, "But what of Don Alonso?"

Cortez hesitated in thought for just a second. "I will deal with that excellent gentleman. Señor Puertocarrero is one of my finest men. He has treated you well?"

"Yes," Malinali replied. "He is a good man."

"I must treat him with the respect he deserves. Until this is resolved, therefore, I must ask of you both that word of my decision not depart this tent."

Malinali and Aguilar both assented.

"One more request," Cortez added. "Señor Aguilar, see that you redouble your efforts to have Doña Marina learn Spanish even more quickly than she already has." For the first time, Cortez smiled at her.

* * * * *

In the days that followed, Malinali and Aguilar resumed their long walks on the beach. Don Alonso was always busy with assignments Cortez gave him. At times, they were joined by one of the soldiers whom Aguilar asked to help Malinali with her Spanish. The soldier and Malinali soon became friends. His name was Bernal Diaz del Castillo.

He told her to call him Bernal. "I am from a region in Spain called Castille," he told her. "My town is small but famous. It is Medina del Campo, and many great battles were fought near it, between Spanish Christians and invaders from Africa whom we called Moors. The Moors believe in a false god named Allah, and they follow a false prophet named Mohammed. Our great Queen, Isabella, and her King Ferdinand of Aragon finally conquered the last stronghold of the Moors in Grenada during the year in which I was born[22].

---

22   In 1492.

My town is where she died[23].

"My father, Don Francisco, was the town Regidor[24]. I grew up hearing stories of a New World on the other side of that great ocean which we call the Atlantic, and so, as a young man of 22, I made my way to our great city of Seville and joined a ship sailing to Darien[25], where I became a soldier. Then I learned that my cousin, Don Diego Velasquez, had been made Governor of the island of Cuba, so that is where I went.

"Unfortunately, I soon found that Don Diego could be of little help to me, so I joined the expedition of Hernandez de Cordoba two years ago, then that of Juan de Grijalva, last year. And here I am now."

"Where is Captain Cortez's home?" Malinali wanted to know. "Is he also from this… Castille?"

"Yes," Bernal replied, "but from a remote region of Castille called Extremadura. Many of us are from there, like Pedro de Alvarado and his brothers, who come from the town of Badajoz. Captain Cortez comes from the town of Medellin, as do Gonzalo de Sandoval and Don Alonso Puertocarrero."

"Captain Cortez and Don Alonso are from the very same city?" asked Malinali.

"Yes," said Bernal, "but I do not think they knew each other until they met in Cuba."

"What is this 'Cuba' you talk about?" Malinali wanted to know.

"It is a large island that lies only two days' sail from the Yucatan where we found Aguilar," replied Bernal. "What is your name for it?"

"We know of no such island. All of the East Ocean is a mystery to us," Malinali admitted.

Bernal stopped and turned to look at the sea, lost in thought. "My comrades and I have wondered about that," he said after a moment. "The people we have seen here, the Mayans, the Mesheeka, your people of Cuatzacualco, they are not *primitivos*, primitive people like those who live on the islands like Cuba. You are *civilizados*, civilized people who build houses and temples of stone, who read and write, make beautiful art, and have a complicated culture. Why is it, then, that no one here has made boats and explored the

---

23   Queen Isabella died on November 26, 1504.
24   Magistrate.
25   Panama.

East Ocean, as you call it? Why is it that we have found you, rather than you finding us?"

Malinali shrugged. "That is a question to ask the gods."

Bernal nodded. "Indeed, Doña Marina, we have asked that very question - and our answer is that the One True God of our Savior has guided us here so that we may bring the Word of God to the Mesheeka and end their worship of devil gods who drink human blood."

"Señor Bernal," she replied earnestly, "you know that I am now a Christian, like you. This is my prayer also, that you and Captain Cortez have come so that the Christian Savior will fulfill my father's dream."

Chapter Ten

VERA CRUZ

Malinali and Bernal returned to the camp to find all the Spaniards assembled in front of Cortez's tent, talking loudly and arguing amongst themselves. In response to Malinali's questioning glance, Bernal smiled. "Ah, the Captain's trap is being sprung."

Taking her aside, he explained. "Remember that I told you that my cousin, Don Diego Velasquez, was governor of Cuba? The truth is that he is a greedy, fat man who has many friends and many enemies - and our soldiers here are made up of both. Those who are friends of Velasquez want to return to their *haciendas* in Cuba. They think that Velasquez will share most of the gold Montezuma has given us with them. The enemies of Velasquez want to stay and found a colony, with lands and haciendas of their own. They will get nothing from Velasquez if they return to Cuba."

"And which side is Captain Cortez on?" Malinali wanted to know.

Bernal laughed long and hard. "Ah, Doña Marina, the stories of Cortez and Don Diego are already legendary in Cuba! I must tell them to you someday. Then you will laugh, as well. No, Cortez made such a fool of Don Diego that he has no thought of returning to Cuba. That is why, a few days ago, he asked for my help, which I was happy to give.

"Have you noticed that the Captain has sent two ships with fifty men each, one led by Francisco de Montejo, the other by Rodrigo Alvarez Chico, to explore the northern coast? That he sent another contingent led by Velasquez de Leon to explore the interior? All these men are loyal to Don Diego. With them gone, we have more men here loyal to Cortez than to Don Diego.

Do not be alarmed now when we get angry with the Captain, for it is like a drama, but only we know the script."

Bernal walked over to join a group of men standing in front of Cortez. Malinali knew them all by name. In addition to her Don Alonso, there were all five Alvarado brothers - Pedro, Jorge, Gonzalo, Gomez, and Juan, as well as Cristobal de Olid, Alonso de Avila, Juan de Escalante, Francisco de Lugo, and Gonzalo de Sandoval. Enraged shouts emerged from the Velasquez men: "Return to Cuba! Return to Cuba!"

Cortez looked out at the men, and suddenly there was silence. They knew he was about to announce his decision. "You leave me no choice," he proclaimed. "I now order that our entire fleet set sail and return to Cuba at once!"

Cortez's confederates in front of him exploded in anger. "You have betrayed us!" they yelled at him. "This land has untold riches and you want us to leave! You want us to abandon the people who live here to the butchery of Montezuma's devil-gods! You want to deny these people knowledge and acceptance of Our Savior!" One after another came the accusations which Cortez had instructed them to hurl at him, while the others raised and shook their fists. Many of the Velasquez men began joining in.

Noticing this, Cortez pretended to plead with them. "But I have no authority from His Excellency Governor Velasquez to establish a colony here."

"Then we will give you the authority, as Spanish law says we can!" thundered Alonso de Puertocarrero in response. "We demand that you form a colony here, in the name of his Most Catholic Majesty Don Carlos, to protect his interests in these rich lands that we alone have discovered. And if you refuse to do so, Captain Cortez, then we will protest your conduct as being disloyal to our king!" At that, most of the Velasquez men found themselves shouting in assent.

Again, they all fell silent, awaiting Cortez's response. "It is true that you do have such authority," he conceded at last. "Years ago, King Alfonso X[26] wrote in his *Siete Partidas*, Seven Chapters of Spanish Law, that a community has the right to form a municipal council and set aside any law preventing them from doing so. But you know how embarrassed I am that I was a lawyer in Spain before coming to our New World."

---

26   1221-1284, King of Castille, Leon, and Galicia from 1252 to his death. For his authorship of the Siete Partidas, Alfonso X is one of the 23 great lawmakers of history whose relief portraits surround the interior of the Chamber of the House of Representatives in the United States Capitol Building in Washington DC.

All tension suddenly vanished as the men laughed at Cortez's joke on himself.

Cortez held up his hands in supplication. "I have no choice but to accede to your wishes," he announced. He beckoned to Padre Diego de Godoy, who served as the King's Notary for the expedition. "By the authority which you have now given me, and with our notary Padre de Godoy as witness, I now declare the founding of a colony for His Majesty Don Carlos, and that its capital city shall be called *Villa Rica de la Vera Cruz*[27]. Do you agree?"

There was a great shout of assent from the men as they raised up their hands.

Cortez nodded. "Very well. Now we must appoint a *Regimiento*, a city council. I would like to nominate Don Alonso Hernandez de Puertocarrero as *Alcalde*, mayor, Juan de Escalante as *Alguacil*, constable, Gonzalo de Mejia as treasurer, and Alonso de Avila as accountant. Do you approve and elect these nominations?"

Again, a shout of assent arose.

Cortez took a deep breath. "Now it is done. I wish to applaud you all for your courage and loyalty to our King in founding this colony. As for me, the military powers given to me by Governor Velasquez have been dissolved." Taking off his hat and sweeping it before them, he said, "With the establishment of Villa Rica de la Vera Cruz and its legally constituted governing body, I now resign my position as Captain and await whatever action you and the Regimiento may be pleased to take concerning me." With that, Cortez bowed before them, turned, and vanished inside his tent.

The men stood in shocked silence. They stood motionless, while the only sounds were the waves on the beach and the cries of the seabirds overhead. Then they all began shouting at once. Don Alonso stepped in front of the group and called for the men to let him speak.

"Gentlemen," he addressed them. "I wish to thank you deeply for the honor you have given me in making me the mayor of our new colony of Vera Cruz. Let the members of our Regimiento step forward, so that we may all thank you." As they did, Don Alonso continued. "It is, of course, impossible that we should establish this colony without Captain Cortez. What role do you gentlemen suggest that he play?"

---

27   The Rich City of the True Cross.

Before any Velasquez man had a chance to speak, Pedro de Alvarado called out, "I propose that the Regimiento appoint Captain Cortez as the Captain-General of His Majesty's Army in the colony of Villa Rica de la Vera Cruz!"

Amidst yells of agreement from the men, Don Alonso asked the other Regimiento members if they agreed with this appointment. When they had all called out their assent, he announced, "I declare by unanimous vote of the Regimiento of Vera Cruz that Captain Cortez is now the supreme leader of all soldiers loyal to His Majesty Don Carlos in the colony of Villa Rica de la Vera Cruz, and that he shall henceforth be given the title of Captain-General."

Juan de Escalante then stepped forward. "A colony requires the rule of law. However much Captain-General Cortez may be ashamed of it, he is as formidable a lawyer as he is a soldier. I propose that Captain-General Cortez be further appointed Chief Justice of Vera Cruz." The Regimiento quickly accomplished this, as well. Then one of its members stepped inside Cortez's tent.

Soon Cortez swept open the tent flap and emerged, to cheers and applause. "Gentlemen," he called out. "I accept the appointments of the Regimiento, with the understanding that my authority comes from it and from you. Together, we will establish a great and prosperous colony here that is worthy of us, worthy of our Majesty, and worthy of our Savior. Let us pray together for His blessing upon us and our endeavors." He knelt on one knee to quietly pray, as did all the others.

When the prayer was over, the assembly began to disperse, and Cortez turned to go back into his tent. A group of men, about twenty in all, remained and confronted him. Bernal, who had returned to Malinali's side, explained that these were the most loyal dependents of Diego Velasquez. "Captain Cortez," she heard one of them say, "we do not wish to remain under your command, and we demand that you return us to Cuba at once."

Cortez courteously replied that anyone who wished to leave the new colony was free to do so, and that he would begin making arrangements for their departure. This satisfied most of the group and, thanking Cortez, they left. But a few men stayed, obviously still angry. Malinali recognized Diego de Ordas, Pedro Escudero, and Alonso de Escobar among them. Pointing a defiant finger at Cortez, de Ordas said, "Captain, we will not let you get away with this. We remain loyal to Governor Don Diego and refuse to accept these false proceedings. Until we are returned to Cuba, we refuse to accept your authority over us. We are no longer under your command."

Bernal moved away from Malinali and approached de Ordas and the others. Malinali noticed that several other soldiers were doing the same.

Cortez looked his adversary in the eye and announced, "Diego de Ordas, you and your colleagues here are now under arrest. If you resist, you will be killed." Cortez looked at Bernal and motioned for their seizure. "Take them to the Santa Elena and place them in chains in the ship's hold," he ordered.

The Velasquez men did not resist, since that was clearly useless. Cortez had obviously been prepared for this possibility. As the captives were led away, Malinali realized that she had witnessed a masterstroke of manipulation. "This is how a king would act," she thought, "how a king would plan in advance to trick his people into doing what he wants, overcoming opposition." She smiled at the thought of how her father would have been impressed with Cortez.

* * * * *

It was a few days later that the ships commanded by Francisco de Montejo and Rodrigo Alvarez Chico returned from exploring the coast to the north, while the contingent led by Juan Velasquez de Leon came back as well. Bernal told Malinali that Velasquez de Leon came close to attacking Cortez, so angry was he to learn of what Cortez had done - and so he, too, had been put in irons, along with Diego de Ordas. De Montejo, however, was quickly soothed when he learned that the Regimiento had appointed him Alcalde, to jointly govern the new Vera Cruz colony with Don Alonso.

The problem now, Bernal explained, was that this "Vera Cruz" did not yet really exist - and could not, on these sand dunes where they were encamped. A suitable location needed to be found, and quickly. Montejo told Cortez about a small protected harbor less than 15 leagues[28] up the coast. In ordering preparations for the march up the coast to this harbor, Cortez sent a detachment led by Pedro de Alvarado to some towns that had been seen but not yet visited by Velasquez de Leon, in order to trade for food and supplies.

---

28   A league equals 3 miles. 15 leagues equals 45 miles.

De Alvarado returned some days later, with every one of his men laden with as many turkeys and vegetables as they could carry. Nevertheless, he seemed quite disturbed by what he had seen. Malinali and Bernal found him walking alone on the beach, deep in worried thought.

"We went to these small Mesheeka towns - I say that because they seemed to speak the same language as Tendile's people..." He looked to Malinali for confirmation.

"Yes, I heard them speak of a Mesheeka area called Cotaxtla," she responded, "which is where you went."

De Alvarado took a deep breath and continued. "All of the towns were deserted, with just a few old people left. There was food left behind everywhere, and that is what we took. Then we quickly departed, for what we saw in those towns was a vision straight from Hell.

"In their temples, we found dozens of bodies - dozens in every temple in every town - of men... and of young boys. Their chests had been cut open and their hearts ripped out. The walls and altars of the temples were splashed with many coats of blood. The arms and legs of the dead had been cut off and were nowhere to be seen. With signs, the old people made it clear to us that the arms and legs had been eaten by the villagers. In every town, it was the same. My men and I never imagined such evil and cruelty could exist. The sight of what these people had done to young boys was the worst. This is indeed the Land of Satan." He crossed himself.

Then he looked to Malinali. "Doña Marina, I have heard of the dream of your father. Now I understand his dream, and our purpose in coming to this land. I vow to you that we are going to make this dream - which I believe was given to your father by our Savior - come true."

All Malinali could do was bow her head. She had always looked up to De Alvarado. He was impossibly handsome, with a beard and long flowing hair that seemed spun of bright yellow gold. It was little wonder that she had heard Tendile and his people call him *Tonatio*, the Sun. To know that these men, these Spaniards, worshipped such a noble and just God gave her a peace inside her soul that she had never known before.

De Alvarado's next words, directed at Bernal, brought her back to the present moment. "What of our rebellious comrades?" he asked. "What is to be done with them on our march north?"

Bernal smiled. "Ah, Pedro, you more than any other know that our Captain-General is a master with no equal at dealing with people. While you were gone, he was busy using that solvent of hardness -- presents and promises of gold -- to bring the Velasquez men over to his side. He has taken them all out of prison - even Velasquez and Ordas, who now swear allegiance to him. He is a *genio*, a genius with people."

De Alvarado returned Bernal's rueful smile. "Yes, Bernal, I am not surprised. Cortez is indeed the master." He looked at Malinali. "It will be very, very interesting, Doña Marina, to see this Great Montezuma, about whom we have heard so much, in the hands of Cortez."

Chapter Eleven

THE SPANISH ULYSSES

Shortly after Bernal resumed his post as look-out over the sandy dunes of the camp, he spotted five native men walking on the beach. With smiles and bows, they approached, and their gestures made it clear that they wanted to be taken into the camp. Bernal sent a messenger to bring Doña Marina and Aguilar to the tent of Captain Cortez, while Bernal took the five men to the Captain himself.

Bernal had never seen such men. While they cut their hair and wore their loincloths differently than the Mesheeka, it was their lip plugs that most distinguished them. They each had a large hole in their lower lip, some filled with a heavy stone disk of turquoise, others covered with thin sheets of gold so heavy that they pulled the lip down over the chin, exposing the teeth and lower gums. Their ears lobes were pierced, as well, with large holes filled with turquoise or gold-covered stone disks, but it was the hideous lip plugs that repelled Bernal.

"*Lopé Luzio, Lopé Luzio!*" they cried out as they bowed deeply to Cortez while rubbing dirt on their foreheads as a sign of supplication and respect. Neither Malinali nor Aguilar knew what this meant, so Malinali asked them if they spoke Nahuatl. Two answered that they did. After talking with them for a moment, Malinali turned to enlighten Aguilar and Cortez.

"These men are Totonacs. They were afraid to come while the Mesheeka were still here. Their city of Cempoala is three days' walk to the north. They call Captain Cortez 'prince' and 'great lord' – *lopé luzio* in their language. They bring you greetings from their king, Tlacochcalcatl (*tla-coach-kal-cottle*), who wishes to invite you and your men to visit his city."

Cortez took off his hat and swept it before him at these words. "Please tell these gentlemen that we are honored by his invitation and that we will be happy to comply."

"King Tlacochcalcatl wishes you to know," Malinali continued to translate, "that he has heard of Lope Luzio's great triumph against the Pontochans. He wishes you to know that his kingdom has maintained its independence from Lord Montezuma and the Mesheeka, but at much cost in tribute. There are many other kingdoms forced to pay tribute to the Mesheeka. King Tlacochcalcatl wishes to discuss this with you as his guest in Cempoala."

Cortez ordered cups of wine for the Totonacs. He informed them that their invitation was very timely, as Cempoala was on the way to where he would establish a settlement for his men. "Let us drink to our being friends and neighbors," he offered, raising his wine cup. They did so, and assured him that this was what their king earnestly desired.

Malinali was seized by an inspiration. Without asking for Cortez's approval, she interjected, "Lopé Luzio says his men are greatly burdened with all the supplies and equipment they must carry. It would be a great act of friendship if King Tlacochcalcatl could supply enough load-carriers to transport this burden to Cempoala and the new settlement."

The Totonacs beamed at the suggestion. "We are sure our king will be happy to provide such assistance. When shall we have the load-carriers come?"

When Malinali told Cortez of her request and the response, he looked at her with undisguised fascination. "As soon as possible," he told her to answer.

Two days later, four hundred Totonac bearers arrived.

* * * * *

As their loads were being prepared, and the camp broken down for the march north, Malinali was summoned to Cortez's tent. Inside, she found Cortez in conference with his closest confidantes: Don Alonso, Pedro de Alvarado and his brothers, Juan de Escalante, Alonso Avila, Francisco Lugo, Cristobal de Olid, and Gonzalo de Sandoval. "Gentlemen," Cortez announced, "I have requested that Doña Marina join us. She has proven her loyalty to us, and has provided us with invaluable advice. I wish to have her continue to do so now.

I have asked Señor Aguilar to assist her Spanish."

They all nodded in assent. Don Alonso looked particularly pleased.

"Doña Marina," Cortez said, addressing her directly, "All of us know of your father's dream. Tell us how you think the Totonacs might play a role in it."

Malinali had been anxious when she stepped into Cortez's tent. Now she found herself calm. She was being treated with respect by these men, the most extraordinary men she had ever known or imagined, men who knew she was not a lowly slave but royalty, a Queen! She stood straight and assumed a regal bearing. But just before she spoke, she heard her father's words: *Ixkakuk! Don't you dare act haughty and superior! You will treat these men with the utmost respect and appreciation. No acting like a queen. Do you hear me, Ixkakuk?*

Her eyes widened at her father's words inside her head. She remained erect, but eased her regal stiffness. Relaxing, she focused on simply answering Cortez's question. "The Totonacs are a rich and powerful people," she explained. "They hate the Mesheeka, who have an army so much larger than theirs that they have no choice but to pay whatever tribute is demanded of them."

"What does this tribute consist of?" Cortez wanted to know.

"Many lengths of cotton cloth, skins of jaguars, green *chalchihuite* stones – which you call 'jade' – maize and other food. But most of all, many, many men and boys for sacrifice to Huitzilopochtli."

Don Alonso spoke. "As we understand it, Doña Marina, your father said that no one kingdom could resist the Mesheeka, but that many could together. He said there were many kingdoms like his who wished they could resist but felt alone. Is the Totonac kingdom such a one? Is that why their king is so friendly to us? Does he want our help against Montezuma?"

She had no doubt that this was so.

"But," Don Alonso continued, "how dependable are the Totonacs as allies and friends? Your father would have known of them, yes? We noted that the Totonacs knew of the Pontochans and our experience with them, so we take it that these various kingdoms are aware of each other."

Malinali thought about this for a few seconds. "My father taught me about many kingdoms. I am trying to remember what he said about the Totonacs. There are people known for their trickery, whom you cannot trust, like those of Cholula. But I do not recall him saying anything like that about the Totonacs." She stopped for a moment as she again heard her father's voice: *Speak for yourself, Ixkakuk.*

She looked around at the men who were all listening intently to her. "I think...I think, though, that you want to know my thoughts, not just those of my father."

As several pairs of eyebrows raised, Don Alonso smiled and said, "Yes, Doña Marina, that is just what we want!"

"Then my thought is that it is possible that the Totonacs could be good friends, that it is possible that they could be the first of many allies against Montezuma, but that it is also possible that they are so afraid of Montezuma that they could turn against you. My advice is that you make them friends, but that you watch and be very careful in doing so."

A dozen heads nodded, a dozen voices murmured in agreement. Cortez, in a formal manner, thanked her. She bowed to them all, stepped outside the tent and breathed deeply, finding herself shaking and breaking out in sweat.

* * * * *

After three days' march, the Spaniards were within a league of Cempoala. Cortez's scouts, who had been sent ahead, came back to exclaim excitedly that the walls of the city and its houses were all made of silver!

Malinali couldn't restrain herself from laughing, and quickly explained to Cortez that it was because the walls were lime-whitewashed and shone so brightly in the sun. Soon, all the Spanish officers were laughing and poking fun at the scouts.

But the laughing stopped when they entered Cempoala, the first real city they had seen in this New World. Tens of thousands of Cempoalans were there to greet them. Hundreds were blowing *atecocoli*, perforated conch shells, as trumpets in welcome. Dozens of Totonac nobles in their finest robes and feather headdresses received them at the city's gates, offering food and roses.

The city had beautiful gardens everywhere, the streets were well laid out, and the shops brimmed with products and produce. When they entered the large central plaza, they were told that the soldiers could camp there, while the officers were given the use of an adjoining palace. More food, including turkeys, plums, and maize, was brought. When everyone had eaten their fill, Cortez gave strict instructions that no soldier was to leave the plaza, nor to give any sort of offense to the Indians.

The Totonac King arrived, borne on a large litter carried by a number of servants. They were shouldering quite a load, for King Tlacochcalcatl was so fat that Cortez nicknamed him, under his breath to Alonso Puertocarrero, "the Fat Cacique[29]." A presentation of gold objects, jewels, robes, and feathers were laid out, with the King proclaiming to Cortez, "Lopé Luzio! Please accept these small gifts. If I had more I would give it to you!"

Cortez bade Malinali to thank the King, and to tell him, "We appreciate your friendship and will repay it by our good works on your behalf, for that is what our King, the great Don Carlos, has asked us to do. He wishes us to protect you from evil and to end human sacrifice."

With that, the Fat Cacique sighed and poured forth a litany of grievances against Montezuma. "The Totonacs are a rich and powerful people. Ours is an ancient kingdom. The kingdom of the Mesheeka only appeared in my grandfather's day. Their armies are too strong for us, their soldiers countless. The Mesheeka take all our gold, much of our food, and so many, many of our people for slaves and sacrifice."

Cortez nodded in sympathy. "Doña Marina, you may tell him that we are to be neighbors. We go to build our city on the coast nearby. When we are settled, I will consider how best to help him."

With this news, Tlacochcalcatl's mood instantly brightened, and he said that he was overjoyed to have the Lope Luzio as his neighbor.

Cortez then told Malinali that he had a question for him. "You are right to complain that Montezuma takes your people to be sacrificed to his gods. Why, then, do you sacrifice your own people to your gods? We passed by temples in small towns on the way here. In each, there were temples splashed with blood and littered with the carcasses of dismembered sacrificial victims. The gods you worship are just as evil as those of the Mesheeka. You cannot ask us to protect you from the Mesheeka until you stop believing in evil gods yourselves."

Malinali translated these words flatly and calmly, knowing how stunned

---

29   *Cacique* was a word for "chief" among tribes in Cuba.

the King would be to hear them. At first, he was speechless at Cortez's audacity and the inescapable contradiction in which he was caught. He struggled to control his anger, his gaze darting between Cortez and Malinali. Something in Malinali's eyes, something in the way she moved her head and looked at him, made him freeze. He realized that she was signaling to him that it would be very unwise to get mad at the Lopé Luzio. Instead of lashing out, he decided to say quietly, "Our gods give us no choice."

Cortez smiled gently, said that he understood, once again thanked Tlacochcalcatl for his friendship, and stated that he looked forward to further discussions.

The Fat Cacique seemed quite relieved.

* * * * *

After getting underway early the next morning, they traveled to the small harbor that Montejo had described to them. When they reached it, a little before noon, they found that there was an impressively fortified Totonac town above it, amidst the towering rocks and cliffs. Malinali discovered that the town's name was Quiahuiztlan (*qwee-ah-weesh-tlan*). Climbing up the steep path to the town, they reached the central plaza, where they were greeted by feather-cloaked town elders with braziers, who proceeded to ceremonially engulf the Spanish officers with incense smoke. There was much bowing, with gestures of friendship. Food was brought, glass beads distributed. The Spaniards had barely finished eating when there was a loud commotion. Through the crowd of Indians, a litter bearing the Fat Cacique emerged. There was fear and panic in his eyes.

"Montezuma's *calpixque, tax-men,* have come!" he announced. "Lopé Luzio, I have come for your help!" he pleaded. "There are thirty towns in our land where the Totonac language is spoken. I told you yesterday how every town is made to provide slaves and sacrifices to the Mesheeka, how in every town the Mesheeka select the most beautiful of our wives and daughters to rape and do what they will to them. Just after you left Cempoala this morning, the tax-men came to tell us that we must be punished for being friendly with you, that we must immediately give them twenty young men for sacrifice, and many more from now on." He broke down, and tears began streaming down his face.

As Cortez began to console him, telling him he would prevent 'these robberies and offenses,' there came another commotion. Cortez glanced at Malinali, who explained, "They are yelling that the *calpixque* followed Tlacochcalcatl here, and are about to arrive."

The Fat Cacique's face turned ashen, and immediately began ordering a reception room prepared with flowers, food, and cacao to drink.

When the *calpixque* arrived, there were five of them. The Aztec tax-men marched through the plaza in a blatant display of contempt and arrogance. Their cloaks and loin cloths were richly embroidered, their hair shining and tightly tied back. Each carried the particular kind of rose that only the Aztec nobility were allowed to possess, and each made a conspicuous display of smelling their flower. They purposely walked right past Cortez and his officers without speaking or acknowledging them in any way, pretending that the Spaniards were invisible.

King Tlacochcalcatl was summoned to the room prepared for the tax-men, and he visibly shook and quavered during the barrage of threats and demands they issued. When Malinali explained what was happening to Cortez, he whispered, "This is a most fortunate day." She could hardly wait to find out why. When Tlacochcalcatl emerged from his berating nearly in a state of mental collapse, Cortez and Malinali escorted him to a quiet place to talk. Malinali arranged for cacao to be brought, which, together with Cortez's soothing words, calmed the King. But not for long.

"I told you that I was sent here by the Great King Don Carlos to punish those who do evil, and that I will not permit either sacrifice or robbery," Cortez directed Malinali say. "I will not allow these tax-men to carry off your wives and children, or to commit violence upon you. Therefore, I command you to arrest these tax-men and place them in a prison."

Malinali could not believe her ears, but she translated the words anyway. The Fat Cacique could not believe his ears either, and simply dissolved into a puddle of fright.

"I will take responsibility for them. I wish that you seize and arrest them now, immediately," Cortez said in a commanding yet reassuringly tranquil manner.

It was almost as if the King were hypnotized. He summoned his assistants and the Quiahuitztlan town chiefs, and gave them the order. Overcoming the initial shock, they quickly carried out the order with great enthusiasm. Quia-huitztlan soldiers roughly seized the tax-men and dragged them into a jail; there, they were tied to long poles, and collars were placed around their necks and chained to the poles. Any of the tax-men who resisted were whipped with a stinging lash.

When this was completed, Cortez gathered the Quiahuitztlan chiefs around him, with King Tlacochcalcatl at his side. Through Malinali, he an-nounced, "From this day onward, the Totonacs will pay no more tribute or obedience of any kind to Montezuma and the Mesheeka. Any Mesheeka tax-men who appear in a Totonac town are to be arrested as these were here. I ask that your King send messengers to all Totonac towns to inform them of this."

Still in a daze, the King explained to his sub-chiefs, "What you have just seen today, the words you have just heard, are so wondrous that no mere hu-man could do or say them. They can only be the work of *teules, gods.*" He cast an anxious, awe-struck look at Cortez. "The commands of the *teules* must be obeyed. Send out the messengers."

As word spread in Quiahuitztlan, the townspeople celebrated with a cu-rious mix of joy and rage. It was not long before there arose a vociferous clamor that the Mesheeka tax-men be killed and eaten. The instant that Cor-tez learned of this, he sent a detachment of his soldiers to guard the Mesheeka captives. "The Mesheeka are not to be killed. I have told you that I will not tolerate any more sacrifices," Cortez angrily admonished the Fat Cacique. "My men will guard them, to see that they neither escape nor come to any harm."

The King meekly agreed.

So did the townspeople. By midnight, they had exhausted themselves, and all were asleep. Cortez sent for Gonzalo de Sandoval. "Appraise these five prisoners, select the two who appear to you the most intelligent, and bring them to me, with no one in the town seeing you," he directed.

A few minutes later, two confused Mesheeka were standing in front of Cortez and Malinali. "Ask them who they are, what country they are from, and what has happened to them," he requested of Malinali.

When they had explained who they were, Cortez feigned ignorance of Montezuma and his empire; when they complained about being arrested,

Cortez answered that why the Totonacs had done so was a mystery to him, and that he regretted their treatment. He then had food and cacao brought for them. He assured them that he was their friend, and that he was at their – and Montezuma's – service. He had now managed to free them, and promised he would protect their companions, freeing them when he could. In the meantime, he urged them to escape now, while there was a chance.

Malinali wasn't sure of the game Cortez was playing, but she was enjoying it nonetheless. There was no trace left of the insufferable arrogance these *calpixque* had displayed earlier. Now they were humbly grateful to Cortez, thanking him for his mercy, and fearful that, in their escape attempt, they might be caught. Cortez ordered six sailors to take a small boat and row the two Mesheeka up the coast, beyond the frontier of Cempoala. As they departed, bowing and thanking him again, Cortez reminded them to relay to Montezuma that he was his friend.

* * * * *

At sunrise, when the Totonacs and their king discovered that two of their prisoners had escaped, they ran to Cortez in a rage. Cortez pretended to be even more furious than they, saying that his guards would be severely punished. He ordered that a heavy chain be brought from his ship, had the three remaining prisoners bound to it and, with a great flourish, announced that he himself would take the prisoners, along with his guards who had allowed the escape, to his ship and have them all put in irons there.

Once on the ship, Cortez at once unbound them all, explained the show to the guards, and bade them take good care of the three Mesheeka. By gestures, as Malinali was not with him, he made them understand that he was their friend and would soon send them safely home.

Returning ashore to find the Totonacs mollified, Cortez was asked by the Fat Cacique and an assemblage of his sub-chiefs how the Lopé Luzio would protect them from death and destruction from the vengeful armies of Montezuma.

Cortez cheerily responded: "Please know that I and my brothers will defend you and will kill anyone who attacks you. Just one of my warriors, armed with a lightning-tube, can destroy a host of Aztecs. If your warriors will fight with us, we will defeat all efforts of Montezuma."

King Tlacochcalcatl and his sub-chiefs quickly vowed to do so. Cortez immediately called for Padre Diego de Godoy to witness, as the King's Notary, the Fat Cacique's pledge. Malinali was asked to make clear to Tlacochcalcatl that he and the Totonac leaders were about to participate in a solemn ceremony whereby, in exchange for protection by Captain-General Cortez and the men of Spain, they would vow allegiance to His Majesty King Don Carlos. A contingent of Spanish soldiers was drawn up and made to stand at stiff attention, adding to the sober aura.

Impressed by the gravity Cortez had created, the King and the entire array of Totonac chieftains swore their allegiance to a king and country of whom they knew nothing, swearing their personal allegiance to Cortez. The Captain-General then asked how many warriors the Totonacs could supply against Montezuma. "Over one hundred thousand," came the reply. Malinali saw the flicker of startled interest that passed through Cortez's eyes.

Later that morning, she found Bernal. With a smile, he said, "I told you he was a *genio*."

"He is beyond words," she replied.

"Actually, there are words," was Bernal's response. "They are words written long, long ago. Thousands of years ago, in a place called Ellada[30], there was a poet named Homero[31]. He wrote a poem about a heroic captain and warrior named Ulises[32]. I wish I had the book of Homer's poem, Doña Marina, for I would teach you to read it. Then you would understand who Captain Cortez is. He is the Spanish Ulises."

---

30   Hellas, the historic name for Greece.
31   Homer.
32   Ulysses.

Chapter Twelve

ANGRY GODS

The Spaniards now devoted themselves to building Villa Rica de la Vera Cruz. On a plain that was half a league from Quiahuitztlan, a fort was erected with high wooden walls and watchtowers, followed by a church, market place, arsenals, barracks, and officers' quarters.

Cortez himself was the first to work, digging trenches and hauling foundation stones. Soon, he cajoled his officers to join him; they all set to work, as did all the soldiers, at whatever task they could best manage – making bricks, nails, and lumber, working the lime kilns – while over a thousand Totonacs labored with them. Within less than three weeks, the new settlement was habitable enough for the colony to be formally founded[33].

A few days after Villa Rica had been established, a delegation of Mesheeka nobles arrived, led by a military commander named Motelchiuh (*mo-tell-chee-you*), and including two of Montezuma's nephews. Motelchiuh grandly presented Cortez with the gilded helmet requested by Tendile at the sand encampment of San Juan de Ulua. It was now filled with gold dust, as Cortez had requested.

"Malinche, please accept this and our other offerings,[34] in thanks from

---

33 June 28, 1519. On the same day several thousand miles away in Frankfurt am Main, Don Carlos of Spain was elected Emperor Charles V of the Holy Roman Empire. The town was relocated south in 1524 and subsequently re-named La Antigua. In 1599, it was relocated once more, back to the original site of Cortez's encampment on the sand dunes of San Juan de Ulua. This is now the city of Vera Cruz, while the site of the first European settlement in North America is an obscure fishing village called Punta Villa Rica, located some three miles south of the Laguna Verde nuclear power plant. About a half-mile inland are the excavated ruins of what was Quiahuitztlan. Cempoala, now a town of 10,000 and spelled Zempoala, is some 20 miles south of Punta Villa Rica.

34 Feathers, cloth, and jewelry.

the Great Montezuma for freeing his servants," Motelchiuh said to Cortez through Malinali. "The Great Montezuma ordered a vast army to destroy you when he learned that you had encouraged his Totonac subjects to commit treason against him and refuse to pay his tribute. Then his servants arrived at Tenochtitlan and explained how Malinche had set them free, and expressed great friendship toward him. So it is that we come now in friendship and not war, and yet we do not understand how you can be living among the traitors of Cempoala and other Totonacs."

Cortez had Malinali respond, "I accept these gifts in the same spirit of friendship. Your other three men have been well fed and cared for, and will now be released to you. I wish nothing but friendship between myself and Lord Montezuma. I must tell you that we are here because of the grave discourtesy shown to us by Lord Montezuma's governor, Tendile. He left us alone without any notice, without food or assistance. So we came here, where the Totonac people befriended us.

"I am sure that Governor Tendile was rude to us without the knowledge or approval of Lord Montezuma. I am sure that Lord Montezuma will understand that the people of Cempoala have rendered great service to us, and that, in so doing, they cannot serve two masters at once. That is why they have stopped their tribute, and I ask the Lord Montezuma not find them guilty and try to punish them. I, together with my brothers, will soon be on our way to visit him and place ourselves at his service. Once this is done, his commands regarding the people of Cempoala will be attended to."

Cortez then had wine served to the delegation, presented them with a number of blue and green glass beads, and had Pedro de Alvarado and other horsemen put on a show of galloping and skirmishing. The Mesheeka nobles expressed delight at the show, and at Cortez's flattery. They departed in a jovial mood.

As soon as the Mesheeka were out of sight, the Fat Cacique arrived on his litter. Announcing that his people were now more convinced than ever that Cortez and his men were *Teules* – for instead of an attacking army, Montezuma had sent presents of gold – he then begged for Cortez's help.

Two days' journey to the west, he said, lay the town of Tizapacingo (*tiz-ah-pah-ching-go*). All the Mesheeka *calpixque* fled there from the Totonac towns that expelled them. A Mesheeka army has assembled there, and had begun destroying the crops of nearby towns and waylaying travelers. "You promised to protect us, Lopé Luzio!" he exclaimed. "You must attack Tizapacingo now. We are ready to march with you!"

When told that two thousand Cempoalan warriors were indeed awaiting his command, Cortez complied. At dusk of the second day of marching, the army arrived at the outskirts of Tizapacingo. A group of eight town elders emerged and asked to speak to Cortez. They were in tears.

Malinali had to ask them to slow their torrent of words. She listened and turned to Cortez. "These villagers are very frightened. They say they do not understand why you would come here to kill them when they have done nothing to deserve it. The people of Cempoala have had a dispute with them for many years over their boundaries and land, and it is under your protection that the Cempoalans come to kill them and rob them of their land. There once was a garrison of Mesheeka soldiers in their town, but have all left. They pray that you will not attack them, and ask instead for the same protection and alliance you have given to Cempoala."

"Doña Marina," Cortez said gravely, "there are many lives at stake here. Do you believe that these men are telling the truth?"

Malinali realized that she was being asked to make a life-or-death judgment, and that Cortez relied upon her and trusted her enough to allow her to make it. The Tizapacingans could be setting a trap. There could be a Mesheeka army waiting to spring upon them. She looked into the eyes of the elders. When she saw nothing there but fear and hope, she looked back at Cortez and answered him with one word: "Yes."

One single word from Malinali decided the fate of the people of Tizapacingo. Cortez instantly called for Pedro de Alvarado, Cristobal de Olid, and several other officers, commanding them to halt the advance of the Cempoala soldiers. They did so, but not in time to prevent the looting of a number of farms surrounding the town.

Cortez ordered the Cempoalan commanders to appear before him. When they had assembled, he thundered at Malinali:

"Tell them I want every single item their men have stolen, every piece of clothing, every bit of food, everything, returned to the farms they have looted. If any of their men enter the town, I will have them killed. Tell them that they and their King have lied to me, and that for using me to try and rob these people, they are all deserving of death. Tell them I will spare them now but that, if they ever deceive me again, I will not leave one of them alive. Tell them to go with their men and sleep in the fields. I will speak with them again in the morning."

Malinali did not have to deliver this with heightened emotion, for the commanders could easily discern how furious Cortez was. Knowing their humiliation was warranted, they meekly complied. Cortez then turned to the Tizapacingo elders, who were beside themselves in gratitude. "You wish to know how you can thank me?" he had Malinali ask them.

They all nodded eagerly.

"You can swear your loyalty to my Lord, King Don Carlos of Spain, as have the people of Cempoala. Even more important, you must stop sacrificing people to your gods. Any god that drinks human blood is an evil god and is not worthy of your worship. This is how you can thank me. Do you agree?"

There was hesitation this time, but they agreed nonetheless.

The next morning, Cortez sent for the Cempoala commanders, who had slept fitfully in terror all night out in the open fields, wondering what Cortez would do. He called for the Tizapacingo elders, bringing them together with the Cempoalans.

"You have been enemies for many years," he told them. "Now you are to be friends. You have sworn loyalty to me and to my Lord, and I now require, in the name of His Majesty King Don Carlos, that you make peace between yourselves. You will settle this dispute of land here and now, quickly, and you will pledge in front of me there will be no more war between you. Is this agreed?"

There was an outbreak of relief, smiles by all, and unanimity in agreement with Cortez's demand.

Once again, Cortez's will had prevailed.

* * * * *

Nevertheless, it was in a black mood that Cortez passed through Cempoala on his way back to Villa Rica. He was met by King Tlacochcalcatl, bearing food and profuse apologies. In the central square stood an assemblage of Cempoalan nobles dressed in ceremonial finery. The King addressed Cortez through Malinali:

"Lopé Luzio, we should not have deceived you regarding Tizapacingo, but it is all to the good, as there now will be peace between our cities. For bringing us this peace, we wish for you to have us as brothers. We wish for you to have children by our daughters. To seal our brotherhood, we have brought seven daughters of my chieftains for your officers to marry, and my very own niece for you."

From the assemblage stepped the eight maidens, dressed in gorgeously embroidered robes, each wearing a golden collar around her neck and large golden rings in her ears. Every one was lovely... with one exception. The King's niece was as fat as he was.

Without hesitation, Cortez swept his hat before the King, smiled, and thanked him for his gracious friendship.

The King and all the nobles smiled with relief in turn. But not for long. Cortez nodded to Malinali to begin translating.

"We are honored by your offer of friendship. Such friendship and brotherhood with you is what we most desire ourselves. We are honored by the offer of your noble daughters. Please understand, however, that for this offer to be accepted, your daughters must become Christians.

"You must also understand that, for us to be your brothers, you must destroy the evil idols which keep your people in darkness. Every day, we see with our own eyes three, four, five Indians butchered on your altars, their hearts cut out and offered to your evil gods, their legs and arms cut off and eaten, the human meat sold like an animal's in your market. If you do not stop this, we can never be your brothers. But if you do, then brotherhood between us will be firmly tied."

The King and the nobles erupted in anger. "Our gods give us good health, good harvests, indeed everything good!" exclaimed the King. "If you dishonor them, we will all perish, and you with us!"

Cortez did not wait for Malinali's translation. He turned to his officers all standing behind him. "We can tolerate this evil no longer," he announced. "How can we accomplish anything of worth in this land if, for the honor of God, we do not first abolish these sacrifices? Tell the men under your commands to be prepared to fight. Even if it costs us our lives, these idols are coming to the ground this very day." With that, Cortez drew his sword.

"Doña Marina," Cortez said coldly, "tell the King to remove the idols from the temple or we will do it ourselves. Tell him that we are no longer his friend but his mortal enemy unless this be done. Tell him to order this or I will kill him where he stands."

Malinali explained this to the Fat Cacique so convincingly that he broke down. "The Lopé Luzio means what he says," she told him. "If you do not do as he says, you will die right here – and worse, the Lopé Luzio will abandon you, Cempoala, and all the Totonacs to the wrath of Montezuma. You must obey him."

"This is not with our consent," came the King's barely audible reply, "but do as you wish."

In an instant, fifty Spanish soldiers raced up the temple to grab the huge statues of the Totonac gods and roll them down the steep temple steps, shattering them to pieces. As the wailing and cries of terror and rage rose from the Cempoalan crowd, Cortez noticed that several detachments of Cempoalan warriors had appeared on the plaza and were preparing to fire their arrows.

Within seconds, Pedro de Alvarado and Gonzalo Sandoval seized the King, flung and pinned him to the ground, and Cortez placed the tip of his sword hard against the King's chest. "Doña Marina," he called out, "tell him if one arrow is fired at my men, I will spit him like a goose!"

The King quickly signaled for his warriors to stand down.

Malinali, who had been holding her breath, dared to breathe again.

The King remained on the ground, too shaken to stand. Cortez had the temple priests brought before him. There were eight. They wore long, black, hooded capes and black gowns that reached to their feet. Their hair was so long that it reached to the waists of some, and down to the knees of others, and it was covered and matted together with blood. Their ears were cut to pieces, as doing so was part of their sacrificial ceremony. They never bathed, so their skin was encrusted with filth, and their stench was overpowering.

"Gentlemen," he had Malinali address them, "you think that this has been a terrible day, and that your gods will curse you for it. But you are not cursed. Instead, you are freed, freed from this evil that has blinded your souls. Some day, and soon, you will celebrate this day as the day when you discovered the One True God, and you will marvel at how you could ever have worshiped gods that drink human blood.

"The One True God does not want your blood. He wants your love, as children should love their Father. All of us, you just as much as myself, are God's children. He does not want your sacrifice. He sent His one and only Son to earth, Jesus Christ, who sacrificed Himself so that all of His children could be saved.

"There will never be another sacrifice at this temple – ever. Instead of your idols, we will leave the image of a great lady, the Mother of the Son of God, Mary. Instead of your sacrifices, there will be flowers. Instead of blood on the temples walls, they will be kept white and clean. And you will be left in charge, to see that this is so."

Startled, puzzled, yet quite gratified that they were not to be horribly punished as they had expected, they humbly agreed. Cortez then ordered the Cempoalans to bring a great deal of lime, to thoroughly remove the thick layers of dried blood, and directed them to whitewash the temple walls.

He had the priests bathed, their heads shaved, bade them to don new white robes , and told them they were to keep themselves and their clothes spotless, as they were now in charge of "the altar of Our Lady." A cross, made by the Spanish carpenters, was placed behind the altar. Cortez then selected the oldest soldier among his men, Juan de Torres de Cordoba, who had developed a severe limp, and assigned him to act as his personal guard over the transformed temple.

The next morning, the Padre Bartholomew de Olmedo performed a Mass, and the transformed priests ceremonially fumigated the altar with incense from burning copal resin. Discovering that the Totonacs did not know how to make what Cortez called 'candles,' the Padre sent for a supply of beeswax, then showed the priests how to make candles from it which, they were told, should always be kept lit on the altar.

The Padre then had the eight Totonac brides-to-be brought before him. He explained through Malinali that they were to become Christians by announcing their faith in the One True God and His Son, Jesus Christ, by renouncing all false gods, and by participating in a ceremony called baptism. When they looked nervously at Malinali, she added:

"Yes, I have become a Christian myself, and I can tell you that my spirit feels free because of it. And do not worry – all that the holy man will do to you is get you wet with water." All eight suppressed relieved smiles, and all eight went through with the ceremony.

Afterwards, Malinali led each by the hand to her promised officer. The most beautiful was the daughter of an important Totonac chief named Cuesco; the Padre baptized her as Doña Francisca. Malinali then led her to Alonzo Hernandez Puertocarrero, who seemed quite pleased. Malinali seemed pleased, as well.

Next, Malinali led King Tlacochcacatl's rotund niece, baptized as Doña Catalina, to Cortez. As she placed Doña Catalina's plump hand in his, Cortez did his best to look happy.

It was Malinali's turn to suppress a smile. She had never seen the great Captain-General embarrassed, or struggling so hard to control his emotions. It was as difficult for her to keep from bursting out laughing as it was for Bernal and the other soldiers who stood nearby.

Cortez detached himself from Doña Catalina as soon he thought it courteous, bowed to her, and stepped forward to address the King and the assembled Totonacs, with Malinali at his side:

"Today we are friends once more. I and my officers are honored to have your daughters among us, and to have you as our brothers. We depart now for our new home, the city of Villa Rica. As your neighbors and brothers, I renew my pledge that we will defend you against your enemy, the Mesheeka of Montezuma. You are free, free of his taxes, free of his sacrifices – and all of you are free of the sacrifices of the false gods that once claimed your blood but never will do so again. May the One True God bless you, my brothers."

The King and the entire assemblage of nobles beamed with pride and satisfaction. As Cortez and his officers walked down the steps of the temple, accompanied by their new brides, Totonacs gathered on both sides, showering them with rose petals. Mounting their horses, and followed by the soldiers on foot, they rode out of the plaza through throngs of smiling, bowing Cempoalans. Soon they were on the road to Villa Rica.

Chapter Thirteen

THE BROMAS

Upon reaching Villa Rica, they were met with a welcome surprise: a ship had arrived from Cuba with a detachment of seventy soldiers, nine horses, and a goodly supply of arms, commanded by Cortez's friend, Francisco 'Pulido[35]' de Saucedo. His nickname came from his handsomeness and immaculate appearance. "I and my men have come to place ourselves at your command and seek our fortune with you!" he grandly declared to Cortez.

All rejoiced at the reinforcements, but when Dandy sat down with Cortez in private, the news was not so good. "Governor Diego Velasquez's *procuradore[36]* in Spain, Friar Benito Martin, has persuaded the Court in Seville to grant him a license for exploring this territory, with the profits going to him," was the message. "Only one-tenth of any gold found goes to the Crown, not the Royal Fifth. You, of course, and those loyal to you, will get nothing."

"My old enemy once again," mused Cortez. He called in Alonso Puertocarrero and his closest officers, had Dandy repeat the news, then said, "Gentlemen, the only solution is to petition the King directly. Here is what I suggest we do..."

Within an hour, before any word of Velasquez's appointment could seep out to his supporters among the soldiers, Cortez had the entire command assembled in the sandy plaza facing the sea. Spread out between them and Cortez was the treasure sent by Montezuma. Gonzalo de Mexia and Alonso de Avila, Villa Rica's treasurers, estimated that the gold and silver, by weight

35   Dandy.
36   Representative.

alone, was worth 22,500 pesos[37].

Cortez began by comparing this to the entire production of Cuba, which for the last several years combined was 60,000 pesos, with the King's Royal Fifth amounting to only 12,000 pesos.

"Yet what you see before you is only the smallest hint of the fortunes that await us. Each of you can look forward to having your own *estancia*[38] and personally amassing a far greater fortune that is here right now. Soon, we will embark on our journey to meet the Mesheeka Lord, Montezuma. But before we do, before we seek our fortune in this new land, we must gain the blessing of His Majesty King Don Carlos, which will secure the fortunes we are about to acquire.

"I propose that the Council of Villa Rica de la Vera Cruz send two *procuradores*[39] to His Majesty's Court at Seville to petition for recognition of our city, and to ask His Majesty's blessing upon our efforts on his behalf."

The Council members, standing together, quickly conferred and gave their assent.

Cortez continued, "I appreciate the Council's decision. The question we must now answer is how much of this treasure before us we should send to His Majesty. Do we send him only the Royal Fifth, or more, so that he can better see the worth of what we are about to achieve?

"I believe that it should be more, for by doing so we will gain in return the direct interest of the mightiest king in all Christendom. The least of us will be Counts, Dukes, and Noblemen. As your Captain-General, my share of this treasure is one-fifth. The remaining three-fifths is yours, to be divided amongst you. I hereby relinquish my share, for the sake of His Majesty. If there be any among you who wishes to keep his share, rather than it be a part of our gift to our King, then he should step forward now, and it shall be given to him by our treasurers."

None among the Spaniards had ever seen such wealth as was displayed before their eyes. They stared at it longingly... but none stepped forward. Cortez stood in silence. The men stood in silence. Still not one stepped forward.

---

37   A *peso de oro* contained about 4.2 grams of gold. 22,500 pesos would represent approximately 200 pounds of gold or 3,000 troy ounces.
38   Estate.
39   Representatives.

"It is decided," Cortez pronounced finally. He paused. "I wish for you all to know that it is my highest honor to lead such men as you. It is both a wise and a noble choice you have made today." He paused once more. "What is left is for us to choose our two *procuradores* to represent us and lay this treasure at the feet of His Majesty. I, for one, can think of no one better than the two *Alcaldes*[40] of Villa Rica, Francisco de Montejo and Don Alonso Hernandez de Puertocarrero."

At this, the men roared their approval. All those standing near the two nominees shook their hands, patted their shoulders, and offered their congratulations. It was clear that their nomination was popular and approved.

Malinali stood motionless in shock. Her face was a mask, but the thoughts swirling through her brain and the emotions swirling through her chest made her dizzy.

Surely Don Alonso would not ask to take me with him, would he?, she asked herself. *No, he must know that only I can talk to the Mesheeka. Besides, he now has Doña Francisca. He will take her, yes? And with Don Alonso gone, then… then…*

She had to find a place to sit down. Her heart was racing as she tried to control her breathing. She knew she had fallen in love with Cortez, but she had never admitted to herself just how much until this moment. Did she dare to hope that they could be together now, and that… that Cortez would return her love?

She clutched the cross she wore around her neck. *Give me hope, give me strength, Virgin Mary,* she prayed. The picture of the Virgin in her mind calmed her. She closed her eyes and focused on it. As the image of the Blessed Virgin soothed her, her breathing slowly returned to normal. When she opened her eyes, there stood Bernal.

"Doña Marina? Are you well?" he asked. She nodded and he sat down next to her. She felt as if he could see her thoughts. "Our Captain-General was quite famous in Cuba," he said quietly after a while. "They tell many stories about him – and many of the stories have to do with women, the most beautiful women in Cuba. They tell one story about him jumping from the balcony of the home of one of Cuba's wealthiest and most powerful men, and hurting his leg. The man had arrived home unexpectedly, and the balcony was

---

40   Mayors.

that of his wife's private chamber."

Bernal turned to look at Malinali with brotherly affection. "Doña Marina, he has won the hearts of many women, all of whom hoped they could win his. You are a great lady, Doña Marina, worthy of Captain Cortez. I hope that he shall prove worthy of you."

* * * * *

A number of Doña Catalina's relatives had accompanied her to Villa Rica. They assisted with the chores and with building the community, along with other Totonacs. The first morning, just after dawn, they assembled at a discrete distance from Cortez's quarters to see the great bulk of Doña Catalina emerge into the day – in particular, to see whether she was smiling when she did. She emerged happy and beaming. Her relatives nodded slightly to themselves and carried on with their work.

As this was observed by many of the Spaniards, it was difficult for them not to furtively glance at Cortez throughout the morning. Cortez, of course, caught the looks, and could easily guess what the men were laughing about, as he saw them in small groups together. When he spotted a large collection of about two dozen of his soldiers loudly guffawing, he strode up to them with a fierce look in his eye. Instantly, in place of the laughter, there was fear and silence.

"Gentlemen!" Cortez announced to them in a stern voice. "Always remember – duty to your King, His Majesty Don Carlos, comes before everything – even in the bridal chamber!"

Then he winked at them.

Before he spun around and walked away, he let them see a slight smile play around his lips. Before noon, every soldier in the camp was laughing with Cortez and not at him. No one, however, laughed louder than Malinali when Bernal told her of the episode.

It was a grand moment when the treasure of Montezuma was loaded onto the ship, including the helmet of gold dust and the great wheels of gold and silver. Then the two *procuradores* boarded and, to the cheers of all the men, the ship sailed away, bearing their gift to the King of Spain.

Malinali had bidden farewell to Don Alonso and returned to his quarters, which she had now to herself. At last she was truly free – and she was alone. Would Cortez come to see her now, stealing away from his obese "wife" in the night? Not that night, she was to discover as she lay sleepless and waiting until dawn. Nor the next. Nor the next.

The following morning, she was bidden to come to the Captain's quarters. Morose and depressed, she dragged herself across the plaza. When she entered the room, she knew something was very wrong.

Cortez didn't even take notice of her. His gaze, instead, was fixed upon five of his men who were hunched on the floor with their hands tied behind their backs.

Bernal took her aside and whispered, "These men plotted to steal a ship last night, to sail to Cuba and warn Don Diego de la Velasquez about our *procuradores* on their way to Spain. Just before they were to set sail at midnight, one of the sailors, Bernardino de Soria, reported the plot to Cortez."

Around the captured men stood members of the Council of Villa Rica. Cortez sat in his chair. "Members of the Council," Cortez addressed them, "stealing a *caravel*[41] is a capital offense. Beyond that, these men wished to have Diego Velasquez intercept our envoy to the King, in the hope of sharing the captured treasure – as if Don Diego would share anything with them! – and steal from us our future in this land. What shall be their appropriate punishment?"

"There is only one thing appropriate, my Captain-General," responded Pedro de Alvarado. "Death by hanging."

"Do you all concur?" Cortez asked of the Council members. They nodded in assent. Cortez looked over to Gonzalo de Sandoval. "Order the construction of a gallows," he commanded. He looked down at the captives, who were all crying and whimpering. "Juan Escudero," he said to one of them, "you have admitted to being the leader of this plot. For that, you shall be hanged by the neck until dead."

Escudero's tears dried up as he spat back to Cortez, "You are just getting even with me for when I was *alguacil*[42] of Baracoa[43], and I had you put in irons for escaping from Don Diego's jail."

Cortez's smile was grim. "Yes, you broke into the church and violated

---

41 Ship.
42 Constable.
43 The town in Cuba where Cortez then had his home.

its sanctuary to seize me, yet I escaped from your jail as well. Even so, I bore you no grudge, and welcomed you on our expedition when you begged to join – and this is how you repay me and all your fellows. You are receiving what you deserve."

He looked at the other captives. One of them, Malinali noticed, was a priest, Padre Juan Diaz. He was especially terrified. "It is what you all deserve," Cortez told them icily. He took a deep breath and stared at them in silence. Nobody moved; there was not a sound, save for the muffled whimpers of the prisoners.

One by one, he recited their names. "Juan Cermeño, Gonzalo de Umbria, Alfonso Peñate, Padre – Padre! – Juan Diaz. I trust the execution of your leader will cause your loyalty to our King to never again be suspect. If it should be, I will immediately have you put to death. For now, I sentence you each to one hundred lashes."

Malinali thought that she would never again see men so grateful to be whipped one hundred times. Padre Diaz passed out and fell over on the floor. It was then that Cortez noticed her presence. "Doña Marina," he called to her, "please explain to our Totonac friends what is about to happen and why. I am sure they understand that every society has its traitors and thieves."

She nodded, but stayed next to Bernal as the captives were removed. Cortez stood up and began to pace in frustration. "Again, Velasquez! How can loyalty to him – he who is loyal only to his own greed – be greater than loyalty to our King, or our loyalty to each other?" He asked this of himself, as much as of his officers. "It is like an infestation among us that keeps eating away at our morale and purpose, like a *caravel* slowly rotted by the *broma* wood-beetle. The Velasquez loyalists among us are like *bromas* who will… who will…" Cortez stopped speaking, struck by a sudden thought.

He turned sharply to Bernal. "Señor Castillo – I wish to see the masters of all of our ships. Bring them here as soon as you are able."

* * * * *

Juan Escudero was hanged in the Villa Rica plaza the next morning. Cortez ordered that the gallows not be dismantled but remain as a caution to others. The other conspirators – save for Padre Diaz, whom Cortez exempted "for benefit of clergy" – received their lashing as the entire Spanish command witnessed. Their wounds were then attended to, and Juan Escudero's body was given a sober Christian burial.

Word then began to spread that Cortez had ordered nine of the twelve ships beached on the sand for repairs. "The ship masters have requested it," went the word, "to scrape for barnacles and examine the hulls." Malinali doubted that their request was simply coincidence, given that they had met privately with Cortez for over an hour, the day before.

Late that afternoon, one of the shipmasters called for Cortez and a number of officers to inspect his ship. With the barnacles and growth scraped from the hull, the ship master pointed out a number of small holes – indeed, the hull was riddled with them. "*Bromas*," he declared.

Shaking his head, Cortez announced, "We have no choice – the ship is unseaworthy and must be dismantled. See that everything of use is taken off – all the sails, anchors, guns, everything – and the wood of the ship and the hull be sawed up and used to build our homes here in Villa Rica."

Over the next several days, one ship after another was found to have had its hull eaten away by the *bromas*. At each discovery, Cortez appeared stunned and disconsolate. "What? Another ship ruined?! How can it be?" he would yell angrily. One by one, the ships were beached and dismantled, until only one remained, that of Dandy Saucedo. The entire command had been put to unceasing work with the dismantlement and the construction of homes and buildings from the ships' remains. It wasn't until only Dandy's was left that they fully realized what they had just done[44].

Cortez assembled his men and officers in the plaza, where he addressed them.

"Gentlemen, I am as confounded as all of you at the misfortune that has befallen our ships. But we must not look upon this as a tragedy, but as the opportunity of history. We can now only depend upon ourselves. Look upon the man to your right. Look upon the man to your left. They are your brothers. Your life depends on them, and their life on you. We must recall the noble words of our greatest hero, El Cid Campeador[45], who began the great

---

44   It is a myth that Cortez set fire to his ships and burned them. The famous "burning of the ships" story began when historian Cervantes de Salazar, in his *Dialogue of the Dignity of Man* (1546) misread a description of the ships being broken apart – *quebrando* – as *quemando* – "burning."
45   Don Rodrigo Diaz de Vivar, 1043-1099.

Reconquista, the reconquering of Christian Spain from the hated Moros:[46]

We must live by our swords and lances Or in this lean land we shall not survive We must move on...

"Just as Caesar proclaimed at the Rubicon, 'The dice have been thrown,' and so we must go forward to make our future and our fortune. Caesar himself did not command braver soldiers than I command today, for you have all proven your worth in battles against vast Indian armies. Today, we go on to further greatness that shall someday be compared to that of the Romans.

"Yet we have a wondrous advantage above those ancient heroes. Caesar's Legions were not Christians. It is our Christian mission to liberate this land from bloody slaughter done in the name of evil gods, and replace that slaughter with the love of Our Lord, Jesus Christ.

"Gentlemen! I call upon you today to serve our God and our King by embarking on a great *Entrada*[47] to bring the Word of the One True God to the Mesheeka capital and to Montezuma himself. Who among you is with me?"

To a man, the entire command shouted in assent.

Malinali stood by the door of Villa Rica's small church as she listened to his words. The word *entrada* rang in her mind. *How else can Cortez conduct his Entrada except with me,* she asked herself. She closed her eyes to thank her new Christian God and the Virgin Mary for giving her this opportunity, and then she called out silently to her father. "*Tahtli! I promise I will make you proud of me!*"

---

46   Moors (after the Latin *maures*, itself after the Greek *mauros*, for "dark skin"), the Arab-Moslem invaders who conquered all of Spain in the early 700s.
47   Entrance, journey.

Chapter Fourteen

HORROR AND HEAVEN IN ZAUTLA

Preparations for departure were made quickly. Cortez assigned his friend, Juan de Escalante, as governor of Villa Rica de la Vera Cruz, and Dandy Saucedo's friend, Pedro de Ircio, as the community's *procurador*. One hundred and fifty men stayed behind to guard Villa Rica, most all of whom were sick, wounded, or sailors with little experience at fighting. Cortez formally assured them that they would share in whatever treasure the *Entrada* was to gain.

One the day of departure[48], Malinali stood next to Cortez as the procession prepared to depart. Three hundred soldiers were divided into companies of sixty each, captained by Pedro de Alvarado, Velasquez de Leon, Alonso de Avila, Cristobal de Olid, and Gonzalo de Sandoval.

There were some forty men with crossbows and twenty with arquebus muskets. Fifteen officers and captains were mounted on their horses. The men wore armor, including cotton padding, chain mail, breastplate, Morion helmet, shield, lance, and Toledo sword.

One hundred and fifty Cuban Indian servants handled the war dogs and pulled the six Lombard guns. Behind the men were a thousand Totonac warriors in cotton armor, their faces painted and hair bedecked with feathers. They carried bows, arrows, and obsidian swords, led by Chief Mamexi. Hundreds more carried the expedition's food and supplies.

Leading the procession was the *Alfarez*[49], Cristobal del Corral, holding the "Cross of Burgundy," a white banner with a jagged red X, the flag of King

---

48   August 16, 1519
49   Standard-bearer.

Don Carlos.

It was an amazing, thrilling sight for Malinali, particularly in the bright sunshine of a clear morning, against the backdrop of the huge rock face of what the Spaniards called *Cerro de las Lluvias*[50], and the turquoise blue of the sea. Wondering if she would ever see the ocean again, she looked up at Cortez. He seemed to be a man of no qualms, of complete self-confidence.

Then the sun passed behind a cloud she had not noticed in the sky, casting a shadow upon the assembly and upon her heart. She felt a cold fright. The force before her looked impressive now, but it was like a small pond compared to the ocean of warriors Montezuma could assemble. How could such a tiny army hope to accomplish what they were embarking upon? Malinali drew in a sharp breath of sudden fear. *This is madness! The Great Montezuma will crush us like a gnat! What chance is there…*

Her spiral into a pit of panic was interrupted by Cortez, who had turned to look at her. Expressionless, without a word, he looked into Malinali's eyes, and the strength of his gaze pulled her out of her spiral.

How does he know what I am feeling? she asked herself. But somehow, clearly, he did. Cortez's glance lasted but a few seconds, yet she found herself straightening her slumped shoulders, and standing tall with an air of regal calm. She vowed never to doubt Cortez again.

King Tlacochcalcatl and the *caciques* of a number of Totonac towns assembled to bid the expedition farewell. Cortez swept off his helmet and waved it to the king with a bow and a flourish. "My brother," he said, addressing Tlacochcalcatl through Malinali, "I cannot thank you enough for your friendship, which I hold dear. I know you will be of good service to the governor of our Villa Rica home, Señor de Escalante, and that you will care for my wife, Doña Catalina, in my absence."

The grotesquely fat Catalina was standing next to the King, and both smiled broadly at Cortez's charming words. With that, the *Entrada* began.

* * * * *

Mamexi, serving as the guide, advised Cortez to head for the Kingdom of Tlaxcala. "The Tlaxcalans are our allies," he said, "and have fought for their

---

50   Rain Mount

independence from the Mesheeka better than any other people." This part of the journey would take several days, and the way would be cold and dangerous.

"Cold?" Cortez repeated in surprise.

Mamexi pointed to the huge, snow-covered mountain in the distance. "Do you see Citlatepetl (*seet-la-tay-pettle*)?[51]" He put the flat of his palm near the ground. "We are low here, near the sea." He raised his palm above his head. "Soon, we will be in the land that rises towards Citlatepetl. Yes, we will be cold."

It was not so for the first day, as they trudged through forests and plantations of maize. The trail got steeper, climbing to the towns of Jalapa and Xicochimalco, which the Spaniards called Flower Cities for their profusions of gardens and flowers. The residents, allies of the Totonacs, welcomed the visitors with smiles and food, thanking them for their liberation from Montezuma's taxes. Mamexi said they could best demonstrate their gratitude by having their soldiers joining the *Entrada*.

Four days after leaving Villa Rica, the expedition stood in front of a mountain mass that Mamexi called Nauhcampatepetl (*now-campa-tay-pettle*) [52]. "We must cross to the left," he said, pointing. "Now we get cold."

They climbed along the southern edge of the mountain to a pass Cortez named *Nombre de Dios, Name of God*. It was a miserable place of icy mists. They emerged onto a high, barren plain that was full of *maguey* cactus plants, and they spent the night in the open, tormented by hail and freezing rain.

The Spaniards called the land *Despoblado*, Desolation, a wasteland with a large salt lake. Trekking to the north of the lake without food or water, they finally reached a string of small communities – in turn, Altotonga, Xalacingo, Teziutlan, and Tlatlauquitepec – none of which had more than a few hundred inhabitants. Yet the townspeople willingly shared food and drink with the travelers.

Turning southwest, they crossed another high pass which the men named *La Leña*, Firewood Pass, and down along a narrow, forested valley to a river that Mamexi called Apulco. "We are now in the Kingdom of Xocotlan (*shocoat-lan*)," Mamexi announced. "The people here are subjects of Montezuma. Let us see how they greet us."

---

51 Now known as Orizaba. At 18,696', it is Mexico's highest mountain.
52 Now known as Cofre de Perote, 14,045'.

After what seemed one of the longest weeks of their lives, the Spaniards arrived at the gates of Xocotlan's capital, Zautla. Greeting them at the gates was the King of Xocotlan, Olintecle (*oh-lin-tek-lay*), and a number of Zautla nobles. While Malinali translated his welcome, she noted that, underneath his friendly smile, there was both fear and anger. As they were escorted to the plaza, she saw that this was a city of many thousands of people, well-fed and well-housed. Yet the food the Spaniards were offered was meager, and the quarters they were given to sleep in were spare.

Cortez seemed not to notice. What he and all the Spaniards could not help noticing was a sight of absolute horror. "It is a *tzompantli*, a skull rack" Malinali explained to Cortez, who looked at her with shock in his eyes.

The Spaniards stood in unmoved silence, staring at row upon row, stack upon stack, of human skulls from sacrificial victims, ringing the plaza. There must have been well over 10,000 skulls, neatly and regularly arranged. In one corner of the plaza, near the sacrificial temple, there were huge piles of human thigh bones. Three priests in hooded black gowns, their long hair matted with blood, stood guard over the bone piles.

Cortez told Malinali that he wished to speak to King Olintecle. They gathered to converse, sitting underneath a huge ceiba tree in a corner of the plaza. "I wish to know," Cortez said, "whether he is a subject of Montezuma's."

The King was taken aback. "Is there anyone who is not?" came the reply. "Is not Montezuma the ruler of the world?"

Malinali realized that Cortez was so infuriated by the sight of the *tzompantli* that he was unable to employ his usual calm diplomacy. Now it was her gaze that calmed him, so that at least his words came out quietly.

"Tell him, Doña Marina, that we are proof that Montezuma is *not* the Lord of the World. We are not his subjects, and neither are our Totonac brothers who accompany us. We are the subjects of His Majesty King Don Carlos of Spain, which lies across the East Ocean.

"Tell him that we have come, at the request of King Don Carlos, to liberate this land from the worship of evil gods and to end the evil practice of sacrificing and eating human beings. We have come to bring the faith of the One True God and the worship of His Son, Jesus Christ, who asks only for love, not blood. We have come so that Montezuma may become a subject of King Don Carlos, as he and his people will be happier in so doing.

"Ask him to look at our brothers, the Totonacs. They have ceased their sacrifices and live more peacefully among themselves. I ask, therefore, that he and his people do the same.

"Just as King Don Carlos sends us to command Montezuma not to kill any more of his people, nor to rob his subjects and steal their land, so I must command Olintecle to desist from his sacrifices, to no longer eat the flesh of his fellow man, and other such evil practices, for such is the will of our Lord God, whom we believe in and worship, the giver of life and death, who will deliver us to Heaven if we obey Him."

Olintecle and the other nobles made no reply. They sat, dazed and mute, far too stunned by such inconceivable words to even think, much less speak. They were also thoroughly unnerved by this woman, whom the Spaniards treated as an equal yet who was like them, this woman who calmly, steadily looked directly into the King's eyes, waiting for an answer.

No answer came. Olintecle's eyes shifted away from Malinali's to stare blankly into space.

Cortez finally broke the silence by turning to speak to Padre Bartholomew de Olmedo, behind him. "It seems that there remains nothing more to do but set up a cross."

The Padre quietly objected, "Captain, I think it would be rash to do so, this soon. These people know nothing of our religion. They will commit sacrilege against any cross we leave, and we intend not to tarry here long. It would be best to wait until they have learned more of our holy faith."

Cortez nodded. "I shall heed your wise advice, Padre. Let us retire, gentlemen." He stood, together with his officers, bowed to King Olintecle, who still sat in a daze, and left for the quarters provided him.

"It has been a long day – a long week," Cortez said to his officers. "It will be good to have a roof over our heads for the night."

They dispersed…but Malinali stayed, as Cortez's gaze invited her to step inside his room.

* * * * *

Alone for the first time with Cortez, Malinali found herself most surprised by what she *wasn't* feeling. Instead of experiencing an emotional tumult of fear, anxiety, heart-thumping excitement, as she had thought might overwhelm her when she dreamed of this moment, instead she felt as serene and calm as still water.

The two of them stood, soundlessly looking at one another. Cortez, too, seemed filled with serenity. Finally, he spoke. "You are unlike any woman I have ever imagined, Doña Marina."

"You are unlike any man I ever imagined, my Captain," she replied.

"There have been many times when I looked at you and it seemed that your beauty would overcome me," Cortez told her. "But I had to bury those thoughts, always and quickly. You were assigned to Don Alonso. I had to completely focus on our purpose in this strange land. Then came my duty to that noble and attractive lady, Doña Catalina."

Malinali couldn't maintain herself and burst out laughing. Together, she and Cortez laughed so hard that tears poured from their eyes. "I must tell you, Captain Cortez, that I laughed myself to sleep many nights, thinking of you with that lovely and so-slender lady." She knew that she wasn't quite speaking the truth, but it did seem funny now.

"Well, I can tell you, my Doña Marina, that I was not laughing during those endless nights! It is such a relief finally to be able to laugh about them." He clasped her hands. "Especially with you." His touch jolted her as the spark of his energy ran through her body.

They spoke not another word. What followed was all that Malinali had fantasized it would be. To join her body with that of a man she adored and admired had been her hidden hope. Now it was real. She felt transported beyond the earth, as if she and Cortez were gods joined together in *ilhuicatl, the heavens*. This was far beyond physical pleasure; it was an act of spiritual rapture. When the final moment came, her soul exploded in fulfillment. As she floated back to earth, she made no attempt to hold back a flood of tears.

Cortez understood. He looked at her with deep tenderness. "Doña Marina," he whispered as he kissed her cheek, "I have never seen anyone as happy as you look at this moment."

She wasn't ready to return to earth just yet. She closed her eyes, the better to absorb Cortez's presence next to her. When she opened them, he was still looking at her. "You seem quite happy yourself, my Captain," she said with a twinkle.

All Cortez could do was smile contentedly and nod.

When they awoke before dawn, Cortez turned to her. "I wish for every night from now on to be like this one," he said.

"It is my wish too," she assured him, and caressed his face with her hand. "But now I have work to do."

Startled, Cortez stammered, "What work?"

Smiling as she put on her robe and prepared to slip out of the room, Malinali informed him, "You'll find out."

She made her way over to the cooking fires of the Totonacs and engaged Mamexi and a number of his warriors in conversation. Thereafter, throughout the morning, the Totonacs struck up casual conversations with a number of Zautla citizens.

When the Zautlans commented on the loud barking of a Spaniard mastiff that had kept them up all night, and asked the Totonacs what kind of animal it was – a lion? a jaguar? – the Zautlans were not told that it was a dog belonging to Francisco de Lugo. Instead, it was 'explained' to them that what they had heard was the voice of a dragon – a dragon that loved the Spaniards and was eager to kill anyone who annoyed them.

The Totonacs also told the Zautlans about the Spanish lightning-tubes, which could kill huge numbers of enemies at great distances, and of their giant deer that could run down and trample enemies to death. The Zautlans exclaimed that the Spaniards must be *Teules, gods.*

"Yes, you are right, they are *Teules!*" the Zautlans were told. "This is how they captured the *calpixque tax-men* of your great Montezuma, and why they ordered that we pay no more taxes and sacrifices to the Mesheeka – and also why Montezuma sent them presents, not a punishing army, in return!"

As the Zautlans' eyes widened in shock at these revelation, the Totonacs followed up by saying, "What is more, they have ended our practice of killing our own people for the gods. We now have the *Teules'* gods, who want flowers and not blood. They are such good *Teules* that they made peace between Cempoala and Tizapacingo, which were great enemies before. Now they have come here... but you have given them nothing. You should run at once and make offerings of friendship!"

It wasn't long before Zautlans began walking up to Spaniards with small gifts: golden necklaces and pendants, cloth, and maize cakes. As word spread about the supposed true identity of the visitors, Cortez discovered a large crowd following him around – and when it was learned that King Olintecle had asked to speak to him, the crowd proceeded to pick Cortez up and carry him reverently on its shoulders to see their King.

Malinali walked beside the crowd with a satisfied look on her face.

As Cortez was set down from the Zautlan shoulders in front of Olintecle, he murmured to Malinali, "Why do I sense that this is your doing?"

"I told you I had work to do," she murmured back, both of them keeping straight and serious faces.

Then King Olintecle spoke to her. Malinali noticed that yesterday's anger was gone from his voice, replaced by a tone of awe.

Malinali translated, telling Cortez, "He wishes you to know that he is grateful that you and your people have come to visit Xocotlan. He regrets that he was unable to fully welcome you yesterday, and he wishes you to know that he and his people will do all they can to provide for you, as you rest here on your way to Tenochtitlan."

"Tell the King that we thank him most gratefully for his hospitality," was Cortez's response, "and that we wish nothing more than peace and friendship between us and the great kingdom of Xocotlan. Perhaps, if he would like, he could tell us more about Montezuma's city of Tenochtitlan."

Olintecle brightened at the opportunity. His hands and arms gestured animatedly as he voiced his description. "Tenochtitlan is the best-defended and most beautiful city in the world. It is a huge city of many, many thousands, built in the middle of a giant lake, with homes on poles in the water so that you must get to them by canoe or over bridges.

"The city can only be entered by three roads, built across the water with a number of openings so that the water can flow through. Each opening has a wooden bridge which can be raised so that no one can enter the city. Montezuma has many great palaces in the city, and is the richest king in the world, with great stores of gold, silver, *chalchihuite jade*, and much more treasure.

"Tenochtitlan is protected by the largest and strongest army in the world. Montezuma has so many soldiers in his army that they are like the leaves of a large forest. The Great Temple of Huitzilopochtli is in the center of the city. Twenty thousand sacrifices a year are made to the Great God, which...."

The King stopped talking as he noticed that Cortez was now staring at him with a look of stabbing anger. He smoothly shifted. "I am sure that the Great Montezuma will be pleased to see you, and will welcome you to his city as we have welcomed you to ours. We thank you for your offer of friendship between us. Please know that we accept this offer because it is what we desire ourselves."

Instantly, Cortez's anger was replaced by a broad smile, a courteous bow, and a wide sweep of his hat. "We are now friends and brothers," he proclaimed.

As the crowd heard Malinali's translation of these words, the Zautlan townspeople again hoisted Cortez on their shoulders and carried him back across the plaza to his headquarters.

As word spread among the Spaniards of Olintecle's description of Tenochtitlan, they became more and more excited to begin marching towards it. But first, Cortez told them, they needed to make certain of their welcome along the way.

He called for Mamexi, asking him to send four Totonac messengers to Tlaxcala. "I wish these messengers to explain to the leaders of Tlaxcala," Cortez told him through Malinali, "that, just as the Totonacs are friends of the Tlaxcalans, so we are the friends of the Totonacs. That we come in the name of His Majesty King Don Carlos of Spain, in order to assist Tlaxcala in her admirable struggle against the tyranny of the butcher Montezuma. That we wish the same friendship with them as they have with the Totonacs."

After the messengers departed, Cortez ordered his men to prepare to march, the next day. All afternoon, Cortez did his best to not be distracted from the need to oversee arrangements and supplies, disciplining himself to refrain from thinking about the night to come.

Malinali did the same.

Chapter Fifteen

THE HILL OF TZOMPACHTEPETL

A ccompanied by twenty Xocotlan sub-chiefs sent by King Olintecle, the expedition made its way down the Apulco river valley to a town where Olintecle told them they could wait for the messengers' return. The King had advised Cortez against going to Tlaxcala. "They are bad people," he said, "traitors against the Great Montezuma. A more treacherous people you will never find." But Cortez insisted, trusting the advice of Mamexi and the Totonacs.

The town was called Izta Quimaxtitlan (_itch_-ta _qwee-mox-teet-lan_) and, when they arrived, all of the elders and nobles had assembled to greet them, proclaiming that they had received word from Tenochtitlan that the Great Montezuma had commanded that the Spaniards should be welcomed in every way the town was able.

As the expedition rested and ate, a group of town elders approached Cortez. "They wish to warn you against the people of Tlaxcala," Malinali explained. "They say these people are very treacherous and cannot be trusted, that the Tlaxcalans know of you and do not care if you are allies of the Totonacs. The Tlaxcalans say that armies have come to their country many times, pretending to be friends but, once inside, have tried to destroy them. The Tlaxcalans do not believe the stories of the Totonacs not paying taxes to Montezuma because of you. The Tlaxcalans say this is not possible, that this is another trick, that their whole country is ready to fight you, to kill you and eat your flesh cooked with chilies."

Mamexi continued to assure Cortez that the Tlaxcalans would be friendly, that these warnings all came from allies of Montezuma and enemies of the Tlaxcalans, and cautioned Cortez to wait until the messengers returned. But the messengers did not return. When they had still failed to arrive by the next morning, Cortez ordered the expedition to set forth toward the Tlaxcala border.

They had gone about two leagues when they came to a stone wall half again as high as a tall man, many paces thick, which ran for several miles across the entire width of the valley. No one was manning the wall, and no one was at the gate in the wall through which the road passed. "What use is this wall with no one here?" Cortez asked Mamexi, who shrugged his shoulders in answer. As they passed through the gate, Cortez sent a few horsemen ahead to scout.

These horsemen had not gone far when they spotted a dozen or so Tlaxcalan warriors, who fled at the sight of them. They sprinted down the valley, the horses after them, Cortez catching up and waving, trying to get them to understand he wanted only to speak with them. Just as they caught up with them, the fleeing warriors turned and began slashing at the horses with their obsidian swords. Cortez and Olid had to cut five of them down.

Suddenly, from gullies on either side of the road, thousands of Tlaxcalan warriors sprang to attack the horsemen in ambush. Their faces were painted in bright colors, and they leapt high in the air in a wild frenzy, yelling war cries and charging at the Spaniards *en masse*.

Cortez noticed, however, that they only fought straight-on, so that no matter how many warriors there were in a group, you only fought the first row of them. When you killed them, then you fought the next row, and the next and the next. Bodies began piling up around Pedro de Alvarado, around Sandoval, Olid, and Avila. Then the Spanish crossbowmen and those with muskets got close enough to cause more damage. The obsidian swords of the Indians were sharp but would easily shatter when hit by a sword of Toledo steel. Faced with scores of dead before them and not one Spaniard casualty, the Tlaxcalans broke and fled.

A number of Spaniards were wounded, however. Cortez ordered that their wounds be dressed with the fat of a dead enemy combatant.

As this was being done, two of the Totonac messengers arrived, and excitedly began exclaiming to Malinali. "They say these warriors who attacked us are not Tlaxcalan," she relayed to Cortez. "They are Otomi, primitives from an area that the Tlaxcalans don't really control."

"Perhaps," was Cortez's only response.

The expedition carried on to a small stream near a town that was abandoned. Deciding to camp there for the night, the Spaniards found a number of the small hairless dogs bred for food wandering about the empty streets. They provided dinner for all. For the entire night, Cortez ordered patrols and scouts to be on alert, and for the horses to be kept bitted and saddled, in case of attack.

Marching off at dawn, the expedition had not gone far when they were confronted by a swarm of Indian warriors. "More of these Otomi?" Cortez asked Pedro de Alvarado sarcastically. "There must be more than five thousand of them." The Indians were shouting, jumping in the air, waving their obsidian swords, banging on drums, blowing shell trumpets, and firing arrows, even though the Spaniards were out of range.

Cortez called for three Otomi prisoners captured the day before. "Doña Marina, tell them to go to these warriors with this message: That we come in peace and as friends, and that we do not wish to make war upon them but to have them as brothers." As they went off, he then asked for Diego de Godoy. "Señor de Godoy, as the King's Notary, you are to record that we pleaded for peace with these people, and that any killing done today will be done in our defense."

Cortez and his men watched as the captured emissaries reached the warriors and talked to them. Whatever message was given, it only increased their fury. They moved closer, and their arrows started to come within range.

Sending Malinali back to the rear, Cortez pulled out his sword and yelled, "Santiago – and at them!" The Spaniards charged. The crossbowmen began hitting their targets, as did the musketmen. The flash and smoke of the muskets caused terror among the Indians, a terror which increased markedly when their fellows began dropping from an unseen force.

As the horsemen in front trampled over three Otomi chiefs, the enemy broke and ran into a ravine. The Spaniards charged after them, entering the ravine before they realized that it was a trap. Thousands upon thousands of enemy warriors were there, waiting for them in ambush.

All the Spaniards could do was cut their way through the ravine. The first to make it through was Diego de Ordaz on his horse. Then came Mamexi and a group of Totonacs to protect him and the others as they arrived on level ground.

As the Spaniards fought off the hordes, using their shields to ward off the rain of arrows and stones, and their swords to sweep down rank after rank of the enemy, more and more of them made it to Mamexi and Ordaz. The exception was one horse and rider. Pedro de Moron was surrounded by hundreds of the enemy in a frenzy to kill. One Indian grabbed Moron's lance, and a dozen more pulled him off his horse. With their obsidian broadswords, they slashed at the horse, cutting off her head at the neck. As the horse fell dead, Cortez and Sandoval made their way to Moron, their horses trampling the Indians around him as they pulled him to safety.

During the charge through the ravine, the six Lombard guns had been left behind. Malinali ordered the Totonacs with her to haul them around the ravine to where the Spaniards had emerged. Once they arrived, Pedro de Alvarado commanded their firing into the masses of enemy warriors swarming out of the ravine. The first discharge decapitated a principal Otomi chief with his giant feather headdress, as well as killing a good many others.

Just that suddenly, the battle was over. In silence, the thousands of attacking Otomi simply turned and walked away.

The Spaniards stared in exhaustion at the retreating Indians, then fell to their knees to give thanks to God. On his knees like the rest, Cortez called out, "We thank thee, O Lord, for coming to our deliverance on this day[53], and pray You will continue to give us the strength to do Your will in this land."

Fifteen men had been wounded, and were treated with the fat of a dead Otomi. Padre Bartholomew gave Pedro de Moron the last rites.

Cortez, with Malinali at his side, then approached Mamexi. "Chief Mamexi," he proclaimed loudly for his men to hear, and Malinali matched his voice so the Totonacs could hear as well, "you and our Totonac brothers have done us great service this day. We all wish to give you our thanks." He pulled his sword from its scabbard and held it high as a sign of respect and appreciation. All those Spaniards who were able did the same. It was a solemn moment. When the swords were again sheathed, Mamexi responded. "You are

---

53   September 2, 1519.

indeed our brothers. Never before have we seen such fighting, so few defeating so many. Only *Teules* could win such a battle. It is our honor to fight with such *Teules* and to have them as brothers."

Nearby was a town with houses that encircled a hill, and temples on top. "That could serve as a fortress," observed Cortez, who ordered the expedition to encamp there. They proceeded to the hill, Cortez on horseback, with Malinali walking beside him. He cast his gaze down upon her and said quietly, "It was important for me to thank Chief Mamexi aloud to his men, not only because it was true concerning how much he helped us, but to save him from the shame that we have been attacked by people that he claimed were his allies. Now, Doña Marina, I must thank you. Do not think that, in the heat of the battle, it escaped our notice that you had the Lombards brought up to secure our victory."

A number of Spaniards, walking nearby, overheard Cortez's words, Bernal among them. They unsheathed their swords and held them aloft as Bernal called out, "We all thank you, Doña Marina!" Malinali looked around at them all and thanked them with her eyes.

The hill was named Tzompachtepetl, (zom-<u>potch</u>-tay-pettle). The expedition ate well that night, feasting on turkeys and the little dogs found in the abandoned town below, and sleeping as much as possible. Fifteen of the enemy had been captured, and the next morning Cortez, Malinali, and Mamexi sat down to question them. Mamexi wanted to know why they had attacked allies of their friends, the Totonacs.

He pointed at two of the prisoners wearing red and white cotton armor. "You are not Otomi," he told them. "You are Tlaxcalan chiefs. You must explain yourselves."

"Our King, Xicotencatl (<u>chico</u>-ten-cottle)[54] believed your messengers," came their reply. "He said that the Totonacs were our friends of many years, so we had to accept these strange men you bring with you. But King Xicotencatl is old, and his son, Young Xicotencatl, disagreed. It is Young Xicotencatl who is the leader of our army, and he ordered the Otomi to attack you. He is our commander and we must obey him."

Malinali began distributing a supply of blue glass beads to them. "Have you ever seen *chalcahuite* stones as rare and beautiful as these?" she asked.

---

54   'Ring of the Wasp.'

"Take them as a sign of our friendship. I am from a kingdom such as yours, one that first saw these strangers as enemies. But I have learned that they do not want war. They wish no harm to you, but only want to pass through Tlaxcala to the land of the Mesheeka so that they may speak to Montezuma. Please take these blue *chalcahuites* to your King and your Commander, and tell them this." She looked at Cortez, who nodded. "You are free to go," she told the Tlaxcalan chiefs.

The following morning, the two chiefs returned. From their arrogant strut and contemptuous expression, Malinali was not surprised when she heard what they had to say. "These men have returned with Young Xicoten-catl's answer," she translated. "He welcomes your request for peace, for the way to peace is for them to gorge themselves on your flesh, and to pay honor to their gods with your hearts and blood. He promises to give you this peace tomorrow, for he promises to leave none of you alive."

Cortez showed no anger. Instead, he directed that more strings of glass beads be given to them, and he had Malinali ask them, in a tone of innocent puzzlement, why the Young Xicotencatl felt this way. Wine was brought to loosen the Tlaxcalan lips.

King Xicotencatl, it was revealed, was blind with age. The Young Xico-tencatl was anxious to gain a great victory over the invaders so that he could be hailed as the new King. He had 10,000 warriors under his command. A great chief named Maxixcatzin (*mah-sheeks-cot-zin*) had joined him with another ten thousand followers, and the same with Chiefs Tecapacanea and Guaxoban. Still more had been brought by Chief Chichimecatecle (*chee-chee-mek-a-tek-lay*), but… but…

Malinali served them more wine.

Chichimecatecle despised the Young Xicotencatl, it turned out, and was intensely loyal to the old King. Other chiefs like Maxixcatzin were also more loyal to the former rather than the latter.

"What is the sign that the warriors of Chichimecatecle follow?" Malinali wanted to know, and was told that it was a banner with a large white bird, its wings outstretched. With that, the Tlaxcalans were thanked, and sent on their way.

As word spread among the Spaniards that fifty thousand Indians would attack them the next day, they began lining up to confess to Padres de la

Merced, Juan Diaz, and Bartholomew de Olmedo. Prayer and preparations for battle went on all night.

At dawn, Cortez issued strict orders. The crossbowmen were warned to use their arrows carefully and to be sure that some of them were loading while others were shooting so that there would be a slow, steady, constant fire. The same direction was given to the musketmen.

The horsemen were told to hold their lances short, and to aim for their enemies' eyes. The swordsmen were to aim at the enemies' bowels. "A man cannot fight when blinded, nor when he sees his intestines pouring out of him and onto the ground, nor when he sees this happening to his comrades," Cortez concluded. "In every encounter in this land, we have prevailed. With God's help, we will do so again today."

They had marched less than half a league from Tzompachtepetl when they came upon the Tlaxcalan army arrayed across a broad plain. Never had the Spaniards imagined an army so large. "There are enough of them to eclipse the sun," one soldier cried out.

"There will be no eclipses on this day!" Cortez thundered in response.

Nonetheless, it was a stunning sight. These were no Otomi barbarians; these were Tlaxcalan warriors in full battle attire, adorned with feathers and war paint, wearing wooden, cotton, and leather armor, brandishing obsidian-toothed swords, lances, slings, and firing arrows. Hundreds of *teponaztli wood cylinder drums* were being pounded, and thousands of blasts from *atecocoli conch shells* sounded. Above this din rose the war cries of tens of thousands of frenzied Indians. Then they charged towards the Spaniards.

Cortez had noted that, among the banners being held aloft within the Tlaxcalan forces, the one with the white bird was off to the right. He called for his men not to fire upon nor attack the Tlaxcalans on their right, but to concentrate on the center and left. Once the charging Indians got in range, the Lombards were set off, one at a time, so that each cannonball hurtled horribly through masses of human flesh, making the maximum impact on the Indians' minds. As they got closer, the crossbowmen and musketmen began their steady fire. But still the Indians came, for there were many thousands more.

Cortez ordered most of the footmen forward to meet the charge, then he and a number of horsemen swung around to the left, crashing into the Tlaxcalan army's flank. This took the Tlaxcalans completely by surprise, as they had never experienced such a tactic. Confusion and panic spread among them. There were so many of them, firing off so many arrows and slung stones, that many of those arrows and stones hit their own men. The Spaniards fought like wild men with their swords, and the Tlaxcalans began to give way. When the entire flank of Chichimecatecle's and Maxixcatzin's forces, which had not been attacked and had held back in the charge, started to withdraw, the panic among Xicotencatl's forces overcame them.

Pedro de Alvarado and his brothers, on horseback, tried to pursue the fleeing warriors but pulled up, so tired they could barely sit in their saddles. The foot soldiers could hardly lift their arms, so exhausted were they from wielding their swords. Strangely, although they knew they had killed count-less enemy, not one Tlaxcalan body lay dead on the field. Every last corpse had been carried off in the retreat. Cortez and his men again dropped to their knees in praise and thanks to God for again, on this day[55], leading them to victory.

* * * * *

Three Tlaxcalan chieftains had been captured, and they were soon brought before Cortez.

"I mean you no harm, and you will soon be set free," he had Malinali tell them, and they were given glass beads, and wine to drink. "I wish for you to give my greetings to my brother, King Xicotencatl, who I know wants peace between us. Please tell your King, as we have been attacked by his son twice, attacks unprovoked by us, that unless his son surrenders to us, we will kill him and every last one of his soldiers. We wish for peace and friendship as you have with the Totonacs. But as you have noticed, because of the treachery of the King's son, the Totonacs now join us in fighting you. A King must be able to control his own son. If King Xicotencatl truly wants peace, and wants his son to live, he must command obedience from him."

During his speech, Cortez made sure that his captives' wine cups were constantly refilled. It was not long before the captives responded by saying they would be happy to bring his message to their King, that Young Xico-

---

55 September 5, 1519.

tencatl had disobeyed his father, but that Young Xicotencatl was certain of victory over the strangers because he claimed he knew their secret weakness.

"And what might that secret weakness be?" Malinali asked very gently.

"That these so-called *Teules* lose all their powers at night. If they cannot be defeated during the day, he will destroy them in the dark. This is what the *tacal naguas*[56] have told him."

The chieftains were complimented for their bravery in battle, reminded once again of the message they were to take to their King, and sent woozily on their way.

When Young Xicotencatl's men, several thousand strong, attacked Tzom-pachtepetl that night, it was the Tlaxcalans who were surprised to find the Spaniards ready for them at the bottom of the hill. The moon had risen, giving enough light for the horsemen to pursue the enemy warriors and cut them down by the score. The attackers fled into the blackness.

When morning broke, however, a great many Spaniards awoke to find themselves in pain from the wounds they had suffered in the fighting of the past several days, and in near-despair over their fate. What if the Indians kept on attacking? How much longer could a few hundred of them, even with several thousand Totonac allies, continue to hold off swarms of warriors as numerous as ants?

To make matters worse, Cortez had contracted a fever, with chills and sweating spells and fits of delirium. There was no salt nor oil to dress wounds, only fat from dead enemies. There was no food to be found any longer, with the turkeys and dogs already eaten. Malinali saw all the signs – the men were losing hope.

She began to walk among them, helping to dress their bandages, bringing them water, but especially talking to them. She told them that the Tlaxcalans were sure to make peace now, after suffering such defeats, and that she had talked with Tlaxcalan prisoners captured during the night attack who told her they had never seen such bravery and were convinced the Spaniards could not be defeated.

Her calmness of manner, her complete lack of fear, soothed and reassured them as much as her words. And it was true, she had talked to the Tlaxcalan prisoners, and they had made such exclamations. But she didn't tell the sol-

---

56 Wizards.

diers what she had said to the prisoners in return:

"Your *tacal naguas* are fools. They play with their stupid magic tricks and pretend to know things about which they know nothing. If they knew anything, you wouldn't be a prisoner now, and many of your comrades wouldn't be dead. Here is what you don't know: These strangers are more powerful than any men you have ever known. They are not *Teules*, they are men, but they have a *Teule*, a God, who is much stronger than your gods. How else do you think a tiny number of such men can always defeat your vast armies?

"The biggest fool of all is your commander, Young Xicotencatl. He is a stupid young boy, full of foolish and dangerous dreams, who does not have the wisdom of his father. You need to go to his father, to your King, and explain this. Explain that if he does not control his son, these strangers will get so angry that they will kill you all. I have seen with my own eyes how the strangers made peace with the Totonacs. They will make peace with you, as well. But your King must heed my words, and quickly, or else Tlaxcala will be doomed."

Then she told the Spaniard guards that Cortez wanted the prisoners released. "Go," she said, "Go to your King and tell him what I have said. Run." And run they did.

Two days passed, with no further attacks, but also with very little food. As Cortez's fever continued, so did the complaints and grumbling of his men. The demand arose, especially among the "Velasquez men," that they all return to Villa Rica and abandon this effort to see Montezuma.

"Almost all of us are wounded. We are sick, we are cold, we have no food," complained their leader, Alonso de Grado. "God has indeed been on our side so far, but it is foolish to keep tempting Him. If these Tlaxcalans fight so well and are so numerous, how can we possibly hope to succeed against Montezuma's forces, who are far stronger and more numerous than the Tlaxcalans? Not even Alexander the Great nor Caesar himself ever attempted to overcome such odds with such a tiny expedition. We must return to Villa Rica. To go on or stay here is madness!"

The dissenters had assembled in Cortez's hut, with Cortez too ill to arise from his sickbed. Weakly, he responded, "Yes, there is much truth in what you say, Señor de Grado. I, too, have asked myself about the wisdom of our course. Yet I have confidence that our war with the Tlaxcalans has ended.

Further, I feel that you are seeking 'a cat with five feet' for, if we retreat to Villa Rica in defeat, our Totonac allies will lose faith in us. They will turn against us and we will have to fight them, too.

"So, gentlemen, if one way is bad, the other is worse. We must remember the ancient truth, 'It is better to die in a good cause than to live in dishonor.' And we must also be inspired by our fathers and ancestors who liberated our land from the hated Moors. They never gave up against great odds. Have you forgotten what they said?" He smiled gently. "When facing the Moorish hordes, they would tell themselves, 'The more Moors, the greater the honor'."

De Grado and the others seemed at least partly persuaded by Cortez's thoughtful words. "There is wisdom in what you say, our Captain. Let us think upon this," came de Grado's reply.

The following day, the men were cleaning their equipment, fashioning arrows, and making other preparations for battle, when a scout on horseback came racing into the camp, yelling that hundreds of Tlaxcalan men and women, bearing loads, were coming in a long procession. Cortez immediately ordered that no one show any alarm or hostility, and directed the men to stay in their huts. As the procession entered the camp, four elderly men emerged, obviously chieftains, judging by their dress, jewelry, and feather headdresses. Cortez stepped out of his hut to receive them.

One by one, they bowed to place a hand on the ground and brought earth to their foreheads. They carried baskets of smoldering copal, and fumigated Cortez with the smoke. Cortez signaled for the men to come out of their huts and assemble to hear what the Tlaxcalan chiefs were about to say. As they spoke, Malinali made sure she translated loudly enough for everyone to hear.

"Malinche, we come as messengers from our King Xicotencatl, who orders that all of the Chiefs of Tlaxcala, all their friends, allies, and subjects, are to place themselves in bonds of friendship and peace with you. King Xicotencatl asks for your pardon for not meeting you peacefully when you came to his land, and for the war that has been waged upon you instead.

"We believed you were friends of the Mesheeka, whom we have been fighting for a hundred years. Many times have the Mesheeka entered our land through trickery and treachery, to rob us of our women and children. We did not then believe the messengers you sent, or that the Totonacs were truly your allies.

"We now see we were mistaken and ask your forgiveness. Please accept this food which we have brought, for there will be more tomorrow. Soon the King's son, the Young Xicotencatl, will come to further prove the sincere desire of all Tlaxcala to enjoy friendship with you."

All four then bowed once more to place their hands on the ground and kiss the earth.

Cortez whispered quietly to Malinali, "Do not be alarmed at what I say." He then spoke loudly so his men could hear, while she explained his words to the chieftains. He spoke angrily:

"I wish for your King to know there are good reasons why we should not listen to him and why we should reject his offer of friendship. Before we entered this land, we sent messengers to offer peace, and to explain that we wished to assist Tlaxcala against its enemy, the Mesheeka. This offer of peace and friendship was not only rejected, we were attacked three times, both by day and night.

"In these attacks, many brave warriors of Tlaxcala were killed, but it is their own fault, just as it is your own King's fault that they are dead. Before you came today, I had decided to stop these attacks by coming to your capital and killing your King myself. But today you have come not to attack us but in peace, and so it is in peace that I welcome you and thank you for the food you have brought."

Cortez then had a number of blue glass beads brought forward and given to the chieftains, along with refilling their cups of wine. "This shall be a sign of peace between us. But just as you at first did not trust us, now we at first shall not trust you. It is only when the Young Xicotencatl comes in friendship and escorts us in peace to your capital that there will be trust between us. Be sure, however, that he comes during the day, for we will kill anyone who comes to us in the night."

Chapter Sixteen

XICOTENCATL – YOUNG AND OLD

Malinali was stunned to hear Cortez speak that way to the Tlaxcalan elders. She knew how close the Spaniards were to giving up, how they feared another attack. But… but… the Tlaxcalans did not know this. They must have believed what she told the prisoners she had set free! Yet how did Cortez learn of that? She had not told him what she had done. Indeed, it must be that Cortez was a *genio* with people, as Bernal said.

Cortez's words had the desired effect on the Tlaxcalan chiefs. They bowed deeply, swore that Young Xicotencatl would come, said that all Tlaxcala would rejoice when the Malinche and his men arrived at their capital, and left, looking relieved and satisfied.

Even more relieved and satisfied were the Spaniards. With turkeys, maize cakes, cherries and other food in abundance, as well as the promise of no more attacks, the camp was full of laughter – and no grumbling, not even from de Grado. Cortez was pleased, and made sure everyone saw he was – but he also made certain that the patrols and scouts continued, day and night, to search for danger. He had no trust in this Young Xicotencatl.

The next day, his fever returned. Lying in his bed, he heard a horse gallop through the camp and stop outside his hut. It was a scout, one he hoped did not bring bad news.

"Captain, a procession is coming – but not from Tlaxcala! They look like Mesheeka nobles!"

Dressing quickly, Cortez sent for Malinali and Mamexi. They informed him that it was indeed a Mesheeka delegation, evidently having come from the direction of Izta Quimaxtitlan, as there were a number of Xocotlans with them.

There were five nobles, dressed in costly cotton robes embroidered with feathers, gold pectorals and arm bands, and large feather headdresses. "Malinche!" they called out. "The Great Lord Montezuma sends you his greetings, and rejoices at your victories over the traitorous Tlaxcalans. The whole world of the Mesheeka has heard of your victories. The Great Montezuma ordered that we come here with these presents from him, in gratitude."

Mesheeka slaves proceeded to spread hundreds of gold and jeweled ornaments on mats in front of Cortez, twenty loads of fine cotton cloth, and dozens of featherwork pieces.

"The Great Montezuma wishes you to know," the nobles announced, "that it is his pleasure to give his loyalty and pay tribute to your Lord Don Carlos, who must be a mighty King to have such men as you. You have only to say how much tribute is necessary each year, in gold, silver, cloth, feathers, and jade, and it will be paid. The Great Montezuma asks in return that, while he is delighted you are now so near to Tenochtitlan, you not attempt to come to his city. The road from here is very bad and dangerous, and there is not now enough food in the city to feed you all. The Great Montezuma wishes the best for you and does not want you to suffer."

The nobles continued, "The Great Montezuma also wishes to warn you against the Tlaxcalans. They are traitors and cannot be trusted, as you have seen in their treacherous attacks upon you. If you trust them, if you go to their city, they will kill you."

Under his breath, Cortez said something in that language the priests used which Malinali did not understand: *"Omne regnum in se ipsum divisum desolabitur[57]".* Then he smiled broadly, took off his plumed red hat to sweep it in front of him with a short bow, and had Malinali tell them:

"I accept these gifts and kind offers from Lord Montezuma in the name of His Majesty King Don Carlos of Spain. The goodwill and friendship shown by Lord Montezuma are deeply appreciated by us all. I also thank Lord Montezuma for his concern for us regarding the people of Tlaxcala. It is true that they have attacked us three times after we asked for peace with them. This is why I ask that you, five great Mesheeka chiefs, accompany us to the Tlaxcala

---

57   "Every kingdom divided against itself will be brought to desolation." The King James Bible translation of Mark 3:25 is: "A house divided against itself cannot stand."

capital so that you may see for yourselves how the war between us and the Tlaxcalans shall end."

Before the startled Mesheeka could reply, Cortez quickly ordered that every courtesy be shown to them and every effort be made to make them comfortable in the camp. He turned to Malinali. "Doña Marina, I am feeling very ill once more and I must retire. These Mesheeka must not see me so. Please see that they are made welcome as best we can." He turned to go into his hut then stopped. "There is something else. For Montezuma to know so much, he must have spies among us. Try to find who they are."

He turned again but, before he could enter his hut, a second scout came galloping into the camp. "My Captain," he called as his horse came to a halt in front of Cortez, "another procession has been sighted – this one from Tlaxcala!"

* * * * *

It was the Young Xicotencatl, with over fifty of his sub-chiefs and officers. They all wore cloaks of maguey fiber, one side of which was colored white, the other side red. Their leader was tall, almost as tall as Cortez, with broad shoulders and heavily muscled arms. His face was coarse and deeply scarred with pockmarks. Ignoring the Mesheeka nobles standing to the side in shock, he stepped forward without hesitation to present himself in front of Cortez.

He did not bow, he did not grovel, he did not kiss the earth. He was expressionless. His eyes examined Cortez, then Malinali, then returned to Cortez, looking him fearlessly in the eye. "Malinche…" He pronounced Cortez's title as a salute, as one warrior to another.

Cortez nodded slightly in acknowledgment.

"Malinche, I come to you today to ask for your forgiveness at the request of my father, ruler of all Tlaxcala. I ask your forgiveness for taking up arms against you. Yet please know this about the people of Tlaxcala. We are free because we fight for our freedom. We have never obeyed anybody, and we value our liberty above all things. We prefer to suffer much hardship, such as no salt or cotton clothes, rather than accept the yoke of the Mesheeka and the commands of Montezuma."

He pointed to the Mesheeka nobles. "They hate us and call us traitors because we refuse to be enslaved by them. We refuse to be enslaved by anyone. But my father believes you do not wish to enslave us, that you come instead to help our freedom, not destroy it. And so I have come to offer my loyalty to you, Malinche, and to your King of Spain."

Cortez smiled broadly, had two chairs brought from his quarters, and welcomed Young Xicotencatl to sit next to him. Malinali stood in front of them. "It is with the greatest pleasure that I accept your loyalty," Cortez said. "We men of Spain admire above all others those who fight for their freedom. For many years and many generations of our fathers and ancestors, the people of Spain fought for their own freedom against a foreign invader. We called this enemy the Moors, and the Mesheeka remind me of them. The Moors came from a far-away land and tried to force the people of Spain to believe in a false god. But we never stopped fighting until they were defeated, so that today there are no Moors in Spain, and His Majesty King Don Carlos rules the richest and mightiest kingdom in the world."

"Your words," Young Xicotencatl replied, "explain why my people and your people are to be brothers. The Mesheeka have come to our land many times with giant armies and never defeated us. How is it then that you with…" he raised his hand as if holding something… "a small handful of warriors can defeat us – and not once, but three times? So we have learned that you cannot be conquered. We have learned that the Totonacs told us the truth about you. We wish to be allies with people who cannot be conquered, so that we will be better protected from the Mesheeka traitors who want to steal our women, our children and our liberty."

Cortez had wine brought for them both. "Let us drink to our friendship and peace between us," he declared. "For although we came to you in peace and you attacked us three times, that is now in the past and I pardon it. Let us drink to a peace that shall last between us, a true peace, for a false peace will give me no choice but to destroy your city and kill you and all your warriors, and this I do not want." Cortez's smile remained as he said these words, but his eyes were like dark ice.

They drained their cups. Young Xicotencatl had seen both the smile and the look. "Malinche," he responded, "our peace will be firm and true. It is the decision of my father the King that this shall be so, and so shall it be. It is the King's desire and mine that you come to our city of Tlaxcala, where it shall be your home. My father the King, all our nobles and priests, all the people of Tlaxcala will receive you with rejoicing. Until your arrival in our city, I and my men place ourselves in your safekeeping and will remain with you as your hostages." As he looked at Cortez, his eyes were devoid of fear.

Cortez stood. With a slight bow, he said, "I accept the invitation that your King has so kindly given us. I must correspond with our city of Villa Rica that we have in the land of our Totonac brothers. As soon as the messengers return from there, we shall depart for your capital. Until then, we welcome you to our camp and to stay as our guests." Cortez was now smiling with his eyes, as well. For the first time, Young Xicotencatl smiled back.

* * * * *

Yet still Cortez could not rest. The instant that Young Xicotencatl left his presence, the Mesheeka nobles rushed up to him again. "Surely you do not believe these false promises," they exclaimed. "It is all a trick by liars and deceivers. Once you are trapped in their city, they will fall upon you and destroy you."

Cortez shrugged his shoulders. "Such tricks do not trouble me. If they should attack us again, it does not matter where or when, by day or night, in their city or in the open, for it is we who shall destroy them. I am determined to go to their city to see whether they are men of truth or lies."

To this they had no reply, and Cortez finally was able to enter his hut, with Malinali following. He collapsed on his bed, shaking and sweating. She placed cool damp cloths on his head and had him drink an herbal potion her grandmother had taught her to make. She would never leave his side until morning.

By then, Cortez was feeling well enough to write a letter to Juan de Escalante in Villa Rica, giving an account of all that had befallen, expressing gratitude to Lord Jesus Christ for their great victories, and asking that two barrels of wine and a box of sacred wafers for Mass be brought to him immediately. He then ordered that a tall wooden cross be erected in the camp.

Six days passed. A new delegation of Mesheeka nobles arrived, with twice as much treasure as before, in gold ornaments and feather-worked cotton robes. They repeated Montezuma's plea that he not go to Tlaxcala where, they assured him, he would be robbed and killed. Cortez received the presents happily, and just as happily told them he was sure the Tlaxcalans would not attack him, for they knew this would mean their death.

Two days later, the wine and wafers arrived from Villa Rica. Cortez had recovered from his fever, and ordered that preparations be made for departure. A scout called out that a huge procession of Tlaxcalans was approaching. Cortez assembled his entire officer corps and mounted his horse to await them. The Tlaxcalan chiefs were carried in litters, hammocks, and on the backs of slaves; they arrived in great ceremony, with priests burning copal to ritually fumigate everyone. From the most elaborate litter stepped an elderly, half-blind man who touched and kissed the ground, and bowed before Cortez: King Xicotencatl.

"Malinche," he called out, "I and the nobles of Tlaxcala have come to personally escort you to our city, where you shall be welcomed with joy by our people."

Cortez dismounted from his horse, stepped to the King, bowed deeply, and embraced him. "We are to be brothers, brothers in liberty," he announced, with the Spaniards cheering his words, and the Tlaxcalans cheering Malinali's translation. Cortez then called for Chief Mamexi and Young Xicotencatl. "The Spaniards, the Totonacs, and the Tlaxcalans are today all brothers!" Cortez shouted. With this rejoicing, the procession of them all to Tlaxcala began. Cortez welcomed the demoralized Mesheeka emissaries to join them.

Chapter Seventeen

FORTES FORTUNA ADIUVAT

When they arrived at the city of Tlaxcala[58], there was an enormous welcoming party to greet the Spaniards. Different clans of Tlaxcalans dressed in differing colors, their maguey or henniquen cloaks painted and embroidered. A contingent of priests with their burning copal performed fumigations, wearing white hooded robes, their hair long and blood-encrusted, blood oozing from their ears, and with fingernails several inches long. The streets and rooftops were thronged with smiling Indians who showered the Spaniards with roses of varying hues.

When they reached the central plaza, King Xicotencatl took Cortez by the hand and led him to a palace, explaining, "This shall be your home in Tlaxcala for as long as you wish." He assured Cortez that all his men, all the Totonacs and Xocotlans, and even the Mesheeka nobles, would be well housed. Upon his signal, hundreds of servants began streaming into the plaza, bearing cooked turkeys, maize cakes, fruits and vegetables for everyone. The soldiers all agreed that it was the best they had eaten since leaving Cuba.

With everyone so joyously happy, Cortez and Malinali retired to their quarters. They had not had any time together since Zautla, so they did not waste any time, making love fiercely and quickly.

Afterwards, noticing Malinali was staring into space, Cortez asked her what she was thinking about.

"*Mixtli*...." was her whispered reply. "Clouds... a bright blue sky filled with small puffy clouds, with the two of us jumping from one to another, like

---

58   September 18, 1519.

stepping stones, playing and laughing." She looked at him. "I am so happy with you, my Captain."

"And I with you, my Doña Marina."

She nestled in his arms. "Tell me about your land of Spain. Señor Bernal says you come from a city called Medellin."

Cortez smiled and raised his eyebrows. "Just what else has Bernal been telling you?" He tickled her, and she squealed with laughter. "Ah, my *España* – it is a very old land. The people of Spain have been there for thousands of years. Many centuries ago – over fifteen – Spain became part of the Empire of Rome. My city of Medellin was founded by the Romans[59]. They called it Metellium, after their general, Metellius. We have many Roman ruins there – a theatre, a bridge, villas. A small river runs by the town, the Ortigas, where my family had a mill for grinding grain. My father, Martin, had been a soldier, and we used to walk along the stream, where he would teach me how to swordfight."

"My father did just the same with me, by the stream that ran by our palace!" Malinali exclaimed.

"Well, we did not have a palace," was Cortez's response. "My father was a *hidalgo*, which is the lowest rank of Spanish nobility. We had a small house in the central square of Medellin, where I was born. My father was the town *regidor* and *procurador*[60]. There was a palace, actually a castle, in Medellin. The closest I ever got to it was with my mother, Catalina. Her father, Don Diego Altamirano, worked for the Count and Countess of Medellin, and she would take me to see my grandfather in the castle when I was a young boy.

"I left when I was twelve[61] to go to school in Salamanca. There was a very famous and very old school there[62], where I studied Latin and the law. You must learn Latin to be a lawyer, because our law comes from Roman law. But I spent more time reading Roman literature and history. A favorite of mine was Terrence[63]. There is a line in one of his plays, *Phormio*, that I decided would be my life's motto: *Fortes fortuna adiuvat*. Fortune favors the brave.

"There was one Roman lawyer, though, who wrote something I will never

---

59   In 75 B.C.
60   Councilor and representative.
61   1496. Cortez was born in 1484. In 1519, Cortez was 35, Malinali was 19.
62   The University of Salamanca, founded by Alfonso IX of Leon in 1218, is the oldest university in Spain and one of the oldest in Europe.
63   Publius Terentius Afer, 190-159 B.C.

forget. He was Ulpian of Tyre[64], the most famous legal mind in Roman history. We had to study this huge book of Roman legal writings compiled by an Emperor named Justinian[65]. At least a third of it was by Ulpian. What I will always remember of his was: *Omnes homines natura aequales sunt*: All men by nature are equal[66].

"When I read this, I said to myself, 'This is something our Lord Jesus would say.' But Ulpian was a pagan Roman, not a Christian! It was then that I understood that Jesus was speaking truths to all mankind, that were true for everyone, Christian and non-Christian, and that everyone could recognize them as true.

"*Omnes homines natura aequales sunt*: All men by nature are equal. You, Doña Marina, me, Hernando Cortez, His Majesty Don Carlos, the Mesheeka King Montezuma, and everyone else are all equal in the eyes of God. As His Son would say, we are all God's children. That is why... that is why..." Cortez closed his eyes and breathed deeply. "That is why I know that our Lord Jesus has sent me here to end this evil eating of man by man, this slaughter of men in sacrifice to Satan..."

He closed his eyes again. When he opened them, Malinali was silently, intently looking into them. He shook his head. "I am sorry. I did not mean to mention such things at a time like this with you." He kissed her gently.

They held each other for a long time. Then Malinali asked, "So, why aren't you a lawyer, back in Spain?"

Cortez smiled. "I tried... but not for long. I returned to Medellin as a 'bachelor of law,' and my family had high hopes of my becoming a *letrado*[67] at the court of the King. But what kind of life was that? A life more boring and dull than that is impossible to imagine. I could not get Terrence out of my mind: *Fortes fortuna adiuvat*. Fortune favors the brave.

"So, to the great displeasure of my mother and father, I left for Seville, the greatest city in all Spain. It was the seat of the royal court of the great Queen of Castile, Isabella, and the great King of Aragon, Ferdinand V, the magnificent heroes who had defeated the hated Moors in their last stronghold of Grenada and sent the brave Admiral Colon[68] to discover this New World,

---

64   Domitius Ulpianus, *fl.* 222 A.D.
65   483-565 A.D.
66   *Digest of Justinian*, 17.32.
67   Legal councilor.
68   Christopher Columbus, 1451-1506.

both in the same year[69]. The joining of their kingdoms[70], along with the expulsion of the Moors, created and united our one land of Spain.

"But I had not come to Seville to be at the royal court. I had come to see my cousin, Nicolas de Ovando, intending to join his expedition to the island of Hispaniola in the New World. But I had an… accident. I hurt my leg from a, ah… fall, and couldn't go."

Malinali couldn't help notice Cortez's hesitation and embarrassment. Something told her… "It wasn't a fall from a balcony, was it? A balcony like the one in Cuba?" Her eyebrows were arched halfway up her forehead.

"Ahhhh – now I know you have been talking to Bernal too much! And it was not a balcony. It was a window, if you must know."

"The window of a Señorita's room?"

Cortez blushed. "Well, her father was very angry, and I had to jump. Actually, her father was also very wealthy, and I had to leave Seville quickly. That was in the Year of Our Lord 1502, and I was eighteen years old. So I spent four years traveling to the great cities of Spain – Grenada, Cordoba, Valencia, Segovia, and Valladolid – working in various law offices, finally returning to Seville when it was safe for me. I learned that a ship, *La Trinidad*, was sailing for Hispaniola, and its captain, Antonio Quintero, agreed to take me. That was in 1506, and I was twenty-two. I have not been back to Spain since."

"You talk of King Ferdinand and Queen Isabella, but never of your King Don Carlos. When did you meet him?" Malinali wanted to know.

Cortez shook his head and laughed. "I have never met the man. He doesn't know I exist."

Malinali's head snapped back in amazement. "What?! Then how…? Then why….?" Her stammering dwindled into speechlessness.

Cortez was still laughing. "I should say, I never met the *boy*. He was only six years old when I left Spain[71]. Besides, he was born in Flanders[72] -- that's over 300 leagues[73] from Spain's northern border. He speaks French, not Spanish. He never set foot in Spain until two years ago – and that was over a year after he became King of Spain! At least his mother is Spanish, but she, sadly,

---

69   1492.
70   Ferdinand (1452-1516) and Isabella (1451-1504) were married in 1469.
71   Charles – Don Carlos I of Spain, Holy Roman Emperor Charles V – was born February 25, 1500 and died September 21, 1558
72   In the Flemish town of Ghent, now in western Belgium.
73   Close to a thousand miles.

is insane."

All Malinali could do, mutely, uncomprehendingly, was stare at him.

Cortez sighed. "All right, I will explain. Ferdinand and Isabella had one son, Juan, who was to be king, but he died young, before he had any children. They also had four daughters. Ysabel married King Manuel of Portugal. She died in childbirth, so Manuel married her sister, Maria, and she is now the Queen of Portugal. Catherine married King Henry VIII of England, so she is the Queen of England[74]. Joanna married Philip, the son of the Holy Roman Emperor Maximilian…"

"The Holy what…?" Malinali managed to interject.

"There is a giant confederation of princedoms and kingdoms throughout Central Europe that the Holy Father in Rome refers to as the Holy Roman Empire. It's a way for the Church to try to keep peace between them. The famous king Carolus Magnus[75] was declared the first Holy Roman Emperor, many centuries ago. The Hapsburg family now leads it. Maximilian is a Hapsburg.

"Flanders is part of this confederation, and that is where Philip is from. Joanna and Philip had a son, called Carlos, or Charles. Queen Isabella died in the year 1504. By then, Joanna had become known as *La Loca*, Joanna the Mad. She poisoned Philip and killed him in 1506. Thus, when I left Spain, this crazy woman and her six year-old son were the only heirs to the Spanish monarchy. When King Ferdinand died three years ago, in 1516, his sixteen-year-old grandson, Carlos, ordered that his crazy mother – who technically was now the Queen of Castile – be locked in a dark room without windows in the Black Castle of Tordesillas[76], so that he could rule unchallenged as the King of all Spain."

Malinali still wore a look of bewilderment. Before she could say anything, Cortez gently put a finger to her lips.

"Yes, my Doña Marina, it is all a ruse, my pretending to speak for Don Carlos, my telling the Mesheeka that he knows about them, that he knows of 'the Great Lord Montezuma.' How could that be true? We, this little band of

---

74 Catherine of Aragon (1485-1536) married King Henry VIII on June 11, 1509. After 23 years of marriage producing no male heir, Henry secretly married his mistress Anne Boleyn in January, 1533 and ordered Thomas Cranmer Archbishop of Canterbury to annul his marriage to Catherine in May. Excommunicated by Pope Clement VII, Henry created the Church of England.

75   Charlemagne, 747-814.

76   Joanna La Loca remained incarcerated there until her death, April 12, 1555.

Spaniards here in Tlaxcala right now, are the first ever to hear of him. Thousands of leagues from here, across the Great Ocean, there is a nineteen-year-old boy desperately trying to keep a country from flying apart, a country that was just put together by his grandparents. It is a land vastly larger than this land here of the Mesheeka and their neighbors.

"Does Pontochan seem a long way from your Paynala? In truth, it is roughly forty leagues. We have traveled perhaps fifty leagues from Cempoala to Tlaxcala. It is at least four times that far from one end of Spain to the other – some two hundred leagues. Moreover, before I left Cuba, we heard that Maximilian was in poor health. Don Carlos is a Hapsburg, through his father. He may be the next Holy Roman Emperor, trying to rule hundreds of kings and princes in a land larger than you can imagine, a land that stretches over a thousand leagues from one end to the other. And so it is that he does not know or care about us. But he soon will."

Before Malinali had a chance to ask how, Cortez answered her.

"My Doña Marina, there is another way of saying that fortune favors the brave. If you really believe that, it means that *a man can create his own destiny.* I am the son of a fine man who was unknown beyond the town of Medellin. I arrived in Hispaniola with only a desire to make a nice, comfortable life for myself. And I did. I saw that the best chance for me was in the new colony of Cuba. I worked hard, raising cattle and mining for gold. I had a beautiful *hacienda*, and I was elected *alcalde*, mayor of the capital city, Santiago de Cuba.

"I had achieved what I wanted, I was successful and respected – and I was no longer a young man. When I first heard the stories of another world, from the men who came back from Cordoba's and Grijalva's expeditions, I ignored them. What did this other world have to do with me? Yet it was I whom Diego Velazquez asked to organize a third expedition, after the failure of the first two. I was prepared to refuse, but when Andres de Duero, Velasquez's secretary, showed me the instructions for the expedition, I hesitated.

"I remember the day[77] so well. The document began by saying that the principal purpose of the expedition was to serve God. We were to bring the Word of the One True God, and of the salvation offered by His Son, to all of those whom we encountered. All Indians we met were to be well-treated, especially women, whom we were forbidden to tease or molest in any way.

---

77   October 23, 1518. A copy is in the Archivo General de Indias (AGI) in Seville, Patronato legajo 15.

We were to place all lands we discovered under the protection of the King of Spain, Don Carlos. It was a *capitulacion*, a formal contract giving us legal authority from His Majesty himself through his agent, Governor Velazquez. This meant that we were acting in the King's name, by his authority, and he must, by law, be informed of all that we accomplished.

"I signed the contract without any more hesitation, for the words *carpe diem*[78] thundered in my brain. I knew, at that moment, that this was my chance to create my destiny, to do what my God meant for me to do, to accomplish a great work of which my God and my King would be proud. Now do you see, my beautiful Doña Marina?"

"Yes," she whispered into his ear. They lay quietly, not saying a word. Then Malinali's forehead crinkled with a question. "But why, now, is Diego Velazquez your enemy?"

A rueful grin crept across Cortez's face. "That is a story for another day," was his reply. "For now, let us just enjoy this time that we have together."

---

78   Seize the day.

Chapter Eighteen

THE TALE OF TACLAELEL

They arose the next morning at dawn. Cortez ordered a small altar to be placed in the plaza, where the padres performed a Mass for the Spaniards. When he returned to his quarters, he found King Xicotencatl waiting there, along with a dignified, elderly man who looked at least as old as the king.

"Malinche," the king said through Malinali, "this is Chief Maxixcatzin, lord of our region of Ocotelolco. He is the military leader of all Tlaxcala, and has protected us from the Mesheeka for many years."

Malinali's eyes widened at the introduction, and she took it upon herself to expand Cortez's brief greeting of welcome.

"El Malinche says that he is honored to meet the famous protector of Tlaxcala," she told them, "and wishes to applaud his wisdom for having his commander, Chichimecatecle, refuse to support the foolishness of Young Xicotencatl when he attacked us on the plain of Tzompachtepetl."

Old Maxixcatzin regarded Malinali with a look of intense interest, then spoke directly to her. "Yes, the king's son can be foolish. So when my flank was not attacked, we did not participate. But how did you know to fight the Tlaxcalan army only on one side and not the other?"

"El Malinche knew that the banner of the white bird was yours," was her reply.

"And how did he know that, and that my forces were the ones to avoid?" Maxixcatzin persisted.

She gave a slight shrug of innocence. "El Malinche knows many things."

She turned to Cortez. "They say that they have much to discuss with you."

Cortez, who had stood watching the conversation between the Chief and Malinali, now regarded her and her words with bemusement.

"Doña Marina, it is evident that *you* have much to discuss with them. But I have learned by now that, when you are up to something, it is best for me to let you continue."

Smiles quivered around both of their lips but were quickly suppressed.

Malinali turned back to the two Tlaxcalan leaders and looked at them expectantly. Having been lost in thought, they blinked, then ordered their attendants to bring cacao to drink. Then, with their refreshments in hand, they all sat on mats laid out on the floor, while the king addressed Cortez:

"Malinche, for many years the gods have spoken to our priests, telling them that, one day, men would come from beyond the rising sun to rescue us from the Mesheeka. Our friends the Totonacs claimed you represented these men, but we did not believe them. It was my mistake to allow my son to attack you. Yet the battles you fought with him allowed us to see how strong, how brave, how invincible are the Spaniards. Now we know you are the men our gods promised to send to us."

Cortez bowed his head in acknowledgement, then nodded to Malinali to begin translating:

"It is true that we come from far away towards the rising sun. It is also true that these battles have allowed us to see how strong and brave are the Tlaxcalans. Now we understand why the Mesheeka have never conquered you, and how, together, the Spaniards and the Tlaxcalans can defeat the Mesheeka. But it is not your gods who have sent us to you. It is the One True God who has sent us, as Christians, to free you from the worship of false gods who drink human blood."

The king sighed. "Malinche," he replied at last, "let us not discuss which god sent you. It is enough for us that you are here. We wish for the Spaniards and the Tlaxcalans to come together" – he splayed his hands, then interlaced the fingers of each – "to create children combining our strengths. I have a very beautiful daughter whom I wish to be your wife. Chief Maxixcatzin and I have spoken to our nobles, and they all desire to have their daughters be wives to your men. The nobles have together several hundred daughters, enough for all of your men, every one of whom can then be our brothers."

Cortez raised his cup of cacao in salutation, and bade Malinali tell him how grateful he was for such a deep expression of friendship. "A daughter is the most precious gift a man can bestow upon another man. Please tell your nobles that we are all honored by this gift, and honored to be your brothers."

Huge smiles broke over the faces of the old king and chief. They stood up. "We have much more to talk to you about, Malinche," said Chief Maxix-catzin. "Perhaps we could show you our city at the same time?"

Cortez pleasantly agreed. As they were leaving and the king was being helped into his litter, as he was too infirm to walk far, Cortez took Malinali aside.

"Doña Marina, I don't care how you do it, but somehow you must arrange it so that I do not have to marry this man's daughter and yet not have him be upset about it. Even though she may be more attractive than the daughter of the Fat Cacique in Cempoala – which would not be difficult – I do not want to endure another Doña Catalina." He looked into her eyes. "I want my nights to be spent only with you."

Malinali felt as if her knees might buckle. She had to look away from Cortez to recover. There were many people around them, and no one must notice her loss of composure. She forced herself to breathe normally. Only Cortez noticed the impact of his words upon her. Without looking up at him, she whispered, "I will find a way, my Captain."

* * * * *

Everywhere the entourage went, throughout the city, they were greeted by beaming Tlaxcalans. Young children stared in wonder at the Spaniards, while many men and women came up to them with the gift of a flower. As Cortez walked alongside the king, who was being carried in his litter, he asked how it was that Tlaxcala had never been conquered by the Mesheeka.

"We are always warned," the king explained. "The men of Montezuma's army are like the leaves of a forest, they are so many. They have attacked us many times, killed many of our warriors, captured many more for sacrifice. What saves us is that so many of Montezuma's soldiers are not Mesheeka. Rather, they are men from kingdoms he has conquered and forced to fight for him. These men do not fight hard, for their heart is not in the battle. Many of these men hate the Mesheeka as we do, and always warn us of a coming attack. So it is that we are never attacked by surprise and are always prepared."

Chief Maxixcatzin further explained, "Nevertheless, we must always be on guard for an attack by night from Cholua. That is a very large city, a day's march towards Tenochtitlan. The Choluans are the most treacherous people we know. Montezuma launches many of his raids upon us from there. He keeps a large garrison of soldiers in every province he rules. These soldiers constantly force the people living there to pay tributes of gold and silver, feathers, jaguar skins, chalchihuite stones, cotton cloth, and always more and more men, women, and children for sacrifice. They take all of this by force, so all of the wealth in his empire is in his hands."

One word of the chief's caught Cortez. "Children? Did he say *children* for sacrifice?" he asked Malinali.

She nodded her head gravely and gave a one-word response: "*Tlaloc.*" Then she bade the chief explain.

"Tlaloc," he said, "is the Mesheeka Rain God. Without his blessing, the crops would wither and die in drought, and everyone would starve. The Mesheeka believe that only the sacrifice of children can gain his blessing. His face is blue, and he wears a crown of heron feathers and a net of clouds. The *Teocalli*, the Great Temple at Tenochtitlan, has two towers – one for sacrifices to Huitzilopochtli and the other to Tlaloc."

When Cortez listened to Malinali's translation in stunned silence, she added, "My father told me about Tlaloc. Only small children satisfy him. The more they cry while being sacrificed, the better, for the more their tears flow, the more Tlaloc will make it rain. That is why the Mesheeka priests rip off their fingernails before killing them, then throw the bloody nails into Lake Texcoco to feed Ahuitzotl, the lake monster."

Cortez and all the Spaniards with him crossed themselves. He stopped walking and stood still, staring at Malinali. Then he looked off in the distance and muttered, *"Madre de Dios,"* Mother of God. He looked back at Malinali. "We must talk of something else," he told her. "Ask them where they came from, how they came here. Anything…"

Both the king and the chief responded to the inquiry with enthusiasm. "We come from a magic place far to the north. It is called *Aztlan*, the Place of the Herons. It was a paradise, but then these savage Mesheeka came and ruined it, so we left."

Malinali interjected, "Ah, this Aztlan is the home of both the Tlaxcalans and Mesheeka. That would explain why they both speak Nahuatl." She motioned for the chief to continue.

"When we reached this beautiful valley, we knew that this should be our home. But there were bad people here, a race of giants called Chichimecas. We had to chase them away. Then the Mesheeka followed us and tried to steal our land. They failed, and we have been enemies ever since."

Malinali gave Cortez a look that told him she was making a great effort to stifle a laugh. "*Chichi* means 'dogs,' and *mecatl* means 'born of' or 'sons of' – and so Chichimecas means…"

"Sons of bitches…" As Cortez supplied the correct response, all the Spaniards in his entourage broke out in loud guffaws. Even Padre de la Merced could hardly contain himself. There was no way either Cortez or Malinali, who by now had become quite familiar with Spanish vulgarities, could contain themselves, either.

When Malinali explained the joke to Chief Maxixcatzin, all the Tlaxcalans laughed just as hard as the Spaniards. It was a sustained moment of shared merriment. After it, the chief commented, "Laughter between people is a sign of true friendship," and Cortez nodded in agreement.

"How did the Mesheeka come to be where they are now?" Cortez then asked.

The king explained. "They name themselves after the chief who led them out of Aztlan, where they had been living in seven caves. He was called Mesheektli, which means 'the navel of the moon,' after *metzli* for 'moon,' and *sheektli* for 'navel.' They wandered for many years, and when they came here, we chased them away, as we had chased the Chichimecas.

"They came to Lake Texcoco but could not find anyplace to live, because there were many strong kingdoms along its shores. But their leader, Tenoch, said this had to be their home, so they settled on a small, muddy island in the middle of the lake[79]. It was called Zoquitlan[80]. The only thing they knew how to do was fight. When they saw that there were always wars going on between the kingdoms around the lake, they offered their warriors to fight for whoever would pay them. This made them rich enough to buy slaves to

---

79   About 1325.
80   Mud-land.

make *chinampas*[81], to make their island bigger. They built it into an island city named after Tenoch, Tenochtitlan[82].

"That took one hundred winters. During that time, they were so busy fighting for these kingdoms that they left us alone. In my grandfather's time, Acamapitchtli (*ah-kama-pitched-lee*)[83] became their first *Huey Tlatoani*[84], followed by his son Huitzilihuitli (*weet-zil-ee-weet-lee*)[85].

"By my father's time, the Mesheeka had grown very strong, and many of the kingdoms had become weak because they let the Mesheeka do their fighting. The Tepanec kingdom was one, with their city of Azcapotzalco. Huitzilihuitli had married the daughter of the Tepanec king Tezozomoc, and their son Chimalpopoca[86] became *Huey Tlatoani* when he died.

"It was when Tezozomoc died[87] that great evil came to Lake Texcoco. The name of this evil was Tlacaelel (*tlah-ka-el-el*)[88], Chimalpopoca's halfbrother, for Huitzilihuitli had many wives. He conspired with Huitzilihuitli's brother Itzcoatl[89] to murder Chimalpopoca so that Itzcoatl could become the Mesheeka king and blame the murder on the new Tepanec king, Tezozomoc's son, Maxtla.

"This gave an excuse to conquer the Tepanecs, which the Mesheeka did, destroying the city of Azcapotzalco and killing Maxtla[90]. It was the first of many, many kingdoms, all conquered under the direction of Tlacaelel. He enslaved the Tepanecs and others, and had them build the causeways connecting Tenochtitlan to land.

"For seventy winters Tlacaelel was the true ruler of the Mesheeka as the Cihuacoatl (*see-wa-ko-wattle*)[91] and Tlacochcalcatl (*tla-coach-kal-cottle*)[92], counselor and military commander to the kings. When Itzcoatl died in the year I was born[93], Tlacaelel made his brother, the First Montezuma[94], king,

---

81 Squares of canes and logs, filled with mud from the lake bottom.
82 *Titlan* means 'the place of.'
83 'Handful of Reeds.' Ruled 1375-1396.
84 Great Speaker, the Aztec ruler.
85 'Hummingbird Feather.' Ruled 1396-1417.
86 'Smoking Shield.'
87 1426.
88 'Manly Heart.' Lived 1397-1487.
89 'Obsidian Snake.' Ruled 1427-1440.
90 1428.
91 'Snake Woman.'
92 'Spear House Chief.'
93 1440.
94 Born 1398, ruled 1440-1469.

followed by Montezuma's son Axayacatl (*Ah-shy-ya-cottle*)[95], then Axaya-catl's brother Tizoc[96]. Before his own death, Tlacaelel had Tizoc killed, as he thought him too weak, and put another son of Montezuma's, Ahutizotl (*ah-weet-zottle*)[97], on the Mesheeka throne.

"It was Tlacaelel who invented the *Xochiyaoyotl* (*zo-chee-yow-yottle*), the Flower Wars. This was an excuse never to stop conquering other peoples. Before Tlacaelel, Huitzilopochtli was the Mesheeka god of the hunt. Animals were sacrificed to him, and only sometimes people.

"Tlacaelel said that Huitzilopochtli controlled the rising of the sun and kept the heavens in one piece, and that he needed food to sustain his labors. It was the holy duty of the Mesheeka to provide him with the only food that would satisfy him – the 'flower' of blood from human hearts. Tlacaelel decreed that Mesheeka warriors must never stop waging Holy Wars – Flower Wars – to capture prisoners for sacrifice.

"He also decreed that other gods were always hungry. Tlaloc needed the flower of babies' blood so that it would rain. Xipe (*she-pay*) needed human skins so that plants would grow. Tlacaelel had the *Teocalli*[98] built in the center of Tenochtitlan. When it was completed, just before he died[99], he ordered a dedication ceremony. Twenty thousand prisoners were sacrificed. It took two weeks to kill them all."

There was silence when the king finished, a long silence. Noting it, the king said, "Forgive me, Malinche, but it is our habit to give long speeches."

"And we thank you for it, King Xicotencatl, for we have learned much by it," came Cortez's response. "The Mesheeka once more remind me of the Moors, who we fought in Spain for so long. They, too, live for Holy War to conquer others and force them to believe in their false god, Allah. But they were not as evil as the Mesheeka, for they do not believe that Allah drinks human blood."

Cortez hesitated and looked at Malinali. She saw that he was making a decision about whether to say something. "Doña Marina, now is the time I must make a request of the king. Tell him I have seen, here in Tlaxcala, the wooden buildings with gratings full of Indian men and women imprisoned in

---

95   'Water Mask.' Ruled 1469-1481.
96   Ruled 1481-1486.
97   'Water Dog.' Ruled 1486-1502.
98   The Great Temple.
99   1487.

them, being fed until they are fat enough to be sacrificed and eaten. Tell him that, if he wants my help against the Mesheeka, he must allow me to break open these prisons and set the prisoners free. What does it matter if Montezuma sacrifices many more people to his gods than he does to his? We will not be brothers, and none of my men will marry any of his women, until all of the prisoners for sacrifice in every city in all Tlaxcala are freed and no more hearts are fed to his gods."

The King was silent for some time upon hearing this. Then he reached up and ran his fingers over Cortez's face. "I am so old that I can only see who you are with my fingers, not my eyes, Malinche," he said. He breathed deeply. "Yes, what our gods said about you is true. You are the one who will kill the gods and bring new gods in their place. We want you to teach us about your Christian gods, the ones you call the True God, and his son Jesus, and his mother, Mary."

Malinali looked up at Cortez, waiting for his reply. "This is not the time to explain the Holy Trinity, nor his misunderstanding of it," he told her. "Just tell him it will be my honor to instruct him. Then ask if we may free the prisoners."

Upon hearing Malinali's translation, King Xicotencatl reached out to explore Cortez's face with his fingers once again. Then he spoke one word.

"Yes."

Chapter Nineteen

THE MARRIAGE OF TECULEHUATZIN

For more than two weeks, every day in Tlaxcala seemed more enjoyable to the Spaniards than the day before. The friendship shown to them by the Tlaxcalans was overwhelming. Children were constantly giving them flowers. Everywhere they went in the city, they were invited into homes to share a meal. Older women, *Señoras*, were always bringing food to their quarters, and there seemed to be a never-ending number of young ladies, *Señoritas*, desiring to share their quarters with them.

One reason for such an abundance of hospitality was the Spaniards' strict obedience to Cortez's stern command to take nothing – nothing – from the Tlaxcalans except what was given to them. They vividly remembered how, when Cortez caught a soldier named Mora stealing a turkey from a village on the way to Tlaxcala, he ordered that the soldier be hanged. Mora would have died, had not Pedro de Alvarado cut the rope with his sword at the last moment.

Now, while the men were enjoying themselves, Cortez spent as much time as possible with King Xicotencatl and Chief Maxixcatzin, teaching them about Christianity. He told them a score of stories from the Bible, mostly about the life and miracles of Jesus. He explained repeatedly that the Christian God was a god of love and forgiveness and salvation.

He also explained how gods like Huitzilopochtli and Tlaloc were like Satan. However, with the advice and admonition of Friar Bartholomew Olmedo and Padre Juan Diaz, he did this gently and patiently. Soon, the two other main Tlaxcalan Chiefs, Citlalpopocatzin (*seet-lal-popo-cot-zin*) and Temilotecutl (*tem-ee-lo-tay-cuttle*), began attending the discussions.

Were Cortez and the other Spaniards sons of gods or sons of men? This was the question that most interested them. "Be assured," Cortez answered, "we are human just like you. All of us are equal in the eyes of the Lord. The only difference between us is that we have the great fortune to be Christians, and thus can be granted salvation. We wish the same for you, and for you to be our brothers in Heaven as you are now here on Earth."

Malinali saw the effect that these words of Cortez had upon all four – but, even more than her translated words, it was the obvious sincerity with which Cortez spoke that touched them the most. In the moment of silence that followed, one of Cortez's officers, Juan Velasquez de Leon, entered the room and asked to speak to Friar Olmedo. They conversed quietly, yet the friar could not contain his surprise at the request the young officer seemed to be making. "It is impossible!" the friar called out. "You and this girl do not speak a word of each other's language. She is not a Christian. Impossible!"

"Then you must baptize her, for marry her I will!" Velazquez de Leon shouted back. All eyes were now turned upon him. He looked at Cortez. "Forgive me, Captain. But I… I…" He glanced at Malinali and blushed. *His youth and passion are showing*, she thought. He stopped stammering and stood up straight. "Captain, I have fallen in love with a young lady, and I wish to marry her – not a marriage of convenience such as, forgive me, Captain, yours to the Fat Cacique's daughter in Cempoala, but for her to be my fully lawful Christian wife."

Cortez said nothing for a moment, just sat and looked at his officer. "Perhaps we should meet this young lady, Señor de Leon," he said softly.

De Leon brightened. "She is outside. Thank you, Captain." He left and quickly reentered with an extremely beautiful woman. Malinali saw Chief Maxixcatzin's head snap back in shock; then a look of intense satisfaction spread across his face. "Otila!" he exclaimed.

The young lady looked at the chief. "*Tahtli!*" she responded.

Cortez and Malinali exchanged glances. "Does this marriage have the blessing of the lady's father?" he asked, looking at the chief. A few words between the chief and Malinali confirmed that it did. Cortez looked up at de Leon. "Then it has my blessing, as well. I wish you both great happiness." There wasn't a person in the room who wasn't smiling. "Friar de Olmedo, please begin making the necessary preparations," Cortez requested. Then he turned back to King Xicotencatl.

"For this, we will need a church. I would like to request of the king that he give us one of his temples, which we will convert into a house of Christian worship and ceremony." The king quickly assented. Cortez immediately ordered Padre Juan Diaz to accompany the king's messenger to the designated temple and begin the conversion – "in the spirit of friendship and cooperation," he commanded of Diaz.

Soon after Diaz and the messenger left, along with Velazquez de Leon and Otila, Pedro de Alvarado made his entrance. Accompanying him was a young woman with a regal bearing whose beauty was simply astonishing. "My Captain," he said, and bowed to Cortez. "May I have the honor to introduce to you the Princess Teculehuatzin (*tay-coolie-wat-zin*), daughter of King Xicotencatl, to whom I am betrothed. I understand you have given your blessing to the marriage of Señor Velazquez de Leon and the Princess Otila. I wish for your blessing upon ours, as well."

Being almost blind, the king could not see his daughter. Cortez's look at Malinali was more intense this time. "Please explain to the king that Don Pedro is as close to me as a brother. He is the finest and bravest man among us. Will the king consent to grant the precious gift of his daughter to Don Pedro?" he asked, and Malinali could see Cortez's mind whirring.

The king called out to his daughter, upon hearing Malinali. "I had promised you to Malinche, my Teculehuatzin. Is this what you wish?"

"Oh, my father," she responded, "if your eyes were only young again and could see him, you would know why I call him *Tonatio*, the Sun – and if you could see me, you would understand that my love for him is as bright as the sun."

"Malinche," said the king upon hearing these words, "I give my daughter to Don Pedro as gladly as I would give her to you, if you do not object."

Cortez closed his eyes and shook his head imperceptibly to himself. He opened his eyes to look at Malinali and murmur, "*Otra vez,*" once again. Their eyes locked for another moment, then he said, "Please tell the king that I am happy his daughter and my brother have found love for each other, and that it is my honor to bless their marriage."

* * * * *

"Should I ask how you did this?" Cortez asked Malinali, when they were finally alone that night.

"Do you need to?" she replied mischievously. "I knew that the first thing to do was meet Teculehuatzin and the other daughters of the nobles. I took one look at her and realized she would require a man as handsome as she was beautiful – and forgive me, my Captain, but Don Pedro, with his hair and beard like the rays of the sun, seems like a god. So all I needed to do was make sure they would meet."

Cortez's grin showed he was enjoying her explanation. "But how did you arrange for Velazquez de Leon to meet the other lady – Otila?"

Malinali burst out laughing. "Oh, that was not my doing. She was with Teculehuatzin and me in the market square when my Totonac friends happened to bring Don Pedro there. Señor de Leon was with him, and while I introduced Don Pedro and Teculehuatzin, Señor de Leon saw Otila. He stood still and silent for a moment and just stared at her. Then he started talking to her loudly, comparing her to the moon, a flower, and a beautiful bird. He went on and on, with Otila of course not understanding a word he was saying. It was so funny, I had to force myself not to laugh. But Otila did not think it was funny. She thought it was wonderful. She asked me what he was saying, I told her, I introduced them, and they walked off into the market, with him holding her hand. When I turned back to Don Pedro and Teculehuatzin, they, too, had wandered off together, and I saw that my job was done."

"You are a magician," Cortez whispered.

She smiled back at him. "Would you like some more of my magic?" she whispered back.

It was an ecstatic night.

* * * * *

The wedding ceremonies and celebrations were the most euphoric and elaborate in the memory of any Tlaxcalan – and it seemed that the entire population of the Tlaxcalan kingdom turned out for them.

A grand parade, led by Cortez, King Xicotencatl, Chiefs Maxixcatzin, Citlalpopocatzin and Temilotecutl, followed by Tlaxcalan nobles in feathered finery, Cortez's officers on horseback, the Spanish soldiers with their armor and swords gleamingly polished, the Xocotlan and Totonac warriors led by Chief Mamexi, wound through the city. Every step of the way, they were surrounded by deliriously happy throngs of Tlaxcalans waving, cheering and showering them with flowers.

The temple that the king had given to the Spaniards had been cleaned and whitewashed, and the statue of the Tlaxcalan god of war, Camaxtli (*kah-mashed-lee*), had been replaced with a cross and a painting of the Virgin Mary. On the very spot where the statue of Camaxtli had stood, there was now a carved stone baptismal font with a basin of Holy Water. In front of the font, waiting for the procession, were Friar de Olmedo and Padre Diaz.

Nearby were the Princesses Teculehuatizn and Otila, together with four other daughters of Tlaxcalan nobles. The first of these four, Toltequequet-zaltzin (*toll-tay-kway-kwayt-zalt-zin*), led the other three to the font, where the priests baptized them. Cortez stepped forward, took Toltequequetzaltzin by the hand, and escorted her to Gonzalo de Sandoval. He then escorted the other three, in turn, to Cristobal de Olid, Andres de Tapia, and Alonzo de Avila.

With that accomplished, the priests conducted a Mass. When a bell rang, concluding the Mass, Juan Velasquez de Leon stepped forward as Princess Otila came to the font. Once she had been baptized by Friar de Olmedo and given the name Doña Elvira, they stood hand in hand before Padre Juan Diaz as he recited a prayer in Latin, read from what he called the Old Testament, recited what he called a Psalm, then read from what he called the New Testament. At last, he turned to Otila, with Malinali on her side to translate.

"Doña Elvira, have you freely entered into the Catholic Church to become a Christian and accept Jesus Christ as your savior?"

She quickly answered yes.

He looked at the couple. "Marriage is a sacred covenant between the two of you and God. Is it your free choice to accept this covenant between each other, to love and honor each other, to be faithful to each other, and to accept the sacred responsibility of the children who may come of this marriage?"

They both eagerly said yes. Cortez, standing by de Leon, handed him a ring, and Malinali did likewise with Otila. Padre Diaz asked them to place the rings on each other's finger. "The exchange of these rings seals the sacred bond between you, which no man may now break asunder. Doña Elvira and Velasquez de Leon, I now pronounce you husband and wife, married in the eyes of the Lord."

The newlyweds embraced, stood and bowed before everyone assembled, then walked to the side of the altar.

Now came the moment that all of Tlaxcala had come to see. People had squeezed into every place to stand, in the plaza in front of the new church, and were crowded onto every rooftop around it. Princess Teculehuatizn stepped forward to be baptized. Malinali turned to the crowd and announced, in as loud a voice as she could:

"The Princess Teculehuatzin, daughter of Xicotencatl, King of Tlaxcala, has now accepted the Christian God as her god, and the Son of God, Jesus Christ, as her savior. The Princess Teculehuatizn has been given the Christian name of Doña Luisa."

As her words were repeated by those who heard them to those who didn't, a murmur arose from the crowd, which was trying to understand the meaning of these strange words. The murmur ceased when Pedro de Alvarado proudly stepped to Teculehuatzin's side. His long golden hair and beard gleamed in the sunlight, and people began shouting the name they knew their princess had given him – *Tonatio! Tonatio!* He flashed a smile and bowed to the crowd, which responded with cheers and yells.

The princess spoke to Malinali, who informed Pedro de Alvarado, "Doña Luisa says the people love you."

He grinned and responded, "No, they love their princess. If they love me, it is because they know that I love her."

Malinali thought for a second, then suggested, "Perhaps we should turn the ceremony around so the people can see the two of you, while I translate Father Olmedo's words to them."

This was accepted by all. Don Pedro – Tonatio – with Cortez at his side, and Princess Teculehuatzin – Doña Luisa – with Malinali at her side faced Father Olmedo and the crowd, while Malinali loudly translated the words of the ceremony. When the rings were exchanged, the final words pronounced, and the newlyweds embraced, the crowd burst into delirious cheers. Thousands of flowers were flung in the air towards the couple. The entire city seemed convulsed in celebration.

The festivities continued far into the night, with the Tlaxcalan celebrants consuming great quantities of *pulque*[100].

* * * * *

Early the next morning, the city was asleep – but not King Xicotencatl, who sent a messenger to request a meeting with Cortez. When he arrived at Cortez's quarters, Malinali thought he looked very somber, as if he had something very serious to say. Yet he did not look angry. Instead he looked calm.

"Malinche, after the uniting of my Teculehuatzin with your Tonatio, many people spoke to me. They were very happy about this uniting, but what they spoke most of was that there was no blood. They thought this very strange at first. They asked, *How can there be an important ceremony without sacrifice? How can one ask the blessing of the gods without feeding the gods their food of heart blood?* Then they talked of how different is this Christian god of yours – a god that does not need blood to give his blessing. Such a god must be very strong, not to require food.

"This is what many of my people said to me. I have talked about this with those who rule Tlaxcala with me. We talked about how such a god must be more powerful than the gods of Montezuma and the Mesheeka. We talked about your words to us that gods who drink human blood are demons. We talked about how strongly we felt the ceremony yesterday in our hearts, yet the ceremony was of such peace. We talked about how happy our daughters are to be Christians now.

"We talked of these things for many hours, Malinche, and now we have made our decision. It is our request that you make us Christians, just as you have done for our daughters."

Malinali could see Cortez was stunned. His eyes went blank for a second, then focused on her. "Doña Marina, please tell the king to forgive me, but I must take a moment to pray and give thanks to God for the king's decision."

Malinali whispered Cortez's words to the king as Cortez got down on one knee, crossed himself, and prayed. He then stood up to embrace the king

---

100   The fermented juice of the maguey plant.

and tell him, "Now you are truly my brother, here on Earth, and forever in Heaven."

After that, Cortez wasted no time. He asked for Padre Juan Diaz to meet him at the new church for an important baptismal ceremony. Before long, a small group had assembled at the altar. With most of the town still sleeping off the revelry of the night before, the crowd of witnesses was small.

Cortez addressed the Padre and the group. "Padre Diaz, we are gathered here by the grace of our Lord God, Who has granted the four rulers of Tlaxcala the wisdom to request that they be baptized as Christians."

At these words, the padre clutched the cross hanging at his chest, crossed himself, and murmured words of prayerful thanks.

Cortez continued, "Doña Marina, please explain to the king and the other nobles that such a sacred ceremony as this requires *padrinos*[101] who will witness and sponsor their initiation into the Church of Christ, and who will guide and walk with them into living a Christian life. That is why I have asked my closest officers, Don Pedro de Alvarado, Don Cristobal de Olid, and Don Gonzalo de Sandoval, to be their *padrinos* this day. Please tell the king that I am honored to be his *padrino*, and that I request that you be his *madrina*[102] and guide in Christ."

It was Malinali's turn to be stunned. Her eyes locked with Cortez's. She nodded her head slightly and knew that her partnership with him was now complete.

Once she related Cortez's words to the Tlaxcalans, Cristobal de Olid took Chief Temilotecutl by the hand and led him to the baptismal font where Padre Diaz christened him with the name Don Gonzalo. Chief Citlalpopocatzin was led to the font by Gonzalo de Sandoval and christened Don Bartholomew.

Pedro de Alvarado then stood in front of Chief Maxixcatzin, flashed his dazzling smile, bowed to him, then bowed to King Xicotencatl standing next to him, and greeted the king with the word *Suegro*[103]. Then he turned to Malinali. "Doña Marina, please tell the king that I call him Suegro, which means he is now a father to me. Tell him that it is my highest honor to welcome him and his chiefs to the Catholic Church of Christ this day – and that it is only

---

101   Godparents.
102   Godmother.
103   Father-in-law

this honor that could have taken me away from his daughter and my wife on this morning."

His words brought smiles of deep satisfaction to both Tlaxcalan faces. Maxixcatzin whispered something in the king's ear which Malinali could not help overhearing: "Now we know why Otila's new husband is not here." The king struggled to suppress a laugh, and both assumed faces of seriousness. Pedro de Alvarado took Maxixcatzin's hand, then led him to the font to be baptized and christened Don Lorenzo.

King Xicotencatl now stood alone. Cortez stepped to one side of him and Malinali to the other. They each took one of the king's hands to lead him to the font. "Padre," Cortez said, addressing Padre Diaz, "I bring to you his eminence King Xicotencatl, ruler of the ancient Republic of Tlaxcala, to be received into the bosom of Christ, to be washed of his sins, and welcomed into our Holy Catholic Church. I say this as his *padrino*, his guide in our faith. I bring also to you Doña Marina, who is to be his *madrina* and witness to this sacred ceremony."

"You both accept the duties and obligations of *padrino* and *madrina* of this new child of Christ?" asked the Padre. Malinali and Cortez nodded. They stepped aside, and the king lowered his head to have the holy water poured over him. After words in Latin and the sign of the cross, the Padre said, "I christen you Don Vincente."

Cortez and Malinali again took the king's hands. They both said to him, *"Mi hermano."*

The king turned to Malinali for translation.

"It means," she said, "that, for both of us, you are now our brother."

Chapter Twenty

THE LEGEND IN CUBA

"Señor Aguilar!" Malinali shouted with a bright smile. She had spotted him sitting under a large ceiba tree at the edge of Tlaxcala's market, eating his mid-day meal.

He returned her smile. "Doña Marina!" he called back. "Would you care to join me?"

She sat down next to him. "It seems so long since I saw you last," she said.

"Yes – well, you learned Spanish so quickly, while I have been so slow at learning Nahuatl, that there was little need to help you translating for Captain Cortez," came his reply. "What I really needed to do was learn to be a soldier again, after being a Mayan slave for those eight long years. So I have been with the soldiers."

"Would you like to learn Nahuatl?" she asked. "I can teach you."

Aguilar considered it for a moment, then answered, "I would like that. Nahuatl is very different from Mayan, but I should try. If I can find the time, that is, for a soldier is kept very busy."

"You don't look very busy to me," came a nearby voice.

"Bernal!" both Malinali and Aguilar exclaimed at the same time.

"Do I understand that Doña Marina is now going to be your teacher, instead of the other way around?" Bernal asked Aguilar with a grin.

Aguilar shook his head. "I'm afraid so."

They chatted happily for a while, then Malinali had a thought. "Bernal, I have a question for you." Her eyes had a mischievous twinkle. "Why are Captain Cortez and Diego Velasquez – the governor, as you call him, of your island of Cuba – enemies?"

Bernal smiled and Aguilar laughed out loud. "Ah, Doña Marina, the soldiers tell many stories about those two," said Aguilar. "But I don't know which ones are true or false, because I was in the Mayan jungles. Let us hope that Señor Castillo can enlighten us!"

Bernal's smile changed to a frown. "It is a good story, yes – but there are certain parts of it that might make Doña Marina uncomfortable."

Malinali gave him a puzzled look. "I have been uncomfortable before. Please continue, Señor Castillo," she said with mocking courtesy.

"Very well. It starts, as stories about Cortez seem always to do, with..." Bernal looked at Malinali and hesitated... "a woman. Her name was Catalina Suarez. She was the daughter of Don Diego Velasquez's best friend, Juan Suarez. She was very beautiful, and she attracted Cortez's eye, and then became his mistress. But Cortez's eyes always wandered, and when he stopped seeing her, she complained to her father that Cortez had broken his promise to marry her.

"Her father complained to Don Diego, who ordered Cortez to marry her. Cortez is not a man you give orders to, so he, of course, refused. And so Don Diego threw him into prison. But Cortez is not a man you can keep in a jail for long. He escaped through a window in his cell, and claimed sanctuary in the church of Baracoa. Don Diego ordered Baracoa's *alguacil*[104], Juan Escudero – yes, the man who was hung at Villa Rica[105] – to violate the church's sanctuary and arrest Cortez anyway.

"Many people were upset about this, so Don Diego decided that he had to get rid of the problem quickly. He had Cortez shackled in irons and placed upon a ship that was to sail for Spain the next day. All of the years of Cortez's work to create a good life and a home for himself in this New World were lost. He was now ruined, destined to return penniless to Spain.

"But the chains on his wrists and feet were loose. For hours, in the dark belly of the ship, he slowly worked his hands and feet free, at the cost of much skin and blood. As he had escaped the prison through a window, he now squeezed through a porthole, lowered himself into the water, and swam ashore.

"It is then that Cortez did what made him a legend in Cuba. Wet and

---

104 Constable.
105 See Chapter Thirteen: The Bromas.

bleeding, he went to his home, cleaned himself, put on fresh clothes, then his armor – chain mail, breastplate, greaves, and helmet – strapped on his finest Toledo sword, saddled his best horse, and rode straight for the mansion of Governor Don Diego. It was very late at night, almost dawn, and the household, including the guards, were all asleep. Cortez stole quietly into the mansion, up the stairs, and into Don Diego's private bedroom. Don Diego was awakened by the cold tip of Cortez's steel sword at his throat.

"'Please do not move or make a sound, Señor Velasquez,' Cortez whispered to the governor. 'We are going to settle our differences here and now.' You can imagine Don Diego's amazement – and his fright. He could see that Cortez was prepared to kill him where he lay, and so he quickly promised Cortez a pardon for his 'transgressions.'

"'What transgressions?' Cortez asked angrily. Don Diego felt the steel press deeper into his skin. 'You are the transgressor – throwing me into jail for breaking a promise I never made, breaking the holy sanctuary of a church to seize me, ruining me and sending me back to Spain in chains. Please tell me, Señor, why should I pardon you and spare your life?'

"Don Diego is fat and greedy, but he is not stupid nor a coward. He looked straight at Cortez and told him, 'Because, if you kill me, you will hang. But if you don't kill me, I will double your property and wealth. All will be forgiven as if none of it, including this moment, ever happened. This I promise to you on my honor as a Spanish *caballero*[106].' Upon hearing these words and that promise, Cortez removed his sword from Don Diego's throat. 'That I can accept,' he said.

"Yet Don Diego continued to look at Cortez. 'I must ask something from you in return,' he said, 'I must ask you to marry the Señorita Juarez.' Cortez angrily sheathed his sword. 'Don Diego – I will not threaten you again, because we now have an agreement of honor. But why do you insist on prolonging the issue that caused our problem in the first place?' 'Because,' replied Don Diego, 'it is a matter of honor between me and the lady's father – and it should be a matter of honor with you.'

"Cortez made a face. 'Honor – for me? Why?' he asked.

"'Because the lady is with child – your child,' was Don Diego's answer."
Bernal braced himself for Malinali's reaction. She gasped in shock. Her

---

106   Gentleman.

gaze turned inward as she took a slow deep breath. Then she looked steadily at him again. "Please continue, Bernal," she said calmly.

"Taken aback, Cortez replied, 'This I did not know.' We who understand Cortez know what he calculated. Marrying Catalina would be his best insurance that Don Diego would continue to keep his word. So Cortez smiled and bowed before the governor in his bed. 'Very well,' he said, 'I agree. The Lady Catalina shall be my wife.' He extended his hand to Don Diego. 'You and I have a *pacto de caballeros*[107].' They shook hands, and Cortez added, 'And the doubling of my wealth and property of which you spoke can be your wedding present to us!' Cortez did not let go of Don Diego's hand until the governor nodded in agreement.

"As word of this episode spread in Cuba and Hispaniola, it made Cortez a figure of legend. But Cortez knew that this could be dangerous for him, as it was so embarrassing to Don Diego. So he married Catalina as soon as he could – this was in the Year of Our Lord 1514 – and worked as hard as he could on his property, raising his cattle and mining his gold, so that before long he had the finest *hacienda* in Cuba, on the River Duaban, and he was very wealthy. He also worked hard at befriending Don Diego, and was so successful that he became *alcalde*[108] of Santiago."

Malinali nodded her head. "Yes, he told me about being an *alcalde* – but not about… the lady Catalina. What about her… and their child?"

Bernal looked at her with sympathy in his eyes – and sadness. "The child was stillborn, and the lady almost died in childbirth. From then on, her heart was very weak, and any work made her very tired. Her health was broken, and some say her spirit, as well. She was never with child again.

"Cortez tried to make her happy. He spent a lot of money on her, and on entertaining her friends and family at his hacienda. His eyes began wandering again, of course, because women flew to Cortez like bees to honey, and how could he resist? At the same time, though, Cortez began attending church more often, going to Mass almost daily and praying.

"He was constantly making new friends, and was so generous with them many were in his debt, yet he never asked to be repaid. One in particular was Andres de Duero, the governor's secretary. When Don Diego announced the formation of a third expedition to this strange new land discovered by Her-

---

107 An agreement of honor between gentlemen
108 Mayor.

nandez de Cordoba and Juan de Grijalva, Andres de Duero convinced Don Diego to name Cortez as the expedition leader. Within two weeks, Cortez had secured six ships and four hundred men – of which I was one. Men raced to join the standard of the legendary Cortez – some even sailing from Hispaniola, like Francisco Rodriguez Magariño, to do so.

"Cortez spent all of the money he had saved on outfitting the ships, and borrowed all of the money he could on his hacienda and other properties. He dressed the part of a great leader, going about in a black velvet cloak with golden knots, and a hat with plumes of feathers. He was in a great hurry, because he knew that all of Velasquez's relatives and friends wanted the expedition taken away from him and given to them. When word came to him from Andres de Duero that Don Diego was about to issue orders canceling Cortez's authority, Cortez decided to sail that very night.

"The one thing he did not have enough of was food for his men. So he went to Santiago's *desolladero*[109] and seized all of the stored meat, along with every pig, cow, and sheep waiting for slaughter. When the butcher Fernando Alonso complained that the city would have nothing to eat, Cortez took off the large gold chain around his neck and gave it to him for 'his trouble.'

"Señor Alonso was afraid of being punished for letting Cortez take the city's meat supply, so he went to the governor's mansion to explain to Don Diego. 'This makes it final,' the governor said. 'Now Cortez is finished.' But it was late at night, so Don Diego went to sleep. At dawn, he awoke and, with a detachment of soldiers, went to the port to have Cortez arrested. He was stunned to see Cortez's ships sailing away on the morning tide! The only ship not yet underway was Cortez's flagship, the *Santa Elena*.

"Don Diego and his men stood helpless on the wharf, calling out to Cortez on his ship, who proceeded to climb down into a small rowboat with two sailors who rowed him to within shouting distance of the governor, but beyond the range of the crossbows or muskets of the soldiers.

"'Captain Cortez, my *compadre*, what are you doing?' Don Diego yelled.

Cortez stood up in the rowboat. 'My Governor,' he yelled back, 'all has been prepared and it is time for us to go. What are your orders?'

Don Diego was so stunned by this question, at Cortez being so *desconcado*[110], that he opened his mouth but no words came out. At his silence, Cortez

---

109 Slaughterhouse.
110 Shameless and daring.

reached for his plumed hat, swept it before him as he bowed to the governor, then had his sailors row him back to his ship. Don Diego and his men stood on the wharf and watched the *Santa Elena* sail away.[111]

"I saw this with my own eyes from the deck of the *Santa Elena*. It was a wonder to behold."

"Cortez is a wonder to behold, true," said Aguilar. "Though I have two questions. How was it that so many Velasquez men came on the expedition, and why did they sail on that morning with Cortez?"

Bernal smiled. "In answer to your first question, you must remember that Don Diego is not stupid. He made sure that many of his friends and of the people loyal to him signed on. Cortez could not object, but he knew who they were. However, in answer to your second question, Cortez convinced them that all of the preparations, including the early departure, were at Don Diego's request. So it is that Cortez has proven himself far more clever than our Governor Velasquez. He has now won over Velasquez's friends to his side. Yet I think we may still see a surprise from Don Diego, who hates more than ever a man who has humiliated him twice and is legendary for it."

"What sort of surprise?" Aguilar asked.

Bernal shrugged his shoulders.

"I think we should not worry about it," said Malinali. "Instead, Señor Aguilar, I think we should thank Señor Castillo for such a long answer to my question." At that, they all laughed together. "And so, Aguilar," Malinali continued, "let us start your lessons in Nahuatl. Bernal, would you care to learn some words with us?"

---

111   November 18, 1518.

Chapter Twenty - One

THE TRAP OF CHOLULA

They spent most of the *siesta*[112] turning Spanish words into Nahuatl. After a while, Malinali realized that she had been having so much fun that it had made her forgetful. She shook her head. "I must leave," she told them. "Our Mesheeka guests have come for their daily ceremony of complaining to Captain Cortez, and I must be there, for it is through me that they address their complaints."

"Have fun," Aguilar joked.

Malinali sighed. "Our talking - *that* was fun. But 'fun' and 'Mesheeka' are two words that don't go together - in Spanish *or* Nahuatl."

Today is our nineteenth day here in Tlaxcala, she thought as she walked to Cortez's quarters. For every one of those days, the Mesheeka emissaries who had accompanied them from Xocotlan had come to complain to Cortez about what terrible people the Tlaxcalans were, how they were all traitors and thieves and poor and wicked and not fit even to be slaves. It was tiresome to hear and translate, and how Cortez could pretend always to be courteous and polite, or even to stay awake, during the daily moaning, she didn't know.

Today, however, when she saw the crowd of soldiers in front of Cortez's quarters, she realized that something was different. A new delegation of four Mesheeka nobles had arrived - chiefs of very high rank judging by their robes, jewelry, and headdresses - and had covered the floor with gifts of gold, jade, and cloth embroidered with feathers. Cortez looked up at her with raised eyebrows and a *where-have-you-been?* expression. Clearly, everyone had been

---

112   The Spaniards' period of rest after the mid-day meal.

waiting for her.

She felt both embarrassment for being late and satisfaction at being so important. Brushing both emotions aside, she walked directly up to the Mesheeka. She quickly determined which of the four nobles was the delegation leader. For all his age and dignity, his eyes briefly widened in surprise to see Malinali's eyes looking into them. Outside of his family, she thought, no woman had ever once looked right at him.

"You are she," he said. "You are the woman who speaks for your Speaker, your *Tlatoani*. You are the woman of whom there is much talk in Tenochtitlan."

Now he was looking back into her eyes, probing for a reaction. She didn't give him any. "But you are not here to talk to me or about me," she replied smoothly. "You are here..." she turned and opened her hand towards Cortez, "to talk to Captain Hernando Cortez of the Kingdom of Spain. You are here to talk to..." she turned back to look at the old Mesheeka chief and let the word hang in the air, "Malinche."

He looked at her as if in a trance. "Yes... Malinche..." he said, almost to himself.

"Doña Marina, do these *caciques* have anything they wish to say to me?" Cortez asked quietly, his eyebrows raised again.

Malinali invited the Mesheeka chief to speak, and out poured a torrent of Nahuatl.

"These men represent the highest nobility in Tenochtitlan," Malinali explained to Cortez. "They come as the personal ambassadors of the Great Montezuma himself to request that you come to see him and be a guest in his palace in Tenochtitlan as soon as possible. The Great Montezuma is afraid for your safety among the traitors of Tlaxcala, and wishes you to leave here quickly, as every day you stay here increases your danger. The Great Montezuma asks that you travel now to Cholula, where you will be among friends who will take good care of you, and from there continue to Tenochtitlan, where everything the Great Montezuma has will be provided to you."

Cortez stood and smiled. "Please tell the ambassadors that I am honored by their invitation and will comply with the wishes of Lord Montezuma immediately. Tell them I regret the misunderstanding between Lord Montezuma and the people of Tlaxcala, whom I have found to be dear and trustworthy friends. I am sure that Lord Montezuma will prove to be a dear and trustworthy friend to me and my Lord, His Majesty King Don Carlos. I thank the Lord Montezuma for sending such high nobles to convey his message. It is my hope that they will stay with us as we travel to Cholula."

Malinali saw the flash of alarm in the nobles' eyes at this last sentence, for it meant that the nobles were to be hostages, and that their lives would be forfeit should there be any trouble in Cholula. Nevertheless, they bowed while the old chief thanked Cortez and said that they, of course, would go to Cholula with him.

So - King Xicotencatl's warning may be right, she thought.

The king was advising that Cortez not go to Cholula, insisting that the best way to Tenochtitlan was by way of Huexotzinco (*way-shot-sing-ko*). "The people of Huexotzinco have been our allies and friends for many years," the king had reminded Cortez repeatedly, "and those of Cholula are the opposite. "We know that you will be safe in Huexotzinco, and we know that in Cholula you will not."

When Malinali told Cortez of her suspicion that the king was right, he brushed her warning aside as he had the Tlaxcalans'. "I do not want an enemy behind me, if Cholula be one as we go to Tenochtitlan," he explained. "We will go there as Montezuma requests, and deal with whatever problems we may find."

Both she and the king were alarmed at Cortez's overconfidence. The king begged him to reconsider, telling him that it was dangerous and foolish to go to Cholula. But Cortez refused to relent. "Then tell Malinche," the king said to Malinali, "that I must send enough of my warriors to protect him, and that he cannot say no to this."

Cortez replied that he would be honored to have Tlaxcalan warriors by his side. *Perhaps,* Malinali thought, *this is what Cortez wanted all along.* But she was still worried.

So also were Cortez's men. They were not anxious to leave the safety and hospitality of Tlaxcala, or to leave behind women they had come to love, instead setting out on the road to danger once more.

As always, Cortez gathered them together and spoke to them in such words of soothing enthusiasm that he managed both to calm and excite them.

"While our time here has been most pleasant, you all know that we must depart. You have heard the descriptions of this great city Tenochtitlan, the capital of the Mesheeka. Compared to it and its riches, Tlaxcala is the smallest and most humble of villages. We have been welcomed to this great city by its Lord Montezuma. It is there that we will be treated like royalty. It is there that our destiny awaits us."

It was an emotional departure between the Spaniards and Tlaxcalans[113], with King Xicotencatl tearfully saying goodbye to his *padrino y madrina*, Cortez and Malinali, and his daughter, the Princess Teculehuatzin, now accompanying her husband, Pedro de Alvarado, as Doña Luisa. Thousands of Tlaxcalan warriors set off with the Spaniards, not simply at King Xicotencatl's command, but as eager protectors of their Princess. At their head was Chief Chichimecatecle. The Young Xicotencatl had refused to go, preferring to stay in Tlaxcala and brood in anger.

Cholula lay only eight leagues[114] from Tlaxcala, but that was too far to reach in a single day's march. Everyone slept out in the open on the first night, by a stream called Atoyac. The next morning, a large welcoming party of Cholulans arrived, led by several nobles, and bringing an abundant supply of maize and turkeys to eat. "We are afraid," announced one of the nobles, "that you have been told bad things about us which are not true. You should not believe what the Tlaxcalans say, for you are welcome among us." Cholulan priests appeared with bowls of burning copal incense, and ritually fumigated Cortez.

When they arrived that night at the city of Cholula, Malinali noticed that the Mesheeka nobles were escorted to a finer palace than Cortez's. Yet their quarters, and those of the other Spanish captains, seemed adequate, as was the food they were given. The Tlaxcalans and Totonacs, however, were not allowed inside the city gates. They were told to camp outside. Malinali had to make clear to their Cholulan hosts that Doña Luisa and the Tlaxcalan wives of the other Spanish "nobles" must be allowed to stay with their husbands, along with a contingent of the Princess's guardians and escorts. The Cholulans not only complied, but upon learning Doña Luisa's royal identity, lodged her and Pedro de Alvarado in a much nicer palace.

Cortez and Malinali discussed the situation before going to sleep. They had spent the previous hour in the clouds of Malinali's *ilhuicatl*, the Heavens,

---

113   October 12, 1519.
114   24 miles.

and Cortez was caressing her face. "I know your fears of being here," he told her. "Yet this place is such a powerful ally of the Mesheeka that I cannot have them at my back. I would be caught in a trap between Cholula and Tenochtitlan. It is better to see what the trap is here, and try to spring it now."

She looked up at him without replying, for she was still in the clouds. He brought her down to earth by telling her, "So you must befriend these people, especially the wives of their leaders, and discover what trap here might await us."

She kissed him on the cheek and whispered in his ear, "Yes, my Captain. I never would have thought to do that without you suggesting it." Then she started tickling him. He, of course, tickled her back, and soon the guards outside had to try to ignore their laughter.

* * * * *

When the Spaniards awoke the next morning and began exploring Cholula, they discovered that it was far larger than any city they had imagined they would find in this "New World." Bernal and Aguilar had arranged to meet Malinali at the market plaza for their mid-day meal, but it was so huge, filled with so many people, that it took them some time to find each other.

"We have lost count of the number of their temples," he told her, shaking his head. "There must be hundreds, all built like pyramids. There is one so big that it looks like a small mountain! I am sure this city is bigger than Valladolid in Spain. It must have 100,000 people or more."

"This is a very old city," Malinali explained. "My father taught me about it. He said it was built one hundred generations ago[115] by people called the Tamoanchan[116] who came from Cuatzacualco."

"Isn't that where you are from, Doña Marina?" Aguilar asked.

"Yes, my father's kingdom of Paynala is in the land of Cuatzacualco. My father said we are descendants of the Tamoanchan, who were the first, as you say, *civilizados[117]*, with stone buildings and cities."

---

115   Around 1000 B.C.
116   The Olmecs.
117   Civilized people.

"So you are related to these people here in Cholula?" asked Bernal.

Malinali laughed. "Oh, I don't think so. *I* am a Tamoanchan descendant. These Cholulans are now a mix of many others, including the Chichimecas and Mesheeka. Yet the Cholulans, it is true, are very proud of their history. They let you know this right away, as many did to me this morning. They think they are much more cultured than the Mesheeka *primitivos*[118]."

"They certainly don't seem as friendly as the Tlaxcalans," noted Aguilar.

"No, they don't, but – "

Malinali was interrupted by a messenger. "Doña Marina, Captain Cortez sends for you. New ambassadors from the Mesheeka have arrived."

When she entered Cortez's quarters, she saw the old Mesheeka nobles who had come with them from Tlaxcala conferring with these new arrivals from, she assumed, Tenochtitlan. When they noticed her entrance, they all stepped forward to face Cortez, who was sitting in his chair, while Malinali assumed her position between them.

The eldest of the nobles spoke. "Malinche, these men have arrived from Tenochtitlan with unfortunate news. The road from Cholula to Tenochtitlan has been ruined, and you will not be able to make your way. The towns on the way have suffered bad harvests and will not be able to feed you and your men. The Great Montezuma has a very large collection of dangerous animals, many jaguars and alligators, and he is afraid that, if they got loose from their cages, they would tear your men to pieces..."

Malinali stumbled over translating these last words as she was desperately trying maintain a serious demeanor and not to laugh. She pretended to cough, and glanced briefly at Cortez. His face was expressionless and his gaze was fixed on the Mesheeka speaker. It was clear that the old man was nervous.

"...and so it is for these reasons, Malinche, that the Great Montezuma desires you not to come to Tenochtitlan, for his concern as always is with your safety."

Then she noticed Cortez was looking beyond the old man, his gaze resting on the new messengers just arrived from Montezuma. They were young men with faces of contemptuous arrogance, and their lips curled in sneers at the sound of the old man's words in Nahuatl. Cortez maintained his bland expression and calmly bade Malinali to interpret his reply:

---

118 Barbarians.

"It is a wonder to me how such a great prince as Lord Montezuma can never seem to make up his mind. One day, he begs us to come to Tenochtitlan. The next day, he begs us not to. He is a powerful king with an empire at his command, yet he cannot keep a few animals in their cages. We have come from the other side of the world, yet he thinks we cannot walk the last short distance to his city. Upon hearing these confused messages, someone might think that there are two different Lord Montezumas. The only way to clear the confusion is for me to leave immediately for Tenochtitlan, to meet the King of the Mesheeka and learn which of the two Montezumas he really is."

Malinali translated these words as unemotionally as Cortez had spoken them, and watched as they caused the sneers to melt from the young messengers' faces, and left the lips of the old Mesheeka noble frozen and unable to speak.

Finally, Cortez said, "Doña Marina, please tell them that it is my hope that they will all be accompanying and guiding us, when we leave for Tenochtitlan tomorrow."

All that the nobles and messengers could do was bow - the messengers quite curtly - and depart.

Cortez then called for a number of his officers, including Diego Ordaz, Cristobal de Olid and Pedro de Alvarado, as well as Bernal. "Gentlemen, I am suspicious," he told them. "These Mesheeka may be brewing some trouble for us. I want you and your men to be on the alert here. I told the Mesheeka that we would leave for Tenochtitlan tomorrow, but we will wait here until we discover what the Mesheeka are conspiring with the Cholulans to do."

He turned to Malinali. "Doña Marina, we were warmly greeted yesterday by Cholulan nobles but not by their king, nor has this man come to greet us today. Could you send a request for this *cacique* to see me?"

She spoke to a Cholulan guard, who returned with a message: "The King of Cholula, Tlaquiach (*tlah-qwee-otch*)[119], is ill and cannot come."

Cortez turned to Bernal. "Señor Castillo, it is a good day for a walk. Please accompany Doña Marina and me on a stroll to see what we might see in Cholula." As they walked through the city, people kept their distance, staring, pointing, and laughing at them. Returning to his quarters at the end of the day, Cortez ordered extra sentries and guards. The evening meal they were

---

119   'Lord of the here and now.'

given was meager, and the Cholulans who brought it surly.

Throughout the next day, Cortez received one dark report after another. No food had been given to anyone. When the soldiers asked for maize, they were given only water and firewood. Three Totonacs came to tell him that there were holes dug in the streets near his quarters, covered over with wood and dirt to disguise them. The Totonacs had uncovered one to find sharp stakes in the hole, designed to kill a horse falling in. Further, they said, Cholulans were gathering piles of large rocks on their rooftops to hurl down on the Spaniards as they passed by.

Then a half-dozen Tlaxcalans who had managed to get into the city appeared to warn Cortez that, the previous night, the Cholulans led by their king had sacrificed seven people, five of them children, to Huitzilopochtli in a prayer that the god would give them victory over the Spaniards. "Since early this morning, Malinche," they told him, "we have seen the Cholulans moving their women and children out of the city and away from danger. Take heed, Malinche, for the Cholulans mean you great harm."

As Cortez conferred with his officers, Malinali slipped outside and walked to a nearby temple. There, she engaged a number of the priests in conversation until she found one who seemed both intelligent and willing to talk. She asked why King Tlaquiach was pretending to be ill and would not see Malinche.

"If I summon him, he will come," he responded, telling her of his importance as a High Priest.

Before long, Tlaquiach and his chiefs appeared at Cortez's quarters. Cortez served them wine, then asked the king why he and his men had been given nothing to eat and were being treated so rudely, when they had been made welcome the day before. The king apologized, explaining that he was acting on the orders of the Great Montezuma.

"I understand," replied Cortez without emotion. "We leave here tomorrow. I must request from you two thousand of your best warriors to accompany us on our way to Tenochtitlan."

The king brightened at this request and quickly - *too quickly*, thought Malinali - complied. After that, the king and his chiefs left, but Cortez bade the High Priest stay.

"Doña Marina, please give these *chalchihuite* stones to this gentleman and thank him for having the king visit us. Perhaps he can explain to us why we are being treated so. Explain to him that I know he will tell us the truth because, as a priest, he is an honest man who represents his gods. Whatever he says to us will not be heard beyond this room, and tomorrow, before we leave, I will be pleased to present him with a large quantity of the finest cotton cloth."

At these words, the priest answered, "The truth is that you are going to die here. The Great Montezuma seems always in two minds over you. One day, his message is to make you welcome with respect, the next day it is the opposite. Now the gods of Tezcatlipoca and Huitzilopochtli have instructed the Great Montezuma to see that your men are killed here in Cholula while you, Malinche, are taken to Tenochtitlan for sacrifice to the gods' honor. To assure this, the Great Montezuma has sent many thousands of his warriors, who are here now outside the city, ready to fall upon you as you depart. This is why King Tlaquiach was pleased to provide his warriors as you asked, for you will be between them and the Mesheeka. You are in a trap, Malinche, from which there is no escape."

Cortez heard this without a flinch of emotion. "Please thank the gentleman for his honesty, and be sure to give him a supply of the best embroidered cloth," he told Malinali. "Please also explain to him that he is not to talk about our discussion with anyone. Should he do so, after we defeat the forces against us on the way to Tenochtitlan tomorrow, I will be forced to return here and kill him."

Startled at hearing these words, the priest said to Malinali, "I thank Malinche for his gifts - and there is one thing more he should know. The Great Montezuma promised that twenty of the Malinche's men will be kept for sacrifice to Huitzilopochtli, here at our temple in Cholula."

* * * * *

After the priest's departure, Cortez asked that the Mesheeka ambassadors and messengers come to see him. Not rising from his chair, he addressed them.

"We have discovered that these people of Cholula are evil-minded and intend treachery upon us. Not only are they planning to kill us, but they will attempt to blame it upon you, saying that Lord Montezuma ordered them to attack and kill us. But I do not believe that Lord Montezuma, as an honorable man, has given any such orders. I believe that Lord Montezuma is a man of his word who wants friendship and peace between us. I know you are shocked to hear of this treachery of the Cholulans, and of their disobedience to the wishes of Lord Montezuma. For your safety, I must ask that you stay in your quarters and not converse in any way with the people of this city. We do not want to have any reason to think that you are part of this treachery, and need to assure that no harm will come to you."

As the Mesheeka stuttered and mumbled objections, Cortez's guards led them to confinement.

With Cortez involved in a huddle with his officers, Malinali was able to slip outside, unnoticed, once again. It was night, and by torchlight she made her way towards the market square. *There must be someone I can find*, she thought, *who can disclose more about our situation.*

That someone found her. An elderly lady approached her. "You are young and beautiful," she said. "You should not die tomorrow. You should come to my house and marry my son, who is to become a rich and powerful chief in Cholula."

"Why might I die tomorrow?" Malinali asked.

"Because the trap is complete, and all these strangers are to be killed. You should marry my son instead of being killed with them," came the old woman's reply.

"How do you know about this?"

"Because my husband is a major commander of Cholula's army. Three days ago, the Great Montezuma sent my husband a gift of a golden drum, and three other commanders were given rich cloaks and jewels of gold, as a reward for organizing the trap." She grabbed Malinali's hand. "All of the strangers will be killed, or captured to be eaten with chiles. This should not happen to you. My son has seen you. He says you are the most beautiful woman he has ever seen, even in his dreams. Come with me. Come to him, now."

Malinali squeezed the woman's hand. "Oh, thank you, mother. Of course I will do as you say, for I do not want to die. I am happy to know that your son is a man of wealth and nobility. I shall be happy to marry him. I would come with you now, but I must get my clothes and my jewels - of which I have many, for I am rich, too! Please come with me and wait outside my room while I gather my property. Then you can help me carry my wealth to your home."

The woman excitedly accompanied Malinali back to Cortez's quarters, where she had the woman sit in nearby shadows. Once inside, she swiftly interrupted Cortez's meeting, and related what had just occurred. Cortez immediately had guards bring the woman to her. Malinali spoke to her:

"Mother, what you just did was very foolish. You are to tell Malinche all that you know about this trap. You were concerned for my life. I thank you for that, and want you to know that no harm is going to come to you. But you should be concerned for your husband's life, not mine. As a commander, his life will be in jeopardy in the battle, for it is your husband and his warriors who will be trapped tomorrow, not us. If you wish to save him, tell Malinche everything you know."

The woman blanched and started breathing in shallow pants. She looked into Malinali's calm eyes and saw that she spoke the truth. Convinced, she divulged every detail of the trap that she had heard. Cortez then had her taken to a guarded room to spend the night.

* * * * *

As dawn broke, several hundred Cholulan warriors, led by King Tlaquiach and his commanders, gathered in the large courtyard of Cholula's Great Temple. The courtyard had high walls surrounding it, with two gates on either side. They were all laughing, joking, and in a merry mood.

The king found Cortez mounted on his horse, waiting for him, with Malinali standing at his side. He called out to Cortez. "Malinche! We are here to escort you to Tenochtitlan! The warriors you see before you are my finest, with many more waiting on the road. Let us depart!"

The king, in his gaiety, did not notice that the Spaniards, wearing their armor and carrying swords and shields, were spreading out in the courtyard and lining along the walls. He also failed to notice the gates being closed and locked.

Cortez, astride his horse, looked down upon King Tlaquiach and addressed him. "I wish to know, O King, why, when we have done no harm to you, you intend to kill us. To what purpose have you prepared long poles with collars and cords, and stored them in a house near this temple? You intend to bind those of us you capture to these poles and drag us to Tenochtitlan for slaughter. Why have you, for the past few days, built barricades to trap us, dug holes in the streets with sharp stakes in the pits to kill our horses, and placed piles of large stones on your rooftops to be cast down upon us? Why have you removed your women and children from the city? Why have you already prepared, this morning, pots of boiling water with salt and peppers and tomatoes? I will tell you why. It is because you intend to kill us, then cook and eat our flesh.

"This is how you repay people who have come to you in friendship and have done nothing to harm you. If you wish to fight us, it would have been far better for you to meet us on an open field in honest battle, as good and brave warriors do, like your neighbors, the Tlaxcalans.

"We know all of the treachery you have planned. We know what you have promised to your false gods. We know that, two nights ago, you sacrificed seven people - including innocent children - to your despicable gods, and that you have promised to butcher twenty of us to your bloodthirsty idols.

"I told you that your gods were false and evil. I told you that they had no power over us, and would lead you to destruction. Now you are about to learn the truth of my words."

Malinali took care that her words of translation came out clearly and were understood by the Cholulans. Then she added, "King Tlaquiach, you know Malinche speaks the truth, yes? Has he said anything that isn't true?"

He recoiled at the question, and his shoulders slumped. "His words are true. But all this has been done at the command of the Great Montezuma! We are not to be blamed!"

Upon hearing this, Cortez replied coldly, "And that is why you were all so happy and laughing when you came here this morning - happy because you thought you had us in a trap, happy that you were going to kill us, happy that you were going to cut our hearts out and cook and eat our bodies. Now it is you and your men who are trapped, and you and your men who will pay for your murderous treachery!"

Cortez signaled for a musket to be fired, and the Spaniards attacked.

The battle was fierce and brief. The Cholulan warriors were cut down like saplings, King Tlaquiach among them. Malinali, protected by a squad of soldiers, pointed out a commander as the husband of the woman from the previous night, based on the description the woman had given. That commander was captured and not harmed. But almost every other Cholulan warrior soon lay dead or wounded.

* * * * *

No Spaniard had been killed but several were wounded. Malinali and the padres began tending to them and the wounded Cholulans. Soon, however, Cortez requested her, for he needed to talk to the captured commander. How many Cholulan warriors lay in wait for them in the streets and outside the city? How many Mesheeka lay in wait, and would they enter the city now? With their king dead, would the Cholulans continue to fight, or surrender to him? Cortez had these and many other questions.

The commander replied that he did not know what the Mesheeka would do, but there were Cholulan warriors barricaded in the streets and on the rooftops above them who were waiting to kill them. As for the dead king:

"You should know, Malinche, that Cholula is a large city with many factions and parties, many of whom do not like Tlaquiach. They will rejoice over his death and those of his followers."

The questioning was interrupted by shouts and cries and the sound of fighting in the streets outside the courtyard. Someone pounded on one of the gates, and a strong voice called out, "Malinche! Malinche!" Malinali recognized the voice. It was that of the Tlaxcalan chief Chichimacatecle.

Cortez ordered that the gate be opened, and the chief and a group of warriors rushed in. He stood proud and beaming in front of Cortez. "Malinche! We have come to defend you against the Cholulan traitors!"

Cortez looked around the courtyard littered with Cholulan dead, then at Malinali. "It does not seem that we need much defending at the moment," he said to her. Then he paused. "What of all the Mesheeka and Cholulan warriors waiting for us outside the city?"

"We entered the city from the side of the rising sun," came the chief's reply. "They are on the side of the setting sun, where you will be going towards Tenochtitlan. We did not encounter them - but my scouts tell me that, once they heard that you had killed King Tlaquiach and his men here, all was confusion among them. The Mesheeka warriors have started walking back to Tenochtitlan, and the Cholulan warriors have no leader and know not what to do. We have blocked them from entering the city."

Cortez smiled, bowed to the chief, and said to Malinali, "Please convey to the *cacique* my deepest gratitude for his assistance."

Chichimacatecle bowed in turn and ran back with his men to exit the courtyard.

Cortez then called for reports from his officers. Word came in that the Tlaxcalans had stormed the Cholulan street barricades, killing every Cholulan warrior they could find, and had begun to pillage. From the courtyard, smoke could be seen rising from several places in the city.

"The temples - they are burning down the temples of the Cholulan gods," observed Malinali.

She looked with alarm at Cortez. "The Tlaxcalans are now free to destroy the city of their hated Cholulan enemies. We have saved ourselves… but we must now save Cholula from our friends. Is not this the Christian way?"

Cortez's brow furrowed as he nodded. "Yes, Doña Marina, it is the Christian way. How do we find the Tlaxcalan *cacique*?"

At that moment, an enormous tumult arose from the Great Temple towering above them. The priests were blowing their *atecocoli* conch shells in alarm. As a horde of Tlaxcalan warriors swarmed over the temple summit platform, priests began leaping to their death, their bodies bouncing down the steep steps in dull thuds. Other priests were hacked to pieces by Tlaxcalan obsidian-toothed swords. The giant wooden statue of Huitzilopochtli was set afire, toppled, and sent rolling down the steps with a flaming roar.

The Great Temple was to burn and smolder for two days, as did the Tlaxcalans who burned with blood lust. Neither the pleas nor the commands of Cortez to Chichimacatecle were sufficient to halt the Tlaxcalan rampage, as thousands of additional warriors arrived from Tlaxcala to join in the rout.

All that Cortez could do was to confine it. As leaders from other districts in the city came to him and asked for his protection, proclaiming that they held no loyalty to Tlaquiach, Cortez send contingents of soldiers to guard their districts. He could not have his soldiers attack the rampaging Tlaxcalans, but he could prevent them from entering the designated sections of the city. Finally, at the end of the next day, he sent Cristobal de Olid to summon Chichimacatecle and all of the Tlaxcalan commanders.

When they were assembled before him, he said, "You have had your vengeance, and now it must cease. You are to leave the city with all of your men, and to camp in the fields as before. You have seized much Cholulan wealth, gold and mantles, feathers, cotton cloth, and salt. I will let you keep those riches - but the captives you have seized, men for sacrifice and women for slaves, you must set free."

The Tlaxcalans erupted in anger, shouting complaints that the Cholulans deserved their punishment for all the horrors Tlaxcala had suffered from them over the years.

Cortez gave Malinali a look of fire.

"Malinche has not finished!" she shouted. The Tlaxcalans fell silent.

"Setting your Cholulan captives free is not all that I demand of you." Cortez brought the Chief Mamexi to his side. "You know the great Totonac *cacique* Mamexi. He has told you all of the peace made between the people of Cempoala and Tizapacingo, who before were enemies. What I now demand is that same peace between the people of Cholula and Tlaxcala."

The Tlaxcalan commanders were too astonished to reply.

"Retire this night to the fields. Take your riches and leave your captives. Tomorrow, at this time, we will meet here again. You will meet with the *caciques* and nobles of Cholula in friendship and peace, and together you will swear that the war and hatred between your peoples is finished."

Chapter Twenty Two

BETWEEN THE SMOKING MOUNTAIN
AND THE SLEEPING WOMAN

The next morning, Cortez assembled the Cholulan *caciques*, commanders, nobles, and priests, together with the Tlaxcalan commanders, in the freshly swept courtyard. Mounted on his horse, he had the Mesheeka ambassadors stand on one side, and Malinali on the other. Behind him were arrayed his officers, resplendent in polished armor, and a contingent of Totonac warriors led by Mamexi, all in their finest feather headdresses.

Cortez began by speaking to the Cholulans sternly, "Two days ago, the king of Cholula was guilty of a great treachery, which he and his followers paid for with their lives. The entire city of Cholula deserves to be destroyed for this treachery, and your enemies of Tlaxcala wished to do so. But you are subjects of the Lord Montezuma, and it is out of my respect for him that I will pardon and forgive Cholula – on one condition: that the Cholulans make peace with Tlaxcala. Nobles and leaders of Cholula, have you chosen one among you to now be your king?"

A tall man stepped forward, enrobed in a beautifully feather-embroidered mantle. "I am he," he announced. "I am Tlachiac[120], brother to Tlaquiach."

Cortez called Chief Chichimecatecle forward to stand next to Tlachiac. "Do you both, in the name of your peoples, forswear war and violence against each other, and pledge that there will forevermore be peace between Cholula and Tlaxcala?" he asked them.

They both answered, "I do so forswear, I do so pledge, in the name of

---

120   'Lord of what is below.'

my people."

Malinali raised her voice to convey Cortez's next words, to be sure that everyone in the courtyard heard her. "From this day forward, the people of Cholula and Tlaxcala are friends. Do you all agree?"

There rose a great shout of agreement from the Cholulans, and perhaps a slightly less enthusiastic affirmation from the Tlaxcalans, but the agreement was made.

"I now request," Cortez announced, directing his words to the Cholulans, "that the people of Cholula, many of whom left the city, especially the women and children, now return to their homes and to the marketplace. Assure them that no harm will come to them. They are to have no fear. Their lives will be more peaceful than ever."

Cortez paused. "I have a further request. The gods of Cholula have proven to be false gods. You should abandon them, for they have abandoned you, and you should accept instead the One True God of the Christian faith. Accept the Son of God, Jesus Christ, as your Savior, Who loves you and wishes for you to dwell with Him in Heaven. The evil idols of your temples are not worthy of your worship. I urge you to destroy them. Yet even if you do not, your practice of sacrificing your fellow human beings to your gods is over. Your gods will never again drink human blood.

"We have heard of many prisons near your temples, cages with thick wooden beams, full of captured men and boys - children! - being kept and fattened for sacrifice. I have ordered my men to search the city for these prisons and to release those prisoners. Anyone attempting to prevent them from releasing the prisoners will be killed. Anyone, any priest, who attempts to murder a person in sacrifice to your idols will be killed. If you do not choose Christ as your Savior, that is your choice. It will not be forced upon you. But we will prevent human sacrifice, and we will prevent your eating of human flesh, by force if necessary.

"My last request is that we be given one of your temples so that we may clean it and erect a cross, the symbol of our Savior, where we and those among you who choose Christ may worship."

Cortez did not wait for the Cholulans to agree. He turned in his saddle to address the Mesheeka ambassadors, as Malinali stepped to their side of him. "Emissaries of Lord Montezuma, I wish for you to carry a message of friendship to your lord. Please inform him that the people of Cholula, to whom we came in peace and at your insistence - for we were warned not to come here by our Tlaxcalan friends - treacherously planned to kill us, but that we have punished those guilty of this plot. Even worse, the Cholulan king claimed that this treachery was at Lord Montezuma's command, as the Cholulans are his subjects.

"Please inform Lord Montezuma that we do not believe this slander, for we know that such a noble prince as he would never conspire in so cowardly a fashion. We know that Lord Montezuma is not a man of cowardice and foul treachery, but a man of strength and honor, one whose promise of friendship towards us can be trusted. This is why our Lord, His Majesty King Don Carlos of Spain, ordered us to cross many seas and distant lands to meet and speak with him. This we shall do, and thus we shall soon be on our way to his city, to give him a complete account of what our King Don Carlos has commanded us to do."

* * * * *

Messengers were sent to Tenochtitlan, and over the next several days, Cholula was re-peopled and life returned to normal. In the marketplace, the famous red and black pottery was sold in abundance – indeed, Malinali was told that Montezuma himself would only eat food served on Cholulan plates. Food was also available in abundance, and the Spaniards were well fed.

The Mesheeka messengers returned with six high nobles carried on litters by slaves. Laying ten large plates of solid gold, an array of gold ornaments, and over a thousand feather-embroidered cotton cloaks before Cortez, then touching the ground before him in reverence, the highest of the nobles spoke.

"Malinche, our Lord the Great Montezuma sends you these gifts and asks that you accept them with the great affection he has for you and your people. The trouble caused by the Cholulans weighs heavily on him, and he is happy that you punished them as they deserve, for the Cholulans are an evil and lying people, as they have proved by blaming him for their wickedness. He wishes to assure you of his friendship, and that you are welcome in Tenochtitlan. Although there will be little food to eat in the city, he will do all of the honor that is possible to you, as his guest. Further, he has ordered all of the towns through which you will pass on the way to Tenochtitlan to give you all that you need."

Cortez had wine served to them all, presented them with a number of glass beads, told them of his gratitude for the gift - "greater than any amount of gold or feathers" - of Montezuma's friendship, and announced that their departure for Tenochtitlan would take place on the following morning.

That night, preparing to retire, Cortez wondered why Malinali was not there. She had not been present at supper, and had remained absent all through the evening. Unable to sleep, Cortez laid in bed, awake, until almost midnight, when Malinali finally came in to slip into bed beside him.

"You missed a wonderful party," she said teasingly. "But then, you weren't invited."

Cortez was not going to snap at the bait. He simply looked at her silently as the flicker of the candlelight danced across her face.

"In truth, I wasn't invited either," she admitted, "but it still was my *fiesta*, my party."

Cortez could see the excitement in her eyes. She could hardly wait to tell her secret, so his silence continued.

"As you know, my Captain, I have made many friends here. The commander and his wife - the old lady who wanted me to marry her son - feel that they owe me their lives. So I told them to have a special dinner *fiesta* for the Mesheeka emissaries and messengers, with the best food and much *pulque*. It is stronger than your wine, and only the priests are supposed to use it, and only for rituals. But I had my Cholulan hosts convince their guests that tonight was an exception. The *pulque* made the Mesheeka tongues very loose, and they talked amongst themselves freely, because the Cholulans left them alone to enjoy themselves. Of course, there were Cholulans serving them, but to them the Mesheeka paid no attention.

"The servants, however, were paying great attention to every word spoken by the Mesheeka, for I had paid them well to do so. So now, my Captain..." She snuggled close to him... "I get to tell you Mesheeka secrets."

Cortez held her tightly and sighed. "Ah, Doña Marina, you are the most astonishing woman I have ever known." He looked into her eyes. "And the most beautiful." He moved to kiss her, then pulled back. "No... my desire for you must wait. You are excited to tell me what you have learned, and I must not delay your excitement."

She snuggled closer. "Yes, I am excited - and pleased with myself. But you may not find what I learned too pleasing. The Mesheeka talked of Montezuma making sacrifices to Huitzilopochtli, and asking the god and his priests what to do. The priests' answer was for Montezuma to invite us into his island city and that, once we are there, he can kill us all, whenever he chooses. The Mesheeka all laughed about how Montezuma would trap us so much better than 'the stupid King Tlaquiach,' as they called him.

"But then they stopped laughing, and talked of the fear and panic among the people of Tenochtitlan, when they heard of how you dealt with the trap of Cholula. They are saying in the streets that you must be the invincible Quetzacoatl, returning to vanquish their gods as Quetzacoatl promised long ago. So the *fiesta* tonight ended not with laughter but in silence, as the Mesheeka kept drinking *pulque* until they fell down asleep."

She reached over to blow out the candle, then whispered into Cortez's ear, "That is what I learned... and now your desire for me need not wait any longer."

* * * * *

As the Spaniards assembled the next morning for their departure[121], Chiefs Chichimacatecle and Mamexi asked to speak to Cortez.

The Tlaxcalan spoke first. "Malinche, we know of your intention to enter Tenochtitlan. We do not think this wise, for it is an island with countless Mesheeka warriors, a place from which none of you may escape alive. Because of our fear for you and our friendship with you, the Army of Tlaxcala wishes to accompany and protect you with 10,000 of its finest warriors."

Cortez rose from his chair to grasp Chichimacatecle by the shoulders. "I am honored by your friendship," he replied. "Yet your fear for me is matched by mine for you. I fear that such a large host of warriors who are enemies to the Mesheeka, in their territory, in their very city, would be too great a provocation for them. A smaller number, say one or two thousand, would not be a provocation, yet would be of great help to us in transporting our equipment and guarding us. Is this acceptable?"

---

121   November 1, 1519.

The Tlaxcalan chief immediately agreed. He departed and Mamexi came forward. "Malinche," he began, in a tone of regret, "I come to inform you that we Totonacs must return to Cempoala. It is our fear that the Great Montezuma will most certainly order our deaths if we accompany you to Tenochtitlan, for he has not forgiven us for ceasing to pay him tribute and imprisoning his *calpixque*[122]."

Malinali saw the flash of concern in Cortez's eyes. "Doña Marina, please explain to Chief Mamexi, to whom I and all of my men owe so much, that he need not have the slightest fear of coming to any harm, for he will be in my company, and the Mesheeka will not dare annoy the Totonacs. I ask that he reconsider."

After she translated these words, she added, "Chief Mamexi, the Spaniards have come to look upon their Totonac allies as their brothers, with great affection. Please stay with us. Your men should know that, besides the great affection Captain Cortez has for them, he promises that they shall be rewarded with Mesheeka riches."

Mamexi did not budge. "We have made a decision, and that is to return to our homes," he stated firmly. "But Malinche should know that there will always be a home for him among the Totonacs."

Hearing this, Cortez responded, "Doña Marina, tell the chief that I regret his decision but that I respect it. He and the Totonacs have done me great service, for which I and His Majesty King Don Carlos of Spain will always be grateful. But he and his men shall not leave for their homes with only my gratitude. I shall order that many loads of embroidered cotton mantles be distributed among them. I wish also that Chief Mamexi take two loads of mantles to my friend King Tlacochcalcatl, and two for himself, and... ah, yes, two for my, ah, wife Doña Catalina and her family."

* * * * *

The gigantic mountain that loomed above Cholula in a mantle of white had been smoking for the past several days. A huge plume of smoke was spewing from its summit, and its roars and shudders could be heard and felt below. As the Spaniards were about to depart, Diego de Ordaz approached

---

122 Taxmen.

Cortez with a request.

"Captain, the mountain above us is well-named: Popocatepetl (*po-po-kah-tay-pettle*)[123]. It is a volcano, like Vesuvius in Italy or Etna in Sicily, which some of our men have seen but never climbed upon. It is my desire to climb upon it, for no man I know has done such a thing, especially when the mountain is exploding. Further, from the heights, I may be able to look down upon the fabled city of the Mesheeka and give you a good account of it."

Cortez was pleased. "Captain Ordaz, what a noble request! Of course, I grant it. My only request in return is that you come back to us in one solid piece. But... do you propose to do this alone?"

"No, sir. Gutierre de Casamori will be my companion, and the Tlaxcalans will find guides for us from a village near the mountain."

Cortez nodded. "We shall be passing close to the mountain on our way. Your report should be very useful to us. *Via con Dios*[124]!"

Malinali had discussed the route with Cortez, after long talks with Chichimacatecle. There was a wall of mountains between them and Tenochtitlan. The easiest route was to go south, below the mountains, then northeast up to the city. But 'easiest' also meant 'the most expected by the Mesheeka.' To go around the mountains to the north was too far. But there was another way, the hardest and least expected: through the mountains, and over a high pass between Popocatepetl and another huge mountain called Iztaccihuatl (*ish-tox-see-wattle*)[125]. Cortez decided that the least expected route was the best.

The expedition set out from Cholula in a joyous mood, rested, well-fed, and expectant. It reached the good-sized town of Calpan by the end of the first day. The town's elders, along with those from Huexotzinco, were waiting to greet Cortez. After the priests fumigated him and the officers, they addressed him.

"Malinche, we welcome you to Calpan. As you are brothers to our brothers of Tlaxcala, you are our brothers, as well... which is why we must warn you of the trap prepared for you. You intend to take the high road between the two mountains. When you come to the top of this road and begin your journey down, you will find not one, but two roads, one leading to the town of Chalco, the other to the town of Amecameca. You will find the road to

---

123 'The smoking mountain,' 17,925 ft. high.
124 Go with God.
125 'The sleeping woman,' 17,159 ft. high.

Amecameca blocked by huge trees cut down by the Mesheeka to prevent you from taking it. The Mesheeka intend for you to take the road to Chalco, for on this road they have prepared a great ambush, with many warriors waiting to fall upon you and kill you all."

Cortez immediately called for wine to be served and glass beads to be presented to the elders. Thanking them profusely for their advice, he also expressed surprise, as he had chosen this route because it would be unexpected by the Mesheeka.

The elders smiled to themselves. "Yes, they thought that you would go the easy way, below the mountain, and had prepared a huge trap for you there. But when they learned that you would come this way, the Great Montezuma, we are told, became very frightened. You must know that he thinks you are Quetzacoatl, returning to destroy his gods. When Quetzacoatl was defeated by Tezcatlipoca[126], he fled over this very road you intend to use.

"All Mesheeka know this story, and of how Quetzacoatl's dwarf and hunchback servants froze to death at the top of the road, which is why they call it the Pass of Quetzacoatl[127]. Why else, then, would you choose to use this hard way and not the easy way, if you are not the Feathered Serpent? So, shaking with fear, he ordered warriors to race to the mountain, block one path and sweep clean the other, and wait to ambush you."

Cortez glanced at Malinali, then shook his head slowly. "With every tale I hear of this Montezuma, the stranger he becomes. Yes, it is true that I have come to kill his gods - but you must know that I am not a god myself, but human, just like you."

They smiled gently at him. "Yes, we know this, Malinche. Our Tlaxcalan brothers have told us. This is why we have warned you, for what need would a god have of our warnings?"

Malinali could not help laughing as she translated this, and soon everyone was laughing with her, Cortez the loudest. He asked for more wine for his friends from Calpan.

Starting off at dawn the next morning, the Spaniards reached the top of the pass by noon. Just as the elders in Calpan had described, there were two roads, one blocked with newly-felled trees, the other freshly swept clean.

126   See Chapter 7.
127   Now known as the Pass of Cortez, or *Paseo de Cortes*. At an altitude of 13,000 ft., it is the starting point for mountain climbers to ascend either Popo or Izta.

They were surrounded by clouds and mists, and it had begun to snow. The Tlaxcalans set to the work of removing the huge trees from the path, and within a few hours the way was clear. Marching down upon it, the expedition came upon a number of stone shelters, where they decided to spend the night. Cortez posted sentries and sent out scouting parties, to make sure that no Mesheeka were about.

As they were embarking the next morning, Diego de Ordaz arrived, excited with news. His men were bearing large, heavy loads in cloth sacks.

"The great mountain has been climbed, my Captain!" he announced proudly. "On our way up, it threw out long tongues of fire, burnt stones that had no weight, and plumes of ash. The entire mountain shook, but soon that was over, and we made our way up through the snow. There is no summit at the top, only a huge crater, very round and a half-league wide. We were far above the clouds, the air was very clear, and we could see a new world in the valley below, with a giant lake ringed with cities and towers. And in the middle of the lake stood a very great city, which must be Tenochtitlan. It was the most wondrous sight! Yet better than that sight was this discovery..."

He bade his Tlaxcalan guides to set down their loads, and he opened one of them. Out poured yellow dirt.

"Sulfur, my Captain! For making gunpowder! We were only able to get this much, but there is far more on the walls inside the crater that we could see."

Ordaz beamed with pride, for he could tell that Cortez was impressed. "You have done well, Diego, very well. My congratulations! This feat of yours shall be remembered. Stories will be told about it, perhaps in song or poetry – or perhaps commemorated on the coat-of-arms granted to your family for the title and estates you shall have in this land one day[128]."

When the Spaniards reached the town of Amecameca, a great crowd awaited them. A number of elders who had assembled in the central square approached Malinali. One of them whispered, "You are the woman we have heard so much of, the one who is named Malina – and it is because of you that we call your leader 'Malinche.' We have heard that we can trust you. Please tell Malinche that we wish to speak with him quietly, so that no spies of Montezuma, no Mesheeka ambassadors who are with you, may hear us."

---

128   This coat-of-arms, depicting a volcano emitting flames, was granted to the House of Ordaz by Charles V in 1525.

The elders led Malinali and Cortez into a corner of the plaza that was shaded by trees. Cortez had guards placed so that no one could disturb them.

The elders poured their story out. "We have come from many cities and towns to speak with you, from here in Amecameca, and from Chalco, Chimaluancan, Tlamanalco, Ayotzingo, and others. We are all of the Chalca people, who have been here since long before the Mesheeka came and made us their subjects. The Mesheeka *calpixque* rob us of all that we have. If our daughters or wives are beautiful, the Mesheeka violate them in front of their fathers and husbands, then carry them away. Our men are made their slaves, to carry wood and stone and maize for them. Our children and young men are carried away for sacrifice to their gods. Malinche! We have heard of your making other people, like the Totonacs, free of the Mesheeka. We ask that you do the same for us."

Cortez looked at each of them intently, in turn. Then he turned to Malinali. "Doña Marina, please tell them that I am honored by their request, and that I have been sent here by my King to achieve their wishes. Explain that I can only do so if they will listen to the words of our holy men, who will instruct them in how to be Christians. Tell them that they must abandon the worship of any gods who are like those of the Mesheeka and who drink human blood. Tell them I must ask for their patience, for my men and I are about to enter Tenochtitlan to instruct Lord Montezuma to abandon his evil ways. I promise them that they will one day be free of the Mesheeka."

When Malinali told them of Cortez's words, adding that "Malinche always keeps his promises," the leaders wept in gratitude.

Two days later, well cared-for, well-fed, and well-rested, the expedition was preparing to embark when an elaborate delegation of Mesheeka arrived, bearing a man on a litter dressed in incredible feather finery. The men before him spread out a treasure of gold ornaments, quetzal feathers, and feather-embroidered cotton mantles before Cortez, then announced that the Great Montezuma himself had come at last to see Malinche.

Malinali and Cortez cast skeptical glances at each other. "Tell them we are honored, then ask our Chalcan friends if this is truly Montezuma," Cortez bade her.

Malinali soon confirmed that the man was an impostor. As the man got off the litter and stood in front of Cortez, Malinali asked, "You are truly the

Great Montezuma?"

"Yes, I am Montezuma, Lord of all Mesheeka, Lord of the World," he grandly replied.

Cortez laughed. "Whoever you are, I ask that you go back to your home. Why do you lie to us? Why are you here? It cannot be that your Lord Montezuma sent you to trick us, that he could be so foolish as to think we could be made stupid, that we could be flattered, that our gaze could be misdirected, that we could be made to turn back, or be destroyed, or be dazzled. Tell us who you are, for you are not Montezuma!"

The man's eyes flared in anger, and he started to speak, but Malinali cut him off. Shaking her head, she looked him in the eye and said, "The game is over. It will be much better if you tell the truth."

He looked away from Malinali's stare and wilted. "I am Tziuacpopocatzin (*tzee-wok-popo-cot-zin*), cousin to Lord Montezuma. He thought you would be satisfied by thinking you had seen him, and that, with the promise of much gold and silver and chalchihuites in tribute to your Lord, you would not advance farther but would return from whence you came."

As she listened to this confession, Malinali noticed that the Chalcans with them were greatly disturbed, glancing about with looks of fright and terror. She asked them what was wrong.

"The Mesheeka have brought a number of *tlacatecolotl*[129], and *teipitzani*[130] to curse you and us all, to make us all sick and die," they replied.

Cortez exploded in anger. "How dare you!" he thundered at the Montezuma impostor, and drew his sword. "I should cut you down where you stand!" He looked over at the trembling Chalcans. "Doña Marina, tell them that these wizards and sorcerers are frauds. Their magic is as worthless as their gods. They have no power over the Spaniards, and I promise that they will have no power over the Chalcans."

He looked back at the impostor. After Malinali had finished reassuring the Chalcans, Cortez pointed his sword at him and said in a voice of quiet rage, "Take your wizards, who are as false as you are, and leave. Leave now, or I will have every one of you killed."

As Malinali translated his words, Cortez looked over to Pedro de Alvarado, who had also drawn his sword, as had all of the officers standing near.

---

129   Owl-men wizards.
130   Evil-blower sorcerers.

"And when you return to your city," he said to the impostor, "please inform your Lord Montezuma that he cannot hide from us, he cannot take refuge from us, and I will hear no more messages from him that one day welcome us and the next beg us to stay away. Tell your Lord Montezuma that we are coming to see him. We shall not fail to look him in the face. He shall hear what I have to say to him."

With that, Cortez sheathed his sword, and the officers followed his lead.

Too shaken and terrified to utter a word of reply, the impostor had to be helped back onto his litter, and within seconds he and his entourage were on their way.

Cortez turned to the Chalcans, spread his arms wide, and smiled. "You see, my friends, there is nothing to fear. It is the wizards who are frightened of us, not we of them. They will never harm you again."

Chapter Twenty Three

MALINCHE AND MONTEZUMA

The next day[131], the expedition reached the edge of the lakes on the valley floor, Lake Chalco, and the town of Chalco[132]. Again, they were welcomed warmly by townspeople who complained bitterly about the hated Mesheeka. "No city in this valley has rebelled more often against the Mesheeka than Chalco," one elder proudly informed Cortez. "Since the days of my father's father's father, we have hated and resisted them."

A new Mesheeka delegation appeared, consisting of four nobles bearing gold and cloth. They promised Cortez much more if the Spaniards would leave. Montezuma was ill. The road was bad. There was not enough food for them. Having heard it all before so many times, Cortez remained polite but insistent. He directed Malinali to inform the nobles that he could not turn back because his King, Don Carlos, had ordered him to meet Lord Montezuma, and would kill him and his men for being cowards if they turned back now.

From Chalco, they followed the southern shore of the lake for less than two leagues before reaching the town of Ayotzingo. Here they were met by still another Mesheeka delegation, this one led by the nephew of Montezuma, King Cacama of Texcoco, after which Lake Texcoco was named.

King Cacama was borne on a litter bedecked with green feathers and embossed with silver and gold. Malinali was informed that each of the litter carriers was, himself, the chief of an important Mesheeka town. They helped Cacama descend from the litter, swept the ground in front of him, bowed to

---

131   November 5, 1519.
132   See map of Lake Texcoco in Map & Illustrations section.

Cortez, and introduced him.

"Malinche!" King Cacama called out. "I and these chieftains have come to place ourselves at your service, and to see that you receive all that you and your companions require. We have come to install you in your home, which is our city of Tenochtitlan, for so we have been commanded by the Great Montezuma, who will welcome you himself upon your entrance to your new home."

Cortez embraced Cacama and thanked him profusely for the friendship and hospitality of Lord Montezuma. There was no mention whatever of the delegation at Chalco, nor of the impostor at Amecameca.

That evening, Cortez waited impatiently for Malinali. She had spent the afternoon and evening talking to the Chalcans whom she had placed among the Mesheeka, and he was anxious to learn what she had found out. Why had Montezuma changed his mind yet again? Was he laying a trap, as the Chalcans and Tlaxcalans had warned?

As Malinali entered, she immediately understood what thoughts were occupying her captain's mind. She smiled, bade him sit down, and insisted that he have a cup of wine.

"You need to put your mind at ease, my Captain," she said to him soothingly. "For I can assure you that the mind of Montezuma is not."

Cortez did as he was bidden. Comfortably seated, with a cup of wine in hand, and with Malinali curled at his feet, he looked down at her and said, "You once told me of how you got lost in my eyes. It is so easy for me, now, to get lost in yours."

There was silence between them as they gazed at each other in mutual adoration.

Then Malinali broke the spell.

"We will succeed in getting lost in a few moments. But first..." She shook her head, wearing an expression of puzzlement. "My Chalcan spies tell a strange tale. Montezuma is a strange man." She looked up at Cortez. "A frightened man. A man who does not know what to do. There was no talk among the Mesheeka of a trap for you, only talk of the meeting that Montezuma called after his trick with the impostor in Amecameca did not work.

"He met with Cacama, King of Texcoco, and with Tetelpanquetzal (*teh-tul-pan-qwet-zul*), King of Tacuba. Montezuma said to them, 'Woe is coming to us! How do we deserve this fate? How did we offend the gods? Who are these men who have come? From where have they really come? Who showed them the way? Our only choice is to make our hearts strong, to bear what must happen, for these men – if they be men – are at our gates.'

"The three kings, I am told, cried bitterly together. Then Montezuma left his palace, and went out into the square before the great temple. People gathered in a large crowd, and he cried before them, with tears flowing down his face. He yelled angrily at the gods for the doom that was approaching, then took out a knife and drew blood from his ears, his arms, and his shins, offering it to the gods and begging them to have mercy on the Mesheeka..." Malinali's voice trailed off into silence as she stared into space.

"What are you looking at?" Cortez asked, then touched his forehead and clarified, "In your mind."

She sighed. "I was trying to imagine what my father would have thought of Montezuma, if he heard this story." She smiled to herself. "I wonder if he would think Montezuma was *loco*[133]. Whatever else he thought, I know one thing: he would have little respect for Montezuma as a king."

* * * * *

The Spaniards continued along the shore of Lake Chalco the next day, through the small town of Mixquic (*mish-qweek*), where people proudly told Malinali that they were Mixquica. "Our kingdom was here long before the Mesheeka," they told her. "But now we must do as the Mesheeka say."

"Perhaps for not much longer," she responded.

Mixquic was built half on the lake shore, half on the water, and the soldiers seemed entranced by its beauty. Continuing on, they came to a causeway which separated Lake Chalco from another lake, called Xochimilco. This led to a small island with a city called Cuitlahuac (*qweet-lah-wok*). The nobles of the city begged Cortez to spend the night.

"It would be such an honor if Malinche stayed with us," they explained to Malinali. "We are the oldest people in the valley, so old that the Mesheeka claim it as their origin, the land of Aztlan. But this is a lie. They came as barbarians from the northern deserts, and made us their slaves."

---

133 Crazy.

Cortez replied that he would be delighted to accept their gracious hospitality – but, at just that moment, the Mesheeka ambassadors who had been guiding them asked to continue the journey. "Please inform Malinche," they said to Malinali, "that a number of great chieftains are awaiting his arrival in Culhuacan, where arrangements have been made for him and his men to stay in various palaces."

"It is better for us to cross the next causeway, rather than be on this small island," Cortez whispered to Malinali. "Please thank these fine people of Cuitlahuac for their offer, but tell them that we will agree to the Mesheeka request."

Thus they continued on the causeway connecting Cuitlahuac to the peninsula of Culhuacan, and to the city of Iztapalapa on the shore of Lake Texcoco. Bernal walked beside Malinali and asked if she had ever seen anything like what was before them.

She shook her head.

"The men tell me that they feel as if they are in a dream," he said. "All these great cities and villages and temples made of stone, rising from the water - the men say it is like an enchanted vision. How can this be described, Doña Marina? It is so wondrous, things never heard of, seen, or dreamed of!"

When they entered the city of Iztapalapa, several *caciques* in feathered splendor were there to greet them, including Tezozomoc, King of Culhuacan. "He is married to a daughter of Montezuma," Malinali relayed to Cortez. "The Mesheeka claim an ancient relationship with the people here, who are called Culhuas - so old that the Mesheeka sometimes call themselves the Culhua."

Iztapalapa was much larger than the valley cities they had been through[134], with about half the houses built on stilts in the lake. The palaces in which the Spaniards were lodged left them in awe. "The stonework and masonry is as good as the best in Spain," Bernal told Malinali.

The structures were two stories high, with roofs of cedar wood, and courts and gardens over which were hung awnings of woven cotton. The paths in the gardens were choked with roses, other flowers, and fruit trees. Large canoes came in to the gardens by way of channels cut from the lake. Beautiful birds of many species flocked to the garden ponds. The palaces shone white with

---

134 About 15,000 people. Chalco was about 6,000, while Amecameca, Mizquic, and Cuitlahuac were about 3,000 each.

lime and were decorated with stonework and paintings. "I never thought I would see such a marvel," said Bernal.

* * * * *

When they woke up the next morning, Cortez and Malinali bathed in the freshwater pool in their courtyard, then strolled among the sweet-smelling fruit trees and rose bushes of their palace garden. "My captain," she said to him, "you have chosen this day to meet the Great Montezuma and enter Tenochtitlan. What do you call this day, and why have you chosen it?"

"This day," he replied, "is the eighth day of November, in the year of Our Lord 1519. There is nothing special about this day. It just happens to be the day we have come here. Why do you ask, my Lady?"

"Because all the people of Tenochtitlan, I have heard, are talking about this day. They each went to sleep last night in terror, including Montezuma, for just as you chose to arrive in the land of the Mesheeka in a 1-Reed year, Quetzacoatl's year of return, so now you have chosen to enter the Mesheeka capital on a 1-Wind day - the one day of the year that bears the sign of Quetzacoatl in his guise of the whirlwind. The whirlwind brings upheaval and destruction. The whirlwind brings, the Mesheeka are whispering, the 'disembowelment of the world'."

"The whirlwind?" Cortez exclaimed with a snap of his head. He stopped, clasped his hands around Malinali's, and held them tightly. "Every Christian who reads the Bible knows the story of the prophet Hosea," he told her. "He warned his people of Israel that God would allow them to be conquered because of their unfaithfulness to Him. This happened many, many centuries ago[135]. Yet his famous warning seems now to be directed at the Mesheeka: *For they have sown the wind, and they shall reap the whirlwind: the grain shall have no stalk; the bud shall yield no meal: and if it does, strangers shall swallow it up.*[136]

"The Mesheeka have sown the wind with their evil. I know I am but a sinful man, not this god with which they confuse me. But the One True God acted through Hosea, and these constant coincidences between me and these

---

135   *ca.* 750 B.C.
136   Hosea 8:7.

legends of Quetzacoatl are perhaps saying that He has sent us as the whirl-wind which the Mesheeka must reap, that we are the strangers who must swallow up their evil."

Malinali's eyes were wide with wonder as they gazed into those of Cortez. "That is what my father prayed for, that is what I prayed for, my Captain, and that is what I now believe. Let us both pray to the Christian God in thanks for this whirlwind."

* * * * *

By early afternoon, all was ready for the march to Tenochtitlan. From Iztapalapa, the Spaniards could see the great city across the lake, a number of its enormous temples looming little more than a league away. They proceeded to the tip of the Culhuacan peninsula and onto a causeway.

When they came to a branch in the causeway, they were met by a delegation. Its members pointed to a large city on the shore of Lake Xochimilco, about a half-league away, towards which the short branch causeway led.

"We have come from our city of Coyoacan to greet Malinche," they told Malinali. "Our city was great and free once, but it was destroyed by the Mesheeka[137]. It is now a place of large gardens and the estates of Mesheeka nobles, while the children of our ancestors are slaves to them. We wish you well."

After thanking the people of Coyoacan, Cortez assembled the expedition for a formal procession along the main causeway. In front were four horsemen in full Spanish armor: Pedro de Alvarado, Gonzalo de Sandoval, Cristobal de Olid, and Velasquez de Leon.

Next came the *Alfarez*[138], Cristobal del Corral, carrying a huge waving banner that Cortez had designed to inspire his men. Depicting a red cross on a yellow field with white and blue flames, it exhorted the Spaniards: *Brothers, let us follow the Holy Cross, for if we have faith, by its sign we shall conquer.*[139]

The infantry followed, with drawn swords, led by Diego de Ordaz. Then came the lancers on horseback, the crossbowmen wearing cotton armor and

---

137   In the 1420s.
138   The Standard-Bearer.
139   See the Banner of Cortez in Map & Illustrations.

helmets with tall feather plumes, the arquebusiers brandishing their lightning sticks, and finally Cortez himself on horseback, surrounded by several horsemen and foot soldiers, with Malinali walking by his side.

Following the Spaniards were two thousand Tlaxcalans in war dress and war paint, many of whom were burdened with the Spaniards' supplies or were dragging the Lombard guns on wheeled carts. A number of them bore a litter on their shoulders, carrying Princess Teculehuatzin, Doña Luisa, wife of Pedro de Alvarado.

The causeway ran arrow-straight to the great city and was at least twice as wide as the others[140]. Although it was easily wide enough for a dozen horsemen to ride abreast, there was such a crowd of Mesheeka along its entire length, all of whom had come to see the mysterious strangers, that the Spaniards felt they were passing through a tunnel.

The Mesheeka spectators were stunned at what they beheld. None of them had ever seen a horse, much less a man in gleaming armor riding upon one. The lead horses kept turning, moving back and forth, jingling with bells on their saddles, neighing and pawing the ground whenever there was a halt. Their riders, Alvarado, Sandoval, Olid, and Leon, were constantly examining the audience from side to side. The huge mastiff war dogs - another new and frightening animal - ran ahead, sniffing at Mesheeka, panting, drooling, and ferociously barking, which effectively cleared the way for the oncoming strangers.

Corral walked by himself, putting on a constant display with his banner, waving it right and left or in a circle, then tossing it up and catching it with a flourish. The Mesheeka were fascinated by the swords, lances, and armor made of an unknown metal which flashed brightly in the sunlight. They drew back from the crossbowmen and arquebusiers, who made a show of brandishing their weapons.

The Mesheeka stood immobile and stared in awe as Cortez passed, then in shock as they witnessed a vast horde of their Tlaxcalan enemies passing by, dressed in their half-red, half-white maguey cloaks and emitting shrieking, whooping war cries.

On either side of the causeway, the lake was filled with canoes hollowed out of tree trunks, some of them so big that they held dozens of people. The

---

140 About 40 feet across.

procession crossed over a number of bridges made of wooden beams, under which the canoes could pass.

The Spaniards passed in silence, themselves dumbstruck by the experience and in awe of their own audacity. Walking beside Malinali, Bernal recalled the many warnings they had received about entering the Mesheeka city where Montezuma would order their deaths. "There are fewer than four hundred of us, Doña Marina," he said quietly to her. "What men in all the world have shown such daring?!"

About a half-league from the city, they came to a fort with two towers, built on the edge of the causeway. Here, King Cacama came forward and asked them to halt. Making his way to Malinali, he said, "The Great Montezuma is coming to greet you here at Malcuitlapilco (*mal-qweet-lah-pilco*). I go now to escort him."

Cortez walked his horse, with Malinali beside him, to the head of the procession. As they waited, she said, "Malcuitlapilco means 'the end of the line of prisoners.' Do you remember King Xicotencatl in Tlaxcala telling us the story of Tlacaelel[141]? That when the Teocalli, the Great Temple to Huitzilopochtli and Tlaloc, was built, Tlacaelel ordered a dedication ceremony in which twenty thousand prisoners were sacrificed on the temple altar, and that it took two weeks for the priests to kill them all?[142] The line of prisoners reached from the temple through the city, out along this causeway, and ended here, and so this spot was named Malcuitlapilco."

Cortez looked out toward the city, noting how far away it was[143], to the Mesheeka throng, to the two-towered fort, to the canoes on the lake, then down at Malinali. "How fitting," he said, "that Montezuma should meet the Spanish whirlwind here."

A great murmur arose from the Mesheeka crowd, as through it strode a number of heavily-muscled warriors with wooden spears, wearing jaguar skins, with their faces encased by a jaguar head skin. They lined up on either side of the crowd, pushing it back and forming a wide, clear corridor. Down this corridor came *caciques* in elaborate robes, sweeping the ground in front of them with brush brooms and spreading cotton cloaks to cover the ground

---

141   Chapter 18.
142   1487.
143   About a mile and a half. If the line wound through the city for a half-mile or so, that would constitute a line of sacrificial victims two miles long.

in front of Cortez and Malinali. Behind them followed four kings: Cacama, King of Texcoco, Tetelpanquetzal, King of Tacuba, Tezozomoc, King of Culhuacan, and Itzquauhtzin, King of Tlateloco. Dressed in magnificent robes and loin cloths, they were carrying a litter with a canopy of brilliant green feathers, its poles thickly decorated with gold, silver, pearls, and jade.

Sitting in the litter, amidst a profusion of flowers and cacao blossoms, was a man wearing an enormous bejeweled green-feather headdress and an extraordinarily embroidered robe and loin cloth of gold and silver threads, studded with pearls and jade: Montezuma.

While all of the other nobles and kings were barefoot, Montezuma wore *cactli* sandals with soles of gold and bindings covered in gems. As he stepped down from the litter, assisted by the regal bearers, Cortez dismounted from his horse. The two walked up to each other, as Malinali placed herself between them, to the side. She noticed that no one among the nobles, save for the four litter-bearing kings, dared look upon Montezuma's face, keeping their eyes turned away.

She, of course, did no such thing, looking straight at Montezuma, just as did Cortez. Montezuma cast a glance at her, and their gazes locked for a second. She kept herself expressionless and emotionless, yet for that second she looked deep into the dark eyes of the Great Montezuma, as if looking into his soul. When Montezuma looked away, she knew no woman had ever looked upon him as she had just done.

He was neither tall nor short, so Cortez stood above him. His skin was copper-dark and smooth, his black hair wavy and long, his nose sharp and prominent, his nostrils large. His head was large, as well, and he had the trim, hard body of a warrior. Overall, he looked younger than his years[144]. Through his lower lip ran a stone plug of turquoise carved into the figure of a hummingbird. Through his nostrils ran another carved turquoise plug, and from large holes in his earlobes hung heavy turquoise ornaments.

"Are you he? Art thou Lord Montezuma?" Cortez asked formally.

"Yes, I am he," Montezuma just as formally replied.

They bowed to each other, then Cortez took off a necklace of pearls and gold chain that he had been wearing, clasped it around Montezuma's neck, and attempted to embrace him.

---

144   In 1519, Montezuma - whose name means 'He who angers himself' - was 51 years old.

At this, Cacama and the other kings rushed up to hold Cortez back, saying that it was forbidden.

Cortez smiled and asked Malinali to apologize.

Montezuma gestured for a servant to present Cortez with a necklace of red snail shells and solid gold pendants wrought in the form of shrimp and crabs. As the servant did so, Malinali quickly told Cortez, "The paintings I have seen of Quetzacoatl show him wearing such a necklace."

"Please tell Lord Montezuma that I am honored by his gift," Cortez instructed Malinali. "Then tell him that my heart rejoices to have seen such a great prince as he. Explain that we consider his coming to greet us in person the highest honor for us all. Tell him that I bring greetings from my Lord, King Don Carlos of Spain, who knows of Lord Montezuma as one of the great kings of the Earth, and wishes him every happiness and long life. On behalf of His Majesty Don Carlos, I am honored to stand before you, O Lord Montezuma."

As Malinali finished her translation, Cortez bowed deeply to the Mesheeka Emperor, whereupon all his horsemen raised their lances with a shout, the infantry clanging their swords upon their armor, the arquebusiers firing a volley of gunshot into the air.

A good many of the Mesheeka crowd fell down in terror at the sounds, and the nobles around Montezuma jerked back in fright, but Montezuma remained expressionless and did not flinch a single muscle. His gaze remained fixed upon Cortez.

"Malinche!" Montezuma called him, without looking at Malinali. "You have finally arrived at your home. Our city is yours and is open to you. You have been sent to us by your king from where the sun arises, and we welcome you." At a gesture from Montezuma, a resplendently enrobed noble stepped forward. "This is my brother Lord Cuitlahuac, son of my father Axayacatl (*ah-shah-yah-cottle*) and my mother Xochicueyatl (*zo-chee-kway-yottle*), and husband to my daughter Tecuichpotzin (*tay-qweech-pot-zin*). He will accompany you to our city of Tenochtitlan. I return to make all in readiness for you. That is all."

With a slight formal bow, Montezuma turned and was helped back onto his litter and carried back towards the city, with the jaguar warriors clearing the way.

As Cortez climbed back onto his horse, he commented to Malinali, "Montezuma's brother is married to Montezuma's daughter?"

She looked up at him with raised eyebrows and a shrug. "Welcome to Tenochtitlan," was her reply.

Cuitlahuac and a number of nobles escorted them along the causeway and into the city. They passed by numerous whitewashed adobe homes and buildings, every roof of which was jammed with men, women, and children gazing down at them. Hordes of people jammed the streets, and even more lined the canals in canoes. Whenever the Spaniards, who were feeling jubilant, smiled at them, people smiled back.

Entering a vast square with massive temples on one side, they were taken to an enormous palace. After assuring that the horses would be attended to, and that the Tlaxcalans would be housed nearby, Cortez and all of his men were ushered inside, through an expansive open courtyard, and into a large room empanelled and floored with sweet-smelling wood.

Montezuma and a number of his attendants stood waiting for him. "Welcome to the palace of my father, the *Tlatoani* Axayacatl," he addressed Cortez, as he walked over and took Cortez by the hand. At the head of the room, beneath an embroidered cotton canopy, stood a gold-embossed wooden chair. Montezuma led Cortez to it and bade him sit down.

"This was the throne chair of my father. It is now your chair. Malinche, you are in your own house, as are your brothers. I ask that you rest here after your long journey. Food and cacao will be brought, so that you may refresh yourselves, while we see that all your men have proper rooms. When all has been done and your refreshment is finished, I shall return."

Montezuma turned to leave, followed by a train of attendants, leaving Cortez sitting on the throne of a Mesheeka King. "If this be a trap," he said to Malinali, "I cannot imagine one more courteous and gracious."

MAPS
&
ILLUSTRATIONS

The only near-contemporary portrait of Cortez was painted by artist Christoph Weiditz upon Cortez's return to Spain in 1529.

There are no portraits or likenesses of Malinali. She was consistently described as having long dark hair and was extremely beautiful. Beyond that, what she actually looked like is unknown.

A manuscript known as the Lienzo de Tlaxcala (Linen of Tlaxcala) contains a number of drawings stylistically depicting her translating for Cortez, drawn by Tlaxcalan witnesses. Cortez, in fact, is never drawn by himself, but always with her by him whether it is at his first meeting with Montezuma on the Causeway.

Meeting with Montezuma in a Tenochtitlan palace.

Conferring with Tlaxcalan nobles.

Huey Ohtli-ipan. Nican oqui namiqui in Tlaloque in Cortes t oqui macaque ixquich cuali. Sobre el camino grande. Aquí encontró el Senado à Cortés y le ministró provisiones.

Negotiating with representatives of other kingdoms.

Or accepting Cuatemoc's surrender.
(The Lienzo de Tlaxcala is held at the University of Glasgow in Scotland)

An Aztec manuscript, known as the Codex Magliabechiano and housed at the National Library in Florence, Italy, depicts human sacrifice on the Jade Steps of the Teocalli in Tenochtitlan.

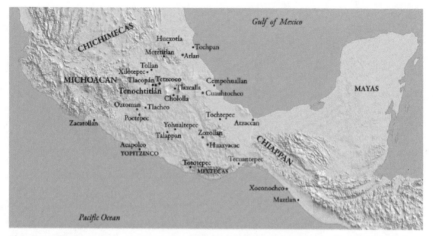

The Aztec Empire at its peak in 1519, the year of Cortez's arrival, encompassed an area of approximately 80,000 square miles, about the size of the state of Kansas. Mexico today is 762,000 square miles.

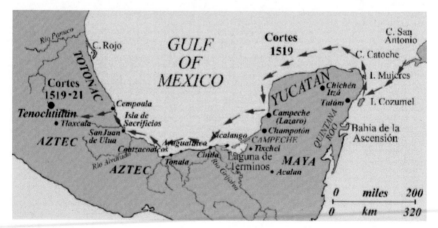

Sea route of Cortez from tip of Cuba, around Yucatan, to first landing in Aztec territory at San Juan de Ulua:

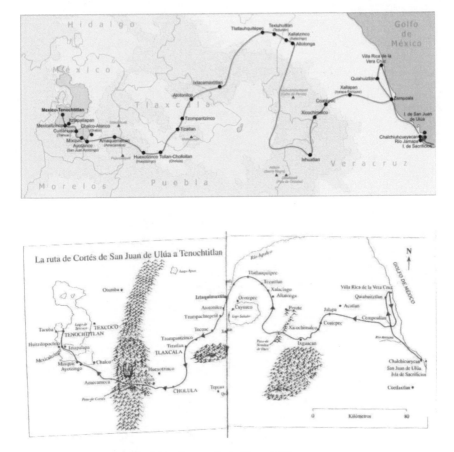

Route of Cortez's Entrada from Cempoala to Tenochtitlan:

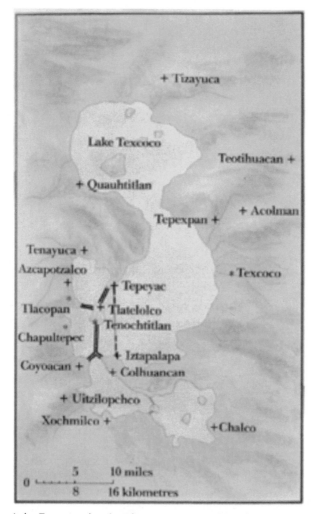

Lake Texcoco, showing the causeways to Tenochtitlan.
The red lines are the earthen causeways, the black dotted
line the dike of Nezahualcoyotl. Cortez's route was along
the southern shore of Lake Chalco and across the short
causeways to the peninsula of Culhuacan and the town
of Iztapalapa. From there, he took the main causeway to
Tenochtitlan.

The Cities of Lake Texcoco

In this map of the cities of Lake Texcoco, note the location of Otumba, west of the ruins of Teototihuacan (then covered by vegetation, thus unseen by Cortez):

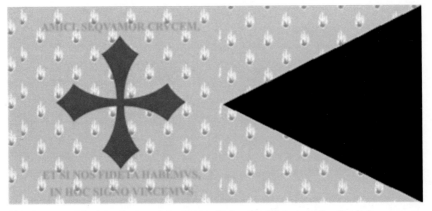

The Banner of Cortez, designed by Cortez to inspire his men. The English translation of the exhortation in Latin is: Brothers, let us follow the Holy Cross, for if we have faith, by its sign we shall conquer.

Chapter Twenty Four

THE JADE STEPS

hen the food arrived – turkeys and maize cakes in great abundance – Malinali ate quickly. She had no time for conversation with Bernal, eager to talk about the wonders of the palace. She cast a knowing glance at Cortez and fled from the room. She returned within the hour, and Cortez was quick to invite her to join the group of officers with whom he was conferring. Everyone looked at her expectantly.

"I heard no talk around this palace or out on the plaza of any trap. I overheard talk between guards, nobles, priests, and common people. They all speak of you by using the word *teotl (tay-ottle)*, which means *wonder, awesome, terrifying power*. They talk of how the strangers are men from another more powerful world, men such as they have never seen before. Montezuma, it seems, can talk of nothing else. There is no anger in what I heard, only *teotl*."

The men had just started to express their relief and appreciation to her when there was a commotion. Several jaguar warriors entered, followed by a procession of grandly cloaked and feathered nobles, perhaps as many as a hundred. In their center was Montezuma.

A number of the nobles were carrying a golden chair even more elaborate than the throne chair of Axayacatl's. It was placed next to the latter. Cortez had come into the middle of the room to receive Montezuma, who then took Cortez by the hand and walked with him to the thrones, where they each sat down. Servants poured into the room and began distributing gifts: gold and silver jewelry and three loads of feather-embroidered cloaks to the officers, two loads of feather-embroidered cloaks to each of the Spanish soldiers.

The enormous hallroom was filled with Mesheeka and Spaniards, who assembled silently at a respectful distance and strained to hear Montezuma and Cortez speak. Cortez had Malinali kneel between and behind the two of them.

"Malinche," Montezuma began, "since the days of my ancestors, we Mesheeka have known we were not natives to this land, but came from far to the north. A great king brought us here to Tenochtitlan, where we settled while he returned to our original home. Many years later, he came back and wanted to lead us on to another land, but we refused. Having married local women, we were raising children and building this city. So he left us, and went across the Great Ocean towards the rising sun.

"And so it is that we have known that his descendants would come back from the rising sun to conquer this land and make us their *maceualli (massy-wally)*[145]. As you have come from across the Great Ocean and the rising sun, we believe you to be those descendants, and that your king is our natural lord, especially because you say he has known of us for a long time.

"We further believe that you are the descendants sent to rule us because of your seemingly impossible victories in battles of so few against so many at Pontochan and Tlaxcala.

"Therefore, be assured, Malinche, that we will obey you as our lord, in place of your king. In this there shall be no betrayal whatever. All that we own is yours. Thus, now that you are in your own country and in your own house, rest now from the hardships of your journey and battles. You must, though, know this – you must believe only what you see here with your own eyes, for I know that those of Cempoala and Tlaxcala have spoken much evil of me. They are my enemies who rebelled against me, and they have said bad things about me to gain favor with you. Now I return to where I live, while here you will be provided with all that you and your men require. Here you shall receive no hurt, for you are in your own land and in your own house."

Malinali translated these words – words that she could not believe she was hearing – as calmly and directly as she possibly could. She made every effort to remain expressionless, and saw that Cortez was doing so, as well.

At the end of Montezuma's speech, Cortez bowed his head with a humble

---

145   'Vassals.'

smile. "Great Lord Montezuma, ruler of all Mesheeka," he began, "your gracious hospitality overwhelms us, for we do not know how to repay you for your favors. It is true that we have come from the other side of the Great Ocean where the sun rises, and that we are the servants of His Majesty King Don Carlos of Spain. It is at His Majesty Don Carlos's command that we are here, for, knowing what a great and noble ruler you are, he asked that we come and beg you and your people to be Christians so that your souls may be saved, as are ours.

"At the appropriate time, I hope to inform you about the One True God and his promise of salvation. But for now, I ask that you have confidence in us, Lord Montezuma, and fear nothing, for we love you greatly. Today our hearts are well satisfied, for we have all wished, for a long time, to see you face to face, to hear you speak in person, and for this we are grateful."

The two stood and clasped each other's hands. Cortez bowed to Montezuma, who then departed with his retinue, the nobles carrying away his throne chair. Cortez sat back down in his golden seat and stared at Malinali, who remained kneeling beside him. She could see that his thoughts were moving so quickly that he could not speak.

"Who is this 'great king' he spoke of?" he finally asked her. "Is it this Meskeetli or that Tenoch our friend in Tlaxcala, King Xicotencatl, told us about?[146] It wasn't their Quetzacoatl god he was talking about - or was he? According to you, he never said the name of any king or god."

Malinali shrugged her shoulders and shook her head. "No name at all. It is as if he was confusing these two legends. Or maybe it is we who have the legends confused. Or maybe he is confusing the legends on purpose, to fool and confuse us. I don't know..."

She thought for a moment, then continued. "I was watching him carefully while listening to him. His eyes were at peace with his mind, and so were the sounds of his words. There is no story I have ever heard about any Mesheeka leader going across the Great Ocean. I think he was talking about Quetzacoatl but that, out of reverence or caution, he wouldn't use the name."

By now several of Cortez's officers had gathered around him. "Did we hear correctly, Captain?" Gonzalo de Sandoval asked. "That Montezuma pledged he was now the vassal of Spain?"

---

146   See Chapter Eighteen.

Cortez stroked his beard. "That is what he seemed to say. He also seemed to say that we are the descendants of a god or ancestor of theirs. Perhaps, however, he was just being polite, as kings can be. Tomorrow, I propose to visit him and discuss - politely - this matter further. I shall want a number of you to accompany me."

As they lay down together that night, Malinali thought Cortez would want to discuss further the puzzle of Montezuma. But the Aztec king was the last thing on his mind. "The morning shall be for Montezuma," he whispered. "The night is for you."

* * * * *

That next morning, Malinali sent a messenger to the *Tecpan*[147] to request a meeting. The messenger soon returned with a contingent of jaguar warriors to escort Cortez and his party. With Cortez were Pedro de Alvarado, Velasquez de Leon, Diego de Ordaz, Gonzalo de Sandoval, and five regular soldiers - one of whom was Bernal.

Bernal couldn't stop talking to Malinali about the soldiers' new home. "We never imagined such luxury!" he exclaimed. "The enormity and number of the rooms and halls, all lined with beautiful polished wood. Each one of us has his own matting bed, with thick furs for blankets, and a canopy! There are hundreds of servants to prepare our food and take care of us. We are being treated like royalty, Doña Marina!"

Yet Bernal's description of Axayacatl's palace did not prepare them for the Tecpan. It was gigantic. The building was not tall, consisting of only two high stories, but it covered an immense area under its roof. It was built of polished alabaster, jasper, and a black stone that contained veins of red and white. The first floor was a beehive of workers, such as potters and featherworkers, servants, and kitchens. Walking through it, Gonzalo de Sandoval said in wonder, "I never imagined a home so large. It must be many thousands of square *valas*[148]."

The second floor was the home of Montezuma and his family. Cortez and

---

147 The Palace of Montezuma
148 A Spanish vala is about 33 inches. One acre is 5650 square valas. The Tecpan of Montezuma was over 30,000 square valas, a quarter-million square feet or almost six acres.

his party were ushered into a large open courtyard that boasted a massive, gurgling stone fountain. Montezuma appeared with a retinue of nobles to conduct Cortez by the hand into his throne room.

On a raised platform stood a huge chair woven out of bundles of reeds. "This is the seat I prefer," Montezuma said to Malinali. For the first time, he looked her in the eye. Until that moment, he had acted as if she did not exist, always looking at Cortez while speaking, and even while listening to her words translating Cortez's replies. It occurred to her that this was probably the first time Montezuma had ever spoken directly to a woman who was not of his close family.

Servants brought an elaborately carved wooden chair for Cortez, placing it next to Montezuma's Throne of Reeds. As they sat down, more servants entered, bearing chairs for the nine Spanish officers and soldiers. Malinali, as before, knelt between Montezuma and Cortez.

"O Lord Montezuma, Ruler of all Mesheeka," Cortez began formally, "we thank you once again for the great kindness you have shown us. We have come today to fulfill the purpose of our voyage here and the orders of our lord, His Majesty King Don Carlos of Spain. That purpose, those orders, are to relate to you in person why we are of the Christian faith.

"Lord Montezuma, I beg you to listen. There are not many gods, a god of the sun, a god of the moon, and of rain, and of earth, and many other things. There is only one god, the One True God, Who once set His Son upon this earth to suffer and die for the sins of us all. Of us *all*, Lord Montezuma, of Spaniards and Mesheeka and Tlaxcalan. It is the One True God Who created Heaven and Earth, and Who placed upon Earth the first of our race, the first man, whose name was Adam, and the first woman, whose name was Eve.

"Every human is the child of Adam and Eve, the First Father and the First Mother. This means that you, Lord Montezuma, and I, Hernando Cortez, are brothers. That all Mesheeka and all Spaniards are brothers. That His Majesty King Don Carlos is your brother, and that, as your brother, he grieves for you because, without the salvation of Christ, you are doomed to burn in the flames of hell upon your death.

"For, as we are all brothers in Adam, so we are all sinners faced with this terrible fate. But the wonderful news which your brother King Don Carlos has sent me to tell you is that, by becoming Christians, you and your

Mesheeka followers may receive the salvation of Christ and eternal life. King Don Carlos has sent me to beg you, Lord Montezuma, to abandon the evil practice of human sacrifice - the sacrifice of your brothers, your fellow man - to evil idols, and instead to accept the salvation that Christ offers you. This is our plea. And in making this plea, we have now done our duty to our king."

Montezuma remained expressionless as he replied with equal formality. "O Lord Malinche, these arguments of yours have been familiar to me for some time. I understand what you said to my ambassadors on the sandhills about the three gods and the cross, and what you have preached in the various towns through which you passed. We have given you no answer, since we have worshipped our own gods from the beginning and know them to be good. No doubt yours are good also, but do not trouble to tell us any more about them.

"Regarding the creation of the world, we have held the same belief for many ages, and so we are certain that you are those who our ancestors predicted would come from the direction of the sunrise. It is for this reason that we welcome you here. If I asked you to cease your attempt to come to our city, it was because my subjects were afraid. They said that you shot flashes of lightning, that you were angry *teules*, gods, and other childish stories. But now I have seen you with my own eyes, and I know you are men of flesh and blood as am I, intelligent and brave men. Therefore I now have a far greater esteem for you than I had from the reports of my subjects."

As they heard Malinali's translation, Cortez and his officers smiled, stood, and bowed to Montezuma in appreciation. The Mesheeka emperor broke out into cheerful laughter.

"Malinche," he said happily, "I know that these people of Tlaxcala, with whom you are so friendly, have told you many terrible things about me – that I am so rich that my home is made of silver and gold and jewels, or that I am a *teule* myself. But you can see that I am a man like you, and that my home is made of stone and wood. So you must take these stories as a joke, as I take the story of your thunders and lightnings."

Cortez responded with a hearty laugh of his own. "Yes, my Lord Montezuma, enemies always speak evil and tell lies about the people they hate, but it is clear to us that we could not hope to find a more magnificent prince than you. We can see that there is good reason why your fame should have reached our king, Don Carlos."

An almost imperceptible nod of Montezuma's head toward an attendant resulted in a number of servants entering and presenting Cortez and each of his officers and soldiers with two elaborate gold necklaces and two loads of richly embroidered cloaks.

"My lord," Cortez said, addressing Montezuma, "the favors you do us increase, day by day, and we hope you will think well of our attempt to repay you by bringing you the good news of which I have spoken. But now it is the hour of your mid-day meal, and it is only appropriate that we depart."

Montezuma thanked them graciously for their visit, and they departed.

On the way back to their lodgings, the Spaniards could talk of nothing but the fine breeding, the exquisite manners, the courtesy and humanity of the Great Montezuma. They all vowed that they would henceforth make every effort to show him the greatest respect.

"We have done our duty," Cortez said to his men as they walked back to their quarters, "considering it is the first attempt."

* * * * *

Before they reached Axayacatl's palace, Malinali cast Cortez a look that told him she was embarking on an *exploración*[149]. She did not return until late in the evening, in a dark mood. Without even looking at Cortez, who was sitting at a table, writing in his journal, she slipped into their bed and lay there silently.

Cortez came over to sit by her and hold her hand. "What have you seen?" he asked gently.

She stared straight ahead without glancing up at him. "*Xochipilli (zo-chee-pilly)*," came her quiet one word answer. Then she looked up at him. "The Aztecs worship a god named Xochipilli, the god of love between men and boys. The temple of this god is filled with young boys, many very young. It is where men come and, and..." Her voice trailed off.

"We call this sinful act sodomy or pederasty," Cortez explained. "Is your witness of this evil the cause of your distress?"

"After living in Xochipilli's temple and being used by men more times

---

149   An exploration of the city.

than people can count, the boys become *ixiptlas (eee-ship-tlas)*, mostly to Tlaloc, but to other gods as well."

"They become what?" Cortez asked.

"An *ixiptla* is someone who is food for the gods, whose heart is fed to the gods, and whose body is fed to the people. I learned tonight that it is not just Tlaloc and Xipe and Huitzilipochtli that must be fed with the living hearts of ixiptlas, of slaves and war prisoners and Xochipilli-boys. There are temples here in Tenochtitlan of dozens of gods, at least 60 or 70 different gods, and all of them require human blood to be kept alive, in the minds of the Aztecs."

Cortez crossed himself and muttered a quick prayer.

"There is no day of the year that is not dedicated to some god," Malinali continued, "and so, every single day, dozens of *ixiptlas* are killed. Their hearts are for the gods, their skins are for priests' robes, their heads for display, their arms and legs for the nobles' meals, and the torsos for the jaguars and other animals kept in an enclosure near the Tecpan. The bodies of these *ixiptlas* are made into the favorite recipes of the nobles - but only certain ones are prepared for Montezuma himself."

When he replied, the softness of Cortez's voice belied the alarm in his eyes. "What do you mean, my Lady?"

There were tears in Malinali's eyes as she looked up at him. It was the first time he had ever seen her cry. "The youngest," she whispered. "The bodies of the very youngest are saved for him. The favorite meal of the Great Montezuma is a human baby child, cooked with tomatoes and chili peppers."

* * * * *

Just after dawn, Cortez directed Malinali to send a request that he be allowed to visit the *Teocalli*[150] of Huitzilopochtli. The message came that he would be met there by the Great Montezuma, who needed to make preparations for his coming.

"That means that Montezuma must ask the gods' forgiveness for allowing you to defile their temple, and must purify it himself with sacrifice," Malinali explained.

Cortez and his entourage were guided to the temple through a series of

---

150   The Great Temple.

large courtyards surrounded by high rock walls and paved with large, smooth, polished white stones. Bernal noted how the courtyards were so clean there was not a piece of straw or a speck of dirt to be seen. "These courts are bigger than the Plaza of Salamanca," he told Malinali.

When they finally stood in front of the huge *Teocalli*, Cortez commented, "It seems higher than the Giralda, the cathedral of Seville[151]." It was an enormous four-sided pyramid, with steep steps leading to a summit platform with two separate buildings. At the base, where they stood, was a large stone disk set in the hardened earth, with a grotesque figure carved into it.

"Coyolxauhqui (*coy-ol-shaow-kwee*)," Malinali explained. "Huitzilopochtli's sister, who the Aztecs say he killed and cut into pieces. That is why she is shown naked, with her head cut off and her body dismembered. This stone, I was told, is called 'Huitzilopochtli's Dining Table.' It is where the bodies of the *ixiptla* sacrifices land when they are tossed from the top of the temple."

The steps were black with a thick crust of dried blood. "Why are the steps so narrow and steep?" Cortez wondered.

"To ensure that the bodies will bounce all the way to the bottom," was Malinali's answer.

Six priests had emerged from the top and made their way down. They were dressed in blood-spattered black robes, their ears cut to shreds, their hair hanging knotted and uncombed to their chests, their faces an ashen gray. Two of them approached Cortez to take him, each by an arm.

"They say they are here to assist you in climbing The Jade Steps," Malinali informed him.

Cortez shook them off in annoyance. "Please tell them that I am in no need of assistance, nor are any of us." Cortez looked at her sharply. "Why are these called The Jade Steps, Doña Marina?"

"Because jade – or *chalchihuite* – has two meanings for the Mesheeka. It means the stone itself but, since the jade stone is the most valuable thing to them, more valuable than gold or jewels, it also means 'precious,' or 'of supreme value.' The steps of the Teocalli are stained with the sacred blood of all those who have died to keep the gods alive. So they call these 'precious'

---

151   It was not. The Giralda Cathedral of Seville was 260' high, while the Teocalli in Tenochtitlan was 150' high, with each of its four sides 250' long at the base. There were 113 steps to the temple platform on the top at an angle of 45º.

steps, The Jade Steps," Malinali explained, her gaze locked with Cortez's as she spoke.

He made no response. Instead, he strode across the stone disk and began climbing, at a measured careful pace. Everyone else followed: Malinali, Pedro de Alvarado, Cristobal de Olid, Gonzalo de Sandoval, Diego de Ordaz, Father Bartholomew Olmedo, Bernal and three other soldiers, accompanied by the priests.

Montezuma was at the top to greet them. "Ah, Malinche, you have climbed The Jade Steps!" he exclaimed. "You must be tired."

Cortez humorlessly replied, "No Spaniard ever is tired."

Montezuma smiled and took him by the hand to a corner of the platform. "This is what I never tire of - looking out from here to our magnificent city below," he said softly. He pointed directly below to a huge square filled with thousands of people. "That is the great market of Tlatelolco," he explained. They could see the lake, the causeways that led to the shore, and cities along the shore with white towers. "There is the causeway of Iztapalapa, by which you arrived." He pointed to another. "That is the causeway to Tacuba." He pointed to a hill off to his right. "And there is the spring of Chapultepec, where we get our fresh water." It was a beautifully clear day, bright sunshine, bright blue sky, bright puffy white clouds, green mountains on the distant horizon. "Can you see why standing here brings me such joy?" Montezuma asked.

Cortez continued to gaze out at the vista while saying to Malinali, "Did he actually say this place brings him joy? Ah, Doña Marina, I am trying so hard to be polite. Please reply to him that yes, Lord Montezuma, the view from here is certainly magnificent."

Nearby stood two square buildings with thatch roofs on the platform. With a sunny smile, Montezuma led Cortez past the first, which Malinali whispered was that of Tlaloc, and into the second. "This is the sacred shrine of Huitzilopochtli, without whom the sun would not rise and the heavens would fall," Montezuma announced.

Their first sight was the *techcatl*, the green execution stone upon which the victims were flung to break their spine and paralyze them, so that the priests - or Montezuma himself - could plunge the obsidian knife into their chests and cut out their hearts while they were still alive. On top of the thick layers of encrusted dried blood everywhere was fresh red blood, a clear sign that sacrifices had been made just before their arrival. The stench was overwhelming.

On either side of the shrine were two stone statues covered with turquoise and mother-of-pearl, wearing gold masks, belts of gold snakes, and necklaces of gold human skulls. One of them, Malinali said, was Coatlicue, Serpent Skirt, goddess of the earth.

Behind the *techcatl* was a stone figure lying on its back, with its head and knees raised, its hands holding a stone bowl. It was painted in a number of colors and decorated with coral and turquoise. Its large, round, mother-of-pearl eyes seemed to stare at them. In the bowl was a human heart. "The *chacmool*," Malinali said. "The receptacle for the heart before it is burnt for the god."

It was gloomy inside the shrine itself, and it took several minutes before their eyes adjusted to the lack of light. They could make out two altars, with a large wooden statue on each. One was Huitzilopochtli, the other Tezcatlipoca. Both were tall and grossly fat, covered with pieces of gold, pearls, and jewels stuck on with seed-paste. Huitzilopochtli was girdled with huge snakes of gold, and in one hand he held a bow, while the other hand held a clutch of arrows. Around his neck were human faces in gold, silver, and turquoise.

In front of the altar was a brazier of glowing copal resin. Three human hearts were smoking as they cooked upon the copal. The walls and floor of the shrine were splashed and caked with blood. "The stench is worse than any slaughterhouse in Spain," remarked Gonzalo de Sandoval in a choked whisper.

The statue of Tezcatlipoca had the face of a fanged bear, with glittering eyes of mirrored glass, and his body was covered with figures in gold of little demons with snake's tails. Malinali explained that, as the god of hell, he was in charge of Mesheeka souls. Five human hearts smoldered in the burning copal in his brazier.

When Cortez turned to Montezuma, Malinali saw that Cortez could no longer hold himself back. His words vibrated with controlled fury, but she translated his words as calmly as she could.

"Lord Montezuma, I cannot imagine how a prince as great and wise as your majesty can fail to understand that these idols of yours are evil monsters.

They are devils, not gods. To worship them is to worship evil, to worship Satan. So that I may prove this to you, I ask that you grant me permission to erect a cross on top of this temple. Let us divide off a part of this shrine where we can place an image of Our Lady, to confront your Huitzilopochtli and Tezcatlipoca. Then you will see, by the fear your idols shall have of her, how grievously you have been deceived."

The faces of the two chief priests standing next to Montezuma contorted in rage. Montezuma himself assumed a look of extreme anger. "Lord Malinche," he replied, "if I had known that you were going to utter such insults in this sacred place, I would never have allowed you to see my gods. We hold them to be very good, not evil. They are gods, not devils. They are good, kind, just gods who give us health and rain and crops and victory over our enemies. They give us the sun, the heavens, and life itself. Because of this, we are bound to worship them and to sacrifice to them, to sustain them so that they can keep giving us everything good. Therefore, I command you to say nothing more against them."

Malinali saw that Cortez had regained his composure. Smiling and bowing, he replied, "I ask your majesty's forgiveness, for what I said was not appropriate. I thank you for bringing us here, to see these things for ourselves, but now it is time for us to depart."

Montezuma's anger was no longer visible but he remained serious. "This is true - but I must stay, so that I may pray and ask the gods forgiveness for the great *tatacul*, sin, I have committed in allowing you to come here and dishonor them."

Cortez bowed once again. "I ask your pardon, O Lord Montezuma," he said, and left the shrine.

Slowly, with precision, he made his way down The Jade Steps. Everyone behind him walked down in silence, as well. When they reached the bottom, Cortez looked at them all. "I swear before the Father, the Son, and the Holy Ghost that I will destroy this temple. I now understand why we have been led here, our true purpose in being here."

He looked at Malinali. "I swear to you, Doña Marina, before Our Lady, that the day will soon come when no one - no one - will ever again be forced to climb these accursed Jade Steps."

Chapter Twenty Five

PRISONER IN HIS PALACE

As they were returning to their quarters in the Palace of Axayacatl, Cortez announced, "If we cannot yet say Mass and have a chapel upon that temple, then at least for now we must be able to do so where we are housed. Doña Marina, please send a request to Montezuma, asking that we be allowed to build a chapel in his father's palace."

When word came quickly back that the request was granted, Cortez assigned his best carpenter, Alonso Yañez, to the task. Early the next morning, Yañez, escorted by Juan Velasquez de Leon and Francisco de Lugo, interrupted the morning meal of Cortez and Malinali. "Captain, we have found something you should see," he said.

Yañez brought them into a small room. "We thought that this room would be appropriate for our chapel," he explained. He walked over to one of the room's walls. "Then I noticed something strange. You can see that there is fresh plaster and paint here, most likely covering up a door – a door to what we think is a hidden room."

Without hesitation, Cortez responded, "Señor Yañez, you are to be congratulated for your sharp eyes. Let us open this hidden door."

Cortez called for torches. When Bernal appeared with lit torches for all, Yañez and his assistant broke through the plastered doorway. Cortez was the first to step into the black entrance of the sealed room, followed by de Leon, de Lugo, Malinali, Yañez, and Bernal.

"*Madre de Dios*," Mother of God, exclaimed de Leon, as they all held their torches aloft. "The treasure of Montezuma."

The flames of the torches flickered over a colossal amount of gold: huge goblets and plates, statues, figures, ingots, all in the hundreds and hundreds, thousands of objects in all, and all solid gold. There were an uncountable number of quetzal feathers, carved pieces of jade, pearls and other jewels.

After de Leon's exclamation, everyone stood in stunned silence. Finally, Malinali spoke. "This is not Montezuma's treasure. It is that of his father, Axayacatl, for this was his palace. There are many legends about this treasure, the greatest treasure that the Mesheeka possess."

"I never imagined that such a treasure trove could exist in the world," said Bernal in an awed whisper.

Cortez finally broke the spell. "Gentleman, the discovery of this treasure will one day bring us great honor in the eyes of our King Don Carlos. Yet such a discovery may now be very dangerous for us. Who knows what Montezuma may do to us, should he learn of our discovery? I propose, for now, that we leave this treasure untouched, just as it is, and that we seal up this room as before. Then we must carefully discuss among ourselves what we shall do."

All agreed. They left the treasure room without taking a single object. Cortez again thanked Alonso Yañez, and bade him to use all his skill to repair their break-in and render it indiscernible.

* * * * *

As word spread quickly among the Spaniards of the great treasure's discovery, the reaction was one not of excitement but of anxiety. Late that afternoon, a number of officers, led by Diego de Ordaz, along with a dozen soldiers, among them Bernal and Aguilar, came to see Cortez.

Malinali was in the midst of giving Cortez a lesson in Nahuatl. The men gave her a collective bow of acknowledgement, and de Ordaz said respectfully, "Doña Marina." Then he turned to Cortez.

"My captain, we have come to speak for all of the men, officers and soldiers. We fear that we have been caught in a telaraña, a spider's web. From the top of that accursed temple, we saw how easily the drawbridges could be raised on the causeways, preventing our escape. We remember all the warnings we received, in every town we passed through, that Montezuma only intended to let us into his city so that he could kill us. We remember his fickleness, one day saying that we should not come, the next day saying we should, the following day saying we should not, again. His heart is not steady, and thus we cannot trust the good will and affection that he is showing us now. If he should decide to attack us, especially if he learns of our discovery of the treasure, we would be helpless. Food and water would be shut off from us. We would be overwhelmed by the vast number of his warriors."

"Do not imagine that I am unaware of these dangers, gentlemen," Cortez replied, "nor that I do not share your anxiety. What do you propose that we do?"

"Captain, we are all agreed," responded de Ordaz. "We must get Montezuma out of his palace with smooth words and brought here, where he must be told that he is our prisoner. That if he orders an attack on us, he will forfeit his life. Our decision is that we take initiative by seizing Montezuma, rather than waiting for him to attack us, for, if he does so, what chance do we have?"

At these words, Malinali struggled desperately to remain calm. Her face remained expressionless but, when Cortez gave her the briefest glace, he could see that her eyes had widened in shock. He then looked at de Ordaz, and into the eyes of each of the men in front of him.

"You have made a bold decision, gentlemen," he said to them. "I commend you for your audacity. Such a course of action will, of course, require very careful thought and planning. Let us confer again, tomorrow morning. And, tonight, let us pray for divine guidance as to how we may succeed."

When Ordaz and the men had bowed in agreement and departed, Cortez looked at Malinali. Her gaze was fixed on him, yet her eyes seemed unseeing and unblinking. Her breathing was quick and shallow. "You are surprised at their decision, my Lady?" he asked her gently.

Her eyes focused on him more clearly, yet still she said nothing. Cortez waited patiently. Finally, she stammered in wonder, "How... how could your men conceive of such a thing?"

"Perhaps it was from a suggestion that Señor de Ordaz received from his commander," Cortez softly replied.

Her brow wrinkled. "From you?"

Cortez's lips formed a hint of a smile. "My Lady, you know that the best way to get men to do what you want is to have them believe it was their own idea."

She nodded. "My father would certainly agree."

Cortez stroked his beard. "Yet I have not decided if this is actually best. Our situation is precarious. Finding this huge treasure has made the men feel their grave vulnerability here. I wanted to prepare them to take action, if necessary. But is it necessary? That is the question I must answer." He took her hand and pulled her into his arms. "What do you think, my Lady?" he asked, with his lips close to hers. "What do you think of this proposal?"

"To try and take the Great Montezuma prisoner in his own palace, to try and do so with a handful of men against an empire of soldiers? My father would say that only gods would try such a thing," she answered.

Their lips now were almost touching. "Am I a god, my Lady?" he whispered.

She looked into his eyes. "No, you are a man," she whispered back. "A man of my dreams, a man that I love."

Their lips met, and they spoke no more of Montezuma.

* * * * *

As dawn broke, the next morning[152], Cortez and Malinali were awakened by Cortez's personal guard, Joan de Caceres. "Captain General, there are two Tlaxcalans here who insist they must see you," he related. "They say it is of the utmost urgency."

"My Nahuatl lessons must be working for Señor Caceres," Malinali noted to Cortez, who told his guard to usher them in as he and Malinali dressed hurriedly.

The Tlaxcalans soon entered, one holding a folded letter that bore a red wax seal. Malinali spoke to them briefly. "They say it was very difficult for them to bring this letter to you," she told Cortez. "It was brought here in great secrecy."

Cortez broke the red seal and read the letter. "It is from a dead man," he said, "the officer I left in charge at Villa Rica, Juan de Escalante. He wrote this as he lay dying. He tells of a Mesheeka governor named Qualpopoca, from a place called Nautla, some seventeen leagues north of Villa Rica[153].

---

152   November 14, 1519, six days after Cortez's arrival at Tenochtitlan on November 8.
153   50 miles. Also called Almería by the Spaniards.

This Qualpopoca demanded tribute from nearby Totonac towns, which refused because, as they told him, 'Malinche has forbidden it.' When Qualpopoca's army began attacking Totonac towns, de Escalante gathered a force of Totonacs to protect them. Near Nautla, there was a battle in which the Spaniards and Totonacs were badly defeated. Six Spaniards were killed, along with many Totonacs. A Spaniard, Juan de Argüello, was taken prisoner, and de Escalante was mortally wounded."

Cortez sighed deeply. "He is dying of his wounds. He doesn't name the others, but I know Juan de Argüello. He is a very large man with a huge head. He grew long, curly hair and an enormous, black, curly beard so that his head would seem even bigger. The other soldiers would tease him, but he was very proud of his head." He looked at Malinali. "Does his being taken prisoner mean what I think it means, Doña Marina?"

Malinali quickly relayed the story to the Tlaxcalan messengers. Now it was her turn to sigh. "They say that, according to the Totonacs, Qualpopoca had this prisoner sacrificed, that his heart was cut out and burnt in thanks to the gods for their victory, that his body was cooked and eaten, and that the large head of which you speak was cut off and sent..." she took a deep breath, "...to Montezuma."

She spoke with the Tlaxcalans further. "All is now chaos," she informed Cortez. "The Totonacs no longer believe that your men are *teules*, various Totonac and Mesheeka villages are fighting one another, and everyone is behaving like wild beasts."

"Doña Marina," Cortez said calmly, "please tell our messengers how grateful I am for what they have done. See that they are rewarded with the finest feather-embroidered cotton cloaks. Señor Caceres, please summon my principal officers."

Within minutes, Pedro de Alvarado, Gonzalo de Sandoval, Juan Velasquez de Leon, Francisco de Lugo, and Alonso de Avila joined Cortez, as Malinali left with the Tlaxcalans. When she returned, after nearly an hour, they were leaving the room. "We are going to morning mass," Cortez informed her, "to ask God's blessing upon our enterprise. What did you learn?"

"There is much talk in Montezuma's palace about the huge head of Señor Argüello. They say that, when it was presented to Montezuma, he became very frightened and ordered that it be sent away to be buried in secret."

"This confirms de Escalante's letter," he replied grimly. "We shall proceed."

At mass, the soldiers were informed of Cortez's plans, and Father Olmedo invoked Heaven's benediction. The bulk of the soldiers assembled in the courtyard in front of Axayacatl's palace, under the pretense of practice drilling and weapons maintenance. A few dozen others were directed to casually spread themselves along the avenue, from their palace to Montezuma's. Two dozen more were instructed to casually stroll in groups of two or three over to Montezuma's palace. Everyone was to be in full armor.

Then Cortez, his five officers, Malinali, and a half-dozen soldiers including Bernal and Aguilar, went to see Montezuma. The Spaniards being fully armed with breastplate, helmet and swords was not unusual, for this was seen as their normal appearance. Montezuma greeted them warmly in his throne room. Only servants attended him. There were no jaguar guards.

Cortez wasted no time. "Doña Marina, please tell Lord Montezuma that I am astonished that such a valiant prince as he, who has declared himself our friend and the vassal of King Don Carlos, would have ordered his governor Qualpopoca to rob and plunder Totonac towns that were under our protection, seizing Totonac men and women for sacrifice, and killing my Spanish brothers who tried to protect the Totonacs.

"Being your great friend and ally, I placed great trust in your friendship towards me and my men. That trust was misplaced. At Cholula, we knew that your captains and warriors were set to capture and kill us at your command. When that failed, you sent them to waylay us upon the road on our way here. That failed as well. Both of these attempts I have overlooked and forgiven, because of my great affection for you. But now your captains and governors have lost all shame and have shown that they wish to kill us, for which the responsibility must be yours.

"Lord Montezuma, I have no desire to start a war or to destroy this city. Everything will be forgiven, provided that you now come quietly with us to our quarters and make no protest. You will be well served and attended to there, as if you were here in your own palace. But if you cry out, or raise any commotion, you will immediately be killed by my men, whom I have brought for this purpose."

Malinali quickly saw that Cortez had made the right decision, for the look in Montezuma's eyes was one of fear, not anger. For a moment, he could not say a word, as his gaze darted between Cortez and Malinali, who both remained expressionless.

At last, Montezuma stammered, "I would never order my subjects to attack your men. Whoever has done so will be punished." He took off a small figurine of Huitzilopochtli from a bracelet on his wrist and called for a servant. "I am ordering Qualpopoca to come before me, with this symbol of my authority. Then we may determine what has happened." Then he turned to look at Cortez. "As for your request, I am not a person to whom orders may be given, or who can be made a prisoner. Further, my people would not tolerate such an insult to their king."

Cortez bowed and said, with a gentle smile, "Lord Montezuma, I have no wish to insult you or your people. My concern is only how best to preserve the affection and respect we have between us."

"What you suggest is not the way to do so, Lord Malinche," Montezuma politely replied. "I must remain here."

Cortez bowed again, maintaining his gentle smile, and was about to reply when Juan Velasquez de Leon placed his hand on his sword hilt and bellowed in a thunderous voice, "What is the use of all these flowery words, Captain Cortez? Either we take him or we slay him here and now. If we do neither, we are all dead men, every last one of us."

As the other officers grabbed their sword hilts and shouted their agreement with de Leon, Montezuma looked at Malinali with terror in his eyes. "What are they saying?" he asked her.

Malinali stepped close to Montezuma and looked directly into his frightened eyes. "Lord Montezuma, I advise you to accompany these men to their quarters immediately, and to make no protest. I know that they will treat you honorably, as the great king you are. But if you stay here, your life is finished. They will kill you where you stand."

Cortez had calmed his men, and all was silence. Then Montezuma said, "Lord Malinche, I understand what you want. I have a son and two daughters. Take them as your hostages and spare me this disgrace. I may not be able to control my chieftains if they see me carried off as a prisoner."

"Doña Marina, please tell him that there is no alternative. The decision has been made," Cortez said quietly.

The look in Cortez's eyes needed no translation. "Lord Montezuma," said Malinali just as quietly, "you could tell your chieftains and people that you have talked with Huitzilopochtli, who instructed you to live with the Spaniards and learn many things from them. It is the gods who command this."

She said this so quietly that no attendant or servant of Montezuma's could hear. They had probably heard little of what had gone on, other than de Leon's bellow, for Montezuma had brushed them off and directed them to stand some distance away. Now he summoned them.

"Early this morning," he announced to his retinue, "I spoke with God Huitzilopochtli, who advised me to live for a while with the descendants of our ancestors, from whom, Huitzilopochtli says, I can learn much of great benefit for my people." He gestured towards the Spaniards. "This caused concern among our friends, who thought they might be unable to assume the burden of my presence." He gestured towards Juan Velasquez de Leon. "Some worried they might not adequately provide for my protection, and swore they would defend me at the cost of their lives. Perhaps they swore this a little too loudly."

Montezuma's attempt at humor elicited nervous laughter from his attendants.

"We leave at once," he commanded. "Prepare my litter."

Attendants scurried away, and the demeanor of the Spaniards changed in the instant when Malinali translated Montezuma's command. They bowed low to Montezuma and each asked Malinali to assure him of their respect.

"I shall protect Lord Montezuma as if he were my own father," said Pedro de Alvarado.

"I regret my outburst of emotion, and I ask Lord Montezuma's forgiveness," said Juan Velasquez de Leon.

"Lord Montezuma shall be attended by his full household, his reign over the Mesheeka will be uninterrupted," said Gonzalo de Sandoval.

"This is but a change of residence for Lord Montezuma," said Francisco de Lugo.

"It will be our highest honor to have Lord Montezuma as our guest," said Alonso de Avila.

Then Cortez spoke. "We hold Lord Montezuma in reverence. His dignity and honor shall be preserved, and he shall be treated with every kindness."

A group of nobles entered the room, bearing the Royal Litter of the Great Montezuma, covered in jewels and quetzal feathers, adorned with fresh flowers and cacao blossoms. The royal feather headdress was affixed, the royal feathered robes were worn, Montezuma was lifted into the litter, and the procession began.

As it made its way towards the Palace of Axayacatl, people gathered in throngs and stared silently, confused by the contrast between the sullen, downcast nobles carrying the litter and the countenance of Montezuma as he smilingly reassured them that he was visiting the strangers who were "the descendants of our ancestors."

The contrast was highlighted by the guard of Cortez's soldiers who surrounded the procession. Word spread quickly throughout the city that something was amiss. As the procession entered the Palace of Axayacatl, a large contingent of Spanish soldiers, including crossbowmen and arquebusiers, formed to block and guard the entrance.

Once Cortez saw that Montezuma was inside and that the guard had formed, he turned to Malinali and said, "From here, Montezuma will continue to govern his empire. But now I will govern Montezuma."

Chapter Twenty Six

CLEANSING THE TEMPLE

Much of the royal household was transferred to the Palace of Axaya-catl. Montezuma's chefs set up the royal kitchens, attendants the royal baths, servants the royal wardrobe, so that he was fed, bathed, and clothed as before. Suitable quarters were arranged for his wives and con-cubines, whom he frequently visited. His retinue of courtiers and counselors was with him throughout the day. Petitioners and ambassadors from various parts of the empire came to plead with him or present him with tribute.

All seemed normal - with one difference. The only guards, of which there were many, were Spanish. There was not a jaguar warrior in sight.

Yet to everyone who came to him with concern, to ask about his obvi-ous imprisonment, Montezuma assured them he was happy and under no restraint. He told them not to disturb themselves or the city, and commanded them not to be distressed, for his 'visit' with the strangers was the will of Huitzilopochtli.

Cortez had instructed his guards to show Montezuma every respect and to see that he received "attention and amusements." Any of the Spaniards who knew any skill, such as juggling, or could provide a performance like sword-play, was asked to entertain him. Montezuma became fond of a young page that Cortez assigned to him, named Orteguilla. The lad was always hap-py and cheerful, with such a quick mind that Malinali had been able to teach him passable Nahuatl. The Aztec Emperor enjoyed talking to Orteguilla, who could always make him laugh. And whatever Montezuma confided to him, young Orteguilla relayed it all to Cortez and Malinali.

After about a week, Qualpopoca and his chieftains from Nautla were brought to the Palace of Axayacatl, where they were presented not to Montezuma but to Cortez. He had them taken to a private room, accompanied by his largest, most menacing soldiers - and by Malinali.

The contrast between the huge, glowering, armed strangers and Malinali's quiet, calm questions caused Qualpopoca to break down and confess that, as Nautla's governor, he had been instructed by Montezuma to recover tribute not being paid by the Totonacs. If any *teules* tried to prevent them, he was to fight and kill them. This would show both his Mesheeka and the Totonacs that the supposed *teules* were not really gods – and if one could be killed, they all could be.

Upon hearing Qualpopoca's confession, Cortez immediately went to see Montezuma. Guards ordered everyone out of the room, leaving Cortez and Malinali alone with Montezuma.

"Lord Montezuma, it is with grave regret that I must tell you that your governor, Qualpopoca, states that it was you who commanded him to attack the Totonacs under my protection, and to kill my Spanish brothers. I must also tell you that I believe him, as it is in keeping with your trickery at Cholula. It is the law of His Majesty King Don Carlos that anyone responsible for deaths such as these should himself die.

"Yet, even though His Majesty would say you deserved such punishment, I cannot bring myself to order it. I now have such affection and concern for you that, even if you were guilty of this crime, I would rather forfeit my life than see you forfeit yours."

Malinali could see in Montezuma's eyes that he had no response to Cortez's combination of threats and kindness. His gaze darted to hers, silently pleading.

"You might command an appropriate punishment for Qualpopoca, for his crimes in Nautla and his worse crime of accusing you of them," she suggested.

Instantly, the look of fright vanished from his eyes. He brought himself stiffly erect, and said, "The Divine Hearth!" Malinali's glance at Cortez prompted him to have the guards let everyone back into the throne room.

When his nephews and courtiers had assembled, Montezuma announced, "I have just learned of the extent of our governor Qualpopoca's treachery.

There is only one punishment for this treason: the Divine Hearth. See that this sentence is carried out upon him and his chieftains immediately - in the Great Square in front of the *Teocalli,* where the people of Tenochtitlan can see what happens to such traitors!"

Cortez bowed to Montezuma, messengers scurried out with the royal command, and Montezuma bade Orteguilla to sit down beside him. Soon they were happily talking, and Cortez and Malinali left.

As they walked out, Cortez commented, "Now he is in my grasp more than ever. And just what is this Divine Hearth, my Lady?"

"It is a punishment the Aztecs use for the worst crimes. You have something like it, I think, for I have heard some of the men talk about how heretics and traitors are killed. They called it *auto da fé.*"

Cortez's eyebrows raised. "The 'act of faith'? Montezuma can be ruthless when he needs to be, can't he? Qualpopoca is to be burned at the stake."

* * * * *

"Isn't there an *arsenal de armas*[154] near the great plaza?" Cortez asked her. Malinali nodded.

"It would be filled with arrows and spears, yes?"

Malinali nodded again.

"If Qualpopoca is to be burned, then his 'Divine Hearth' may as well be made of these wooden weapons. They could never be used against us if they are ashes. Send a messenger with some guards to this arsenal, my Lady, with these instructions..."

As she went off to do so, Malinali noticed that Cortez was lost in thought. When she returned and found him again, he was accompanied by a soldier carrying leg irons. Cortez looked grim and in no mood for talk, so she walked silently with him back to Montezuma's chambers, where Cortez ordered his guards to stand between Montezuma and the courtiers and attendants.

"Doña Marina," Cortez requested, "please inform Lord Montezuma that, as much as I regret it, our law requires punishment for his being a cause of the violence perpetrated upon my men and those under my protection. I have no choice but to order this."

---

154 A weapons storehouse,

He nodded to the soldier holding the leg irons, who proceeded to fasten them around Montezuma's ankles. Montezuma seemed too shocked to move or protest. A haze formed over his eyes and he said not a word.

With a curt bow, Cortez turned and left, motioning for Malinali to follow. She was too stunned to say anything herself, and so they walked in silence until they reached their quarters.

"I have seen something far beyond my dreams - Montezuma placed in chains," she finally said. "Why did you do this?"

"To break his spirit," came Cortez's reply. "No matter how gracious he is, he cannot be trusted. He really did give Qualpopoca a secret command to attack us and the Totonacs. It is as if he is two people in one. That is too dangerous for us, a mere handful of strangers surrounded by tens of thousands who would shed our blood at his command. Our only chance is *audacia*, audacity, my Lady. *Fortes fortuna adiuvat.*"

He paced the floor. "I get no joy from humiliating him. I, like all of my men, have become very fond of him – at least, of the part of him that is like a child. But there is another part of him that is a monster, worshipping evil gods soaked in blood. I had no wish to do this - any more than I wish to watch those Aztec nobles burn to death. I have asked the guards to inform me when it is over."

"Thank you for sparing me the sight as well, my Captain," Malinali replied quietly.

Cortez continued to pace the floor in silence until a guard entered the room and nodded. At that, Cortez strode out of the room, saying, "And now, my Lady, we shall see how good a judge of people I truly am."

They found Montezuma surrounded by his attendants, all of whom were weeping. They were holding up his shackled legs with their hands, and had inserted bits of cloth and quetzal feathers between the iron and his ankles to protect his skin. Montezuma's face was a frozen mask, his eyes open and unblinking.

Taking the shackle key from a guard, Cortez rushed up to Montezuma and unclasped the irons. "Doña Marina," he called out, "please inform Lord Montezuma how much it pained me to do this, but it is our law. I deeply regret it, and no longer wish to keep him away from his palace. He is fully free to return - or to remain here with us. It is his choice."

As he heard her translated words, Malinali saw a tear form in Montezuma's eye. "Malinche," came his reply, "it is better that I remain here. Once I return to the Tecpan and am at liberty, many nobles and chiefs will demand that I fight you. If I do, there will be much bloodshed and destruction in our city. If I refuse, they may fight me, to replace me with someone else. So the better course is for me to stay here, at the command and wish of Huitzilopochtli."

He spoke these words with clarity, but without any tone of resolve or authority. They were the words of a broken man. Once again, Cortez had been right.

After she relayed Montezuma's reply, Cortez threw his arms around the emperor and embraced him. "Ah, Lord Montezuma," he called out, "how right I am to love you as I love myself!"

Montezuma smiled weakly and asked to see Orteguilla.

* * * * *

From that day on, after every morning Mass, Cortez made it his habit to visit Montezuma, accompanied by his main officers, Pedro de Alvarado, Juan Velasquez de Leon, and Diego Ordaz. He wished that Gonzalo de Sandoval were there, but Cortez had sent him to govern Villa Rica and reestablish Spanish authority, a task which de Sandoval was easily able to accomplish, as word of Qualpopoca's fiery execution had spread among the Nautla Aztecs and the Totonacs. Malinali made sure that Bernal was with them, as well, for she enjoyed his company.

Having finished his morning meal of fruits and vegetables, Montezuma would greet them, whereupon the Spaniards, including Cortez, would take off their mailed caps or helmets, flatter him with compliments, and show him every courtesy. Montezuma began to take a particular liking to Pedro de Alvarado, and called him by his nickname, *Tonatio*, for his bright yellow hair and his bright, sunny smile. The emperor continually showered gifts of jewels, small bars of gold, feathered cloaks, and beautiful women upon the Spaniards. When he presented Bernal with one such beauty - "the daughter of an important man," the emperor noted - Bernal kissed Montezuma's hand in gratitude.

Cortez would wile away hours with Montezuma, playing *totoloque*, a Mesheeka game with small gold pellets tossed at small gold slabs from some distance away. Whoever landed his pellets closest to the slabs won.

As the days and weeks passed, Tenochtitlan adapted to Montezuma's new circumstances, and life returned to normal. The gigantic market of Tlatleloco, with thousands of vendors selling every kind of merchandise to be found in the land, carried out its orderly business. The *capullec*, city district leader, of each district met every day at the *calpixcalli*, assembly area, and received the orders issued by Montezuma's deputies. People held parties with dancing and singing until late at night.

The sacrifices continued, as well. Cortez pretended to ignore them.

He had given orders to Gonzalo de Sandoval to send word to Villa Rica, directing that everything that could be salvaged from the scuttled ships - sails, tackle, mariner's compasses, pitch, chains for anchors – should be transported to Tenochtitlan. When it all arrived, Cortez told Montezuma that he wished to have two sailboats built, for use upon the lake.

Agreeing, Montezuma ordered that oak and cedar trees be cut down and hauled to the lake shore.

There, the Spaniards' master carpenter, Martin Lopez, oversaw teams of Mesheeka craftsmen, instructing them in how to cut and shape the wood, to caulk and tar the planking, to cut the sails, and to set up the mast and rigging. An awning was provided for shade. In a few short weeks, the boats were done, whereupon Cortez invited Montezuma for a cruise on the lake in the "brigantines."

They sailed to a small island in the lake called Tepepolco, Montezuma's private hunting preserve. The emperor was thrilled to glide over the water so quickly that there was a breeze on his face, so much faster than his canoes with oars could travel. Cortez had been teaching him how to use a crossbow, and the emperor was delighted to discover how much game he could kill with it on his island - deer, hares, and rabbits. At the end of the cruise, Pedro de Alvarado ordered the ship's two brass cannons to be fired off as a salute to Montezuma, who thanked him and the Spaniards for "a most wonderful experience."

Cortez was pleased. "Montezuma has had such a pleasant adventure," he told Malinali, "that he will never object to our brigantines exploring the lake and learning as much as possible about it and the towns on its shores. Perhaps he will not notice that we are no longer trapped on this island city, and can escape by boat, should the need arise[155]."

The morning visits to Montezuma continued. Over a game of *totoloque* one morning, Cortez commented that Montezuma looked troubled.

"Malinche, there is something I must tell you," came his response via Malinali. "My nephew, Conacochtzin (*kona-coach-zin*), arrived here last night from Texcoco, asking for refuge. His brother, Cacama, King of Texcoco, is organizing a rebellion against me. He has arranged a meeting with the kings of Coyoacan, Tacuba, Iztapalapa, Toluca, and Matalcingo in order to form a rebel army, march on Tenochtitlan, kill all of you, kill me, and make himself ruler of all the Mesheeka."

"Let us march upon him first!" Cortez instantly responded. Before Malinali translated this, she looked warily at Cortez. "My Captain, how many of your men would march on Texcoco and how many would remain on guard here? Are there enough to do both?"

Cortez hesitated, then answered, "No. I was being impetuous. What do you suggest, my Lady?"

"Lord Montezuma," Malinali asked, "why did Conacochtzin ask you for refuge?"

"Because he is loyal to me, his uncle, the rightful ruler of the Mesheeka," came the emperor's answer.

"Does Cacama know what his brother has done? Could Conacochtzin return to Texcoco unsuspected?"

Montezuma thought for a moment. "I will have to ask him. What are you thinking?"

"There must be a way..." She cut off her own answer. "Lord Montezuma, where is this meeting of the rebel kings to be held - in Texcoco?"

"No," the king replied, "in a secluded wood some ways away, called Tepetzinco."

"How does one get to this place?" she asked. "By a road where there could be an ambush?"

"No, you must go from Texcoco to Tepetzinco by canoe," the king answered.

---

155   In total, four such sailboats were built during this period, each roughly 40 feet long and able to carry four bronze cannons, 75 men, equipment and horses.

Malinali smiled. "By canoe! So if Conacochtzin returned to Texcoco, seemed to join his brother's rebellion, took charge of the arrangements for this canoe, and paid off the people rowing it, the canoe could transport Cacama – not to Tepetzinco, but to Tenochtitlan, where he would be in our hands."

It was Montezuma's turn to smile. "Excellent! I shall give these instructions to Conacochtzin immediately!"

Cortez looked at Malinali with his eyebrows raised, not having understood their conversation in Nahuatl. "I think the problem may be solved," was all she would say.

* * * * *

Later, when Malinali explained the plan to Cortez back at their quarters, he could only respond, "Your father taught you well." And her plan did go well. Once back in Texcoco, Conacochtzin colluded with another brother, Ixtlilxochitl (*ish-tleel-zoh-cheetle*) to arrange the canoe. Cacama boarded the canoe without suspicion, which in turn delivered him to Montezuma and Cortez. Montezuma then ordered the arrest of the other rebel kings, and soon all were in the prison of Axayacatl's Palace, attached to an iron anchor chain left over from the building of the brigantines.

Feeling more secure with the rebellion quelled, Montezuma announced to Cortez that he needed to visit the *Teocalli*, to make the devotions to the gods that was expected of a Mesheeka ruler. Cortez replied that he was welcome to go - but that he must not murder any human beings, for that was a "sin against God." He also informed Montezuma that a guard of the best Spanish officers would be provided for his 'protection.'

Accompanied by a grand assemblage of his nephews and nobles, Montezuma was carried in his litter to the Teocalli. At arms' length from him were Juan Velasquez de Leon, Alonso de Avila, Pedro de Alvarado, and Francisco de Lugo. Surrounding the entire procession were a hundred and fifty Spanish soldiers. Father Bartholomew Olvedo walked up the steep steps of the temple, following Montezuma, who was assisted by the temple priests. But when they reached the top, Father Olvedo discovered that four victims had already been sacrificed. Their hearts were burning in the copal fire, and their corpses were stacked in a pile, waiting to be thrown down the Jade Steps.

Moreover, two young men and a boy not more than 10 years old were being held by the priests in front of the *techcatl*, the blood-encrusted sacrificial stone. The priests handed Montezuma a jewel-handled flint knife, seized the three victims and hurled them onto the *techcatl* with such force that their spines snapped with loud cracks. Montezuma quickly stepped between the victims and plunged the dagger into each of their chests. The priests then inserted their own knives into the victims' open chest cavities to cut out the hearts, held them up in reverence, and placed them in the *chacmool*.

None of the Spaniards, including Father Olmedo, could believe what they had just seen. It had happened so quickly and shockingly that they remained motionless. With the ceremony completed, Montezuma was carried down the Jade Steps and back to the Palace of Axayacatl in his litter, followed by the sullen, wordless Spaniards.

Upon their return, Montezuma was in a cheerful, happy mood, smiling and laughing. He ordered gifts of jewels to be distributed to the Spanish officers and guards.

Cortez and Malinali had stayed in their quarters during this episode. When informed by Andres de Tapia of what had transpired, Cortez said calmly, "Señor de Tapia, I feel like taking a walk. Would you accompany me?"

The two of them and Malinali, joined by ten guards, including Bernal, walked out of the palace and into the huge courtyard facing the Teocalli. Cortez pointed to a building nearby. "Doña Marina, would you tell Señor de Tapia the purpose of that building?"

"It is the children's prison, where children to be sacrificed to Tlaloc are kept," she replied.

He pointed to another building. "And that one?" he asked.

"That is the victim's kitchen, where the priests cook the arms and legs of the victims and prepare them as meals for Montezuma and the nobles."

They reached the foot of the Teocalli. "Señor de Tapia, let us climb these Jade Steps and examine the shrine at their top," Cortez said all too casually.

When they reached the top, they walked into the shrine of Tlaloc. Cortez stood in front of the huge, goggle-eyed stone statue of Tlaloc, caked with blood nearly three inches thick. Around Tlaloc's neck hung the skin of a human head.

The temple priests were in an uproar. "*Silencio!*" Cortez ordered. They fell silent. "Doña Marina, please inform these gentlemen that I wish this shrine to be washed free of blood, and to replace this evil statue with one of the Christ and of the Virgin Mary."

The priests laughed. "If that were done," they replied, "all of Tenochtitlan and the entire Mesheeka kingdom would rise up and destroy you."

Hearing this answer, Cortez took Bernal's spear. "Something must be done for the Lord," he called out, and began defacing Tlaloc, jabbing out its round mother-of-pearl eyes and knocking off its gold mask. Bernal and the other guards prevented the priests from interfering. When he judged the statue to be sufficiently defaced, Cortez calmly turned to his men. "Now, let us pay a visit to Lord Montezuma."

By the time they reached Montezuma's substitute throne room at the Palace of Axayacatl, the emperor had already been told of Cortez's outrage and was livid. Cortez quickly brushed Montezuma's anger aside.

"Lord Montezuma, how many times have I begged you to cease these evil practices and to give up sacrificing human beings to your gods? You assured me that there would be no such sacrifices if you went to worship at your temple. Not only did you permit your priests to perform these evil deeds, but you murdered three victims yourself, one of them a little boy, right in front of my men.

"This will now end. If you do not order the removal of your gods from this and other temples in Tenochtitlan, and allow us to replace them with statues of Christ, the Virgin Mary, and the Christian cross, then I will do it by force. I am asking that you give the order, for I do not want to have to kill any priests who try to stop us."

His anger replaced by alarm, Montezuma called out, "Malinche! How can you wish to destroy our whole city? Our gods would be enraged against us and would not spare our lives - not even yours!"

"You worship devils, not gods, and they bring you bloodshed and slaughter," came Cortez's iron reply. "Their time is at an end. Will you give the order?"

Montezuma's shoulders sagged. "We must take our gods where they will be safe. You must not touch them. No more dishonor must be done to them."

"It shall be as you request," Cortez replied.

The next morning, several hundred black-robed priests gathered at the base of the Teocalli bearing ropes, wooden rollers, and woven maguey mats. Silently ascending the temple, they created a bed of the mats down the steps, removed the statues of Tlaloc and Huitzilopchtli from their pedestals, and carefully lowered them with ropes and rollers down the mat-covered steps. They did this in harmony and silence - none of the priests said a word. At the bottom of the Jade Steps, the statues were placed on litters and carried off to a sacred, secret cave outside the city.

That afternoon, the Spaniards began cleaning the temple, washing away the blood before whitewashing the walls. Cristobal de Olid, overseeing the operation, discovered in an alcove another statue of Huitzilopochtli made of maize and various vegetables held together with human blood. He ordered it destroyed and burned on the spot. He further ordered that the blood-encrused *techcatl* sacrificial stone and the *chacmool* receptacle demolished.

It took several days for the temple to be thoroughly cleaned and prepared. Effigies of Christ and Mary were put in place, and the Spaniards celebrated, with Father Olmedo leading them in singing the ancient Christian hymn of *Te Deum*. They then proceeded up the steps to what was now a Christian church, and celebrated a Mass.

As Cortez and Malinali led the procession, he noted that even the steps had been cleaned, the encrusted blood removed. "These are no longer The Jade Steps, my Lady," he said. "Never again will a human being be butchered here."

The priests, shaven and bathed, had been given clean new white robes. They were instructed by Cortez not to touch the altar, but to keep it swept clean, to burn incense, to keep wax candles burning there, day and night, and to decorate it with branches and flowers.

The people of Tenochtitlan witnessed all of this in quiet shock. The day after the first Mass was held atop the Teocalli, townspeople began placing dried stalks of maize at the base of the temple. Malinali explained that the stalks were an offering and prayer to the new Christian god for rain. It had not rained in a long time, and their crops were withering.

The next morning, the people of Tenochtitlan woke up to a pouring rainstorm. "Of course their prayers were answered," Cortez told Malinali. "Today, after all, is Christmas[156]."

---

156   December 25, 1519.

Chapter Twenty Seven

"I SHALL CUT OFF CORTEZ'S EARS!"

O ver the next several weeks, the Spaniards marveled at how easily the Mesheeka seemed to accept the loss of their gods. Perhaps, they surmised, it was because the Mesheeka had been taught by their priests that, if their old gods were not fed the blood of human hearts, the sun would not rise and the world would collapse into darkness and chaos – and yet, day after day, week after week, despite the fact that there were no sacrifices, the sun kept rising. Therefore, maybe the priests were wrong. Maybe the new gods of the strangers were more powerful than the gods of old. Malinali heard these whispers, and did her best to encourage such thoughts among the Mesheeka.

When Cortez expressed a desire for his men to explore the country, Montezuma had a large map of sisal cloth prepared, on which were drawn the coasts along the East and South Oceans[157], and the rivers than flowed into them. The emperor seemed happy to provide escorts for the exploration parties. Gonzalo de Umbria and two soldiers were sent to the gold mines at Zacatula, on the south coast. Andres de Tapia and Diego Pizarro were sent to the mines of Tuxtapec, southeast of Mesheeka territory. Diego de Ordaz, along with ten soldiers, went to explore the southern part of the east coast, seeking a good location for a new harbor and port.

All were instructed by Cortez to locate sources of gold, to determine where the best land was for raising crops and cattle, and, most of all, to judge the attitude – as best they could, as they would have no translators – of the

---

157   Atlantic (Gulf of Mexico) and Pacific.

peoples and kingdoms they passed through, regarding the Mesheeka.

Within a month, all had returned safely, and reported that they had been treated well by the peoples they met, and had received numerous presents of gold and jewels. The Mixtecs of Zacatula, reported Gonzalo de Umbria, hated the Mesheeka. Diego de Ordaz had been warmly welcomed by a king named Tochel, who proudly took him to a place called Cuylonemiquis (*coo-eel-o-nim-eee-keys*): The Place Where We Killed The Mesheeka. He offered his kingdom's help in any resistance to the Aztecs.

Andres de Tapia and Diego Pizarro brought back two chiefs of the Chinantecs from the region of Huaxyacac (*wash-yah-cock*)[158]. They, too, pledged their loyalty to Cortez, saying that they loathed the Mesheeka so much that they would not mention them by name.

If Montezuma had learned of this, he didn't show it. On the contrary, his mood seemed to get better by the day. A worried Orteguilla came to see Malinali and explained why.

"Doña Marina, I am afraid that Montezuma is plotting something. He has been having meetings in secret with several of his nobles, meetings which I am not allowed to attend. All I have overheard is how important it was that the *Acatl* year was over, and that a new year, *Tecpatl*, has begun. And Montezuma keeps talking about how he must be free of his prison so that he can perform the ceremonies of *Tlacaxipeualiztli* (*tlah-kashee-pay-wal-eesh-tlee*). What does all this mean?"

She explained, "Captain Cortez and his men arrived here in what the Mesheeka call an *Acatl* or Reed year[159], which they look upon as a year of misfortune. That year has gone, and we are now in a *Tecpatl* or Flint year[160], which they see as a year of good fortune.

"The first month of this new year, *Atlcahualo*[161], is ending, and the second month, *Tlacaxipeualiztli*, is about to begin. This month is a very sacred one, during which the hours of day and night become equal[162], and many important ceremonies must be performed. Sacrifices must be made to the god Xipe so that the plants will grow. Montezuma and the highest nobles must impersonate the gods in a sacred dance, wearing a particular costume."

---

158   Which ended up being spelled by the Spaniards as Oaxaca yet pronounced *wha-hock-ah*.
159   See the end of Chapter Seven.
160   The Aztec year began on our February 14. This conversation took place in early March, 1520.
161   'They Leave the Water.'
162   The spring equinox, March 21st.

She paused, sighed, and put her hand gently on the young boy's. "Thank you, Orteguilla, for coming to me and telling me of this. The costume that Montezuma and the nobles wear for the dance is made of human skins, flayed from the bodies of captives. *Tlacaxipeualiztli* means 'The Flaying of Men'."

* * * * *

As he had no intention of being skinned alive, Cortez quickly went to see Montezuma, along with Malinali and several of his captains such as Cristobal de Olid.

The Emperor no longer seemed a broken man. He smiled broadly, and announced, before Cortez had a chance to speak, "Malinche! It pleases me so much that you have come, for I have a proclamation that you must hear. Huitzilopochtli and our other gods have spoken to me, and have commanded me to make war on you for all the insults and evils you have inflicted upon them. I told the gods that I was so fond of you that I could not allow such an attack unless I first gave you a chance to depart from our land and return to your home across the East Ocean. So I must ask you to prepare your departure immediately."

Montezuma said this so gaily, in such a carefree tone – as if he were merely asking Cortez to join him in a game of *totoloque* – that Cortez hesitated before responding. Malinali knew that Cortez had planned a show of anger and intimidation, but saw that he had now decided against it.

Cortez used this moment of hesitation to look into Montezuma's eyes, where he saw a look of amusement. Instantly, Cortez mirrored Montezuma's expression and attitude. He smiled as broadly as Montezuma, and his stiff posture melted into one of relaxation. "Lord Montezuma, we will of course comply with your wishes," he said happily. "We will now begin preparations for our departure from Tenochtitlan. Our difficulty in returning to Spain across the East Ocean, however, is that we have no ships. May I ask, therefore, that you assign carpenters to our shipbuilder, Señor Martin Lopez, as you so kindly did to make the small sailboats on Lake Texcoco? I will then send them with Señor Lopez to the coast to build three ships large enough to carry us back to Spain."

Montezuma appeared overjoyed with this response. "As many carpenters, logs and supplies as you require, they are yours. You will have them tomorrow. I also wish for you, Malinche, to take two loads of gold with you, back to your home, and one load each to all of your men, as my personal gift."

Cortez bowed his head. "Of all the great lords in the world, you, Lord Montezuma, are the most gracious and generous. I assure you that the world will soon know of your magnificence. The ships will be built, we shall sail back across the East Ocean, and it will be my great honor to have you accompany us as our guest, so that you may meet His Majesty King Don Carlos."

Malinali saw Montezuma's look of amused indifference vanish. Before he could say anything, however, Cortez bowed deeply from the waist, stepped backwards a few steps, turned and departed.

Back in his quarters, Cortez instructed Cristobal de Olid to have Martin Lopez organize the shipbuilding at Villa Rica. "He is to have wood cut, timbers made, and the Mesheeka carpenters kept busy - but he is to see that the work proceeds slowly. He is always to appear to be doing something, so that the Mesheeka suspect no delay. In time, God our Lord, in whose business we are engaged, will provide men, help, and a remedy so that we do not lose this good country."

* * * * *

A month passed, and one ship was slowly nearing completion on the Actopan River, near Villa Rica. Malinali was taking her afternoon walk through one of gardens in the Palace of Axayacatl when Geronimo Aguilar found her. With him was Orteguilla.

"Ah, here you are, Doña Marina!" he called out. "Happy Maundy Thursday!" Seeing Malinali's puzzled expression, he elaborated, "Surely you remember that this is the day[163] of our Lord Jesus Christ's Last Supper," he said with a smile. "Tomorrow is Good Friday and Sunday will be Easter. I thought certainly that you would recall this day because it was on Maundy Thursday, one year ago, that you first met me, along with Captain Cortez. Remember? On that day, the Mesheeka chiefs came aboard the *Santa Elena* at San Juan de Ulua and asked for the *Tlatoani*. It was you who understood, and Captain Cortez asked who you were."

---

163   April 5, 1520. Maundy Thursday in 1519 was April 20. See Chapter 7.

"Oh, yes, I do remember, very well!" Malinali exclaimed. "You said that Maundy Thursday was a very auspicious day – and it certainly was for me!"

"It was for all of us, Doña Marina," Aguilar said, with a respectful bow. But when he lifted up his head, his expression had changed. "Unfortunately, this day may not be as fortunate as a year ago…"

It was then that Malinali noticed the worry on Orteguilla's face. "I asked Señor Aguilar to find you, my Lady, for I have more upsetting news about Montezuma," the young page told her. "Montezuma has received a cloth sent to him by his governor Tendile - remember him? - from San Juan de Ulua. On it were painted eighteen Spanish ships, five of them crashed upon the sand. Montezuma quickly sent runners who speak some Spanish to investigate. They found hundreds of Spanish soldiers camped on the dunes at San Juan, and spoke to their leader, a Captain Narvaez. They told him about Captain Cortez, and complained that he had imprisoned their king. Narvaez then declared that he was Cortez's enemy, and stated that he had been sent by His Excellency Don Diego Velasquez to punish Cortez for his disobedience and his crimes against the Mesheeka.

"The messengers ran back to Tenochtitlan and, the very day of their return, Montezuma ordered a huge amount of food, cloth, and gold to be taken by porters to Narvaez and his men. Runners were sent to Narvaez with the message that he was most welcome to come to Tenochtitlan and rescue Montezuma, and that Montezuma wished for Cortez to be killed or captured. Narvaez replied that he would soon be on his way." Orteguilla looked at Malinali with anxious eyes. "I do not believe that Captain Cortez knows of this, my Lady."

"No, he does not," she answered, "but he will now. Come."

When the trio related the story to Cortez, he shook his head. "Panfilo Narvaez. What better man for Don Diego to send against me? They have been friends since their childhood in Spain. Now he is Don Diego's second-in-command. And he looks commanding - very tall, with yellow hair like Pedro de Alvarado and a huge bright red beard. His voice is deep and hoarse, as if it came from a vault. He is a very brutal man who has committed many massacres of the Cuban Indians. He is arrogant and self-important, cunning but not very intelligent, especially when dealing with people. He is indeed my enemy, but the many soldiers he brought with him are not. Perhaps Señor

Narvaez has brought me the great blessing I have prayed for."

Cortez and Malinali went to Montezuma and confronted him with their news.

The Mesheeka emperor showed no embarrassment. He produced the painted cloth and said, "Now there is no need for you to build any ships. You can all return to your homeland together on these ships, with no more excuses. I see now that the people of Spain are not united and do not have the same lord. Still, the ships are here and you must use them."

Cortez feigned surprise. "My Lord Montezuma, as a great ruler yourself, you well know that while you are the Lord of these lands, there are people within them who reject your rule. I have known this Narvaez for many years. He is a *vizcaino*, a bad man who brings misfortune because he steals whatever he can. He has rebelled against his king, His Majesty Don Carlos. How would you regard those who rebelled against you?"

"I would deal with them harshly," came Montezuma's reply.

"Yes, but first, since your Lordship is a wise ruler," confided Cortez, "you would give them a chance to repent. You would reason with them before destroying them. This is what I shall do with Señor Narvaez. I shall go to see him, along with a detachment of my men, and I shall reason with him. Once there is peace between us, we all can leave on the ships, but only then."

Montezuma, trying to cover a smirk with a smile, noticed Malinali. She, in turn, knew just what he was thinking - that the Spaniards would fight against and destroy each other.

"You are a wise leader yourself, Malinche," he said. "Go, and make peace with your countrymen."

* * * * *

Cortez was not about to do anything blindly. He dispatched Andres de Tapia to confer with Gonzalo de Sandoval at Villa Rica, and sent Father Bartholomew Olmedo as his emissary to Narvaez at San Juan. Walking by day and carried in a hammock by Tlaxcalan runners by night, Tapia was at Villa Rica in three days. There he found that Sandoval had matters well in hand.

Narvaez had sent a notary, Alfonso de Vergara, a priest, Father Antonio Ruiz de Guevara, and a soldier, Antonio de Amaya, to Villa Rica to demand the surrender of the city. Guevara called Sandoval and his men 'traitors,' and threatened them all with dire punishment.

In response, Sandoval promptly arrested them, placed them in wooden cages built to be carried, and had them taken to Tenochtitlan on the backs of Totonac porters. They arrived in the Mesheeka capital on the day that Tapia arrived in Villa Rica.

Cortez promptly apologized for their treatment, lodged and fed them like royalty, filled their pockets full of gold, and pumped from them all they knew of Narvaez's command - how many men, the names of the officers, a description of the existing dissention between the commanders, a list of the supplies and armaments they possessed, and much more. In this way, he learned that Narvaez's forces were over three times the size of his own, with close to one hundred horsemen with their horses, eighty musket-men, a hundred and twenty crossbowmen, and over eight hundred infantrymen, plus artillery.

It was disclosed that Narvaez was not popular among his officers, and that presents of gold might be usefully distributed among them. After three days of such discussion, Guevara, Vergara, and Amaya were carried royally by hammock back to San Juan, accompanied by Cortez's Cuban servant, Santos, and a horse loaded with as much gold as it could carry.

By the time they arrived, Father Olvedo had been there several days, regaling Narvaez's officers and men with descriptions of the fantastically wealthy Kingdom of the Mesheeka.

Guevara and his two companions described Tenochtitlan as El Dorado, a 'mountain Venice,' the richest and most beautiful city in the world, a 'paradise on earth' that Captain Cortez had at his disposal. Santos distributed the gold, telling the men that Cortez would make them as rich as their dreams. Over a thousand pesos' worth of gold was given to each of Narvaez's key officers, Baltazar Bermudez and Francisco Verdugo, as well as to the artillery chief, Rodrigo Martinez.

Such was Father Olvedo's report to Cortez upon his return to Tenochtitlan. And Narvaez himself? "He has declared himself Captain General and Founder of the Colony of San Salvador, the town he is constructing at San Juan de Ulua. All the descriptions of Tenochtitlan and of your success here served only to infuriate him. His last words to me before I left were: 'This land now belongs to me and to Don Diego Velasquez. Tell that traitor Cortez to come and fight. If he comes, I shall cut off Cortez's ears'."

That night, as they lay in bed, Malinali caressed Cortez's ears. "You will make sure you keep them, won't you?" she teased.

He had earlier ordered arrangements to be made for a march upon San Juan de Ulua. "Of course," he whispered, "for you will be with me to ensure that I do."

She was surprised. "I am not to stay here?"

Cortez shook his head. "I am leaving Pedro de Alvarado here, in command of a hundred and twenty men. The rest of my forces I must take to confront Narvaez. This is a tiny number to keep Montezuma a prisoner and maintain our position here, yet it is a chance I must take, for the opportunity of adding Narvaez's men to mine, once I defeat him, is a gift from God. I will not, however, take any chances with your well-being. You will be safer with me than here."

Malinali kissed Cortez in gratitude, then in passion, and they spoke no more.

* * * * *

It was early May by the time Cortez was ready to depart. He had given Pedro de Alvarado strict instructions not to provoke the Mesheeka, and to respect Montezuma.

Mischievously, Malinali could not prevent herself from translating Montezuma's words as she wished, when he bade Cortez goodbye. "Malinche! I, the Great Lord Montezuma, King of all Aztecs, am pretending to show great sadness at your departure. It is with my blessing that you depart in the hope that the *vizcainos* you go to fight will kill you, but not before cutting off your ears. Please allow me to offer a hundred thousand of my best warriors to accompany you, so that they may kill whomever among you and the *vizcainos* may be left after you and they have finished killing each other."

Malinali saw that Cortez's officers had bowed their heads down, and that several were experiencing sudden coughing fits, all in an effort to suppress their laughter. Cortez, familiar with her sense of humor, merely bowed, stepped forward, and embraced Montezuma.

"My brother, Lord Montezuma, I thank you for your most generous offer, but all the assistance we require is the help of God. I only ask that you ensure the care of the picture of the Holy Virgin Mary in the Great Temple, and see that she continues to be surrounded by flowers and lit wax candles."

Setting out for the coast with a force of three hundred and fifty men, Cortez traveled fast and light, leaving behind both his cannons and his musket-men. The heavy weapons of the latter would slow them down.

A Totonac runner arrived *en route* with a message from Tlacochcacatl, the Fat Cacique of Cempoala, saying that Narvaez had moved his forces into Cempoala and taken over his city. "Please come and rescue us, Malinche!" was the message.

Within ten days, Cortez and his men were encamped at Tanpaniguita, some eight leagues[164] from Cempoala. His first actions were to send spies into Cempoala, and to distribute pocketfuls of gold among his soldiers, who well knew how much gold had been spread among Narvaez's forces.

A few days later, they were joined by Gonzalo de Sandoval, Andres de Tapia, and fifty soldiers from Villa Rica. Beaming with satisfaction, Sandoval brought with him some two dozen defectors from Narvaez, led by a Narvaez officer, Pedro de Villalobos. Sandoval had sent some of his men into Cempoala, disguised as Totonacs. Hearing bitter criticism of Narvaez among the soldiers there, they revealed themselves and persuaded Villalobos and others to defect, taking with them a number of horses, as well.

Father Olmedo was again dispatched to negotiate with Narvaez, who angrily and insultingly dismissed his efforts. Geronimo Salvatierra, Narvaez's quartermaster, announced that, once Cortez's ears had been cut off, he would eat them.

Cortez continued his espionage and bribery campaign. He moved his camp to a spot less than two leagues from Cempoala. Totonacs sent by the Fat Cacique brought food, to make sure the Spaniards were well fed.

On the afternoon of May 28, Cortez assembled and addressed his men. "My fellow Spaniards, loyal to our good King Don Carlos, you all know of how I was sent here by the authority of the King's governor of Cuba, Don Diego Velasquez. And you all know that, once Don Diego learned of the great riches of this land of New Spain, he decided to take them for himself. Now he has sent a large force, under Panfilo Narvaez, to seize from us all that we have

---

164 Twenty-four miles.

achieved with so much suffering and hardship.

"This force is much larger than ours. They have artillery and musket-men, which we do not. They have many more horsemen, crossbowmen, and infantry. But we have faced far greater odds in this land and have prevailed. Our skill and discipline in battle are superior to theirs. Moreover, they have no loyalty to their captain, Narvaez. Many of them stand ready to take our side. That is why, on this night, we shall win a great victory, with as small a loss of life to ourselves and our fellow countrymen who oppose us as possible.

"Tomorrow, we shall celebrate this victory of which I am confident, for tonight our lives and honor are in your hands, and in those of God."

The men erupted in cheers, picking Cortez up and carrying him around on their shoulders while shouting *"Viva Cortez!"*

Soon thereafter, it began to rain. Cortez divided his men into five groups. Diego Pizarro would lead sixty men to seize Narvaez's artillery. Three groups were assigned to target specific officers and their commands: Velasquez de Leon and sixty men for Don Diego's nephew, Diego Velasquez; Diego de Ordaz with a hundred men for Salvatierra; and Gonzalo de Sandoval with eighty men for Narvaez himself. Cortez and the remaining fifty would hold themselves in reserve, ready to go wherever they were most needed. Once all of this had been explained, Cortez told everyone to get some rest.

But finding repose proved hard to do, in the pouring rain. Cortez had planned to attack prior to dawn, but soon decided that, as his men weren't getting any decent rest anyway, he might as well launch his attack in the middle of the night, when it would be least expected. So decided, he roused the camp, and the men set off just after midnight.

As the force was about to split off into their five groups, a Totonac messenger arrived with a message from the Fat Cacique: Narvaez and his bodyguard were in the shrine at the top of Cempoala's main temple. Salvatierra, along with a number of officers and crossbowmen, was established on a platform of that temple. Some two dozen musket-men were in the enclosure at the temple entrance.

Cortez once again wished his men well, and reminded them to be careful about killing any of their fellow Spaniards. "Try to capture them, if possible. Give them a chance to surrender, for many quickly will."

As the force continued on their way, they came upon two Narvaez sentries, Gonzalo Carrasco and Alonso Hurtado. Hurtado ran away, while Cortez grabbed Carrasco, fastening his fingers around the sentry's throat. Carrasco, choking, revealed that Narvaez's artillery and cavalry were outside of the town, while Narvaez and the officers and men were presently asleep around the temple.

Sandoval's group left immediately. The rest of the force proceeded to the edge of the city, where their horses were left in the care of Cortez's page, Juan de Ortega. Malinali stayed there, as well, with a small guard to protect her. Father Olmedo conducted a short mass and read a general confession as the men knelt down and prayed.

By this time, the sentry Hurtado had run back to the city and up the steps of the temple, to awaken Narvaez. As Narvaez and his guard groggily grabbed their clothes and arms, they heard a shout: *"Viva el Rey, Spiritu Santo!*[165]*"* Gonzalo de Sandoval, Andres de Tapia, and their men had silently snuck up the pyramid steps.

Reaching the small, square top of the pyramid, they attacked Narvaez and his guard, who numbered about thirty. Still not fully dressed, Narvaez began swinging his huge *montante* two handed-sword, but did so wildly, as he could not see in the dark. Blind confusion prevailed among his men.

Amid the fighting, shouts and the clash of steel were heard from below. De Leon and de Ordaz's men had arrived, attacking young Diego Velasquez and Salvatierra's commands around the temple and on the temple steps. Then one enormous bellow caused a pause in the fight on the top of the pyramid. "Holy Mary, I am killed!" cried Panfilo Narvaez. "My eye! They have destroyed my eye!" A Sandoval pikeman, Pedro Gutierrez, had plunged his pike into Narvaez's right eye.

Although blinded, Narvaez ignored Sandoval's demand that he surrender. In response, Martin Lopez, as good a soldier as he was a shipbuilder, set fire to the shrine's thatch roof. Trapped by the flames, Narvaez and his men capitulated. Tapia and Sandoval walked Narvaez down the steps, to where Cortez awaited them.

Blood was pouring from Narvaez's eye and flowing over his nightshirt. Standing in front of Cortez, he demanded a doctor.

"*Traidora y revolvedor*, traitor and troublemaker, you have received better

---

165   Long Live the King (Don Carlos) and the Holy Lord.

than you deserved," responded Cortez, then took a moment to calm himself. "Nonetheless, you shall be well treated. Who is your doctor, sir?"

Narvaez answered that his name was Maese Juan.

Cortez turned to Sandoval. "Gonzalo, this man is your prisoner. Locate the doctor, Maese Juan, and bring him here to treat him."

The battle was not yet over. Narvaez's artillerymen were attempting to fire their cannons, but the well-bribed Rodrigo Martinez had stuffed wax in the firing holes. As a result, Diego Pizarro and his men were soon able to seize control. Cortez had also arranged for his Totonac friends to creep in and cut the cinches of the cavalrymen's saddles. When the cavalrymen mounted their horses, they soon found themselves on the ground. Finally, with shouts of "Viva Cortez and his victory!" resounding throughout Cempoala's center, only one group of Narvaez men remained unconquered, barricading themselves in a small temple.

When Cortez had Diego Pizarro fire a few cannonballs at the temple, the resistance soon ended.

As dawn broke, Cortez assembled his forces in the central plaza, together with all of the captured Narvaez men. There were many more of the second than the first. Cortez himself sat in a chair, wearing a long orange robe over his armor – a gift, he said, from Emperor Montezuma. He directed that another chair be brought so that Tlacochcacatl, the Fat Cicque, could sit beside him. Malinali stood between them, to translate for the Totonac king.

"We are all Spaniards here," began Cortez, "all loyal to our King, His Majesty Don Carlos. The victory won here by my men is not a victory over fellow loyal Spaniards, but over the disloyal delusions of their former commanders. Those men, Señors Narvaez, Salvatierra, and others, are now in irons, where they belong.

"Those of you who suffered under their delusions now have a choice. You may return to Cuba – not in irons like your commanders, but where a disloyal and untrustworthy governor may yet place you in irons, in his outrage at what has transpired. Or you may join us in our return to the great Mesheeka city of which you have now heard, and share in the uncountable riches of this land of New Spain. To do so, you must acknowledge me as your Captain-General and as the *Justicia Mayor* of New Spain. Let us all join together as brothers, and put aside this recent past. Do you agree?"

As one, all of the assembled men cheered wildly in agreement.

Cortez stood and invited the men of both groups to mingle with each other. Then he went among them, himself, clasping hands, dispensing compliments, telling jokes to make them laugh, and entertaining them with tales of the Mesheeka paradise high in the mountains. Then he went to see Narvaez.

"After seeing Panfilo, I must meet privately with my officers, to congratulate them," he said to Malinali walking beside him. "Next to God, it is to them that we owe this victory."

"Not to you, my Captain?" asked Malinali.

Cortez glanced at her with a small smile, and said nothing.

Although Narvaez was in irons, his wound had been cleaned and bandaged well, he had bathed and been given fresh clothes, and his cell was clean, with a comfortable bed. "Your men have sworn allegiance to me," Cortez informed him. "You will remain here until I deem it appropriate to return you to Cuba. That may be a while."

Narvaez's one good eye regarded Cortez with hate and anger. "Captain Cortez," he said in his bellowing voice, "you must consider it a great thing to have beaten me and made me a prisoner."

"On the contrary, Panfilo," replied Cortez coldly, "compared to the other things that I have accomplished here, it is one of the least things I have done in New Spain."

Malinali could not resist. Looking at Narvaez, she reached up and touched the side of Cortez's head. "Don't you think, Señor Narvaez," she asked sweetly, "that Captain Cortez has the nicest ears?"

Chapter Twenty Eight

THE FATE OF MONTEZUMA

ortez moved swiftly to commandeer the ships and supplies of Narvaez's fleet. Under the command of Francisco de Lugo, the ships were
brought to Villa Rica, where everything of use was brought ashore,
and great quantities of wine, bacon, flour, cassava bread and other perishables
were carefully stored.

He also moved quickly to merge the men and commands of Narvaez's
men with his own. He detached Juan Velasquez de Leon and a hundred and
twenty men, one hundred of whom were Narvaez men, to explore the coast
to the north of Villa Rica and establish a colony near the Panuco River. He
directed Diego de Ordaz to lead the same sort of contingent south to establish
a colony near the Coatzacoalco River.

He placed Rodrigo Rangel in charge of Villa Rica, made sure that Narvaez and Salvatierra were securely imprisoned there, and ordered Gonzalo de
Sandoval to make all necessary preparations for the remainder of the command to return to Tenochtitlan.

Everything changed, however, when Malinali brought one of Narvaez's
officers, Botello Puerto de Plata, to Cortez. "Señor de Plata has disturbing
news, my Captain," she told him.

Cortez had been hearing about him. A *hidalgo* from Santander on the
north coast of Castille, de Plata had become a Latin scholar while studying
in Rome; he also had a reputation for being a *prestidigitador*, a magician who
could predict the future.

"Señor Cortez, I must warn you to leave here immediately," de Plata announced. "The officer you left in command at Tenochtitlan, Pedro de Alvarado, and all of your men there are in grave danger. The Aztecs are making war upon them, using ladders to attempt to climb into their quarters. They wish to kill them all. You must return there quickly."

Cortez showed no emotion at this, simply thanking him for the information. When de Plata left, Cortez asked Malinali, "Why should I believe this fortune-teller, my Lady?"

"Because just such a rumor is being talked about among the Tlaxcalans," she replied. "Somehow, de Plata heard of it and insisted that he tell you."

"Talk to your Tlaxcalan friends more," Cortez responded. "Find out whether they know this to be true."

Later that afternoon, when four Mesheeka nobles arrived on litters, borne from Tenochtitlan, Malinali hurried from the Tlaxcalan camp to Cortez's quarters. She entered with a quick nod of her head which Cortez knew meant that the rumor was confirmed.

Crying profusely, the nobles cried out, "Malinche! Malinche! Tonatio[166] attacked us during our festival of Toxcatl. Many have been killed. Blood has run like water on our streets. The Great Montezuma requests that you come to Tenochtitlan immediately to end this calamity."

Malinali saw a sad smile briefly flash across Cortez's face. She knew he was asking himself, *Why this, and why now?* At the very moment when he had triumphed over both his Spanish and his Aztec enemies, this new disaster had come. Then she saw the sad smile and the thoughts behind it vanish.

Cortez ordered that the nobles be housed appropriately and handled with every courtesy. Messengers were sent to Ordaz and Velazquez de Leon, telling them to abandon their coastal explorations and march immediately to Tlaxcala, where he would meet them. He instructed Sandoval to prepare everyone to depart Cempoala on the following morning.

It was a forced march all the way to Tlaxcala. The soldiers were encouraged, however, by the warm and friendly reception they received in Jalapa and in every other town along the way. The commands of Ordaz and Velazquez joined them before reaching the Tlaxcalan capital, whereupon Cortez formed up his entire force for an impressive entrance parade.

The Spaniards totaled over one thousand three hundred men-at-arms,

166   Alvarado.

eighty crossbowmen, at least eighty musketmen, and nearly a hundred horses. They were welcomed by thousands of Tlaxcalans, who showered them with flower petals. King Xicotencatl wept as he embraced Cortez. He grasped Malinali's hands and called out, "*Madrina!*[167]" Then Chief Maxixcatzin explained the seriousness of Alvarado's situation.

"*Tonatio* is in true danger, Malinche. Seven of your men have been killed, and the Aztecs set fire to your quarters. The attacks were very fierce but stopped once Montezuma learned that you had defeated your enemies in Cempoala. Now your men are starving, as the Aztecs will not allow food to be delivered to them. Our warriors there tried to fight, but there were so many Aztecs that they were lucky to escape. They were under King Xicotencatl's orders to bring our daughters, the Princesses Otila and Teculehuatzin, here to safety."

Once Malinali related this to Cortez, she asked him, "Shall we send for Señor de Leon?"

Cortez agreed.

By the time de Leon arrived, his wife was waiting for him. "Otila!" he cried out. "Our Savior has answered my prayers!" But their embrace was brief, as they were quick to leave.

King Xicotencatl again took Malinali's hand. "If only my Teculehuatzin were now as happy. Please tell Malinche," he implored her, "to bring back her husband, her *Tonatio*. I have ordered two thousand of my warriors to go with you."

Nevertheless, after the rigors of the forced marches and the rumors of troubles in Tenochtitlan among the men, especially those of Narvaez, Cortez decided to first let everyone enjoy Tlaxcalan food and hospitality – and the pleasures of Tlaxcalan ladies – for three days, before departing.

The next day, Malinali brought a Tlaxcalan message to Cortez: the brigantines built by Martin Lopez to sail on the lake and provide an escape had been destroyed by the Aztecs.

In light of that news, Cortez decided on the northern route around Lake Texcoco, avoiding the southern route via Cholua. "We need to see this territory, and to enter across the shortest causeway, that of Tacuba across from the city of Tlacopan on the other side of the lake," he explained to Malinali.

---

167   Godmother.

"Should it be necessary to fight, we must know the quickest way out, now that the ships have been burned."

When they finally reached Tlacopan, the chiefs of the city begged Cortez to stay there. "Malinche - you are our only hope! We ask you to stay here, where you will be safe. Send for Montezuma to meet you here and to bring Tonatio and your men with him. If you go into the city, we fear that you may never come back, and all hope of our being free of the Aztecs will be lost."

Cortez had Malinali thank them profusely and tell them how much he appreciated their wise advice - but explain to them, as well, that he could not trust Montezuma, and that it was his duty to rescue his men.

Cortez's soldiers kept up the spirits of the Narvaez men during the march to the Aztec capital by regaling them with stories of Aztec riches and predictions about how warmly they would be received…but what actually greeted them, as they crossed the Tacuba causeway and entered Tenochtitlan, was eerie silence.

It was the day dedicated to St. John the Baptist[168]. The horses hooves echoed in the streets, canons were fired, and gunshots rang out as the Spaniards tried to make their return one of celebratory victory. But the streets were empty, and the Aztec townspeople shuttered and hidden. Only when the cavalcade reached the Palace of Axayacatl did the celebration become genuine, as Alvarado and the besieged men greeted them in exultant relief.

A messenger arrived, saying that Lord Montezuma was anxious to see Malinche. Cortez had Malinali reply that he would be unable to see the Aztec King until the food blockade was lifted and his men were sufficiently fed.

Within an hour, a supply of turkeys and tortillas began arriving. Still, Cortez delayed, not wishing to see Montezuma until he had first talked with Alvarado.

He had already learned much about the Aztec festival of *Toxcatl* from Malinali: "Toxcatl is the month of Dryness[169] and is dedicated to the god Tezcatlipoca. It is celebrated with a sacrifice of an *ixiptla* to him - a young man chosen for his good looks and good manners a year before. For that entire year, he is treated like the god himself and is given four women, who represent the goddesses of food, drink, sexual love, and salt. For the Aztecs, these are the four basic physical pleasures of life.

---

168   June 24, 1520.
169   It corresponds to May 4th-23rd.

"The day of the sacrifice is one of sacred dances. The Aztec noblemen dress in their finest feathers and ornaments, then dance in long, curving lines in front of the *Teocalli*. Then the *ixiptla* proceeds up the steps of the temple to the priests, where his heart is offered to Tezcatlipoca."

Malinali had also told Cortez a dark tale that he hoped was only a Tlaxcalan rumor, spread in their desire for revenge against the hated Aztecs. The bloody story claimed that, as the Aztec nobles were dancing in their feathers and jewelry, with one long line of them forming circles like a coiled snake around the huge, pounding drums in the Temple Courtyard, Alvarado and his men, in their armor, had attacked without warning. The Tlaxcalan claimed that hundreds of nobles had been cut down by Spanish steel swords in a massacre that, in turn, ignited the Aztec insurrection. Cortez was determined to hear Alvarado refute the tale before he confronted Montezuma.

When Alvarado finally entered, Malinali was startled to see a changed man. Previously, it had not been solely for his long golden hair and beard that he was called *Tonatio* - his personality had shone like the sun, as well: his smile, his charm, his confidence, his carriage. Now it seemed that a cloud pressed down upon him. He was in the shade of it, although he was pretending otherwise.

Cortez sat silently, waiting for Alvarado to speak.

"My Captain, it is my great regret that this insurrection took place, but perhaps it was to be expected since, as a result of your departure to fight Narvaez, our garrison here was so very small. We learned that Narvaez had sent a message to Montezuma, claiming that you would soon be destroyed, and encouraging him to destroy us, also. At Montezuma's court, the page Orteguilla also overheard that we would be attacked just after the end of a festival, in the Great Temple courtyard. We heard that great quantities of arms had been secretly stored nearby for that purpose.

"The day before the festival, the kitchens near the temple were very busy. This is where the arms and legs of the *sacrificios* are cooked. There were many huge pots and much water for boiling, as if they were preparing for many bodies, many *sacrificios*. We were told that they were for us - that after the one sacrifice made for the festival, we would be killed and our bodies cooked with garlic and chiles, to be eaten by the Aztec nobles.

"It is true that I gave my permission for this festival - but only with Montezuma's promise that there would be no sacrifices. Now we saw that they had no intention of keeping this promise, and that they planned for us to be sacrificed, as well. Our only chance, I decided, was to fall upon the Aztecs and kill their nobles before they could kill us."

"You decided *what?*" cried Cortez, and then slumped in his chair. "So it is true," he said, and stood up, with an angry sigh. "Señor de Alvarado, you have done badly. Your conduct was that of a madman, and has brought a great doom upon us and upon all of our hopes for life in this new land."

He walked out of the room, leaving Alvarado standing alone. Malinali followed him.

* * * * *

They made for Montezuma's quarters in the Palace of Axayacatl. Entering, she saw upon the Aztec Emperor's face a look of bewildered helplessness. "Doña Marina," Cortez requested, "please ask Lord Montezuma if there is any way to repair the grave damage that has been done in my absence."

"I can do nothing, Malinche," was all the king could say.

"What you can do is order the market of Tlatelolco opened. We are thankful for the food that was delivered, but we are told that the market is closed so we cannot get any more," Cortez responded.

"I can do nothing," Montezuma repeated. "I am afraid my people would reject my appeal. Perhaps they would hear an appeal by my brother, Cuitlahuac, who is with me here."

Cortez nodded his approval. He turned to Malinali. "Doña Marina, please tell Lord Montezuma that I am in deep regret over what has happened."

On the way back to his quarters, lost in thought, his only comment to Malinali was, "I am afraid I broke him too much."

Calling all his officers together, Cortez announced, "Gentlemen, the time for regrets and recriminations is past. We must ask for the help of our Savior, for with that help we shall yet overcome these difficulties, and triumph. We shall spend the remainder of this day preparing our defenses. Tomorrow, after dawn, I am commanding Señor Diego de Ordaz to lead a strong force to the Tlatelolco market to secure the food we need. Gentlemen, let us pray."

That night, Malinali lay quietly next to Cortez in their bedchamber.

"Fortune favors the brave," he mused to her, "but not always. I did not know the extent of Alvarado's foolishness. His was the spark that has set the Aztecs on fire against us. We are in very great danger, my Lady. We are trapped inside this island city, and we must fight our way out."

Ordaz set out the next morning[170] with over three hundred men, several dozen crossbowmen and musket-men, and a few horses. Cortez's instructions were to act peacefully and request food "without disturbance." The command had not marched a hundred paces when it was attacked by hordes of Aztec warriors coming at them from all direction, with other warriors firing sling-stones and arrows from rooftops.

Eight soldiers were killed immediately. Ordaz desperately tried to retreat, but swarms of the enemy surrounded him. He and his men had to fight, step by slow step, back to their palace. Desperately, they cut through the Aztec masses with their steel swords, firing their muskets and crossbows point blank, until they reached the safety of the palace. Four more men died on the way, and scores were wounded. Ordaz himself was bleeding from three separate wounds.

For the rest of the day, the shouts and war cries of the Aztecs were incessant. A constant rain of arrows and stones was hurled over the walls and into the palace courtyard. The noisy uproar continued throughout the night, as the Spaniards dressed their wounds, put out fires, and repaired breeches in the palace walls and defenses.

Late that night, Cortez called for Martin Lopez. "Señor Lopez," he said, "there is a war machine used in sieges in Europe called a *mantelete*[171]. Are you familiar with it?"

"Yes, my Captain," Lopez replied. "It is a stout wooden box under which a score of men can move, protected, with apertures through which they can fire muskets and crossbows." He paused. "How many do you want built, my Captain?"

"Three or four," Cortez answered. "I want them to protect men hauling the Lombard guns which can destroy the homes and buildings around this palace, since it is from those places that we are being attacked. How much time do you need?"

"You shall have them before the sun sets tomorrow."

---

170 June 25.
171 The Mantle

Malinali had spent the day helping the wounded men. She had had no time to worry. But now, at this late hour, after Lopez and his men left, she looked at Cortez questioningly.

He embraced her, holding her tight. "My Doña Marina," he whispered, "have no concern. God did not bring us to this land to die, but to conquer the evil that curses it. We are being tested now but, through us, His Will shall be done." He loosened his embrace and looked down upon her, deep into her eyes. "I love you, Doña Marina."

They were the words she had dreamed so many times to hear. Her fears were swept away by joy, and the rest of the night was spent in glorious passion.

They arose before dawn, and Cortez assembled his officers. "Gentleman," he proclaimed, "while Señor Lopez is constructing the *manteletes*, I propose we test the enemy's strength. Tell your men that I shall lead whoever wishes to accompany me into the streets, to kill as many of our attackers as possible. It is only through fear of Toledo steel that we will be given safe passage from this city."

Hundreds of men quickly volunteered and, with Cortez at their helm, poured out of the palace gates. The Aztecs attacked in human waves, climbing over stacks of their just-killed compatriots to throw themselves upon the Spaniards, who methodically cut them down. The fighting and killing went on, hour after hour, until mid-day, when Cortez signaled their return to the palace. Due to their armor and discipline, only two Spaniards had been killed, although many were badly wounded. The streets around the palace were covered in Aztec corpses.

Cortez went to see Montezuma, still wearing his blood-smeared his armor. Several bloodily-clad officers were with him. "Doña Marina," he said, "please tell Lord Montezuma that it is not my wish that a thousand or more of his countrymen now lie dead in Tenochtitlan's streets, or that I am covered in their blood. Yet this will happen every day, from now until we are granted safe passage from the city."

Montezuma broke down and cried. "Malinche!" he screeched. "What do you want of me? I have no power to grant your wish! I curse the day that you and your people came to our land. I no longer wish to live because of you."

Shaking his head in silence, Cortez turned and walked away. Proceeding down the corridor to their quarters, Malinali said, "The Tlaxcalans are hearing that the Aztecs have renounced Montezuma and have elected his brother Cuitlahuac as *Huey Tlatonani*. Montezuma is no longer King."

"A king betrayed by his brother? It's a familiar tale in Europe," Cortez commented. "That explains his disintegration. Still, we must give him a chance to speak to his people. Perhaps they retain enough respect for him to obey his command to let us go."

The afternoon had to be devoted to caring for the wounded men and repairing defenses. At dusk, with the first two of Lopez's *manteletes*, a group of canoneers quickly sallied out and blew up a number of houses near the palace with their Lombards. Cortez seemed pleased with the test.

At sunrise the next day[172], as Cortez stood on the palace parapet, preparing another attack on the attackers, he saw on the far side of the square facing the palace a dozen elaborately dressed Aztec nobles, with high feather plumes, each man covered in gold and silver armbands and chestplates. One of them was being protected by shields of gold plate by the others, who were all paying reverence to him it was if he were... Montezuma.

"Doña Marina," Cortez called out. "That man in gold, directing and being bowed to by the others - is he Cuitlahuac?"

It was some distance away, but she was able to answer yes.

"So it is true," said Cortez. "They have a new king." Leaving the parapet, he said to Malinali, "The time for Montezuma to speak to his people is now. Who among our men would Montezuma most listen to, right now? Not me. Who most has his confidence?"

She thought for a moment. "You also mean respect, for although Orteguilla has his confidence, he is a boy."

Cortez nodded.

"Among all of the others, I think Cristobal de Olid and Father Bartholomew de Olmedo. They have a real affection for Montezuma, and he knows it and trusts them."

Cortez nodded again. "Go to them and have them convince Montezuma that he must speak to his people to end this bloodshed. We wish to leave in peace. Meanwhile, I must prepare for fighting should it be necessary and Montezuma fails." He turned, then stopped. "One thing more. They are to

---

172   June 27.

make sure that Montezuma is well-protected."

Malinali found Olid and Olmedo, explained matters to them, and accompanied them to see Montezuma. "This is your chance to reassert your authority, to regain your throne, and to end this bloodshed," all three of them implored him. Malinali took his hand. "Lord Montezuma," she said looking into his eyes, "it is time for you to be *Huey Tlatoani*, the leader and ruler of your people, once again."

Tears welled in his eyes, and he agreed.

Arrayed in his finest feather headdresses and feather robes, Montezuma was escorted to the roof of the Palace of Axayacatl by Olid, Bernal del Castillo, and two other soldiers, Leonel de Cervantes and Francisco Aguilar, all holding up their shields to protect him.

As soon as the Aztecs saw Montezuma on the rooftop, all of those waiting to attack ceased their shouting. They became quiet, and a huge crowd quickly assembled in the square below.

"My people," Montezuma called out, "you all know how much I love you, and how much I grieve at the many deaths you have suffered. There is no cause for this war, for the Spaniards have promised to leave our city, to leave our land forever, and to let us live in peace. I am now commanding you to put down your weapons and end this war, to let the Spaniards go, so that we may be rid of them, and so no more of you need die."

There was an unmoving silence from the crowd below. Then four nobles came forward, and one of them addressed Montezuma. "O Great Lord Montezuma," he called up to him, "we weep for your misfortune and the disaster that has fallen upon you. But we must tell you that we have chosen your brother, Cuitlahuac, to be our King.

"The Great Lord Cuitlahuac has commanded us to continue this war until every one of the foreigners is dead. He has told us that the gods Texcatlipoca and Huizilipochtli hunger for the hearts of the foreigners, which we must feed to them. So we beg for your forgiveness, O Lord Montezuma, but we must refuse your command and obey the Great Lord Cuitlahuac instead."

During this reply, which the Spaniards did not understand, the men guarding Montezuma rested their shields, as the crowd seemed so quiet and peaceful. However, the instant that the noble below finished his speech, the crowd erupted with a sudden shower of thrown and slung stones that rained upon the rooftop.

The Spaniards protecting Montezuma could not raise their shields in time. Three large stones crashed against Montezuma's head and body.

He was quickly carried below, where Father Olmedo and his attendants cleaned and bandaged his wounds. Regaining consciousness, Montezuma saw around him a crowd of anxious Spaniards, including Cortez. Malinali was holding his hand. He shook his head weakly and said to her, "I have nothing to live for. My own people have killed me."

Father Olmedo held up a crucifix to him. "Will the Lord Montezuma redeem himself in the eyes of Jesus Christ and ask for his Christian salvation?" He looked beseechingly at Malinali. "Doña Marina, I beg you, please help me to save his soul."

Montezuma understood what was being asked. "I have but a moment to live," he told her, "and I will not, at my end, desert my gods."

He shuddered and sighed. And with that, Montezuma, the Emperor of the Aztecs, was dead.

Chapter Twenty Nine

THE NIGHT OF TEARS

alinali looked at each of the men standing silently around her. Several of them were weeping. She caught Bernal's eye. "We mourn for him, Doña Marina," he said quietly to her, "and not just those of us who were unable to protect him from his own people today. All of us are in sorrow, for he showed much kindness to us."

That she would be holding the hand of an Aztec Emperor as he died, that the Aztecs themselves would murder their King, that these mysterious men from another world who had come to conquer his kingdom would weep openly over his death – she found all of these thoughts overwhelming. She crossed herself and prayed silently to the Virgin Mary for comfort and understanding.

It was Cortez who broke the silence. "Doña Marina, please select a noble from Montezuma's entourage and have him deliver a message to the people of this city: He is to tell them that their Lord is dead at their hands, that they have killed their king. They must now give him the funeral and burial rites he deserves and, after that, they must allow us to leave the city in peace.

"They must know that our hearts are broken over what they have done. It was only our respect for Montezuma that prevented us from destroying this city, and now that his own people have killed him, that is what we will do if they refuse to let us depart."

In a short while, six nobles, all members of Montezuma's family including his son Chimalpopoca, carried his body on their shoulders out of the Palace of Axayacatl and into the great square. Malinali went with them, accompanied by only a single Spaniard soldier, Bernal. The four chiefs who had addressed Montezuma as he stood on the roof stepped forward to take the body.

Malinali had one of the nobles with her deliver Cortez's message to them. Then the noble added his own message. "This was your doing," he told the chiefs. "Yours and that impostor, Cuitlahuac. We saw with our own eyes how the Great Montezuma died of the wounds from your stones. His death is your great shame, the great shame of the impostor Cuitlahuac. We, his closest family, demand that you renounce him and your choice of him as *Huey Tlatoani*. We demand that you choose one from among us as the new Huey Tlatoani, as our law and the will of the gods require. Until you do this, we will not live among you, the killers of our beloved Montezuma."

With that, they all turned and, with Malinali and Bernal, walked back inside the palace.

That night, Malinali and Cortez lay beside each other silently. "Cuitlahuac will not accept your shame," she said finally. "He will use Montezuma's death against you, and accuse you of it. The Mesheeka will never accept the truth – that they killed their own king – and so they will believe him. Now they will make war upon us, more than before. They will not let us leave their city in peace."

Cortez took a deep breath. "All that you say is true, my Lady. I thought my boast that we would destroy their city might make them hesitate or be more cautious about attacking us. But yes, we must fight our way out. The question is how and where? I already know where - by the shortest causeway, to Tacuba. But how? That is what we must find out."

They embraced and fell asleep in each other's arms.

* * * * *

Well before dawn, Cortez arose and called a meeting with his officers. "Gentlemen, we must prepare for our departure. We must clear the way to the Tacuba causeway by destroying all of the homes and structures along it, from which our enemies would otherwise rain stones and arrows upon us. We must kill so many of them that they may relent in their attack.

"We shall use the *manteletes* constructed by Señor Lopez. Our horsemen will lead the assault to break through the enemy's ranks, and will spear as many of them to death as possible. We are being tested, gentlemen. Have no doubt that we shall prevail. God did not bring us to this land to fail. Our faith in Him shall ensure our ultimate success."

As they discussed how this assault was to be conducted, one of Montezuma's entourage entered and spoke to Malinali. She relayed the message to Cortez and the officers. "It is as suspected. The Aztecs are more enraged than ever. They say that we shall pay for the death of their king and our insults to their gods. They vow that none of us will leave this city alive, and that our hearts will be eaten by the gods while they will feast upon our cooked arms and legs."

Soon thereafter, Cortez led the charge out of the gates of Axayacatl Palace with a number of horsemen, followed by several dozen men in three *manteletes*, then a contingent of crossbowmen and musketmen. They made straight for the Tacuba causeway, under a constant shower of stones and arrows from the Mesheeka. Four Lombard guns were dragged by some of the remaining Tlaxcalans to bombard houses and buildings along the way. After managing to destroy and set fire to more than twenty such houses, the Spaniards had to cut their way through masses of attacking Mesheeka on their return to the palace.

Once again, as the Aztec dead piled up, more Mesheeka warriors crawled over their bodies to attack the Spaniards in crazed frenzies of rage. The horses trampled them, the horsemen speared them, the Spaniards shot them down with crossbow bolts and musketballs, and dismembered and gutted them with swords. The way back to the palace was one of blood, entrails and slaughter. Somehow, the Spaniards made it back to the palace, with many men and horses wounded but all still alive.

Cortez was among the wounded. One of the obsidian-toothed wooden swords of the Aztecs had slashed his left hand, and it had to be heavily bandaged. The rest of that day and into the night, everyone tended to their wounds, fending off the incessant attacks upon the palace walls, and repairing their weapons and equipment. Malinali visited as many of the men as she could, making sure that their wounds were cleaned and taken care of, as best she could. Neither she and Cortez got much sleep, that night, and both were up again before dawn.

"Gentlemen," Cortez announced to his officers, "I propose that we depart this city tonight at midnight via the Tacuba causeway. As the Mesheeka have destroyed two of its bridges, we shall require a number of heavy beams and planks to repair them. Carpenter Alonso Yañez will oversee whatever in this palace needs to be dismantled. The hooves of our horses must be muffled with cloth. Our departure must be carefully organized and quiet. Do you agree?"

The men all nodded grimly in assent.

"We must spend this day in preparation. Our silence will likely get us closer to the mainland, but at some point we are sure to be discovered, and then we will have to fight to reach safety. Every man must be prepared to do so."

Gonzalo de Sandoval spoke up. "Captain Cortez, the Narvaez men never cease to complain of their fate, and in the bitterest of terms. They are most bitter towards you, feeling that you led them here on the promise that they would be welcomed by the people of this city in, shall we say, a friendlier manner than that which has transpired."

Sandoval's comment brought both smiles and sneers from the other officers. Cortez managed to suppress both from his face, but not his eyes. "Señor de Sandoval, please inform these men that events do not always turn out to one's liking - as happened when they first came to this land, expecting to steal from us all that we have achieved here. Such complaints will not save their lives from the Mesheeka. Please inform them that their only hope now is to fight like true soldiers of Spain."

Cortez looked around at his officers and gave them a cheerful smile. "And yet, as we prepare, we must also distract. You may have noticed that there is a temple next to our quarters here..."

He cast a glance at Malinali, who interjected, "The temple of Yopico, where the priests store the skins of sacrificial victims."

Cortez continued, "The Mesheeka have turned this temple into a fortress. From the top, they can look down upon us. On its steps, they mass their warriors, who rain down their arrows and stones upon our quarters. I propose to lead a small group of a few dozen men to rid ourselves of this annoyance. None of the senior commanders may accompany me, as they are needed in preparation for tonight. Who else among you wishes to amuse himself with me in this endeavor?"

Two of the lesser officers stepped forward, Pedro de Villalobos and Gonzalez Ponce de Leon. Cortez told them to gather twenty men each. As they turned to leave, he added, "But no Narvaez men. We wouldn't want to interrupt their complaining." Everyone laughed.

* * * * *

There was a small window on the second floor of the Palace of Axayacatl, from which one could see the Temple of Yopico close by. Malinali sat there nervously as she watched Cortez and his band run out of the palace gates and charge the mass of Mesheeka warriors swarming over the steep temple steps.

He had tried to calm her fears before he left. "I cannot let the fear of these Narvaez men infect the rest," he explained. "That is why I asked Gonzalo to raise the subject, to bring this into the open. By showing absolutely no fear of these Aztecs, by doing something audacious and attacking them, it will give all of our men the confidence that we can depart this city with our lives - which we shall, my Lady."

She made no reply, just letting Cortez hold her tightly. Then he was gone. She had never worried about him before, but now she did. *How can he fight without the use of his left hand?* She tried to calm her heart, but it had a racing, pounding mind of its own, as she watched this little group of Spanish soldiers - forty or so men - run straight into what had to be over a thousand armed and angry Aztecs.

She spotted Bernal next to Cortez, and remembered that he had smiled at her before they left, trying to reassure her as well. She saw them start to cut their way up the temple steps in a wedge, their swords slashing and slicing. Aztecs fell down the steps by the dozens, then by the hundreds. Within minutes, the point of the Spanish wedge led by Cortez reached the top platform of the temple. The thatch roofs of the shrines were set on fire, and statues of Aztec gods were pushed over and sent tumbling down the steps to crush Aztecs in their way.

Malinali was surprised to see so many black-robed priests on the temple platform. As they resisted the Spaniards, they found themselves being thrown off the summit. Malinali saw Gonzalez Ponce de Leon grab a number of them and hurl them into space. *They look like black ants,* she thought, *bouncing down the steps to their death.*

With the temple shrines destroyed and most of the priests killed, Cortez signaled for his men to start back down. Vicious hand-to-hand fighting erupted along the entire length of the steps, and she saw several Spaniards overwhelmed and butchered into pieces. Cortez and Bernal were not among them, although every one of the Spaniards had wounds streaming with blood by the time they reached the bottom of the steps,.

Fighting off the still-attacking Aztec horde, and carrying the most severely wounded, Cortez's band finally made it back inside the palace gates. Malinali grasped the cross she always carried with her, thanking the Virgin Mary and her Savior, who had answered her prayers.

* * * * *

Once more, many wounds had to cleaned and bandaged. As she cared for them, Malinali learned that over a dozen Spaniards had been killed on the steps of Yopico. At least, she *hoped* they had been killed; if any had been captured alive, they would soon be watching, paralyzed with their spines snapped, as their beating hearts were torn out of their chests in sacrifice.

How Cortez had survived with only a few bloody yet shallow cuts, she did not know. Bernal told her that, during the fighting on the platform, two Aztec warriors managed to grab Cortez and were just about to throw him to his death, but Bernal was able to slice through the back of the Aztecs' knees with his sword.

As she cleaned a gash on Gonzalez Ponce de Leon's neck, he smiled at her and said, "This was no night to be in bed, Doña Marina."

In wonderment, she realized that the men were now cheerful, even joking about their battle. Cortez had been right again.

For the rest of the day, everyone focused on preparations for their midnight departure. Cortez paid particular attention to the gold and jewels that had been accumulated, including the Treasure of Axayacatl which they had discovered in the secret palace room[173]. Some time before, a soldier named Alonso de Benavides, trained in smelting, had been assigned by Cortez to

---

173   See Chapter 25.

melt most of the Aztec gold down into hundreds of small flat bars.[174]

Now Cortez ordered an aide, Cristobal de Guzman, to have all of the gold bars, all of the silver, all of the gold chains and jewelry, all of the precious jewels and pieces of jade, all of the robes and quetzal feathers, brought together in the great hall of the palace.

First, he portioned off the 'King's Fifth' with Alonso de Avila and Gonzalo Mejia, King Don Carlos' official notaries. With the Tlaxcalans carrying the bars, the King's Gold was placed in over a dozen straw and wooden boxes, and loaded onto two large mares.

Then another horse was loaded with Cortez's portion, and a fourth loaded with that of the officers.

With this done, there still remained a tremendous pile of treasure in the room. Cortez had Malinali tell the Tlaxcalans - of whom there were only about 100 now - that all of the embroidered robes and quetzal feathers were theirs. The Tlaxcalans whooped with loud glee. "The plumes of the quetzal are more valuable to them than gold," explained Malinali.

Cortez then called for every soldier to assemble in the great hall. "Within a few hours," he addressed them, "we shall depart this city. I promise to you that we shall soon return to rid this city of people who murder their own king, to liberate this land of butchers who kill in worship of their evil gods, and to replace this slaughter with the blessings of our Lord Jesus Christ. Upon my honor, this we shall do.

"With His Majesty King Don Carlos' notaries, Señor de Avila and Señor Meija, as witnesses and under their supervision, the Royal Fifth of the treasure we have acquired has been apportioned. The same has been done with the portion due to me and to your officers. Now you see before you what remains. It is worth many tens of thousands of pesos. Take what you will of it. It is far better for you to have it than these Aztec dogs."

The soldiers stood motionless, stunned by Cortez's words and the dazzling, shimmering sight of the enormous treasure before them. Before any of them moved towards it, Cortez added, "But I must warn you not to overload yourselves. He travels safest in the dark night who travels lightest."

---

174   Roughly about a foot long, two inches wide, and a half-inch thick - weighing about 5 pounds of solid gold each. As this would weigh about 72 troy ounces (a troy ounce is about 10% heavier than an avoirdupois ounce), at a 2010 price of $1000 per ounce, each bar would have a present-day value of $72,000.

Malinali noticed that it was the Narvaez men who moved first. They fell upon the hoard, wrapping gold chains around their necks, and stuffing as many of the gold bars inside their cotton armor as they could. Cortez's men were far more cautious.

She saw Bernal pick up a few light *chalchihuite* jade pieces and nothing more. Most of the others took but one or two gold bars, a few jewels, or a light gold breastplate. *Cortez knows his men well*, she thought, *and knows who among them value their lives more than money.*

Shortly after midnight[175], after a Mass was performed for the expedition by Father Olmedo, the gates of the Palace of Axayacatl quietly swung open. Earlier, Malinali had sent out Tlaxcalan spies, who soon came back to confirm that the city was asleep, with no Mesheeka warriors or sentries in sight, perhaps because of the unusual cloudy mist that shrouded the city, accompanied by a cold drizzly rain.

Cortez had carefully planned the order of march. First out were sixty soldiers under the command of Francisco Magariño, carrying a portable bridge made from palace ceiling beams. They quickly carried it to cover the Tepantzinco canal in the Tacuba causeway.

Next to follow was a vanguard of some two hundred men whom Cortez had directed must be "valiant and young," led by Gonzalo de Sandoval, Diego de Ordaz, Francisco Acevedo, and Andres de Tapia. They carried additional planking and beams for the causeway breaks, and were charged with protecting Malinali, Princess Teculehuatzin (Alvarado's wife Doña Luisa), and Fathers Olmedo and Diaz. "You shall be the first to reach safety, my love," Cortez told her. "I shall follow. Have no fear."

After the vanguard came Cortez, leading several hundred soldiers composed of detachments commanded by Cristobal de Olid, Francisco de Morla, and Alonso de Avila. Just behind Cortez rode his aide, Cristobal de Guzman, with the horses carrying the gold. In the center of this group were Montezuma's family members including his son Chimalpopoca, and other Mesheeka nobles.

The rearguard of the rest of the soldiers, several hundred strong, was commanded by Pedro de Alvarado and Velasquez de Leon. At its tail were most of the remaining Tlaxcalans, pulling the wheeled Lombard guns.

---

175   The night of June 29-30. Taking place after midnight, the date of *La Noche Triste*, the Night of Tears, is June 30, 1520.

The expedition of well over a thousand men marching a dozen or so abreast snaked across the deserted great square and through the empty streets to the Tacuba causeway as silently as it could. The muffled tramp of the horses softly echoed into the mist, as did the light footfalls of the men.

The vanguard crossed the Tepantzinco canal with Magariño's bridge, then the Toltec canal, thanks to Sandoval's planking, and reached the safety of the first village on the mainland, Popotla. There was now a hint of the summer's early dawn, and Malinali could barely make out Cortez's mounted figure in the swirling drizzling mist as he and his men began crossing the Toltec gap of the causeway.

All was quiet. She could hear nothing but her heart. Then, in the next moment, she heard shouts - loud voices shouting in Nahuatl. The Spaniards had been spotted. Suddenly, the priests' *atecocoli* conch shell horns began sounding the alarm from the tops of temples, as were the deep, pounding thuds of the priests' huge war drums.

Cortez and the other horsemen immediately spurred their horses forward and called upon his soldiers to run. Reaching the vanguard at Popotla, Cortez placed it under the command of a minor officer, Juan Jaramillo, and told him to guard Doña Marina with his life. He then instructed five horsemen – Sandoval, Olid, Ordaz, Morla, and Avila – to follow him. Together, they raced back to the causeway.

It was a murky chaos. The lake on either side of the causeway was thick with canoes filled with Aztec warriors, who were crashing their crafts into the rocky side of the causeway, then swarming upon it to attack the Spaniards. At least their white cotton armor made them easier to see in the drizzling gloom. The planks Sandoval had put down to bridge the Toltec gap were broken, and Spaniards by the dozen, then the hundreds, were left floundering in the water, trying to cross. Aztecs in canoes, surrounding them, were clubbing them to death.

Cortez and his captains drove their horses into the water and began attacking the canoes. They quickly discovered how to get their horses to overturn them. The chaos was made worse by the noise, the din of shouts, yells, war-cries, and the horrible gurgles of dying men as hundreds of Aztec and Spaniards lost their lives.

The mist was now lifting with the early grey of the morning, and Cortez could see that the battle was raging along the entire length of the causeway. The flash of the Lombards would briefly light up the rear of the battle, but no matter how many Aztecs were blown apart by the canons, still more followed, until at last the big guns fell silent. In those flashes, Cortez had seen how hopeless the struggle of the rearguard had become.

Malinali saw it, as well. A torrent of Aztecs was flooding over the rearguard, who were jumping into the lake to save themselves... but they were drowning, instead. They could not seem to keep themselves above water. *It is the Narvaez men,* she realized, *with all of that heavy gold that they insisted on placing under their armor.*

She saw Cortez place himself and two horsemen on one side of the Toltec canal, and three more on the other side, with the water up to their horses' bellies. Urging the soldiers who were fleeing and fighting on the causeway to ford the gap, they fought to protect them as the men obeyed, cutting down Aztecs who tried to get through.

Malinali could not tear her gaze away from the slaughter, nor could she prevent the tears pouring down her face. The sight transfixed her: all of these men whom she had come to care for, dying right in front of her, screaming, struggling, clubbed, speared, drowned -- and her Cortez trying in desperation to save them, swinging his sword tirelessly, with Aztec after Aztec falling before him... and yet they continued to come, in endless numbers.

Then she spotted Pedro de Alvarado. Alone, chased by a crazed Aztec horde, with all of the men under his command already either escaped or killed, de Alvarado was running for his life down the causeway. She saw Cortez yell to him but, with his horse in the water, that was all he could do.

Alvarado was running towards the Toltec gap, but Malinali could see that he was trapped, for if he jumped in the water, the Aztecs would follow and he would be theirs. He grabbed a long lance from the ground beside one of his slain companions.

Everything suddenly seem to stop.

All of the Aztecs recognized *Tonatio*, the golden Child of the Sun. The battle ceased for this moment as every eye turned to him, seeing that he was about to die. The Aztec horde chasing him stopped. The Aztecs attacking in their canoes stopped. Cortez became silent. All that could be heard was the wretched sound of men dying and drowning.

Alvarado looked back at his pursuers. Then he burst forward towards the canal, jumping into it as far as he could. As he reached the top of his arc, he jammed the lance into the mass of bodies that had piled up in the middle of the gap, and vaulted all the way over to the other side.

Landing, he sprang to his feet and looked back in triumph at his pursuers. The Aztecs began chanting, "*Tonatio! Tonatio!*" And, just like that, the battle was over. The rage and frenzy of the Mesheeka was dispelled, and now they noticed that all around them were wounded Spaniards whom they would rather capture for sacrifice than kill. They focused upon them, enabling Cortez to shepherd the rest of his men to the safety of Popotla.[176]

In the early morning light, Cortez surveyed the disaster. After confirming that Malinali was untouched, he asked about Martin Lopez. Assured that, although he was wounded, he would surely live, Cortez said, "Of all those among us, it is that skillful and clever man who will gain us victory over these rebellious Aztecs."

The reports were calamitous. Only four hundred men and thirty horses were accounted for, which meant that some sixty horses had been killed, and close to eight hundred men were dead or captured. Among the dead were Velazquez de Leon, Francisco de Morla, Francisco "Dandy" Saucedo, Montezuma's son Chimalpopoca, and the rest of the Mesheeka nobles in their protection.

The Lombard canons were lost, The musket-men had lost all their guns and gunpowder. Every man among them was wounded, many horribly. Then came news of the final blow: the horses carrying the gold had also been lost. The great treasure of the Aztecs was gone, sunk into the mud of the lake.

The remains of the expedition assembled underneath a huge ceiba tree in Popotla. "We shall call this terrible night *La Noche Triste*," The Night of Tears, Cortez announced. "We shed these tears for the loss of our beloved countrymen and friends, so many of whom perished this night.

"Yet their deaths shall not be in vain, for we have no fear of the Mesheeka. We know that, in the end, the One True God will enable us to vanquish them and their evil gods. Have faith that this is so. Have faith that our Savior brought us here not to die but to save this land."

---

176   In Mexico City today, the *Calle de Tacuba* road follows the path of the Tacuba Causeway. A portion of it is named *Puente de Alvarado*, Alvarado's Bridge. Along it is a small bridge named *El Salto de Alvarado* commemorating the exact spot of Alvarado's Leap.

Cortez looked out among the shattered remnant of his forces, defeated, wounded, oozing blood and sorrow. "*Vamos, que nada nos falta,*" he said. "Let us go forward, for we lack nothing."

Chapter Thirty

THE GLORY OF OTUMBA

They set off as dawn broke, and stumbled into Tlacopan, where the chiefs of the city met them with fear in their eyes.

"Malinche!" they addressed him. "We warned you to stay here, where you would be safe, and not to go to Tenochtitlan. Now you have been destroyed, and we with you, for the Aztecs will soon follow to kill you and us."

Cortez stood arrow-straight and calmly spoke to Malinali. "Doña Marina, inform these gentlemen that we greatly value their friendship and shall see that they do not suffer for it."

The chiefs remained worried. "You must not stay here, Malinche, for the Aztecs are sure to attack. Not far from here is the temple of Otoncalpulco, with a large courtyard surrounded by a wooden wall. There you will be safer. I will order our people to carry your wounded on litters, and to help in whatever ways we may."

Cortez thanked them profusely, and the chiefs issued their orders.

One of them turned to Malinali. "Malinche must know that we are Tepanecs, not Aztecs. Our kingdom was the first to be enslaved by them[177]. It was our hope that Malinche would be the answer to our prayers to be free of their rule." He looked pleadingly into Malinali's eyes. "Is there any hope left?"

Malinali returned his gaze. "As long as Malinche is alive, there shall always be hope."

Crossing the two small streams of Tepzolac and Acueco, they reached

---

177   1428. See Chapter 19, The Tale of Taclaelel.

Otoncalpulco by noon. There they were met by a chief of great dignity. After speaking with him for a few moments, Malinali announced to Cortez and the men: "We have been welcomed here by the Lord of Teocalhueycan (*tee-oh-kal-way-con*), which is not far. He asks that you should rest, for you are weary and have suffered heartaches. Water, maize, tortillas, eggs, turkeys, and fruit will be provided for us all. Here you may be at peace and restore yourselves."

Everyone collapsed in relief.

Malinali spent the rest of the day tending to the men, cleaning and bandaging their wounds, bringing them water and food. It wasn't until evening that Cortez summoned her to where he had set up his quarters in two rooms of the temple.

"My Lady, I know that my men are grateful to you for all that you have done for them. Now I need for you to do one thing more."

She raised her eyebrows but said nothing.

"That one thing is to answer a question of the utmost importance to us. We cannot stay here for long. Our only hope is to reach the sanctuary of Tlaxcala. But… will the Tlaxcalans welcome us, or fall upon us? In our weakened state, we shall be defenseless against them. Hundreds of them have been killed fighting with us, and there are but a few dozen left. Go among them to gauge their mood, to see whether they remain willing to guide us by the safest paths to Tlaxcala, and to learn how we will be greeted there."

Nodding silently, she slipped away.

After an hour, she returned. "You need not worry," she reported. "The Tlaxcalans burn with desire for revenge upon the Mesheeka. All they talk of is getting you safely to Tlaxcala, from whence you can lead an army of their warriors to sweep Tenochtitlan from the face of the earth."

Cortez said nothing, silently looking at her, and Malinali could see the emotion his eyes were expressing, the look of admiration. This was how she had always dreamed that a man would look at her. Then she saw the look change. The admiration was still there, joined by something more - desire. She took his arm and led him into the adjoining room, where a sleeping mat of straw and blankets had been prepared.

All the next day[178], everyone rested and ate well. That evening, the chief of Teocalhueycan arrived to advise that a force of Aztecs was on the way, and

---

178   July 1, 1520.

that the Spaniards should soon make their way to his town, for it sat on a fortified hill, protected by a barrier of rocks.

They set off in the midnight darkness, moving slowly, with those best capable of fighting in the front and rear, and the wounded in the middle. Although the distance was less than two leagues[179], it was after dawn before everyone was safely within the rocky protection of Teocalhueycan.

After another day of rest, the chief came again. "You must keep moving north to go around Lake Texcoco to reach Tlaxcala," he said. "My brother is the Lord of Tepotzotlan and will provide for you there. Beyond that, the land of the Tepanecs end. May the gods smile upon your journey, Malinche."

From the description, Cortez judged the distance to Tepotzotlan to be about five leagues. He decided to keep his men where they were for one more day, then march them through the entire night to reach the town by dawn.

It proved too much. Many men were too weak, even when helped by the Tepanecs. Many of the horses could not be ridden, due to their injuries, and had to be walked. By daylight, they were still a league away from their destination -- and the Aztec attacks began, a string of small ambushes, with a few Mesheeka throwing rocks and firing arrows. But several hit their mark, and four Spaniards never reached Tepotzotlan.

When the Spaniards did arrive, they found the town deserted. The Tepanecs from Teocalhueycan explained that the inhabitants were afraid of the Mesheeka and so had run into the mountains nearby. Nonetheless, great stores of food had been left behind, and the Spaniards feasted well.

Unfortunately, few of them had yet recovered from their wounds, and hardly any of them had escaped suffering a wound or injury of some kind. Their Tepanec helpers said that they could get them to the next town, Zitlaltepec, which lay at the top of Lake Texcoco, but that then the Spaniards would have to strike out to the east for Tlaxcala by themselves.

Another night march brought them to yet another abandoned town - but this time there was no food. As the group headed east, guided by the Tlaxcalans, men began to die of their wounds. The Spaniards had to forage for food and found only wild cherries, corn stalks, and grass. The harassing Aztec attacks continued, picking off one man at a time.

As they approached a small range of mountains that the Tlaxcalan guides

---

179   Three miles to the league.

said needed to be crossed, there was yet another ambush, one in which the Aztecs shot a number of bolts into the horse of Cristobal Martin de Gamboa. The Spaniards drove them off but the horse died.

"We shall all have meat tonight," declared Cortez pragmatically. He had the horse divided carefully so that all had a portion, cooking it in fires among the mountain rocks. "We shall soon be in the land of meat and bread, among our friends and the beautiful women of Tlaxcala," he told the men as he walked among them to raise their spirits. Not once did he show any concern or worry, nor share even with his officers what Malinali had told him earlier.

All through the day, the harassing Aztecs had shouted constantly at them, and it seemed always to be the same words. When Cortez had asked her what it meant, she replied, "They say, 'You are going to a place where you will perish to a man'."

"Have you asked the Tlaxcalans what this means?" he asked.

She hesitated., then said, "Yes. They say that the only way to Tlaxcala is through a valley on the other side of these mountains, and that the Mesheeka know this and will be waiting there, to destroy us."

"Does this valley have a name?" asked Cortez.

"It is called Otumba." She lowered her eyes. "I did not want to concern you, my Captain."

He lifted her chin and met her gaze. "Nor I you, my Lady. You need have no fear. This valley of Otumba, it shall be our glory."

* * * * *

Malinali walked among the men, who were gathered in small groups around the cooking fires. *How many of them will be alive by tomorrow night? Perhaps none at all,* she reflected, for she had not told Cortez all that she had heard. The Tlaxcalans were also saying that Cuitlahuac had formed the largest Mesheeka army ever known, an ocean of warriors who would be waiting to meet them at Otumba.

What possible chance did these men have? Every one of them is sick and weak and wounded... She had seen them win before when it seemed impossible, but now it seemed ridiculous even to hope. What she understood least of all was how Cortez could remain so calm -- even confident! – when faced with such doom.

"Doña Marina!" a voice called out. It was Bernal. He was with Aguilar, both enjoying their bit of horseflesh. When she sat down next to them and stared into their fire, Bernal observed, "You seem full of worry tonight."

She looked up at him. "You are not?"

He had a sad smile. "Of course we are, all of us. But of what use is that? We know what we may face tomorrow -- yes, Aguilar has been talking to the Tlaxcalans, too -- yet what can we do but fight our best? We must trust that our Father in Heaven has brought us here for good reason, and that He will guide us and Captain Cortez tomorrow."

She could not hold back her tears. Clutching her crucifix, she said, "Thank you, Bernal. I need to have that trust myself." She looked at them both. "If I don't see you again, if this is the last.... Thank you both for being my friend. Your friendship has meant so much to me. I... I..." She could not continue. Before they could respond, she stood and walked away.

She stumbled through the camp wiping away her tears. She felt a firm hand on her arm, steadying her, and heard a voice. "May I be of assistance to you, Doña Marina?" It was Pedro de Alvarado. He bade her sit down.

She looked at him in wonder. "How... how can you face tomorrow so calmly?" she asked at last.

He gave her the dazzling smile for which he was so famous. "Ah, Doña Marina, how can I not be, when I face it with all of my brothers? The five of us are here - wounded, yes, but all in one piece. Our Lord did not have us all survive thus far in vain!"

She looked at all of them - Garcia, Gomez, Gonzalo, Jorge, and of course, Pedro. It was astounding that they had survived even *La Noche Triste* together. They seemed almost... happy.

"You still seem puzzled, Doña Marina," said Pedro. "Shall we tell you a secret?"

She nodded.

"We are professional soldiers, trained to fight with military discipline. These Aztecs, they can fight like maniacs, but they do so without training, without discipline. Yes, we have armor and Toledo steel, but these traits are even more important. And let me explain something else." He walked over to his horse tethered nearby. "No Aztec has ever faced the charge of one of these in battle," he continued. "They have no idea what it is like to face being trampled by a charging war horse. They have only seen them walking along the streets of Tenochtitlan."

"But there will be so many," she said.

"True, but they will not be led by Captain Cortez," he replied. With that, he stepped up to her and whispered in her ear, "He needs you tonight, Doña Marina."

All of her worries and weariness suddenly vanished. All she wanted was to be with Cortez, on this night above all others.

* * * * *

The Spaniards broke camp at dawn and made their way through the mountain pass in the early morning hours. When they reached the other side and gazed upon the valley floor of Otumba, they were stunned and speechless.

As far as their eyes could see, there stood an ocean of men wearing white cotton armor, so that it looked like an angry sea of frothing whitecaps. They carried brightly feathered shields, and many wore fantastically feathered headdresses. All were brandishing obsidian-toothed wooden swords and other weapons, and all had painted their faces and bodies in a wild array of colors.

Cortez asked for a count of his own forces. They were down to three hundred and forty-seven men, twenty-seven horses, and some sixty Tlaxcalans. They had no cannons, muskets, or crossbows, only swords and a few lances. Everyone was suffering from wounds and hunger, some so sick that they could barely stand. Before them, over a hundred thousand Mesheeka warriors had gathered, all wanting their blood.

Cortez had Father Olmedo lead the men in a Mass, then placed him, Padre Juan Diaz, Doña Luisa, and Malinali in the protection of a dozen Tlaxcalans who had sworn to guide them safely to Tlaxcala, should disaster occur. Malinali dropped to her knees and began praying to the Virgin Mary.

Cortez, astride his horse, addressed his men. "Gentlemen! It has been the highest honor of my life to lead you, for you are the most courageous and honorable men I have ever known. But know this! Today shall not be our doom." He pointed to the sea of Aztecs. "It shall be theirs! Today will be a day about which the poets of Spain will compose songs, songs sung for centuries. Have no fear, but know that our God and Savior stand beside us. Gentlemen, today will be our glory." He turned his horse towards the Aztec army and raised his sword. "Santiago - and at them!" he yelled, then spurred his horse and charged.

Three hundred and forty seven men attacked an army of a hundred thousand warriors.

Cortez had given orders for his horsemen to aim their lances directly at the faces of the enemy, not their bodies. The soldiers had been told to thrust through the bodies of their foes with their swords, rather than swinging and striking. The horses were to charge as hard as they could, crashing into the enemy and trampling them, with the soldiers to follow.

They plunged straight into the morass of Aztecs, cutting a wide swath of crushed and bloodily mangled bodies before them. For a moment, it seemed that their foes would panic, but there were far, far too many. Soon, the Spaniards were enveloped, a small island surrounded by the enemy's sea.

And yet... and yet...

Malinali watched as the island remained. It was not washed over by waves of warriors, and it began to move, slowly cutting its way across the plain.

As always with the Aztecs, only the warriors directly at the front of their mass mattered. The ones behind them did no fighting. As the Spaniards cut down an Aztec, another would immediately take his place, yet still they only had to fight one warrior at a time.

Moreover, the Aztecs seemed terrified of the horses, especially the one ridden by Gonzalo de Sandoval. He would plunge forward crushing foes, then quickly wheel his horse around to charge others. He kept darting back and forth, as did the other horsemen, helping to push the island forward.

But this only served to engulf them more deeply within the enemy sea. An hour passed, then another. *They cannot keep this up*, Malinali thought. The island was still there, still moving... but too slowly. Many of the men had fresh wounds. Cortez bore a large gash on his head, with blood streaming down the side of his face. Several men had died, with the Aztecs carrying away their bodies in whooping delight.

As the sun rose high in the sky, Malinali saw that the men were at last getting too tired to fight. The horses were falling back to protect the men, rather than charging and pushing forward. The screams and war cries of the Aztecs became louder, as they sensed that the annihilation of the hated Spaniards was near.

Malinali saw Cortez rise in his stirrups and look over the battlefield. He could only do this for a few seconds before he was forced to fight again. The third time he did this, however, he froze, staring intently at something.

Turning, Malinali saw that, some distance away, on a slight rise in the plain, a group of magnificently dressed nobles had appeared. One in particular wore a robe of gorgeous feathers, with a huge feather headdress into which were woven jewels that sparkled in the sun. Strapped to his back was a staff, on top of which was a spectacular banner of bright yellow feathers that waved above him. He was carried on a litter, held high so that he could see the battle.

Yes! It was the *cihuacoatl*[180] of the Aztec army. It might even be Cuitlahuac, but at this distance she could not be sure. She was certain, however, that this was the commander. The banner was the emblem of his authority. Cortez had spotted him. Did Cortez recognize who he was?

Cortez quickly wheeled his horse around and charged through the melee to five other horsemen. Even this far away, she could see who they were: Gonzalo de Sandoval, Pedro de Alvarado, Cristobol de Olid, Alonso Avila, and the fifth... the fifth, yes, was Juan de Salamanca. Cortez pointed his sword at the Aztec nobles. Then, as one, the six horsemen charged.

They slashed their way through the surprised Mesheeka, crushing and spearing and cutting down all in their way. In mere moments, it seemed, they had reached the nobles. Cortez's horse slammed into the litter, knocking the commander to the ground, and scattering the litter bearers and the other nobles, who were cut down by the remaining horsemen.

As the commander tried to spring to his feet, Cortez drove a lance into his shoulder, pinning him to the ground. Juan de Salamanca jumped off his horse and stabbed the commander to death with his sword. Then, tearing the staff and banner from the dead commander's back, he thrust it into Cortez's hand.

Standing in his stirrups astride his horse, holding the captured banner high above him so that all could see, Cortez shouted a bellow of victory.

All eyes, Spaniard and Aztec, turned to him. By now, the litter bearers

---

180 Commander.

and nobles who had escaped from the killing horsemen were running away, screaming. The Mesheeka warriors with whom they collided started doing the same. The Aztecs gazed in horror at the sight of Cortez, for they knew it meant that their commander was dead, and now they did not know what to do.

The Spaniards gazed in astonished joy, then fell upon the enemy horde with ferocity. Malinali saw lines of panic radiate through the Mesheeka mass. Suddenly, an ocean of bodies began fleeing in every direction, trampling and running over each other.

The Spaniards and the Tlaxcalans followed in vicious pursuit, their energy renewed. Cortez and the other horsemen raced across the battlefield, cutting down as many of the enemy as they could. All that the Aztecs could seem to think to do was to run away, and they were cut down as they ran.

Finally, the slaughter was over. Thousands upon thousands of Aztec bodies lay dead on the plain. Those who had escaped were vanishing in the distance. The Tlaxcalans danced around those of rank and gathered up feathered booty.

Malinali slowly made her way, with the padres and the guard, to where Cortez was assembling his men beside the body of the Aztec commander. Her mind seemed blank, her body numb. Her prayers had been answered, but she still could scarcely believe it.

As she got close to the body, she saw that it wasn't Cuitlahuac. She wondered why he hadn't commanded his own army. Well, no matter. This man had obviously been a noble and commander of the highest rank, and he was dead at Cortez's feet.

She had expected that Cortez would be shouting and exultant, along with all of the men with him. Instead, he waited silently until all the men stood around him in a crowd. He asked for a count of the Spanish and Tlaxcalan dead. After a moment, it was provided by Cristobal de Olid: "Eighteen dead, Captain, plus twenty-four men of Tlaxcala."

Cortez looked out upon the vast battlefield, strewn with so many thousands of Aztec corpses, then looked to his men. "Let us pray to the Lord of Hosts for granting us this victory," he said, and to a man, they all got down on one knee and bowed their heads while Father Olmedo pronounced a prayer in Latin.

When they stood again, Cortez began walking among his men, murmuring a word here and there, seeing that those with fresh wounds were cared for, grasping the shoulders of his officers. Then he came to Malinali. Standing before her, his armor splattered with Aztec blood, his own dried blood caking his beard, he said not a word, just gazed into her eyes while he briefly ran the tips of his fingers down the side of her face. Then he mounted his horse.

"Now let us make our way to Tlaxcala," he announced. "And, as we do so, let each and every one of you reflect on the greatness of your achievement here on this eighth day of July in the year of our Lord, one thousand five hundred twenty."

Leaving behind a small burial detachment and Padre Juan Diaz to hold services over the slain Spaniards, the expedition began marching east, with the sun at their backs, across the plain of Otumba.

Chapter Thirty One

THE SPANISH PHOENIX

B y nightfall, the expedition reached the town of Xaltepec on the far side of the valley. It was deserted, and everyone had to forage for food. Malinali tried to clean the bloody gashes on Cortez's head and the deep wound in his left hand, but Cortez shook his head. "To a man, all of us are wounded, exhausted, and hungry," he told her. "Organize help for them, tend to them... then you may have all night to tend to me."

When Malinali returned, she found Cortez fast asleep. At dawn the next morning, she tried again to clean and bandage him as best she could, but he was anxious to get underway. "Our only hope of safety lies in those mountains of Tlaxcala," he said, as he gazed at them looming above Xaltepec. Slowly, slowly, the expedition trudged up into the mountains to the Tlaxcalan frontier fortress town of Hueyotlipan.

There to greet them were King Xicotencatl, Chief Maxixcatzin, and Commander Chichimecatecle.

"Malinche! Malinche!" they cried out when they saw Cortez. Chief Maxixcatzin threw his arms around him. "How grieved we are at your misfortunes, and the number of our own people who have been killed with yours," he told Cortez through Malinali. "We warned you not to trust the Mesheeka, but you did not believe us and went to their city. Now all we can do is help with your wounds and give you rest and food. Here you are home."

Commander Chichimecatecle was the next to speak to Cortez. "Malinche! It is not a small thing that you escaped from the Mesheeka city across its bridges. If we thought of you as great and brave warriors before, we think of you much more so, now. Your gods are truly powerful to have delivered you from more Mesheeka than we have ever seen before, at Otumba."

Then the half-blind King Xicotencatl was brought before Cortez. He ran his fingers across Cortez's face. "We have made common cause together, Malinche," announced the king, "and we have common injuries to avenge. Whatever fate awaits us, know that we will prove true and loyal friends, and stand by you to the death."

Cortez placed his hand on the king's shoulder. "As shall we," he replied.

"You shall rest here for only two nights," the king announced. "Then you shall come to our capital, where everything is being made ready for your return. We leave you now to see to these preparations. Eat well and rest." The king's retinue began distributing maize cakes and turkeys to the hungry men, as the Tlaxcalan leaders climbed onto their litters and were borne back to Tlaxcala.

"They seemed anxious to leave," Malinali observed to Cortez.

"The hour is late," was his response. "Even at the speed the bearers run, it will be far into the night when they reach their home."

"It was more than preparations they wanted to get back to," she said skeptically.

"Ah, My Lady," said Cortez as he put an arm around her shoulders. "You should not be concerned for the Tlaxcalans tomorrow. Let us be concerned for ourselves tonight."

She complained no more.

Everyone did eat and rest the next day, but many were badly wounded and sick with a number of ailments, and the townspeople were too few to help them. They were therefore relieved when, on the morning of the following day, a large contingent of Tlaxcalans arrived with hammocks to carry the wounded and sick to Tlaxcala.

Upon their arrival in the capital, they were warmly greeted by people everywhere. Comfortable quarters had been arranged for all, with abundant food and drink. Cortez noticed that, as soon as they had been shown their quarters, Malinali vanished into the crowd of townspeople in the adjacent city square.

She did not return until evening. "There was a delegation of Mesheeka nobles here yesterday, sent by Cuitlahuac, promising Tlaxcalans peace and riches if they killed us," was her revelation. The look in her eyes was saying to Cortez, *You see? I was right.*

Cortez said nothing, just sat in his chair waiting for the rest.

"The Young Xicotencatl was delighted," she continued, "arguing forcefully for an alliance with the Aztecs, and urging that we all be killed quickly, which would be easy, given our 'beaten condition.' But Chief Maxixcatzin argued against him, saying Tlaxcalans should not commit treachery upon people to whom they had promised friendship."

Malinali's voice became more excited. "Then Chief Maxixcatzin, in front of the Mesheeka nobles, talked of the 'habitual treachery' of the Aztecs. He said that, given their 'customary arrogance,' they must be desperate indeed to plead for help from their enemies. He ordered them to leave, but the Young Xicotencatl demanded that they stay and that an alliance be agreed to - and then..." She shook her head in amazement... "the old Chief Maxixcatzin pushed the Young Xicotencatl to the ground and ordered him out, as well. No one there had ever seen such a thing. The young prince had to leave in shame and disgrace. The Mesheeka nobles hurried away, back to Tenochtitlan."

Cortez wore a self-satisfied smile. "Now do you believe that we are among friends we can trust?" he asked her.

"It is foolish to doubt you, my love," she replied.

The next morning, the king requested to see them. "Ah, my *padrino* and *madrina*," he exclaimed.

They both smiled broadly. "Don Vicente," greeted Cortez, using the king's Christian name, as they bowed their heads towards him.

The king held Malinali's hand. "Madrina, we know that Malinche has heard how we refused the Mesheeka's offer of alliance and refused to betray you to them. We wish instead for an alliance with Malinche, and we ask now that it achieve certain things."

"Whatever Don Vicente wishes of us, he has only to ask," responded Cortez.

"The kingdom of Cholula must be in alliance with us," was the first request. "It is too close and large a danger to us if it is not. It must be kept free of Mesheeka control."

Cortez was silent for a moment. "The Cholulans have already sworn loyalty to me and to His Majesty Don Carlos. They must be treated fairly. They must be made your allies, not your servants. You must trade fairly with them and not demand tribute," was his reply. "If you agree, then I will demand an alliance between your two kingdoms, and see that it remains free of the Mesheeka."

The king nodded. "This is agreed. Next, we wish to fight with you to conquer Tenochtitlan. In return, we ask that a permanent garrison of our warriors be established in that city, to prevent the Mesheeka from ever attacking us again. We ask that we share equally with you any riches that come from conquering the city. And we ask that, whoever rules Tenochtitlan, we be free from any tribute demands made by it."

Cortez looked at Malinali. "Doña Marina, please tell his Excellency that I am only too happy to comply with all that he says. Tell him that, with his help, we will see that no people in all this land pay tribute and sacrifices to the Mesheeka ever again. We will liberate the entire Mesheeka Empire."

The old king reached up and put his hands on Cortez's shoulders, and Cortez returned the gesture. "It is agreed," he said.

"It is agreed," confirmed Cortez.

"Rest now, Malinche," the king commanded. "Rest and regain your strength, you and all your men, for soon we fight together."

Even with his half-blind eyes, he can see, thought Malinali. Cortez's wounds on his head and hand looked serious. It would take time for them to heal.

* * * * *

It would, in fact, take two weeks. The expedition's doctors treated Cortez's two terrible head wounds and were especially worried about his left hand. The injury to it at Otumba was not healing properly. Two fingers, the little and ring fingers, remained paralyzed[181]. He fell into an alarming fever, and lay helpless and delirious in bed for days. Malinali remained constantly at his side, and when he finally woke, the first thing he saw was her, looking into his eyes.

He gazed back at her for a long time. Then he asked, "How are the men?"

She hesitated. "Many are getting better, but others are not. They are mostly the ones who are not getting better, here," she said as she pointed to

---

181 They would remain so for the rest of Cortez's life.

her heart. "They have even written a letter to you."

"Who are they?" asked Cortez.

"The Velazquez men, together with the Narvaez men, led by Andres de Duero."

"My friend, Andres..." Cortez shook his head weakly. "Tell them to present their letter. I wish to speak to them."

Malinali frowned. "No, my Captain! You must rest. You can only see them when you are better."

Cortez frowned back. "Now," he ordered. "I will not feel better until after I have seen them."

She went to fetch de Duero, who came with the letter and a number of its signers. They were startled to find Cortez so weak, lying propped up in his bed. De Duero bowed to him, said, "With greatest respect, Captain-General," and handed him the letter.

It was a summary of their catastrophes and dire situation. "Our heads are broken, our bodies rotting and covered with wounds and sores. We are weak and naked in a strange land, sick and surrounded by enemies. Our horses are dead, our artillery is lost, our ammunition is exhausted, and we are lacking in everything to continue this war... We cannot believe that these people of Tlaxcala are truly our friends. They are but lulling us into a sense of false security, and then they will assault us and finish us off...

"Further, Your Excellency, our leader and general, is badly wounded. The surgeons say you may not survive. Yet we are informed that you intend to continue this war against the Mesheeka, which will surely lead to our destruction... We therefore respectfully request that you order our departure from this city, and that our entire army leave at once for Villa Rica de la Vera Cruz, where we may be saved, either through reinforcements or by returning to Cuba... If you will not agree, then we now make formal claim against Your Excellency for all damage, deaths, and losses which may occur as a result."

Cortez studied the letter carefully and summoned his strength. He might have looked weak, lying in his bed, but Malinali could see the fire in his eyes. "I understand why you would write such a letter and make such a request, given what our circumstances seem to you," he began.

"I ask you, what nation which has ruled the world has not at least once been defeated? Never would that nation have risen to greatness, had they let a defeat destroy their destiny. Tell me, where in our history has our honor and valor faltered before an enemy? If that were so, our people of Spain would remain today ruled by the Moors, slaves of infidel Mohammedans. Is there not one among you who would not take it as an insult if he were told that he has turned his back, losing his honor to run away?

"And what would be the practical consequences of such a retreat as you propose? It would show our Mesheeka enemies that we lack the courage to face them, and our Tlaxcalan allies that we lack the courage to support them. Retreat is the one thing that will guarantee that the Tlaxcalans, if they do not fall upon us, at the least will fail to protect us from Mesheeka fury.

"We must always remember, gentlemen, that 'fortune favors the brave.' It is the bravery of those Christians who trust in the goodness of God that achieves His will – and it is indeed His will that we bring His word and His freedom to this Satan-ruled land. How else could we have accomplished the great feats that He has blessed us with thus far? To retreat now would be to retreat from His will. Our Lord God has a purpose for us in this land, and we must fulfill it as true Christian knights and gentlemen.

"As for my wounds, I pronounce myself cured of them. I will be at your service to lead you in accomplishing our Lord's will, to lead you in such victories that all of Europe - indeed, all of history - will behold in awe, if you choose to follow me. I have faith that, in your honor and valor, you will do so."

Malinali watched the men standing above the bed-ridden Cortez exchange questioning glances. After some moments of silence, Andres de Duero announced, "We thank Your Excellency for his faith in us, and shall give him no cause to doubt either our honor or our valor. Let us agree to postpone our request, pending future developments."

"Please forgive my inability to stand and thank you appropriately, Señor de Duero," Cortez responded. "Allow me to do so as soon as I am able."

The men nodded in assent and departed.

Cortez held his hand up to grasp Malinali's. "My Lady, I am as a child in your hands, needing to be cleaned and fed and brought back to strength. Let us see if we can do this quickly, for I must soon visit the Tlaxcalan king and his nobles in order to avert disaster."

It took her two days. By then, Cortez still felt weak but did not show it. "By the hour I feel my strength returning," he said as he embraced her, "thanks to you. Now, let us see the king."

He explained that the men could not remain in Tlaxcala. He needed to give them a mission, working in concert with the Tlaxcalans, in order to re-energize them, keep the malcontents occupied, and weaken some part of the Mesheeka Empire in the process. Something not too ambitious, but that will excite the Tlaxcalans. "If we talk to the king carefully, we will discover what this mission may be," he told her. Malinali felt a warm satisfaction, knowing that the 'we' meant she and Cortez, working together.

They found King Xicotencatl conferring with Chiefs Maxixcatzin and Chichimecatecle, as well as a third chief who was introduced to them as Tian-quizlatoatzin (*tee-ahn-qweets-la-twat-zin*). All expressed their happiness at seeing Malinche well once more.

"My great and honored friends," Cortez began, "we have agreed that Cholula shall be ruled no longer by the Mesheeka. Yet how secure can this be, when in nearby lands there are kingdoms that remain under Mesheeka control? It would be far easier to secure Cholula by removing one or more of these kingdoms from their control, and such an action would contribute to weakening Mesheeka power over all its subjects."

Maxixcatzin spoke. "There is much wisdom in what you say, Malinche. Please excuse us for a moment."

The four Tlaxcalans huddled together while Malinali and Cortez stepped away. They seemed to reach a decision, and Maxixcatzin came forward to say one word: "Tepeaca" (*tep-ee-ah-ka*)[182].

At Malinali's and Cortez's raised eyebrows, Chichimecatecle explained. "Tepeaca is a kingdom very valuable to the Mesheeka. It lies on the other side of Matlalcueye (*mat-lal-kway-yay*)[183] from us. It is east of Cholula and is a very rich land, providing vast amounts of tribute to the Mesheeka and many sacrifices for Huitzilopochtli. Further, all of the tribute paid by conquered kingdoms beyond Tepeaca goes through it. Take Tepeaca from the Mesheeka and they lose not only its tribute but all of the tribute from those kingdoms, as well. It would be a mortal blow to Mesheeka power."

Chichimecatecle then asked Chief Tianquizlatoatzin to speak. "There are

---

182   'Nose of the Hill.'
183   'The goddess who wears a green skirt.' It is a 14, 632' foot volcano with a ring of green forest around its lower slopes, now named La Malinche on the map of Mexico.

many Mesheeka warriors at Tepeaca. The Tepeacans themselves have a large army whose commanders owe their allegiance to Tenochtitlan. These commanders will order their men to fight us alongside the Mesheeka. My king has ordered me to lead a Tlaxcalan force to accompany you, a force large enough to defeat the Tepeacan-Mesheeka army."

Cortez gave Tianquizlatoatzin a respectful bow and said to Malinali, "Please tell the chief we welcome him and his warriors as our brothers-in-arms, and ask him his opinion of the Tepeacan warriors. Do they owe allegiance to the Mesheeka as do their commanders?"

Malinali could see by the look in Tianquizlatoatzin's eyes that Cortez had asked a good question. "Malinche understands the weakness of Tepeaca's rulers. The people of Tepeaca hate the Mesheeka and are forced to fight for them. And, in truth, there are commanders who feel the same."

"Then we must tell these people that we come to bring them liberty," said Cortez. "That, if they join us, they will never have to pay tribute and sacrifices to the Mesheeka again. With this message, the Tepeacan commanders will not be able to trust their own men, or may even join us."

Tianquizlatoatzin smiled broadly. "Our spies will spread the message. When does Malinche wish to march?"

"Tomorrow," Cortez said, and did not see Malinali's head snap back at that reply.

* * * * *

Two thousand plumed and painted Tlaxcalan warriors, armed with shields, spears, obsidian-toothed wooden swords, and bows and arrows, stood in the morning sun for King Xicotencatl's blessing, then awaited Tianquizlatoatzin's command, who in turn awaited Cortez's.

By the king's side were his daughters, Princess Teculehuatzin – who had said a loving goodbye to her *Tonatio*, Pedro de Alvarado - and Princess Otila, who was still in mourning for her beloved Juan Velasquez de Leon, lost on the bridges during *La Noche Triste*.

Malinali could not believe that Cortez was off to do battle again[184]. How could he have recovered so soon, after nearly dying? How could the wounds

---

184   August 1, 1520, little more than a month after La Noche Triste and three weeks after Otumba.

of so many of his men have healed so fast? As it was, several of the wounded men had to be left in Tlaxcala, including Bernal.

But Cortez had told her that he could not leave soon enough. "Inaction is deadly for us," he had explained. "Only action can save us, bold action, and quickly." He had made love to her so passionately through the night, and again at dawn, that she still felt his embrace. She looked up at him, resplendent in his polished armor astride his black horse. He looked down at her with an imperceptible nod, then called out the command to depart.

Cortez wheeled his horse around, followed by his mounted officers, who now had scarcely more than a dozen horses between them. Barely three hundred Spaniard soldiers began marching, with not one musket-man among them, and only a half-dozen crossbowmen. Even with the two thousand Tlaxcalans, it didn't look like a force formidable enough to conquer a kingdom.

She was, however, quite grateful to King Xicotencatl for arranging the luxury of her being borne on a litter by Tlaxcalan bearers. She felt like a princess again! His *madrina*, the king had said, should not have to walk.

Slowly circling Matlalcueye, they camped at the Tlaxcalan town of Tzompantzinco, then Zacatepec. When they reached the Tepeacan town of Acatzinco, Cortez had Malinali send a message to the rulers of Tepeaca, announcing that they were no longer subject to the Mesheeka, and that, if they were to pledge their allegiance to the King of Spain, they would be forever free of the need to send tribute and sacrifices to the Mesheeka of Tenochtitlan.

The reply he received was far from pleasant. It stated that the rulers of Tepeaca were hungry, and were looking forward to having Cortez and his men for dinner, cooked with chiles.

Two days later, in the mists of early morning, Cortez drew up his forces outside of the city of Tepeaca, in a maize and maguey field. Facing him was an array of several thousand Tepeacan and Mesheeka warriors. Cortez turned to Pedro de Alvarado astride his horse beside him. "Your opinion, sir?" he inquired.

"A small force, compared to Otumba, my captain," de Alvarado replied with a smile. "There cannot be more than 10,000."

Cortez turned his horse and addressed the men behind him. "Gentlemen! We fight today alongside an army of our Tlaxcalan allies. Let us show them how Spaniards conduct themselves in battle! Santiago, and at them!"

He turned his horse again and, together with de Alvarado, Cristobal de Olid, and the other horsemen, charged. They made immediately for the group of commanders with large feather banners being held above them. As the warhorses plunged into the mass of the enemy, their riders swinging huge swords of heavy, sharp metal, those who were not trampled or cut down broke in panic and fled.

The horsemen were upon the commanders in a moment, and the banners were seized, while Cortez yelled an order that the commanders were to be captured, not killed. It took him a while, however, to halt the killing of others. The Spaniards ceased as the order spread among them, but the Tlaxcalans were in blood-lust, and were not satisfied until hundreds of the enemy lay slain on the field.

Cortez ordered an immediate march upon the town, commanding his men to conduct themselves with military discipline and restraint, and asking Malinali to request that Tianquizlatoatzin do the same. Tepeaca was a good-size town. As they marched through, the streets were empty, its citizens in hiding. When they reached the central square, however, an assembly of some two dozen nobles and chiefs were waiting to greet them. As Cortez rode his black horse slowly toward them, they all knelt and touched their foreheads to the ground.

The most distinguished of them rose and then stepped forward. "Malinche!" he called out. "I am Chichitzin, Lord of Tepeaca. We have heard of your great power, but we did not know how great it was until we saw it today. We renounce our Mesheeka overlords, pledge our allegiance to you, and ask for your protection, both from the Mesheeka who will want our tribute as before, and from the Tlaxcalans, who will now ask that we pay tribute to them."

"King Chichitzin and honored gentlemen of Tepeaca," began Cortez's reply, "I accept your allegiance, not to me alone, but to His Majesty King Don Carlos of Spain, for I am but his humble servant. In His Majesty's name, I and my men of Spain pledge to you that Tepeaca shall no longer pay tribute or provide sacrifices to anyone ever again, neither to the Mesheeka nor to the Tlaxcalans. You are now a free people."

Malinali saw tears springing from the eyes of several of the elders.

"The price you must pay for this freedom," Cortez continued, "is to expel all Mesheeka warriors and tax-men from your land. I call upon you to send word to all of the cities and towns of the Tepeaca kingdom to do so, and to affirm that they are now under the protection of the King of Spain."

Malinali could not resist rephrasing this a bit, so that the Tepeacans heard that they were now "under the protection of Lord Malinche and his King of Spain."

Chichitzin bowed low and said, "It shall be done, Malinche." He looked up. "You are welcome in our home, Malinche. You are now our guests."

After the Spaniards were comfortably housed in palaces of the king, Cortez called for Tianquizlatoatzin. "Let us walk," he told the commander, as the two, accompanied by Malinali and followed by a mixed bodyguard of Spaniards and Tlaxcalans, strolled out into the city square.

The square had returned to life, filled with people. Cortez pointed to them, and said, "Commander, you recall that the inhabitants of this city were hiding in fear of us when we arrived. It is necessary that the Tepeacans not be afraid of us, neither of me nor of you. I would like to explain why."

The Tlaxcalan chief looked curiously at Cortez and said nothing.

"I know that, as allies of the Mesheeka, Tlaxcala has looked upon the Tepeacans as enemies," Cortez continued. "But I wish to ask you this – can my small army and that of Tlaxcala, by ourselves, defeat Tenochtitlan and rid the world of the Mesheeka Empire?"

Chief Tianquizlatoatzin stared hard at Cortez, and at last replied, "No."

"Then our only path to victory over the Mesheeka is to change their allies into our allies, yes? To have them join us, ally after ally, throughout the Mesheeka Empire, so that it is the Mesheeka who will be all alone, and Tenochtitlan will fall into our hands."

Malinali found it very difficult to translate these words of Cortez's. Her heart was pounding, her throat was dry, her brain on fire. She was watching her father's dream come alive, before her eyes. In her mind, she was shouting, *Tahtli! Tahtli! Are you listening, my father?* Then she calmed herself, smoothly translated Cortez's words, then held her breath, waiting for the Tlaxcalan chief's reply.

It was a single word: "Yes."

They continued walking in silence. Then Cortez asked, "Commander, how large is this kingdom of Tepeaca?"

"Do you remember Citlatepetl,[185] far in the distance to our left as we approached the city?" the chief asked in return.

Cortez nodded

"All the land between Citlatepetl and here is that of Tepeaca, and beyond..." He waved his hand, pointing west. "...towards Cholula. It is a rich land. They grow much food."

"What of all of the tribute that must pass through Tepeaca, in addition to the tribute Tepeaca itself must pay to Tenochtitlan?" Cortez next inquired.

The chief cast up his hands as if to say that the amount in question was inexpressibly large. "That is where the great wealth of the Mesheeka lays. Much of the food, feathers, and other items that the Mesheeka value is stolen from lands like Huaxyacac[186] where the Zapotecs live. The Mesheeka made the Zapotecs their subjects not long ago, when I was a young man. All of that wealth comes through here, Malinche."

Cortez reached out before him with his open hand, then slowly closed his fingers together, as if choking someone by the throat. "Then it is here that we shall begin strangling the Mesheeka, my friend. For that, however, we must work together, and so I ask you to command your warriors to no longer look upon the Tepeacan warriors and the Tepeacan people as their enemies but, rather, as their allies against the Aztecs. Can you do this?"

The chief hesitated, then finally replied, "It is not an easy thing for which you ask. We have been poor and hungry for so long, and the Tepeacans have such fat bellies. But I see the wisdom of your words, and I will do my best."

"Thank you, my friend. Just remind your warriors how much more they will be able to stuff their bellies – and how much better the food will taste – in Tenochtitlan than here, when they are victorious over the Mesheeka."

Upon returning to his quarters in Chichitzin's palace, he summoned all of his officers together. As they stood before him, he announced, "Gentlemen, I have a proposal for your consideration. It is that we establish ourselves here in Tepeaca. Tlaxcala is a poor land and we cannot ask the Tlaxcalans to feed us for much longer. Here, food is abundant and we shall not be a burden to our hosts. Of even greater importance, however, is that from here..." He

---

185   The giant snow-capped volcano now known as Orizaba, Mexico's highest peak at 18,646', referred to in Ch. 14, *Horror and Heaven in Zautla.*

186   "Place of guaje trees," conquered by the Aztecs in the 1490s. Huaxyacac, pronounced *wash-yah-kahk*, was altered in spelling and pronunciation by the Spanish to Oaxaca, *wah-hah-ka.*

raised his hand to make the strangling gesture. "...we shall begin to choke the Mesheeka Satan-worshippers into defeat. The wealth of the Mesheeka Empire passes through here. All we have to do is stand in the way ...and collect it."

As the officers digested this, he continued. "As you know, we cannot depend merely upon the Tlaxcalans. We must forge an alliance between several kingdoms that are subjected to the Aztec yoke, for it is they who will be motivated to join together in a common struggle for their liberty. You know that we have already met many rulers of such kingdoms. Here is where we begin to forge this alliance. Here is where I propose that we begin fulfilling the mission that our Savior has given us. The mission is to rid this rich land of the horrible evils inflicted upon it by these Mesheeka, these hated Aztecs. We have been blessed by God, Who has given us - us! - this sacred opportunity. It is here that we may start on our road to victory for our King, His Majesty Don Carlos, for our country of Spain, and for our Christian religion. What say you, gentlemen?"

Who could resist such a call? Malinali asked herself. And, to a man, the officers yelled and shouted their agreement.

* * * * *

Cortez and Malinali then went to see King Chichitzin. "I have agreed that your people shall keep for themselves all tribute of food and goods paid to the Mesheeka," Cortez said to him. "My Tlaxcalan friends have agreed to an alliance with Tepeaca, and to protect your people from Mesheeka armies. But Tlaxcala is a far poorer land than Tepeaca, which has so much more food. Does it seem fair to you that Tepeaca share its abundance of food with Tlaxcala, in order to make secure such an alliance between their two peoples and to ensure that Tepeaca shall remain protected from the Mesheeka?"

The king was cautious. "Who will command our army?" he wanted to know. "Must our warriors be ruled by Tlaxcalan commanders, as they were by Mesheekan?"

"This is to be an alliance of equals," Cortez replied. "You are no longer subjects of anyone."

"Then it is agreed," concluded the king. "And let us test this alliance by sending out joint commands of our combined forces to disperse the several

Mesheeka garrisons placed across our territory. They are not large, for their main garrison was here, and so they should be easily removed - yet it should be a good test. As we do this, I shall order shipments of food carried to Tlaxcala."

Over the next few weeks, the king proved right. Cortez sent some of his officers, such as Gonzalo de Sandoval and Cristobal de Olid, along with small detachments of his soldiers to lead joint Tlaxcalan-Tepeacan forces and guide their cooperation. The Mesheeka garrisons were easily dispersed, without the loss of a single Spanish life. The chiefs and elders of dozens of Tepeacan towns swore loyalty to Cortez, thanking their gods that they were rid of the Mesheeka.

He was keeping his men so busy, and so well fed and cared for, that none of them asked about all of the tribute that they were supposed to collect as it flowed through Tepeaca from other kingdoms on its way to Tenochtitlan. Cortez had Malinali plan with the king and his council to have Tepeacan nobles litter-borne to those kingdoms with the formal message that no further tribute or sacrificial victims were to be sent to the Mesheeka.

Often, the message had to be delivered in secret, for if Mesheeka commanders garrisoning those subject kingdoms found out, they would have had the Tepeacan nobles killed. Gradually, the flow of tribute passing through Tepeaca began drying up. And Malinali arranged for whatever did arrive to be sent on to Tlaxcala.

As Cortez gained allies – for the Tepeacan nobles were returning with messages from kingdoms such as Huaxyacac, stating that they wished to ally with him against the Mesheeka - he was also gaining reinforcements.

During this time, six different ships arrived at Villa Rica. Two were sent by Diego Velazquez to assist Panfilo Narvaez, about whom Velazquez had as yet heard nothing. Cortez's man in charge of Villa Rica, Alonso Caballero, smoothly talked the ships' captains, Pedro Barba and Rodrigo de Lobera, and the men onboard into joining Cortez in Tepeaca. Their much-needed supplies were carried by Totonac bearers.

Three ships arrived, sent by the Spanish governor of Jamaica, Francisco de Garay, in the hope of establishing a colony similar to Villa Rica. Caballero performed the same feat of persuasion with their trio of captains, Diego de Camargo, Miguel Diez de Aux, and Francisco Ramirez, who were heartily welcomed by Cortez in Tepeaca - especially since they brought with them horses, muskets, gunpowder, crossbows, and the soldiers to use them.

The best of them all was a large ship captained by Juan de Burgos from the Canary Islands, full of almost everything that Cortez needed – including more horses – sent by his father, Martin, back in Spain.

Altogether, this added two hundred more soldiers to Cortez's force, bringing it to over five hundred, now well-equipped and with all officers on horseback. They were all assembled now in Tepeaca, including Sandoval and Olid, back from their campaigns, and all of those who had been left to heal in Tlaxcala. Malinali had been delighted to see Bernal once again.

Every day, messengers from various kingdoms and cities arrived, asking for Cortez's decision on some issue or dispute. Chichitzin had provided him with a palace of his very own, in which he received this constant stream of supplicants.

"My Captain, you are becoming the ruler of your own empire," Malinali teased.

"Yet how could I do so without you?" he asked. "For I only know what all of these people want through you."

"Perhaps it is I who should rule this new empire, then," she teased.

He smiled. "I wonder how much you already do."

One day, in what Cortez had told her was October, a messenger arrived from a place called Huaquechula. It was some distance south of Cholula, in a remote corner of Tepeaca, next to Mesheeka territory. A very large Mesheeka army had been assembled there, since it was positioned on an important tribute route between the south and Tenochtitlan. The *Tlatoani* of Huaquechula was requesting that Malinche come and destroy this invading army. If Malinche did so, the people of Huaquechula were ready to rise up and fight, risking their lives against the Mesheeka.

Cortez was overjoyed at the news. "At last, just as we needed it," he whispered to Malinali, "an opportunity to use our new army." He instructed her to tell the messenger that he would soon be there.

While they were on their way, however, with a combined force of over five thousand Tlaxcalans, Tepeacans, and his own men behind Cortez, Malinali became worried. "This may be a trap," she warned him. "The Tepeacan commanders tell me that this is a very well-guarded place. It is at the end of a deep valley, between a river with a high bank and the mountains. A stone wall as high as three men blocks the only entrance to the city. And there is not simply one Mesheeka garrison - there are two. One is in the city, behind a wall, and a second, much larger one sits on a hill above the city. As we are fighting the first, the second could fall upon us, trapping us between them."

"First, then, let us see if these people will fight the Mesheeka themselves, as they swore to," was Cortez's response. "Then we shall see what sort of trap this is, and for whom."

Huaquechula proved to be about 12 leagues[187] from Tepeaca. Late on the fourth day following their departure, they camped on a field outside the city. It was, as Malinali had described, deep in a valley, with a protective wall. A good-sized city, she was told that it held some thirty thousand inhabitants. Above the city on a flat hill was the main Mesheeka force.

Early the next morning, Cortez ordered his forces into battle formation. As they were doing so, a great tumult arose from inside the city - the sounds of battle and fighting.

The same messenger whom they had seen in Tepeaca came running through an opening in the wall and up to Malinali, off to the side of the formation, surrounded by a large bodyguard. Cortez rode over to them. "The people in the city have begun killing the Mesheeka," she related. "The Mesheeka are retreating to the *teocalli*, the city temple."

The temple could be seen above the wall - and now all could see hordes of fighters struggling on its steps. Smoke had begun to pour from the building on its summit. That was all Cortez needed to see. Exclaiming, "It is as they so swore," he called for his key officers. He commanded Pedro de Alvarado to hold most of the force in check and be prepared for an assault, pointing to the Mesheeka army on the hill above. He had Sandoval command the rest and follow him. Then he charged through the opening in the wall and into the city.

Dead Mesheeka warriors were everywhere. The fighting continued on the *teocalli*, where there seemed to be more bodies of Huaquechulans on the steps than of the enemy, who were putting up a fierce defense. Soon, however, Spanish soldiers were running up those steps, followed by swarms of inflamed

---

187   36 miles.

Tlaxcalans and Tepeacans. The Mesheeka were slaughtered to a man.

"We have no time to congratulate ourselves," Cortez called to Gonzalo de Sandoval. "This battle is far from over." He ordered the forces back out of the city as quickly as possible.

Once outside the wall, his men saw the reason. The main Mesheeka garrison was far larger than they had supposed. Thousands of Mesheeka were assembling at the bottom of the flat hill where they camped, while thousands more were pouring off the hill and down steep trails toward the valley floor. Altogether, the Mesheeka numbered at least twenty thousand or more.

Cortez spurred his horse at a full gallop towards Pedro de Alvarado. "Attack! Attack now, before their forces are assembled!" he yelled, to which de Alvarado bellowed an excited assent. All the Spanish horsemen raced across the field at full run, with the Spaniard footmen, Tlaxcalan and Tepeacans charging behind them.

Spanish warhorses smashed into the surprised Mesheeka, who fought back bravely but could not withstand the assault. Next, the rest of the force slammed into them, and they were overrun. Gonzalo de Sandoval and Cristobal de Olid then swung their commands around to the side, to attack the enemy's flank. In disarray, the Mesheeka broke and tried scrambling up the steep trails to escape to their camp.

But there was no escape. The trails became a scene of mass confusion as the Mesheeka who were running up collided with those who were running down. Soon they were all in terror, pursued by Tlaxcalans and Tepeacans intent on revenge for all of the horrible suffering perpetrated upon them over so many years.

The Mesheeka fought desperately but it was not enough. Slowly, step by step, they gave way to the foe surging up from below, up the hill ever higher, until the ridge was reached – and on that flat hill, not one was left alive.

Cortez had long since recalled his men, who stood watching the bloody drama unfold above them. The elders and nobles of Huaquechula came out of their city to bow and express their thanks and loyalty to Cortez, even as the slaughter continued on the heights. Food and drink was provided to the Spaniards as they waited for the bloodshed above to end.

It was near sunset before that was achieved. The Tlaxcalans and Tepeacans began descending the hill, loaded with as much Mesheeka booty - featherwork, jewelry and weapons - as they could carry.

"The beginning is over," Malinali overheard Cortez say to Pedro de Alvarado.

At camp, over the evening meal, Cortez called for Martin Lopez. "Señor Lopez, perhaps you have been told that, at our darkest moment, under that tree after our defeat of *La Noche Triste*, I asked if you were safe – and, when informed that you were, I said that we then lacked for nothing."

Malinali could see Martin's face blush in the light of the campfire. "Yes, I heard that, Captain-General, but I did not understand."

"It is because, Señor Lopez, we shall not defeat Tenochtitlan across its bridges. What need is there to assault this city-on-an-island when we can simply isolate it into submission, preserving it without the sort of bloody terror that we saw today, so that we can then present it as a glorious prize to our majesty King Don Carlos. Indeed, we have been informed by our new arrivals that he is now even more than a king – he is the Emperor of the Holy Roman Empire, Charles V.[188]

"Señor Lopez, as the master shipbuilder of this expedition, you are the key to our victory over Tenochtitlan and the Mesheeka Empire. So it is that I now task you with proceeding at once to Tlaxcala. From there, I wish you to send for all of the tools and materials you need from the ships now in Villa Rica. I wish you then to seek a place where you can cut much wood – oak, evergreen oak, and pine – and fashion it into the pieces necessary to build thirteen brigantines. This will all be transported to streams flowing into Lake Texcoco. There, the ships will be assembled, and we will control Lake Texcoco with them. Tenochtitlan will fall into our hands."

"It shall be done, my Captain-General," was all that Martin Lopez needed to say.

Bernal, sitting next to Malinali, leaned over to whisper, "Doña Marina, do you remember my saying that Captain Cortez was the Spanish Ulises?[189] He is more than that. There is a legend about a magic bird that cannot be destroyed. When it seems to die, it burns into a pile of ashes, only to rise anew from those ashes, stronger than before. Our captain is like this magic bird. He is the Spanish Phoenix."

---

188   See Ch. 12, Angry Gods. See also Cortez's explanation of the Holy Roman Empire to Malinali in Ch. 17, *Fortes Fortuna Adiuvat*.

189   See the end of Ch. 11, *The Spanish Ulysses*. Ulises is the Spanish version of Ulysses, which is the English version of Ulixes, which is the Roman version of Odysseus, hero of Homer's *The Odyssey*.

Chapter Thirty Two

"WE HAVE KIL LED MALINCHE!"

Cortez lay awake in his bedchambers at his headquarters in Tepeaca. He and his forces had returned from Huaquechula in time to celebrate All Saints Day[190] and pray to those who had achieved the beatific vision in heaven that this "ultimate end of human existence" might possibly be granted to them when they die.

That was yesterday. Today, they held the Feast of All Souls Day, to pray for those departed Christian souls being cleansed of their sins in *purgatorium*. For some reason, he had felt a strange uneasiness during the prayers at Mass, which he expressed to Doña Marina. Now he was even more uneasy, for where was she? Gone on one of her evening learning expeditions. But this one was taking too long. He wished that she was next to him right now.

Suddenly she was. She burst wordlessly into the room, quickly removed her dress, and snuggled up to him in their bed.

A look into Cortez's eyes told her what he had been thinking. And when he looked back into hers, he knew something was wrong. He waited for her to tell him.

"My Captain, I have unfortunate news," Malinali said. "Chief Maxix-catzin has died."

Cortez closed his eyes and sighed. "So that's who was missing in my prayers today. He was a good man and a good friend. He lived a very long life and we must be grateful that he ended it as a Christian. I shall pray for him at Mass tomorrow." He looked at her. "But you have more to tell me."

---

190   November 1, 1520.

She caressed his face and looked at him with love. "Yes, but nothing unfortunate. Just the opposite." She paused mischievously, while Cortez gave her a look which told her that he was deciding whether to listen or ravish her without another word. She, in turn. gave him a smile that told him she wanted him to choose the latter.

And he did. For a wonderfully long time.

Afterwards, Malinali could not stop smiling and giggling. Cortez tried to get her to talk but she tickled him unmercifully instead. So he tickled her back, and soon they were laughing so much that neither could speak. Finally, she calmed down. "Actually, there is much to enjoy in what I am going to tell you," she teased.

"First," she continued, "the Aztecs have a new king. Montezuma's brother who overthrew him, Cuitlahuac, is dead, replaced by their cousin Cuauhtemoc (*coo-awe-tay-mok*). He is the son of the king who came before Montezuma, the brother of Montezuma's father, Ahuitzotl[191]. He is young, not much older than me[192]. He had all of Montezuma's sons killed, including Axoacatzin, so that he would have no rivals to the throne. It is strange, though, for Aztec nobles and priests to let someone with such an unlucky name rule them, for Cuauhtémoc means 'setting sun'."

"Let us ensure then that his name is prophetic," commented Cortez, "and see that the sun sets on his evil empire. But what, my love, is there to enjoy in this?"

"Ah!" she exclaimed with a smile. "Cuauhtémoc has sent ambassadors to a number of other kingdoms to ask for an alliance to defeat you - and has met with disaster after disaster. Of these, the one which all of the Tlaxcalans are talking about is Puhrepecha. The Aztecs call it Michoacan, the place of fishermen, because of its big lake with many fish, and they have never been able to conquer it. It is some distance..." she pointed west... "beyond Tenochtitlan.

"When Cuauhtemoc's ambassadors came to Tzintzuntzan, the Puhrepecha capital, they brought many presents to Zincicha, the Puhrepecha king - giant obsidian mirrors, much turquoise and rare feathers. They said, 'Let us fight together against the strangers in our land.' Zincicha got very angry. 'What do you mean *our* land?' he asked. 'The Mesheeka have been trying to steal the land of the Puhrepecha for themselves since my grandfather's time.

---

191 See Ch. 18, The Tale of Taclaelel.
192 Malinali would turn 21 in December 1520.

Now someone threatens your land and you dare to ask for our help. I have no desire to help the enemy of my people.' So Zincicha ordered the Aztec ambassadors sacrificed.

"I am told," she concluded, "that Cuauhtemoc's ambassadors have met similar rejection from several other kingdoms as well. The Tlaxcalans are overjoyed with this news, for it means that their great Mesheeka enemy has no friends. Are you not overjoyed yourself, My Captain?"

If Cortez was, he did not show it. His eyes were staring at her, but she knew he was looking at the thoughts inside his head. She said no more and let him think.

"We cannot stay here in Tepeaca any longer," he said finally.

Malinali's brow furrowed. "But it is safe here," she objected.

Cortez grimaced in scorn. "I have no intention of being safe. We must *carpe diem*, as the Romans said – seize the day."

It was her turn to grimace. "You have created your own kingdom here. It may fall apart if you leave. You cannot afford to let this land, so rich and valuable to the Mesheeka, fall back into their hands."

Cortez stroked his beard and looked at her intensely. Wagging a finger at her, he said, "You are right about that." He stroked his beard some more. "Very well," he decided. "I shall stay here for a few more weeks, until Tepeaca is governed and garrisoned properly. Then we leave for Tlaxcala - and then for Texcoco."

Malinali was startled. "Texcoco?! That is the Mesheeka's second largest city. For it, Lake Texcoco is named. It is in alliance with Tenochtitlan!"

"Then we will test that alliance," Cortez responded. He closed his fingers in the choking motion. "For my plan to succeed in strangling the island of Tenochtitlan, we must control the lake in which it sits. For that, we must have a base on the lake. It must be on the Tlaxcalan side of the lake in order for the brigantines to be transported and launched. We cannot have a large enemy city nearby. So to make that city ours solves both problems." When he saw the worry in her eyes, he kissed her cheek. "You must not fear," he counseled. "We shall not go to Texcoco alone. We will have several thousand Tlaxcalan warriors beside us."

She smiled at him with love. Then the smile turned into an invitation to resume their previous activity, an invitation Cortez was happy to accept.

* * * * *

Almost every day for the next several weeks, Cortez and his officers, with Malinali to counsel and interpret, met with King Chichitzin, organizing and ensuring the security of Tepeaca. He placed his commander of artillery, Francisco de Orozco, in charge of a Spanish garrison of some sixty men. Then, on what Cortez told Malinali was the 13th day of December, he and his small army left for Tlaxcala. King Chichitzin was happy to see all but a few of the thousands of Tlaxcalan warriors go with him.

It was a happy Christmas for everyone in Tlaxcala. Cortez and King Xicotencatl had cried together over the passing of Chief Maxixcatzin, but they, along with Spaniards and Tlaxcalans alike, felt that they had much to be grateful for, much to celebrate, and much to look forward to in the coming year.

Malinali had never been happier. All of the Spaniards treated her with such respect. Indeed, the officers were always asking for her advice and suggestions regarding how best to get along with the Tlaxcalans - their Tlaxcalan lady-friends in particular. The Tlaxcalans, in turn, revered her and treated her like nobility, like the princess she was. Everyone acknowledged the value of her counsel to Cortez. She only wished that he wasn't meeting with Martin Lopez all of the time, so that he could spend more time with her. She had to remind herself frequently of how important the proper building of the brigantines was to their well-being and Cortez's plan.

King Xicotencatl offered Cortez an enormous number of warriors, tens of thousands, to accompany the Spaniards to Texcoco. "Every man in Tlaxcala wishes to go and fight the Aztecs," the king explained.

"But how can we feed that many?" Cortez asked Malinali during the conversation. "Please thank the king, and tell him that we require a smaller force for Texcoco, a city which we hope will welcome us, not fight us. Would the king assent to several of my officers staying here and training his warriors on how to best fight the Aztecs when we get to Tenochtitlan?"

The king nodded.

Two days after Christmas, ten thousand Tlaxcalan warriors arrayed in brilliant feathers and warpaint, and led by Chief Chichimecatecle, stood in the sunlit central square of Tlaxcala, facing the city's main temple. The Spaniards seemed very few next to them – five hundred and fifty soldiers, eighty crossbowmen and musket-men, and forty cavalrymen on horseback.

Cortez stood on the lower steps of the temple to address them, with Malinali to translate for the Tlaxcalans. "Today is a momentous day," he began, "for it is on this day that the men of Spain and the men of Tlaxcala join together in a noble cause, to rid this land of a barbarian evil, the curse of the Aztec Mesheeka. The people of Tlaxcala, like so many other peoples in this land, have suffered greatly under this curse. Now, you men before me are going to end this suffering.

"We men of Spain also wish to offer the great blessing of faith in Jesus Christ to all people of this land. So it is with pride and happiness that I announce to you that the great commander of the Tlaxcalan army, Chief Chichimecatecle, has, like King Xicotencatl before him, now embraced the Christian faith.

"This noble mission of ending the Aztec Mesheeka curse and bringing the blessings of Christianity begins with our march on Texcoco, to which we will come in peace but are prepared to fight if we are not received in peace. It is from Texcoco that we start our capture of the Mesheeka capital, Tenochtitlan.

"I wish you all to know the rules of conduct for this campaign. There is to be no blasphemy by any soldier, no dueling, and no gambling. No town is to be pillaged, no woman is to be violated, no one is to be robbed of his possessions. We must gain the natives of this land as allies, not enemies, for it is by such alliances that we will defeat the Mesheeka.

"If we conduct ourselves thus, there will be great honor and riches earned by all of you, men of Spain and men of Tlaxcala. Honor and riches are things which very rarely can be found in the same bag. Let us now go forward and earn them both."

As the force set off from Tlaxcala, Bernal walked alongside Malinali. "All of our men are in high spirits," he told her. "They wish to avenge themselves for the disaster of *Noche Triste*, yes, but it is much more than that. They feel that they are about to accomplish something truly extraordinary, something that history will remember."

Malinali smiled at her friend. "I believe that too, Bernal. I believe that Lord Jesus and His Mother have answered my prayers – indeed that They have answered the prayers of my father, as well, even though he didn't know to whom he was really praying. So, yes, I am happy, as are you. Yet Captain Cortez says to keep a hand on my emotions like..." she made a pulling motion with her hands... "a horseman must hold his horse from not running too fast."

"Ah, holding the horse's reins, yes. Why did the Captain say this, Doña Marina?"

"He said we must be patient. He has talked much with his officers of 'the wisdom of patience.' Now that we are close to this great goal, he says, we must be careful, we must 'go quickly slowly,' which I laughed at when I heard him say it, and he frowned at me. But now I understand. It will take some time, even months, for the brigantines to be built and launched, then more time for his plan to blockade Tenochtitlan into surrender. All this time must be used to gain more allies, bring more kingdoms now under Mesheeka rule to join us. Captain Cortez wishes to capture Tenochtitlan, not destroy it. He wishes for the Mesheeka to surrender, not to have to kill them. 'There are more riches in peace than destruction,' he says. With time, with the blockade, with the other kingdoms as our allies instead of theirs, the Mesheeka, he hopes, will finally choose surrender, not war."

They walked for some time in silence as Bernal considered her words. Then he voiced his thoughts. "What our Captain wishes for is what we all wish for, Doña Marina. He is right to ask for our patience. Yet I think, the more patience we have and the more allies we gain, the more determined the Mesheeka will become to make war to the death. People who rule others never wish to give that power up, and the more evil their rule, the harder they fight to keep it. The Mesheeka know how much they are hated by those they rule. Surrendering to those they have ruled would mean to be at their mercy, and the people of this land are not merciful. No, Doña Marina, Captain Cortez's wishes are those of a Christian, noble and good, but I think, in the end, that enough blood will have to be spilt to fill Lake Texcoco to end Mesheeka rule."

Malinali shivered in the warm sun at Bernal's words, for she was afraid that he was right.

* * * * *

It was midday. The sun shone relentlessly hot and bright, high in a cloudless sky, yet for Malinali it was the blackest of nights. There was no light in her soul; it was filled with fear and pain instead, and her mouth tasted of ashes.

How long had it been since they had left Tlaxcala for Texcoco, so happily and optimistic? Half a year. The Spaniards said that this black day was the 30th of June[193]. She stared vacantly at the sparkling blue water of Lake Texcoco. So much had happened, so many near disasters, so many triumphs, until victory over the Aztecs had seemed certain... until now.

They had expected a fight when coming to Texcoco, but they were met on the way by the king's brother, Ixtlilxochitl (*ish-tleel-zoh-cheetle*)) who offered to be Cortez's ally. Then a group of nobles met them, carrying golden banners of peace, and saying that "Malinche" was welcome. Yet when they entered the city, the streets were empty, and King Conacochtzin (*kona-kotch-zin*) was nowhere to be found.

Texcoco was a beautiful city with many canals and palaces. They stayed in the largest palace, that of an earlier king, Nezahualpilli (*nesha-wal-pilly*), and Cortez sent Pedro de Alvarado and Cristobal de Olid to the top of the biggest temple to see what they could observe.

What they saw was most of the city's people fleeing across the lake in canoes. When the Tlaxcalans learned that King Conacochtzin had fled as well, they became enraged and began to loot the city. It took a while before Chief Chichimactecle and his sub-chiefs could make them stop.

Yet she and Cortez had celebrated what he called New Year's Eve with a night of bliss. "This new year, my love, shall see your father's dream come true," he vowed to her.

Three days into this new year, the rulers of two cities within the Texococan kingdom, Huextola and Coatlinchan, arrived and pledged their support for Cortez. They brought a gift of several Mesheeka messengers who had been sent by Cuauhtemoc to demand that they fight with him against the Spaniards. "Do with them what you wish," they told Cortez.

Cortez had Malinali reply that he welcomed the rulers' support but that he wished to end Mesheeka control over other kingdoms peacefully, that he wished to be a friend of the Mesheeka, and that he did not want to be forced to destroy Tenochtitlan and kill its people. He therefore instructed the Aztec messengers to return to Tenochtitlan and tell Lord Cuauhtemoc that, as a

---

193   1521.

new leader of his people, he should put the past behind him, value the lives of his people foremost, and begin living in peace with all of those who resided in this land.

That Cortez did not have the Aztec messengers killed, and instead sent them unharmed back to Tenochtitlan with a plea for peace and not war, highly impressed the rulers. It was not long before several other Texcocan towns asked for Cortez's protection against the Mesheeka and vowed their support - for they had soon learned that Cuauhtemoc, in a fury over Cortez's offer, had ordered his own messengers slaughtered on the sacrificial altars.

Ixtlilxochitl became king of Texcoco, and sent word to all those who had fled that it was safe for them to return to the city. He informed all of the Texcocan nobles that they must choose to either stay in a free Texcoco, free of Mesheeka rule, and ally with the Spaniards, or flee to Tenochtitlan, as had Coanacochtzin.

They stayed.

No sooner had the city returned to normal than Cortez and Ixtlilxochitl set off to explore the south of the lake, from Texcoco to the finger of land that led to the main causeways to Tenochtitlan, and the city that controlled it, Iztapalapa.[194] They took two hundred Spaniards and several thousand Tlaxcalans.

The Mesheeka broke a dike to flood the city and drown Cortez, but everyone escaped. Upon their return to Texcoco, all the talk was of a duel between Ixtlilxochitl and a chief of Iztapalapa who had been ordered by Cuauhtémoc to capture him and bring him to Tenochtitlan for sacrifice. Ixtlilxochitl killed him.

In the following weeks, city after city such as Ozumba, Tepecoculuco, and Mixquic sent their nobles to Texcoco, pledging their alliance with Cortez and against the hated Mesheeka. The largest and most important of these were Chalco and Tlamanalco, who begged for help in getting rid of the Mesheeka army garrisons in their midst. Cortez sent Gonzalez de Sandoval with two hundred Spaniards and many Tlaxcalans. They destroyed the Mesheeka garrisons.

Sandoval returned with the rulers of Chalco and Tlamanalco, who wished to personally thank Cortez. They wept in bitterness and relief as they told of

---

194   For the location of cities around the lake, see The Cities of Lake Texcoco in Maps & Illustrations.

how Mesheeka commanders had a habit of seizing the most beautiful women and violating them in front of their fathers, mothers, or husbands - and that now this would happen no more.

During this time, a canal many feet deep and wide was being dug for the brigantines, as Cortez insisted that they be built safe from attack by Aztec canoes. It reached from Texcoco to the lake, about a half-league away.[195] Ixtlilxochitl had devoted many thousands of workers to constructing it, and now it was near completion. So once Sandoval returned from Chalco, Cortez sent him off to Tlaxcala to bring the logs and planks now cut for the brigantines safely to Texcoco.

It was a thrilling sight, one which Malinali told herself she would never forget, as thousands and thousands of Tlaxcalans arrived, marching in a line at least two leagues long, bearing the cut timbers and materials for the brigantines. They had managed to carry them for twenty leagues[196] over the mountains, and now they were all dressed in their best cloaks and feathers. As they entered the city, they chanted *España! España*[197]*! Tlaxcala! Tlaxcala!*

Cortez said that it was the middle of February. She, in turn, told him that, for the Aztecs, the month of Atlcahualo was beginning, during which many young children would be sacrificed to the rain god Tlaloc.[198] He then informed her it would take another month or more to construct the brigantines, during which time he intended to make another exploration around the north of the lake.

"Before you return," she warned him, "it will be the Aztec month of Tlacaxipehualiztli, the Flaying of Men. Any of your men whom the Aztecs capture will be skinned alive, and their skins worn by the priests."

Cortez's departure was delayed by the almost daily arrival of emissaries and nobles from one city after another, coming to pledge allegiance to him and ask for his protection from vengeful Aztecs. To each of them, Cortez had her give the same reply: He was grateful and thankful to have them as allies, and would protect them under one condition – that they pledge allegiance to one another. Only by abandoning age-old hatreds between themselves and uniting together to fight the common enemy of them all could they hope to

---

195 The hand-dug canal was some 12 feet deep, 12 feet wide, and 1½ miles long, as there are roughly 3 miles to the league.
196 60 miles.
197 Spain! Spain!
198 See Chapter 18, The Tale of Taclaelel.

defeat the Aztecs.

"You must embrace each other. If you wish to ally with me, you must ally between yourselves. Then, together, we shall be victorious, and all shall gain their freedom." That was his message and demand. It amused Malinali to see how such a demand shocked these emissaries, as they were so riven with rivalries of war and hate between them. Yet such was their greater hatred of the Mesheeka, and such was the hope Cortez was offering, that none refused Cortez's demand. All agreed. Malinali was seeing her father's dream become real before her eyes.

By the time Cortez left with three hundred and fifty of his men and many thousands of Tlaxcalan and Texcocan warriors, the month of Tlacaxipehualiztli had begun.[199] When he returned, two weeks later, all he could talk to her about was liberating Azcapotzalco – once an independent kingdom and now the great slave-market of the Aztecs, where he set "so many thousands" of slaves free – and of ambushing a great horde of Aztecs who attacked them during their return. "It was a beautiful victory," he said with a happy smile.

Yet Bernal told a different story. "We fought all the way to Tacuba, Doña Marina, and all the way back. Thankfully, we lost almost no men of ours, and our allies killed amazing numbers of Aztecs. We learned, however, that the Aztecs seem to have endless supply of warriors determined to fight to the death. In Tacuba, Captain Cortez made a mistake and almost caused us to be trapped to our doom on the *La Noche Triste* causeway. We were surrounded by innumerable canoes from which came a thunderstorm of arrows, spears, and stones. One of our men, Volante, was carried away. As he is a man of huge muscles and very strong, he broke free from his captors and swam back to safety with us. 'They shall not skin me today!' he shouted. Every hour of every day returning here, we had to fight attacking Aztecs. Captain Cortez said that he wanted to see how strong the Aztecs still are, on the other side of the lake. Well, he has found out."

Malinali asked him to tell her about the 'ambush.'

Bernal smiled. "Ah, yes, the Captain was tired of these attacks, so he had two detachments of cavalry and infantry hide in thick bushes while the rest of our army continued on. I was with one of the hidden groups. When the force of attacking Aztecs, several thousand of them, followed unsuspectingly,

---

199   March 5.

we burst out of the bushes to put them to the sword and lance. Then our allies turned and fell upon them, as well, so that no Aztec left the battle alive. Yes, it was a beautiful victory, for it was sweet recompense, and the attacks upon us ceased."

When Malinali queried Cortez about Aztec determination and strength, all he would say was "Watch" and "Patience." He was far more interested in making love to her, an interest with which Malinali joyously complied.

Indeed, they now made love with more joy, passion, and frequency than ever, as if they could not get enough of each other. For this, she needed no 'patience' as Cortez advised. *Martin Lopez can take all the time in the world to complete the brigantines*, she thought, *while this bliss continues.*

But she did watch, as emissaries from cities and kingdoms arrived to swear fealty to Cortez – not just several a week, now, but two or three, every day. Of course, she did more than watch, for she had to interpret for them all, and carefully, for they spoke Nahuatl with an array of different accents and dialects.

With them, Cortez made a new demand. Not only must they pledge allegiance to him and to that mysterious king he now called "*Emperador Carlos el Cinco*"[200] and pledge not to fight each other. They were now required to pledge to fight *for* each other.

"You all ask for my protection from the Mesheeka, which I shall give to the best of my power," he would tell them. "But as there are so many of you, I and my men cannot do this for all. What you now must do is to form protective alliances between yourselves. In the past, you fought amongst yourselves. Now you must join together so that the Mesheeka cannot defeat you. Each of you must come to the assistance of the other when attacked by the Mesheeka. Do you agree?"

They all did.

Part of the reason they agreed so easily was Texcoco's new King Ixtlilxochitl, who showed each visiting emissary, noble, chief, and king every hospitality, and talked to them about how much more peaceful and prosperous Texcoco was now, freed from Mesheeka subjection. He showed them, as well, for with the increased trade from many kingdoms, some very distant, his prosperity was obvious. So was the peace, for here were thousands of Tlaxca-

---

200   King Don Carlos of Spain, who was also Holy Roman Emperor Charles V.

lans, their former enemies, working together with them to construct the canal and engage in trade.

Another part of the reason was the arrival in Texcoco of a man from an island in the East Ocean that Cortez called Hispaniola.[201] Rodrigo de Bastidas was an old friend of Cortez, and very wealthy. "All the men in the islands[202] have heard of your triumphs," he told Cortez, "and wish to join you, but they are prevented by your enemy, Diego Velasquez. I decided to ignore that fat man, so here I am, at your service."

De Bastidas did not come alone. He brought three ships, hundreds of muskets, crossbows, and swords, a huge supply of gunpowder, two hundred fighting men, and sixty horses. Cortez was very pleased to see him and his cargo.

Indeed, Cortez was so pleased that he decided to write another long letter to his king and emperor in Spain, describing his achievements on the king's behalf, and requesting support for the governance of 'New Spain.' He sent Diego de Ordaz and Alonso de Avila to personally carry the letter in one of Bastidas' ships, which was laden with Aztec riches - featherwork, jewels, and gold artifacts - as gifts for the king.

Malinali knew that her bliss could not last for long. Cortez announced that he would be leaving on a third exploration – this one completely around the lake – after the Mass of Easter Sunday.[203] At least she would be going with him to interpret. But she knew that she would see little of him. It also upset her that he was ignoring her advice not to venture into the wild mountains far to the south of the lake. An emissary from the Tlahuica kingdom had come, appealing for Cortez's help. The Tlahuicas wished to ally with Cortez but could not do so because of a very large Mesheeka garrison in their capital of Quauhnahuac (koo-_wan_-a-wok)[204]. She had then made the mistake of telling Cortez that Quauhnahuac was a place of legendary beauty.

Even though they had thousands of Tlaxcalan and Texcocan warriors, and were joined by thousands more from Chalco - Bernal said they must have numbered some twenty thousand - they were molested by Aztec attacks all the way through the mountains. Moreover, when they came to Quauhna-

---

201   The largest island in the Caribbean, now comprised of the countries of Haiti and the Dominican Republic.
202   Cuba, Jamaica, and Hispaniola, by then thoroughly colonized by the Spanish.
203   Easter fell on March 31 in 1521.
204   The Spaniards changed the pronunciation to Cuernavaca, "cow's horn."

huac, it was surrounded by deep ravines, and the bridges across them had all been broken.

The most astonishing thing then happened. Ixtlilxochitl, the Texcocan king, spotted two huge trees on either side of a steep narrow ravine that so leaned towards each other that their tops intertwined. He ordered one his warriors to climb across this 'tree bridge' high in the sky. When he did so, several hundred Tlaxcalans and roughly twenty Spaniards followed. With the wind swaying the tree tops back and forth, the men negotiated the waving branches, and a number of them slipped and fell to their deaths. Once across, however, this force was able to surprise the Mesheeka garrison from behind. With the Mesheeka thus distracted, Cortez had one of the broken bridges quickly repaired so that he could bring the rest of his forces across, and soon every Aztec warrior was killed.

After a difficult trek out of the mountains, the expedition reached the southern shore of Lake Texcoco, where Malinali made another error in judgment. A little distance offshore was a large island city called Xochimilco[205]. The Xochimilca people had been conquered by the Aztecs fairly recently, only a few winters before she was born, and had all been made Mesheeka slaves. So Malinali had told Cortez that she did not expect the Xochimilca to join the Mesheeka in fighting them, just as the Tlahuicas had not in Quauhnahuac.

She was wrong. They fought their way across the short causeway to the island city, which they quickly captured. Once inside the city, however, innumerable Mesheeka appeared in canoes to surround and trap them. When Cortez led a charge against them at the entrance to the causeway, he was surrounded and thrown from his horse. But then, as the exultant Aztecs seized him, a Tlaxcalan warrior and a Spaniard, Cristobal de Olea, sprang with such ferocity upon his captors that Cortez was able to break free.

For two more days, they had to fend off unending attacks by swarms of Mesheeka. Finally, Cortez lost his patience and agreed to the demands of the Tlaxcalans and other allies that they destroy much of the city and put it to the torch. With the rubble from the destroyed houses, he had the breaks in the causeway made by the Mesheeka filled in, then ordered his troops' departure, leaving Xochimilco a smoking ruin.

Thankfully, they made their way all the way around to Texcoco, through

---

205   The Field of Flowers.

Coyoacan, past Tacuba, and along the northern lake shore, without major incident.

Cortez was pleased with his expedition. Malinali, however, was not. "We have circled the entire lake now, and with this knowledge from our reconnaissance, I am confident of beginning the *estrangulamiento*[206] of Tenochtitlan," he told her.

"You were almost killed. This expedition was not worth the risks you took," came her reply.

He embraced her and held her tightly. "Ah, my Doña Marina, you must not worry for me. Our Lord in Heaven has a purpose for me here, and I shall be safe until I complete it."

She felt his strength around her and hoped it was true.

At first, it certainly seemed to be. After their return to Texcoco at the end of March, the flood of requests and offers for alliance from cities and kingdoms increased. The Aztec Empire was falling apart more quickly than Malinali had ever dared to hope. The peace between all of these places, many of which had been blood enemies for generations, was also more than she could have imagined – as was the amount of work being accomplished in Texcoco.

Bernal was as astonished as she. "The Captain is taking no chances," he told her. "He sent a pattern for our arrowheads to all of the towns of this region, which have now supplied us with fifty thousand copper arrowheads. The same with the kind of wood we want for arrows. He placed Pedro Barba in command of our crossbowmen, and he has made sure we have all the spare bowstrings and glue we need for repairing arrows. All of our armor must be polished and padded, lances and swords sharpened, the horses shod. Cavalry and footmen are training harder than ever. We are ready for war, Doña Marina."

Finally, the brigantines were ready. There were thirteen in all, and Malinali was surprised by how big they were.[207] Each could carry some thirty soldiers, along with twelve rowers for the oars – six on each side. The brigantines had one or two masts for canvas sails, as well as a small bronze cannon in the front, while Cortez's ship carried two large iron cannons from Spain. The ships' bottoms were flat, to accommodate the shallow lake.

They were launched in a ceremony at the end of April. Thousands of Tex-

---

206 Strangulation.
207 Cortez's flagship was the largest, over 60 feet long, the others over 50.

cocans and Tlaxcalans, dressed in their feathered and painted best, cheered, whistled, and blew whistles and conch shells as the ships fired their cannons and unfurled their sails.

Malinali had never seen Cortez prouder. "I have a navy of Roman galleys," he boasted to her, "except that the Romans had no cannons or gunpowder!"

The next day, Cortez assembled his force in another grand ceremony: Bernal counted eighty-four mounted horsemen, six hundred and fifty soldiers, each with a sword, shield, and lance, and one hundred and ninety-four crossbowmen and musket-men, all with well-quilted armor, leggings, thick sandals, and a steel helmet and gorget[208].

He placed Pedro de Alvarado in command of one hundred and fifty soldiers, thirty horsemen and eighteen crossbowmen and musketeers who, together with 8,000 Tlaxcalans, were to set up an attacking position in Tacuba, and block its causeway to Tenochtitlan.

He placed Cristobal de Olid in command of one hundred and seventy-five soldiers, thirty horsemen, and twenty crossbowmen and musket-men who, with another eight thousand Tlaxcalans, were to establish a camp at Coyoacan, blocking causeway access to the Aztec capital from there.

And he placed Gonzalo de Sandoval at the head of another hundred and fifty soldiers, twenty-four horsemen, and fourteen crossbowmen and musket-men who were to march to Iztapalapa with some ten thousand warriors from Chalco and other allied cities, blocking the third causeway.

The remainder of the force would be with Cortez on the brigantines.

When Malinali reminded Cortez that there was a fourth causeway out of the island, north of Tenochtitlan to Tepeyac, he smiled and said, "Ah, that is to be our '*puente de plata.*' It is always good to leave your enemy a 'silver bridge' of escape. I want to starve the Mesheeka into retreat, not to death, my Lady."

As the three detachments made their way around the lake and established themselves, Malinali was able to enjoy another period of bliss with Cortez. Their lovemaking was more intense and long-lasting than ever. She felt as if the two of them were gods, making love in heaven. She knew it had to end… and it did, the day after the Mass of Corpus Christi.[209]

---

208   Collar to protect the neck.
209   The Feast of Corpus Christi fell on May 31 in 1521.

But it did end gloriously, for it was the day Cortez 'set sail' with the brigantines across the lake. It was a sight she would never forget, the shimmering blue sky dotted with clouds, the shimmering blue lake dotted with hundreds of Texcocan-warrior-filled canoes, the rowers and the wind making the brigantines race across the water. She felt the wind and sun on her face, just as she felt Cortez's love for her and his pride in what he had achieved, as he stood next to her in his *capitana*[210].

She glanced at Martin Lopez, who had 'worked like a slave' to build these ships, and at King Ixtlilxochitl, whose support had made this possible. They stood on the other side of Cortez, and she could see the pride and wonder in their faces. She thought back to that terrible day when she had been seized by the slave traders, on orders from her mother, and changed from a princess to a slave. But if that had never happened, she would not be here now.

Malinali clutched the crucifix hanging on her neck and thanked the Virgin Mary for the blessing of her life. Her heart shouted with joy, *"Tahtli! Tahtli! I have made you proud of me, haven't I?"* She looked up at Cortez with a smile, which he broadly returned.

Then their eyes focused on a steep pile of rocks jutting out of the center of the lake, the island of Tepepolco. Smoke was coming from the top of it, signals from the Mesheeka garrison there to Tenochtitlan, telling of Cortez's movements. Reaching the island, Cortez leapt out, led some hundred men up the rocks to the top and, after some fighting, eliminated the garrison.

When hundreds of Mesheeka canoes full of warriors arrived, too late to protect the garrison, Cortez had the brigantines sail straight into them, crushing and sinking many, the crossbowmen and musket-men shooting down upon them, so that the water was full of dead and drowned Aztecs. The few surviving canoes retreated to Tenochtitlan. Cortez ordered his fleet to Iztapalapa and the camp of Sandoval.

On the way, he turned to Malinali. "Doña Marina, with our victory just concluded on the lake, I have a request. The causeways of Coyoacan and Iztapalapa join to form the main causeway to Tenochtitlan. Tell me of the place where they join."

"It is called Acachinanco, and there is a strong fortress there, with two towers and a thick wall, all of stone. It is called Xoloc," she answered. "The

---

210 His flagship.

Aztecs will have a garrison there. We passed by it on our first entrance to Tenochtitlan, and you met Montezuma on the causeway."

"Yes, that is what I am thinking of, the fortress. We should establish our encampment there instead of at Iztapalapa. We can control the causeway much better from there." Cortez redirected the fleet to Xoloc. When all of the brigantines had landed, the Mesheeka garrison quickly fled up the causeway. Xoloc was theirs. But it would not be easy to keep it.

For the next several days, the Mesheeka poured down the causeway and surrounded Xoloc with canoes, firing arrows and stones. The brigantines smashed the Mesheeka canoes, and the Tlaxcalans battled with them, day after day. Then Cortez learned that his "silver bridge" was working in reverse: the Aztecs were using it to bring food and supplies into their city. He decided to send Gonzalo de Sandoval and his men to Tepeyac to block its causeway. And he decided to send Malinali with him.

"You will go with Gonzalo to Tacuba, to be with Señor de Alvarado and Doña Luisa[211]," Cortez explained to her. "It is there that you are most needed, I am told, for negotiating with the Mesheeka - and there you will be safer than here. This is where the fighting will be most severe, and I want you where there will be less danger than in this small fortress."

She began to protest, but one look from Cortez told her that he had made his decision. "The danger will be getting worse," he continued. "I cannot hold our vast multitude of allies to simply defend us from Aztec attacks much longer. They came to fight and rid their world of Aztec enslavement. Soon, we must carry the battle into the city itself from here." He caressed her face. "I must have you safe. Please go with Señor de Sandoval, my love."

And so, reluctant and fearful, she went to Tacuba.

Cortez was right, of course. Pedro de Alvarado and his brothers had built a very strong position, and had so many allies that the Mesheeka could not really attack them, although there was much fighting on the Tacuba causeway every day. And she did enjoy being with Doña Luisa, whose husband provided them both with every comfort he could. Yet she found herself afraid - not for herself, but for her beloved Cortez. She felt a doom approaching that she could not make go away. Every night, she prayed in tears to the Virgin Mary, but the fear remained.

---

211   Princess Teculehuatzin, daughter of Tlaxcala King Xicotencatl, whom Pedro de Alvarado married in Chapter 19.

And then the fear came true.

Every day, the fighting had grown more vicious, more violent. The Mesheeka fought like wild animals. During breaks in the fighting, she would go out onto the causeway, accompanied by Pedro de Alvarado and a strong guard, to call out to the Aztec commanders, asking to speak with Lord Cuauhtémoc. "Malinche does not want you all to die. Please let us end this in peace," she would plead.

All she ever got back was shouted insults.

Every day, more of the great city, the magnificent Aztec capital of Tenochtitlan, was being destroyed. Cortez had penetrated into the city square, and the Palace of Axayacatl was burned to the ground by the Tlaxcalans. Since a principal Mesheeka method of fighting was to assault the attackers with a hail of stones and arrows from rooftops, the Tlaxcalans and other allies leveled more of the city into rubble each day. The allies did so happily, so great was their hatred for the Mesheeka.

By the end of June, more than half the city was a ruin, and the end for the Mesheeka seemed near. In fact, Cuauhtémoc had moved his forces and most of the population out of the city proper and into the northern section known as Tlatelolco. The allies sensed victory. All the cities around the lake had joined Cortez. So many warriors from so many kingdoms swarmed over the Spanish camps that it was an 'embarrassment,' joked Pedro de Alvarado.

When Cortez arrived by brigantine at Tacuba, Malinali was filled with excitement and relief. He held a meeting with all of his officers to decide on the 'final action,' as he called it. To a man, the officers argued for assaulting Tlatelolco from all sides, with Alvarado and Sandoval coming from the Tacuba causeway – Sandoval from that of Tepeyac, and Cortez and Olid coming through the main city. "We will trap them between us and crush them for good," Gonzalo de Sandoval predicted.

Cortez shook his head. "It is we who could be trapped," he responded. "The Aztecs still have an endless number of men - how I don't know, but they do. There are many canals that have to be crossed. If the enemy manages to cut them off, it is we who would be surrounded with no escape."

Every one of the officers disagreed loudly, so impatient they were to 'finish it.' After being assured that the allies would be with them to prevent any breaks over the canals, or repair any that were made, Cortez assented. "If that is your wish, gentlemen, then we attack tomorrow," he announced. Then he left, sailing back to Xoloc, leaving Malinali with only a quick caress.

Her fears were now greater than ever.

The morning of June 30 had no sunrise. Dark clouds on the horizon obscured it. Yet the men were in high spirits, anxious for Pedro de Alvarado's command to move forward. They crowded onto the Tacuba causeway, waiting to rush into the city and on to Tlatelolco. Thousands of allies were behind them, painted and feathered, howling their war cries, for this was to be their day of triumph.

Masses of Mesheeka warriors could be seen in the city, silent and waiting.

De Alvarado had been told to give Cortez time to complete his journey through the main city, as well giving time for Sandoval to reach the northern outskirts of Tlatelolco, before his attack, so the assault would come together jointly. As they waited, they heard the sounds of fighting in the city, cries, shouts, the shots of musket-men. Soon the sounds would be close enough – Cortez would be close enough – for de Alvarado to sound the charge.

Then the sounds changed. No more shots. A great din, a loud roar arose, coming towards them. Drums, trumpets, horns, crowds of men exulting. The masses of Mesheeka warriors awaiting them were suddenly no longer silent. They were dancing and yelling and preparing, not for defense but for attack.

Five Mesheeka, wearing gaudy feather headdresses, burst out in front of their compatriots. Each was holding and waving a bloody severed head – the head of a Spaniard. They were shouting, screaming, *"Malinche! Malinche! We have killed Malinche!"* They tossed the severed heads onto the dirt of the causeway.

Malinali, watching from campside, fell to her knees in horror. One of the heads was indeed that of Cortez.

The Mesheeka attacked in fury. The allies behind Alvarado broke and fled in panic. As Alvarado and his men braced for the enraged Mesheeka racing towards them on the causeway, everything went black before Malinali's eyes and she slumped unconscious to the ground.

Chapter Thirty Three

REAPING THE WHIRLWIND

"*Doña Marina! Doña Marina!*"

Someone was screaming at her, shaking her violently. Blinking, Malinali saw that it was Doña Luisa. Dazed, Malinali stared up at the woman in confusion.

"You must not stay here! The Aztecs are attacking!"

She heard the words with no understanding. She felt herself being pulled roughly to her feet and pushed into a run. When they reached a stand of trees, she looked around in bewilderment. There was an incredible noise ringing in her ears, but it seemed far away.

She looked in the direction of the noise and saw the Tacuba causeway. It was filled with screaming Aztec warriors, swinging their *macuahuitl* obsidian-edged wooden swords as they raced towards Pedro de Alvarado and his men. Somehow, the sight of it seemed as distant as the noise…

Suddenly, like the wave of a storm, the full sight and the sound of the battle crashed upon her. She heard claps of thunder, but the sky was clear. Then she saw the brigantines in the lake on either side of the causeway, firing their canons into the Aztec mass. She recognized the captain of one of the ships, Juan Jaramillo, the officer who had protected her during *La Noche Triste*.

Next, she saw Pedro de Alvarado leading his horsemen in a charge straight into the Aztecs, as the musket-men and crossbowmen took up positions on the edges of the causeway and fired into them. So many Aztec warriors had streamed onto the causeway in their fury and determination to get at the Spaniards that now they couldn't move. They simply became targets for the cannons, the muskets, the arrows, the hooves of war horses. They died by the hundreds, and by more hundreds, until at last they gave up the assault, retreating back into the city, shouting insults and taunts, proclaiming that they had killed... had killed....

Then the terrible sight that had caused her to faint appeared before her eyes, the bloody head of Cortez bouncing and rolling in the dust, and she screamed in horror. Doña Luisa embraced her, and she clung to the Tlaxcalan princess, sobbing uncontrollably. "My Captain, my Captain..." she moaned in desolation.

When she could finally let go, she whispered her thanks and walked alone along the shoreline to stare vacantly out upon the waters of Lake Texcoco.

The realization of her dream, of her father's dream, of liberation from the Aztecs, who were hated so deeply by everyone in this land, had come so close. *How can the Lord Jesus have brought Cortez to this land, only to have the dream end like this?* She clutched her crucifix and prayed to the Virgin Mary for understanding.

How long she sat there looking out upon the lake, reliving memories now turned so bitter, she did not know. The sun was still high in the sky, beating down upon her. Then there was a shadow. Doña Luisa had come to sit beside her. She was smiling – a happy, joyous smile. How could she? How could she bear to smile when....

"Cortez lives."

Malinali heard the words as sounds only, as if they were of some strange language she didn't understand.

Doña Luisa grasped her hand tightly. "Andres de Tapia has just come to our camp from Xoloc. Cortez and his men were trapped, and a number of soldiers were killed or captured. But Cortez and many others escaped. The head that you saw – that we all thought was that of Cortez – was the head of another soldier who looked somewhat like him from a distance. The Aztecs fooled us. Doña Marina, Cortez is alive - *Cortez is alive!*"

A flood of tears poured down Malinali's face as she silently gave her thanks to the Holy Mother. She cried for a long time, with Doña Luisa next to her, holding her hand.

The sun was now well behind them. They walked back to the camp, to Pedro de Alvarado's quarters, where Malinali was housed. There she saw

Andres de Tapia and Gonzalo de Sandoval, both bandaged and limping from various wounds.

Immediately, de Tapia approached her. Bowing courteously, he said, "Doña Marina, I know of your concern. A tragedy has befallen us, but I wish to assure you that Captain Cortez is well. It was a terrible battle, with Captain Cortez and a small detachment separated from the rest and trapped between two canals in the city. A horde of crazed Aztecs fell upon us, yelling, 'Malinche! Malinche!' and seized our Captain. He was saved by Cristobal de Olea, who cut off the hands of Cortez's attackers, as he did when saving the Captain at Xochimilco.

"Although wounded badly in the leg, Captain Cortez killed his other attackers and was finally rescued by another detachment led by Antonio de Quinones. I regret to say, however, that the noble gentleman who saved Captain Cortez's life twice, Cristobal de Olea, was himself killed by the Aztecs. But our Captain was able to rally us to beat off the enemy and retreat in good order back to Xoloc. He then sent me to inform everyone here of what had happened. We give thanks to God that our Captain is safe, Doña Marina, but we weep for those of us who have been killed this day, and weep more for those who have been captured."

* * * * *

Although her prayer had been answered, the following days were nightmares. Cortez had insisted that she stay where she was. She would be safer there than at Xoloc, where he had to stay because of his wounds. Their allies from dozens of cities and kingdoms, numbering in the countless thousands, had nearly vanished. Bernal told her that King Ixtlilxochitl and some forty Texcocans, along with Chief Chichimecatecle and another forty Tlaxcalans, remained with Cortez at Xoloc. There were similar handfuls of allies with Sandoval at Tepeyac, and with them here at Tacuba. That was all.

"We are alone, then?" she asked Bernal.

"Yes, Doña Marina, we are alone, and there is scarcely a man among us who is not wounded, and badly. All we are waiting for now is for the Aztecs to pour out of their city and annihilate us, which we expect will happen as soon as they complete their sacrifices to Satan."

The sight of those sacrifices were the most horrible of her life. From the Tacuba causeway, they could see the temple of Tlatelolco with its steep steps and sacrificial platform on top rising in the distance. She stood with Bernal, Doña Luisa and Pedro de Alvarado, and watched as one captured Spaniard after another, stripped naked to expose his white skin, was dragged up the temple steps to the platform and held down on the *techcatl* sacrificial stone, where their chests were sawn open by the priests with an *itztli* flint knife. Their hearts were then ripped out as an offering to Huitzilopochtli, and their bodies thrown off of the platform to bounce to the bottom of the steps. There, other priests were waiting to cut off the arms, legs, and head, whereupon the body was flayed for its skin.

Interspersed between the sacrifices of the captured Spaniards were those of the captured Texcocans, Tlaxcalans, and other allies. Hour after hour, this went on, the booming drums of death never stopping their pounding, the conch shell trumpets never stopping their blowing, the cries of agony from one victim after another never-ending. At night, they went on, the entire scene lit by huge bonfires.

This went on for five days. Sixty-four Spaniards were counted as sacrifices, along with hundreds of allies, mostly Texcocans and Tlaxcalans.

When finally the drums and the trumpets and the screams of sacrificial victims stopped, a group of Aztec warriors rushed down the Tacuba causeway to toss out the roasted legs and arms of several Spaniards. The warriors yelled, "Look! This is the way you will all die, as our gods have promised us. Eat the flesh of your brothers, for we are glutted with it. Stuff yourselves with our leavings. Make yourselves fat, for we shall soon eat you all."

When Malinali heard those words and told Pedro de Alvarado what they meant, she made a decision. "I wish to be taken at once to Xoloc," she told him. "If I am to die now, it will be with my Captain."

De Alvarado nodded in assent. "Señor Andres de Tapia and a small detachment will soon be leaving with messages for Captain Cortez. You may accompany them, Doña Marina."

She thanked him, then embraced Doña Luisa for what she feared would be the last time.

* * * * *

The instant she saw Cortez, however, all her fears vanished. She could not, of course, throw herself into his arms as she wanted, for he was far from alone, consulting with his officers. She clutched her crucifix instead, in gratitude and relief.

When he saw her, he broke into a cheerful smile. "Gentlemen!" he proclaimed to his officers. "Doña Marina is with us again!"

Several of the men had been sitting in chairs or on stools around Cortez, who was immobilized on a couch with his wounded leg. They all stood up and warmly bowed to her.

"We were discussing, Doña Marina, the fact that it has been several days since our catastrophe at the *puente de dolor*, the bridge of sorrow," Cortez said to her. "Our allies, save for a valiant few, have left us. We all, without exception – including myself, as you can see – are wounded. Yet the Aztecs, who number in the multitudes, have not poured forth from their city to destroy our pitifully small force. Yes, they have been celebrating their victory and commemorating it to their satanic gods, and they have led numerous small harassments against us. But the main attack has not yet come to finish us. When do you think it will?"

Just then, King Ixtlilxochitl stepped inside Cortez's tent. As all eyes turned to him, Malinali replied, "I think we should ask the ruler of Texcoco," and she translated the question to him.

"Malinche! My answer is that the attack will not come at all!" was his response. "I, too, have been downcast these past days, with the death and sacrifice of so many, and so many of my people and others giving up our struggle. But now I have come to tell you not to be distressed. The Aztecs have fed on your bodies and on the power of their victory, but that is over. Cuauhtémoc's mistake was to place his huge army within Tenochtitlan to defend it. That army is now running out of supplies.

"My spies tell me that food is very scarce in the city. It is only a matter of days before there will be none. There is also no water, for the water in their wells now has too much salt. All they have to drink is rainwater. What you must do, Malinche, is stay in your camps for some days and rest your wounds. You, *Tonatio*, and Sandoval must keep your big canoes[212] busy. Day and night, keep them busy, preventing Aztecs canoes from bringing food and

---

212   The brigantines.

water into the city. If you stop their food and water, how can they go on? They will suffer far more from hunger than from war."

Cortez said to his aides, "Help me to my feet." As he stood, he opened his arms and motioned the king forward. They embraced, and Cortez said, "Doña Marina, please tell this noble gentleman how much I value his friendship and wise counsel. He is a king worthy of his people. I am honored to be considered worthy of his friendship."

As he stepped back from Cortez's embrace, King Ixtlilxochitl responded, "Malinche, there is more that you should know. Cuauhtémoc has sent messengers to many kingdoms, telling them that all is forgiven for joining you against him, and asking that they now join him to destroy you. They have refused. Your allies may have left you for now, but all they are doing is waiting, waiting to see what happens between you and him. Their hatred of the Aztecs remains. If Cuauhtémoc cannot destroy you soon, your allies will return to you."

He glanced at Malinali with a look of hesitation, as if there was something he was not sure he should say. "Please continue," she told him.

"The Aztecs are using the sacred plants," he said. Malinali translated this with a puzzled frown. "Not just the *tlamacazqui*[213]. Cuauhtémoc has ordered that the entire store of sacred plants kept by the priests be given to the warriors to keep them fighting in spite of their thirst and hunger. This is why the Aztecs seem to fight so crazily, and is why they will do so until they die. They are drinking *ololiuhqui* and *tlitliltzin* water[214], eating leaves of the 'fear-conqueror' *sinicuiche*[215], and taking much, much *peyotl*[216]. Cuauhtémoc and all the nobles are taking much *teonanocatl*[217], the god-mushroom, drinking it with cacao and honey."

Cortez noticed Malinali's puzzlement and saw how her eyes widened in amazement while translating Ixtlilxochitl's words. He looked at her, prompting her to explain.

She blinked several times before answering. "The Aztecs believe that the gods live in these plants, and that they are eating the flesh of the gods when

---

213 The priests and nobles.
214 Two varieties of morning glory seeds, *Rivea corymbosa* , and *Ipomoea tricolor*, containing a hallucinogenic alkaloid tryptamine d-lysergic acid amide or LSA, a chemical cousin of lysergic acid di-ethylamide or LSD.
215 *Heimia salicifolia*, leaves of which containing the hallucinogen cryogenine.
216 Peyote, the buttons of the *Lophophora williamsii* cactus containing the hallucinogen mescaline.
217 *Psilocybe* mushrooms containing the hallucingens psilocin and psilocybin.

they use them, so they are normally eaten only by priests and nobles. Even then, they are eaten only in the most important ceremonies and sacred rituals. These plants, they say, let them see the gods themselves, as well as many wondrous things.

"For Cuauhtémoc to give such things to his warriors, and for him and the other nobles to be eating them without the sacred ceremonies, means an agreement of suicide with the gods. It means that the Mesheeka are all willing to die in order to kill you. It means that we are fighting those who are 'divinely insane,' who believe that they are no longer human but fight with the courage and strength of gods."

No one spoke for some time after Malinali's words. Then Cortez sighed. "I did not want to destroy this beautiful city. I did not want so much death. The Aztecs have brought the doom about to befall them upon themselves. Their gods are evil and false and have no power to protect them. We must kill their gods. It will be a tragedy if we must kill all of the Aztecs, as well. But if that is the path they have chosen, then we will take it. Whatever crazy things they have made their brains drunk with, it will do them no good when they are at the end of a sword of Toledo steel."

He drew his sword. "Gentlemen! We shall not relinquish this land to evil. We shall liberate it to the glory of Spain and the glory of our Lord in Heaven."

All of the officers drew and raised their swords in silent assent.

* * * * *

That night, Malinali could not hold Cortez tightly enough. There were no words. He held his arms around her and she clung to him in silence, as they lay in bed through the hours of darkness. As dawn was arriving, they finally made love.

It was only afterwards that they talked. "Andres de Tapia told me that you came here to die with me," said Cortez as he caressed her face. "Sometimes, our Lord in Heaven tests us in ways that seem unbearable. Yet, when you thought all was lost, and that your father's dream was finished, you chose to be with me." Malinali saw such love and wonder in Cortez's eyes that she was stunned and could say nothing.

He kissed her with greater passion than ever before. Then he smiled.

"But, just as I am still very much alive, so is your father's dream, my love. You understand, don't you, that your father wasn't simply dreaming?"

She waited for him to answer his own question.

"It was a *presagio*, an omen, a premonition, sent to him by God. Just as God sent me here to liberate this land, God sent you to me, for without you, I could not achieve His purpose. And how could you enable me to do so without your father's dream? It was much more than a dream, and it is a great tribute to your father that he had the courage to accept such a gift from God, to make it his own. He must have been an extraordinary man. I wish I could have known him. You are truly your father's daughter, my Lady."

She closed her eyes against the tears that sprang out of them. She could see her father in her mind so clearly, looking at her and calling her *Ixkakuk*. "*Tahtli! Tahtli!* " she whispered.

"This dream shall soon cease to be but a dream," Cortez continued. "That is why the first thing I must do this morning is speak to Chief Chichimecatecle."

"He left for Tlaxcala last night," she told him.

Cortez's head snapped back. "Left! You mean...? Why didn't you tell me?"

Her smile was gentle. "He shall soon return. He said, 'Tell Malinche I won't be coming back alone'."

Relief replaced alarm in his eyes. "Malinche... It still seems strange to me that I am known in this land by your name, not mine. Does it amuse you?"

"Yes." Her smile broadened, then she tickled him. He tickled her back, and in an instant they were making love again – carefully, however, for his leg was still healing.

* * * * *

Later that morning, a soldier appeared at Cortez's tent, requesting to speak with him. Introducing himself, he said, "Captain-General, my name is Francisco de Montano from Ciudad Real.[218] I wish to make a request of you."

Cortez bade him to continue.

"We are in a desperate situation," the soldier said. "Not one man among

---

218   A province of south-central Spain.

us has less than two wounds from fighting off the continual harassing attacks of these Aztec mad dogs. The one thing that protects us, and that lets us kill so many of the attackers, is fire from our muskets and from the cannons on the brigantines. But we have almost no gunpowder left. For our own supply, we have depended on gunpowder made in Cuba and sent in ships. I propose to you, Sir, that we make our own."

Cortez, Malinali could see, was taken aback. "You have a way do this, Señor de Montano?"

"Yes, Captain. There are many caves in this region where we can acquire *sal de piedra*.[219] I saw them in the mountains during our expedition to Quauhnahuac. Making charcoal is easy. The problem is the sulfur. Captain, do you remember Diego de Ordaz and Gutierre de Casamori climbing the great smoking mountain[220] and returning with a few bags of sulfur?"

Cortez nodded.

"Well, Señor de Ordaz said that there was not much on the volcano's rim, but that he could see large amounts of it down on the walls inside the volcano. Señor de Ordaz is now on his way to Spain with your message to His Majesty Don Carlos. But Señor de Casamori is here, and I have spoken to him. I asked him if a man could be lowered with ropes into the volcano to collect a large amount of sulfur. He thinks it is possible. I ask your permission to do this."

"Señor de Montano, if I could easily stand, I would embrace you!" Cortez exclaimed. "This is exactly the kind of courageous initiative I most admire. When do you wish to depart?"

"Immediately, Sir," came de Montano's reply. "Señor de Casamori and the Tlaxcalans who guided them on the mountain, along with several others, are ready as well."

Soon after Montano left, there was a great noise in the camp. Malinali went out to see what it was, and soon returned - with Chief Chichimecatecle. The look on Cortez's face was a combination of happy relief and puzzlement. *How could the Chief have returned from Tlaxcala so quickly?* she knew he was wondering.

"Malinche! It was a great shame for me to have my men leave you," the

---

219   Saltpeter or salt of the rock, potassium nitrate. Gunpowder is 75% potassium nitrate, 15% charcoal, and 10% sulfur.
220   Popocatepetl - see Chapter 22.

chief announced. "Thus I went for them and found many on the way, before they reached Tlaxcala. I told them of my shame, and that it was theirs also. I told them if we gave up this struggle now, we would give up our chance to be free of Aztec rule forever. Thus many of my warriors have returned here with me today, and many more will return in the days to come."

Cortez insisted having his aides help him stand so that he could embrace the chief. "My noble friend," he had Malinali say to him, "how can your people fail to succeed when they have champions like you to lead them? Tlaxcalan poets will sing songs in praise of you for generations to come."

Later that afternoon, a runner arrived with a message for 'Malinche.' "This man is from Quauhnahuac,[221]" Malinali informed Cortez and his officers. "He says that a force from the nearby kingdom of Malinalco has attacked them. The king of Malinalco is the cousin of Cuauhtémoc, and is sending his army to attack you from behind. 'Because we are the ally of Malinche,' he says, 'the Malinalcans have attacked us on the way, burning our maize fields and killing our children for sacrifice.' He begs you to come to the rescue of your ally, Quauhnahuac."

The officers looked at Cortez. "The greater our weakness," he said, "the greater need have we to cover it with a show of strength. We must comply." Casting his gaze across the men before him, it fell on Andres de Tapia. "Señor de Tapia, assemble a force of the most able-bodied, a few dozen if you can, and a dozen cavalry. Several hundred Tlaxcalans will accompany you. See that you are gone no longer than ten days."

The following morning, another runner appeared, bearing a similar message. He came from Otomi allies to the west, with apologies for their desertion and a plea for rescue from an army from Matalcingo, whose king was also a cousin of Cuauhtémoc. Cortez dispatched Gonzalo de Sandoval with a force similar to De Tapia's.

That night, Cortez expressed a worry that, by depleting his forces so much by going to their allies' rescue, he was inviting the Aztec to attack. "So many of our men are still wounded, we need more Tlaxcalans returning. King Ixtlilxochitl promises that many Texcocans will come soon. We must hope so, because we are still weak, my Lady."

"Yes, but the Aztecs are weaker, as well," Malinali responded. "King Ix-

---

221 Cuernavaca. See Chapter 32.

tlilxochitl's spies tell him that many Aztecs are reduced to eating straw and grass. Their water is so foul that it is making them sick."

"Yet they continue to attack with wild vigor," Cortez objected. "They are not in such huge numbers that we are unable to defend ourselves, but their ferocity..."

"*Peyotl* and the other sacred plants make them so, but their supply will soon be gone."

Cortez thought about that for a minute. "Then we must pray that Our Lord in Heaven grants us a few more days – time for the men to heal, and time for Señores Sandoval, Tapia, and Montano to successfully return from their missions. So strengthened, we can then demand that the Aztecs surrender and live." He looked at her with an expression of concern. "They will surrender, won't they? There has been far too much death. They can't all want to die, can they?"

She tapped the side of her head. "*Peyotl* changes you here. It has made them death-crazy."

Cortez's only response was to draw Malinali's head down to rest upon his chest.

* * * * *

She was delighted to see Bernal. He was in good spirits, just returned from a 'triumphant' expedition with Gonzalo de Sandoval. "We routed the Maltacingans completely, and captured two of their highest nobles," he enthused. "And we hear that Andres de Tapia has done the same with the enemy forces of Malinalco."

"Yes, he returned yesterday," she responded. "And much else has happened in the days you were gone. Francisco de Montano has returned with much sulfur! He told a very exciting story about being lowered deep into the mouth of Popocatepetl and almost choking to death from the smoke and fumes. 'Hanging in space above the depths of hell,' he said it was like, as he scraped bag after bag of sulfur from Popo's skin.

"We have even more gunpowder, as well! Another ship arrived in Vera Cruz, with a good supply of it, as well as additional men with crossbows and horses. I spoke to one of the men. He said that they were on an expedition of two ships led by Juan Ponce de Leon to a place called Florida. They were attacked by people there called Caloosas, and Señor de Leon was struck by a poisoned arrow. They think he may die. His ship sailed back to Cuba, while the other ship came here.[222]

"And there is more good news! Chief Chichimecatecle led a force of Tlaxcalan warriors to attack the Aztecs right in the center of Tenochtitlan! By himself, with no Spaniards! They killed many Aztecs and captured three commanders."

Bernal looked at her with satisfaction. "It is good to see you happy once again, Doña Marina. When I saw you last at Tacuba, you thought you were coming here to Xoloc to die. Now you can see that we are going to live, and victoriously, thanks to the blessings our Lord Jesus has bestowed upon us."

That evening, Cortez held a meeting of his officers and a number of men in his camp, with Chief Chichimecatecle and King Ixtlilxochitl also in attendance. Malinali stood by them to translate Cortez's words.

"Our fortunes have changed much in the twenty days since our disaster at the *puente de dolor*. Things are now much better, thanks to the support and courage of our great friends from Tlaxcala and Texcoco, to the skill of my officers such as Señores de Tapia and Sandoval and their men, the great daring of Señor de Montano, and to the good fortune of more supplies and men.

"Thanks to this, our many allies who left us after the *puente de dolor* are returning, as they see our own strength return. It is wise for us to wait until they do so in sufficient strength for us to complete our task here quickly and with finality. All of us - including myself, as you can see - have recovered from our many wounds and are ready for this task. Yet I wish to make one last effort to propose peace with the Aztecs and their king Cuauhtémoc. We have captured two nobles from Maltacingo and three noble Aztecs. I wish to have them brought before us."

As soon as the five captives were standing in front of them, Cortez spoke to them through Malinali.

"Please convey to King Cuauhtémoc my great respect for him. He and

---

222   Juan Ponce de Leon (1460-1521) from Santervas de Campos, Valladolid, Spain, accompanied Columbus on his second voyage of 1493. He was the first European to reach a land he called *La Florida*, "flowery" in 1513. He led a colonizing expedition to settle there in 1521 with 200 men, 50 horses, and supplies. Attacked by the Caloosas in the estuary of the Caloosahatchie River (Charlotte Harbor), he died shortly upon reaching Cuba. The myth that he was searching for a legendary "Fountain of Youth" arose in the early 1600s.

his people have fought like true warriors. Yet now the time has come to cease fighting and killing. It is time for there to be peace between us. It serves no one, not the Aztecs, not us, not anyone in this land, to have the great city of Tenochtitlan, the most beautiful place in the world, destroyed.

"We know that the Aztecs have neither food nor water, that they are dying of hunger and thirst. King Cuauhtémoc must know by now that he has no hope of defeating us. He deserves the same fate as those of our brave men who fell into his hands. Yet it is not our way to butcher defeated enemies like animals and feed them to false gods. Our Lord in Heaven would condemn us to Hell for such blasphemy against Him. The Lord Jesus commands us to forgive our enemies for their sins against us.

"So it is that I forgive King Cuauhtémoc. He has been poorly advised by his priests, and he behaves foolishly because he is so young. If he accepts my offer, I will spare his city. It shall not be destroyed. I will pardon all the Aztecs and there will be peace. All of this I offer if he will agree to personally surrender to me and order the fighting to cease. I give him my word as a Christian that he will be treated with honor and dignity."

The captives were escorted into Tenochtitlan and released. The next day, a force of Aztec warriors, led by several high-ranking commanders adorned with an array of gorgeous plumes denoting their rank, led an attack down the Iztapalapa causeway towards Xoloc. Although they attacked with maniacal rage, they were soon overwhelmed by a larger force of defending Texcocans led by King Ixtlilxochitl. In the course of the battle, Ixtlilxochitl himself captured the Aztecs' main commander. He insisted on bringing this commander to Cortez.

"Malinche!" Ixtlilxochitl called out as he entered Cortez's tent, still splattered with blood from the battle and holding the captured commander firmly in his grasp. "I bring you my brother Conacochtzin, who would still be King of Texcoco, not I, if he had not abandoned his people and become a traitor for the Aztecs."

Malinali could not help but see the great pride in Ixtlilxochitl's eyes as she translated his words. Cortez could see it as well. "Great Lord Ixtlilxochitl, is there no end to your nobility and heroism? I have been learning much of Texcoco history from Doña Marina, who tells me that your kingdom was blessed with a great ruler, your grandfather Nezahualcoyotl (*nesha-wal-coy-*

yottle).[223] He was not only a great warrior but a man of extreme wisdom, a *filósofo*[224] who worshipped not false gods as do the Aztecs but one single Unknown God, Ipalnemoani. On the roof of the temple of Texcoco, I am told, Nezahualcoyotl outlawed human sacrifices, replacing them with offerings of flowers and incense to the Unknown God.

"Great Lord Ixtlilxochitl, you are a king equal to your renowned grandfather. I believe that the Christian God was working through him and works now through you. I believe that your people through the ages will revere you as they do him."

The Texcocan king stood in silence and looked intently into Cortez's eyes. Then he said solemnly, "You have been taught well, Malinche." The slightest smile curved his lips. "My grandfather would have liked you."

He thrust his captive forward. "But now, Malinche, my brother has much to tell us."

Conacochtzin began speaking, Malinali translating.

"Malinche, our lord Cuauhtémoc received the message you sent to him. He called for all his nobles and commanders to discuss it. I was among them. Everything he had tried to defeat you had failed, he said. Should he surrender himself to you? he asked them. They grew very angry with him. Every man among them said no, the fighting must continue, that it would be better for all Aztecs to die, even the women and children, than to lose their kingdom to their enemies.

"These men were Tlacotzin, the *cihuacotl*,[225] Petlauhtzin, the *tlillancalqui*,[226] Coyoueuetzin, the *tlacochcalcatl*,[227] Temilotzin, the *tlacatectal*,[228] Auelitoctzin, the *ezhuahuancatl*,[229] and several high lords such as Tetlepanquetzatzin, king of Tacuba, and myself. We all agreed to die fighting you, Malinche, and our king then agreed with us."

Cortez grimaced and shook his head. "So how is it that you are still alive, captured by your brother? Your days of fighting are over, and soon they will be over for all Aztecs."

---

223 Lived 1402-1472.
224 A philosopher.
225 "Snake Woman," chief advisor to the king.
226 "Master of the House of Darkness," deputy advisor to the king.
227 "Blood-Shedder," commander of the army.
228 "Cutter of Men," deputy commander of the army.
229 "Chief of the Eagle and Prickly Pear," chief judge.

The next morning,[230] Cortez was up before dawn, telling Malinali he had a 'surprise' prepared for the Aztecs.

He and his men were back before noon. Bernal was with them, and he was smiling. "This was a good day, Doña Marina. Captain Cortez decided that a trick was in order. He and Gonzalo de Sandoval collected thirty horse-men and one hundred of us soldiers, along with a thousand Tlaxcalans, and we entered Tenochtitlan very early. Sandoval ordered most of our force to hide in some of the larger houses. Then Cortez, with a few horsemen, cross-bowmen, and musket-men, advanced deeper into the city. It was not long be-fore they were attacked by many Aztecs. Spotting our captain, and seeing that his force was so small, they began yelling, "Malinche! Malinche!" Quickly, great swarms of Aztec warriors appeared, all wanting to kill him.

"So Cortez retreated, slowly at first, then seeming to panic and run away. This put the Aztecs into a wild excitement, chasing after him. Racing past us, Cortez had two shots fired as a signal for us to come out of our hiding places to fall upon and destroy them. Not one of the Aztecs was left alive. The Tlaxcalans saw to that."

Cortez, however, was grim and incommunicative. "Too much death," was all he would say. For the next four days, she saw little of him. The fight-ing, he said, was continuous but, at last, much of Tenochtitlan – including the entire area between Xoloc and Tacuba – was cleared of the enemy. Then, as the sun broke upon the city the next morning,[231] they stepped out of their tent to see a plume of smoke rising in the distance.

"It is coming from the summit of the temple of Tlatelolco," Malinali observed. Cortez nodded. "Which means that Alvarado has taken both it and the Tlatelolco marketplace. Soon, my Lady, we shall be leaving here and moving there."

But not that day. Francisco de Montano and Gutierre de Badajoz, she learned, had fought their way to the top of the temple and placed Cortez's flag[232] there, but the fighting had been so fierce all around the marketplace that Alvarado had to call a retreat at sunset. The following morning, Cortez sent swarms of Tlaxcalans and Texcocans into the marketplace and beyond, to remove all of the Aztecs from it.

---

230 July 22.
231 July 27.
232 See Chapter 23.

She expected him to look triumphant when he returned to Xoloc that evening, but his mood was dark. "My officers and I rode around the entire square of Tlatelolco. Then I myself climbed the steps of the temple. When I reached the summit and the sacrificial platform, it was the blackest sight I have yet seen. A dozen heads of my countrymen were displayed amidst the gore and stench. When I had climbed down from that home of Satan, I fell to my knees and prayed to my God for the strength to resist a desire to wipe these evil Aztecs from the face of the earth, to resist the desire for bloody revenge."

He looked at her with a plea in his eyes. "I ask that you help me resist this desire, as well. I need your strength as I need your love."

She looked into his eyes. "This is still the one thing I understand the least, when it comes to the Christian faith – this demand for forgiveness of enemies. Always and everywhere, people wish to annihilate their enemies. Why are Christians so different?"

Cortez gave her a small, sad smile. "Why is Jesus Christ so different, is what you mean - why are His teachings so different from other religions' founders. For centuries, my land was ruled by *Moros*[233] from Africa who believed in a religion of hatred and destruction of *infielos*[234], because that is what the man who created their religion taught. After all of those centuries, it wasn't until my lifetime, when I was a young boy, that Spain finally rid itself of this pestilence."

Cortez looked pensive. "That was the great moment in our history. In the year of our Lord 1492, our king and queen, who had united all of Spain,[235] secured the surrender of the last Moro king, Boabdil.[236] Yet this triumph was without bloodshed. When Boabdil saw that the situation was truly hopeless, he surrendered his great city of Granada. It was done peacefully and he was treated with great respect. This is what I wish to do with Cuauhtémoc and the Aztecs but, as you say, they are crazy with *peyotl* or some sickness in their heads."

He focused again on her. "You ask why we are required to forgive our enemies. It is for our own salvation, my Lady, not our enemies'. Hatred, the

---

233   Moors, Moslems.
234   Infidels.
235   Ferdinand of Castille (1452-1516) and Isabella of Aragon (1451-1504).
236   1460-1533.

desire for destruction, is a poison, a spiritual poison that can kill one's soul. Jesus knew this. He knew that in forgiveness we save ourselves. It is a teaching that is hard for many to accept, too hard for many who call themselves Christians and truly believe they are."

He closed his eyes in pain. "*Why? Why?*" he cried out. "Why must this carnage continue? Why at the least doesn't Cuauhtémoc let the women and children leave Tenochtitlan? Must they all starve and die, too?"

She could see the depth of his anguish in his eyes when he opened them. "So many thousands of Aztecs have died in this siege - but it is as nothing to how many more will perish if I cannot persuade Cuauhtémoc to surrender. If he refuses again, I will not be able to hold back the Tlaxcalans, the Texcocans, and the hosts of other allies arriving in vast numbers every day now. At dawn, we shall leave here to establish new headquarters in Tlatelolco. It is from there we will reach out to Cuauhtémoc - we, Doña Marina, you and I, for I can only talk to him through you. We must convince him. We must."

Malinali had never looked upon Cortez with more love than in that moment. Many times, she had heard the men talking among themselves, telling stories of heroes of old, whom they called "knights," and who were said to be not just great warriors but also men who acted with great honor and nobility. Here was just such a knight, brought to life from those old stories…and he was looking at her – at *her* – with love and longing in his eyes.

They talked no more.

* * * * *

When they arrived in Tenochtitlan, Malinali was not prepared for what she saw. She was walking with Bernal and a large contingent of soldiers… but where was the city?

"Such a sad sight," said Bernal. "Our allies have been busy taking their revenge on the capital of their oppressor."

The only way to prevent the incessant attacks from roof tops, he explained to her, had been to bring those roofs to the ground. The only way to prevent the incessant attacks from canoes along the canals that wound through the island city like a maze had been to fill them up with rubble from the leveled buildings. Not a building nor a palace had been spared, and not a canal remained.

"Every house is a fortress, every street cut by canals," Bernal explained. "There was no choice except this. After the disaster at the *puente de dolor*, Captain Cortez decreed, 'To my shame and regret, I must command that our allies convert the water into dry land.' And that, Doña Marina, is why you are now walking across what used to be this great city and is now a pile of rubble – but you are walking safe and unmolested."

When she entered the city's great central square, she stood frozen in shock. On one side loomed the huge temple with its twin towers for sacrifices to Texcatlipoca and Huitzilopochtli, and the blood-encrusted Jade Steps leading up to them. The area was now devoid of priests, abandoned and empty, as was the entire square. Every single great building around the square, save for the stone temple itself, was gone.

The walls surrounding the enormous square[237] were gone, the palace of Tillancalqui, the two palaces of Montezuma, the palace of Axayacatl where they had stayed the year before, the children's prison where children were kept for sacrifice to Tlaloc, the victim's kitchen where the priests cooked the arms and legs of victims for meals for the nobles, the huge *tzompantli* containing so many thousands of victims' skulls[238] -- all vanished, nothing left but bare ground with scattered bits of rubble.

"With each passing day," Bernal continued, "more allies from more cities and kingdoms arrive, wishing to participate in the demolition of a city that once was a wonder of the world - as you can see..."

She certainly could see for, though the square was empty of buildings, it swarmed with people busily carrying away rubble with which to fill in the remaining canals. A contingent of Tlaxcalan warriors approached, led by Chief Chichimecatecle, who announced that he would personally escort her to Cortez in Tlatelolco.

"The Aztecs are dying in numbers we cannot count every day now, dying of hunger. They have eaten all the rats and lizards until there are no more, even of them," he told her as they walked.

"Is this the fate for the Aztecs that you wished for?" she asked the chief.

He stared straight ahead and was silent for a long moment before replying, "For the women and children - some of whom, when they die, are being

---

237   The temple square of Tenochtitlan was about 1,000 feet on each side.
238   The skull rack below the sacrificial temple contained some 60,000 victims' skulls.

eaten - no. As for the men, my heart feels nothing. I only wish for this accursed place to be gone, so that my people's dream of a Tlaxcala free of it will be true."

He breathed deeply. "And it soon shall be true, thanks to Malinche..." He looked at her, straight into her eyes. "...and to you."

Malinali realized what a great compliment he was paying her, and she held his gaze and slightly nodded her head in respectful acknowledgement.

As they walked through the destroyed city, she was reminded of its enormous size[239] -- and was startled to find that she could walk straight across it without any Aztec threat. The almost total control Cortez now had over the city was evident when she was escorted behind the market square of Tlatelolco, on the opposite side of the Tacuba causeway, and taken to a large home that she learned had belonged to an Aztec noble named Atzauatzin. On the spacious roof of this home, Cortez had established his headquarters in a large tent of red cloth. Only his eyes told her that he was happy to see her, for he did not smile.

Next to him was Pedro de Alvarado, along with several skeletal figures so emaciated that it took her a moment to realize they were Aztec nobles. "They came to us, crying for 'Malinche,' Doña Marina," Alvarado informed her. "We have waited for you."

There were such nightmares in their eyes she had to force herself to look at them. "You are the children of the Sun!" one of them called out, looking wildly at Cortez. "But the Sun is swift, it can go across the earth in a single day! Why, then, do you delay so long in putting an end to our miseries? We wish you to kill us at once, so that we may go to our god Huitzilopochtli, who waits for us in heaven!"

Cortez stared out at the ruined city and the lake beyond. After some time, he began to speak. "When I first looked at this city spread below me, it was in the company of Lord Montezuma, from the top of the Great Temple. It was a city of such beauty, with its magnificent buildings, laced with canals, flower gardens and bright trees too numerous to count, that I wept. Never before had I seen anything so beautiful. Now, when I look upon this city, I am weeping once more."

He turned to face the starving creatures, and Malinali noticed that, al-

---

239   Tenochtitlan covered an area of some five square miles, with over a quarter-million inhabitants.

though there was a pretended sternness in his voice, there was nothing but sadness in his eyes.

"It was not just the beauty of your city that made me weep, standing there with Montezuma," he continued. "It was knowing that this incredible beauty was built on a foundation of evil and blood. As the Son of God, Jesus Christ, is my witness, I did not wish to destroy this city. I wished only to destroy the evil that infected it like a horrible disease, a disease of the soul."

He stepped forward to look at them intently. *"I do not want you to die! I want your gods to die!"*

Then he pointed at the Great Temple of Tenochtitlan, soaring in the distance. "Look! The building remains but its gods are dead and gone, and they are never coming back." He swept his arm in an arc over the ruined city. "Look! Your city is destroyed. Your people are eating worms and insects. They are dying in such multitudes that the stench of their decaying bodies is overwhelming, even where we stand here. And why? *Why?* Because you continued to believe in evil gods, rather than live in peace with your neighbors. Look again! It is your evil gods that have done this to you - not me! I do not want you to die. I want you to *live* - live in peace with your neighbors, instead of believing that your evil gods wish you to conquer them and sacrifice them to your bloody Huitzilopochtli."

Cortez looked at Malinali imploringly. "Doña Marina, I beg you to make them understand that *Huitzilopochtli is dead*, not waiting for them in heaven. Only the One True God can save them, and for that they must live, live and ask for His forgiveness."

But when she tried to convey that message, all she got in return were expressions of terrified bewilderment.

"They are too hungry to think," Cortez concluded. "Let us feed them and, when their bellies are full, persuade them to go to Cuauhtémoc. Have them tell Cuauhtémoc that I do not know why he will not confer with me to arrange an end to all this death, when I could crush him and all his people in an hour if I desired. I give my Christian word that he will be treated with every respect and that we will confer in complete safety."

As the Aztec nobles ate ravenously, she talked with them as soothingly as she could. She pointed to the sun. "You say that Malinche is the child of the Sun and, yes, he could indeed kill Cuauhtémoc and all Aztecs before the Sun's journey ends on this day. Think! The only reason he will not is because he does not want to. He wants peace, not death. Let us do this together. You go to Cuauhtémoc and persuade him to meet with Malinche. Then, from that meeting, where I will be the one who talks between them, there will come new life for the Aztecs. I ask you to live for this, not to die."

Full of food and cacao, they nodded in agreement.

"You must return as soon as you are able, with Cuauhtémoc's answer," she reminded them. "You now carry the fate of your people in your hands."

After the nobles left, she stood with Cortez, facing east. They were in a section called Amaxac, in the northeastern corner of the city. Most all of the huge city lay behind them and to their right. Only this small portion lay in front, bounded on two sides by the lake.

"All that is left of the Aztec people are stuffed into there," he told her. "Tens and tens of thousands alive, and even more dead. If you go in there, you cannot take a step without treading upon a dead body. It is a Hell on Earth, more terrible than I could have imagined." He looked at her in pain. "I do not think your father meant for a dream like this."

All she could do was whisper, "No."

As they waited, hoping for the return of the nobles, Cortez issued a series of orders to his officers. Alvarado was to hold himself in readiness for an assault, and Sandoval was to ready the brigantines for a cannonade upon the houses nearest the water.

Hours passed and it was mid-afternoon before two of the nobles reappeared. "The Great Lord Cuauhtémoc will meet with Malinche," was the message they bore. "Tomorrow, when the sun is highest in the sky, in the market square of Tlatelolco."

Cortez and everyone else breathed a sigh of relief. Immediately, he sent word for all of his officers to stand down and withdraw their forces. The next morning, elaborate preparations were made. A stone platform in the square was covered with mats and carpets. A banquet of delectable food was laid out. Cortez and his officers arrayed themselves in their finest polished armor and waited, erect on their horses.

Five Aztecs nobles came…but no Cuauhtémoc. The nobles prostrated themselves in front of Cortez and apologized, saying that Cuauhtémoc could not come because he was very sick. Cortez refused to show any disappointment, and instead said to Malinali, "Doña Marina, tell these gentlemen that they are welcome as our guests. Tell them please to enjoy all that has been prepared for them."

The nobles fell upon the feast with such hungry ferocity that the Spaniards averted their eyes. When they had finished, Cortez ordered more food brought, wrapped in bundles. "Please take these provisions with you, and return for more when you want. Also, please convey to Lord Cuauhtémoc my hope that his health will soon return. I have instructed my soldiers to withdraw from their positions. There will be no attack from us while he recovers. When his sickness is over, I will welcome him as I have you – welcome him as a brother with whom I wish to live in peace."

After the Aztecs left, however, Cortez turned to his officers on horseback. "This Cuauhtémoc is just as devious and untrustworthy as Montezuma. Gentlemen, everyone is to be on guard, but on no account are they to provoke any attack. We shall give Cuauhtémoc several days to consider his situation. I shall return to Xoloc. The stench of death arising from below that roof in Amaxac is intolerable."

As they passed through the Great Square of Tenochtitlan on their way to Xoloc, Malinali saw that it was filled with thousands of Tlaxcalan, Texcocan, and other allies' warriors. "Look at their eyes," Bernal said as he walked with her. "They have the eyes of wolves, eager and ready to tear the Aztecs apart. They are waiting here, waiting for the final kill," he said, and Malinali shuddered.

She shuddered in a different way when at last she was in Cortez's arms that night. "I wanted you far away from that awful place," he told her. "Here we can be at peace for the next several days. Let us put aside all of the horrors we have seen, and use these days to enjoy our love."

Those days were complete bliss. Malinali not only thought she was living among the clouds of heaven, but that she was as light as a cloud herself, or a golden ray of sunlight shining through them. Cortez was like a thunderbolt, overwhelming her with his passion, indefatigable, never-ending. During all of the time they had been together since that first time in Zautla, she had used a preparation of herbs taught to her by her grandmother, Ciuacoatl, so as not to be with child. Dare she stop doing so now? Yes, she decided. She prayed to the Holy Mother for the blessing and honor of Cortez's child.

She had never seen Cortez happier. "The rest of the world does not exist," he said. "Only you." Only they existed, for day after day after day after...

Then it ended. A messenger arrived, saying that a group of Aztecs nobles had appeared in Tlatelolco, asking for 'Malinche.'

As Cortez began putting on his armor, he kissed her gently and said, "Now, at last, we shall see how this finishes."

* * * * *

They arrived in Tlatelolco by mid-day. "Lord Cuauhtémoc wishes to meet with Malinche," the nobles said, "but it is already late in the day. He will come tomorrow."

Malinali was so incredulous she didn't translate their words. She pointed to the sky. "The sun is still high. It is not late. Your Lord must come now," she argued.

They shook their heads. "Tomorrow," was all they would say, and left.

On the next day, a banquet was laid out in the square, as before. The nobles came, but no Cuauhtémoc. "Our Lord has decided he will not meet with Malinche," they said. "We cannot discuss this further."

Cortez remained cordial. "He will surely come to see me, as he understands how well you are being treated, and sees how you come and go unharmed. He has nothing to fear from meeting me, and it is the only way to cease this bloodshed. Please go to him and ask him to reconsider. Think of all of the lives of your people that may be saved if you convince him."

Nodding in agreement, they departed.

Early the following morning, the nobles arrived at the home in Amaxac and were escorted to the rooftop, where they announced that Cuauhtémoc would indeed meet Malinche at noon in the Tlatelolco market square. The preparations were made yet again, and noon found Cortez astride his horse, along with several officers, with Malinali standing by.

No one came – no nobles, no messengers, no Cuauhtémoc. Three hours passed, without a word or a person from the Aztecs. Cortez was infuriated.

Then a cavalryman galloped into the square. "Captain Cortez, the Aztecs are mounting an attack!"

Immediately, Sandoval was dispatched to take charge of the brigantines, while Alvarado and Cristobal de Olid were sent to prepare their forces. Cortez then had King Ixtlilxochitl and Chief Chichimecatecle brought to him. "Doña Marina, please instruct these gentlemen to assemble their warriors for battle - and to order their warriors that under no circumstances are they to do harm to women and children, the old, the weak, or the sick. If any of their warriors does this, my soldiers will kill him. Do they understand?"

Malinali gained their agreement, and soon the square was filled with thousands and more thousands of warriors in gaudy warpaint and bright feathers, Spaniard soldiers and horsemen. The horses reared and neighed, as if sensing what was about to happen.

A heavy guard escorted Malinali to the rooftop headquarters. From there, she watched as Cortez led the forces into the warren of Amaxac's narrow streets. A vast tumult of war cries erupted from the Aztecs, who charged down the streets to attack them, as clouds of arrows, darts, and stones were fired and cast from the rooftops. The musket-men began shooting, along with the crossbowmen, and Malinali could hear the successive booms of the canons on the brigantines in the watery distance.

Then came the screams.

She knew that they were not the yells of men, but the shrieks of women - and children. She knew what must be happening. The Spaniards were unable to control their allies, who were killing any Aztecs they could find, old, young, sick, woman, baby, it did not matter. Buildings were being torched, first a few, then hundreds, and soon they were crashing in burning ruins and clouds of dust and smoke.

This was not a battle, but a slaughter, the Aztecs demented to have started it, and too starved and weak to oppose it. Wave after wave of allies poured into Amaxac like an immense storm of murderous fury.

Malinali sank to her knees. She was witnessing the final destruction of the Aztecs, in a maelstrom of blood and fire and smoke and vengeful hate. "*Tahtli! Tahtli!*" she called out to her father, "I did not mean for your dream to come true like this!"

And yet her dream came true, on that day[240], right before her. She couldn't take her eyes off it. Finally, she saw the Spaniards march out, and the allies with them When Cortez returned to the rooftop, he took off his

---

240   August 12, 1521.

blood-splattered armor and sat in silence. At last, he said, "Never did I see so pitiless a race as the people of this land, or anything wearing the form of man so destitute of humanity."

He looked up at her. "Let us return to Xoloc. Tenochtitlan is an *osario*."[241]

* * * * *

That night, neither of them wanted to celebrate what had happened with love-making. All they wanted was to hold each other tightly in silence. But it was different in the camp. All along the causeway, there were bonfires, laughing and singing was heard everywhere.

"The men are so happy," Malinali noted.

"Not over the horror of today," Cortez advised. "Over the knowledge that this war is over, and that they have been victorious."

They arose at dawn to make their way to Tlatelolco. Alvarado, Sandoval, Olid, Ixtlilxochitl, and Chichimecatecle were waiting. Cortez addressed them, with Malinali translating for the chiefs. "Gentlemen, it is on this day, the 13th day of August in the Year of Our Lord One Thousand Five Hundred Twenty One, that we achieve victory and extinguish the Aztec Empire.

"Our goal today is not, however, to butcher as many Aztecs as possible." He cast a glance towards the two chiefs to make sure they knew he was talking about them. "Rather, it is to capture Cuauhtémoc alive. If we do that, this war is over. Señor de Sandoval, instruct your brigantines to be on their most careful watch for fleeing canoes. Our quarry may be among them. He must not escape to lead a rebellion against us elsewhere. Señores de Alvarado and de Olid, the purpose of your forces is to push the Aztecs towards the water, to capture those who surrender and to see that they are not killed. By pushing and trapping them, we can force the leaders and Cuauhtémoc himself into canoes, where we can seize them."

He turned to the two chiefs. "Lords Ixtlilxochitl and Chichimecatecle, I know that your men were beyond your control yesterday, and for that I do not blame you. But I do not expect that to happen again today."

---

241 A charnel-house. Estimates are that 40,000 Aztecs were killed in this single battle, upwards of 150,000 during the entire Siege of Tenochtitlan.

Reluctantly, they nodded.

At that moment, a delegation of Aztecs appeared, led by a man who was obviously of high rank.

Malinali spoke to him, then announced, "This is the *cihuacoatl*, commander of the Aztec army."

Cortez gave him a courtly bow. "Sir, it is you above all, save for Cuauhtémoc himself, whom I wish to meet. You and I are both leaders of armies. It is our life's work. Surely you know that you must surrender to us, rather than have what remains of your army destroyed. Let us talk together and come to an understanding of peace between us."

Malinali could see that the Aztec was a defeated man who could not keep the sadness and disappointment from his face. "Malinche! How I wish for this!" he replied. "Yet my king, Cuauhtémoc, forbids it."

Now disappointment was on Cortez's face. "Surely, your king will not stand by and see your people perish, when we can so easily save them. I beg you to go and bring him to me so that we can end this war."

"Lord Cuauhtémoc sent me here to tell you this – that he is ready to die where he is, and will never meet with you."

Cortez sighed. "*He* can die, but why must he have his people die with him? It is his belief in evil false gods that is the cause of this. So I have no choice."

In a tone of deep resignation, the *cihuacoatl* replied, "It is for you to work your will."

Cortez stiffened in his saddle. "Go, then, and prepare your people and your king for the end. Their hour has come."

As the *cihuacoatl* left, Cortez said to his commanders, "Nonetheless, let us wait a while. I do not want a repeat of yesterday. Let us give time for Cuauhtémoc to try his escape. And that means, Señor de Sandoval, that you and your men must be extremely vigilant."

The commanders left to organize their forces, while Cortez and Malinali went to the rooftop headquarters. The hours went by until by noon, when Cortez decided he could wait no longer. He directed Francisco Verdugo to give the signal, then watched as Alvarado's and Olid's forces entered Amaxac, which seemed deserted except for the uncountable number of Aztec corpses lying amid the shattered, smoldering rubble of what had once been buildings.

Cortez had assigned Luis Marin to keep him informed. In less than an hour, Marin ran back to report, "Countless men and women have come to us to surrender. They look like skeletons, wearing filthy rags. It is beyond our men's understanding how they could have endured such misery. We are gathering up as many of them as possible and guiding them to a safe area. Most of the Aztecs have been pushed near to the water, where some have jumped in and drowned. We are doing our best to prevent the allies from killing as before, but one group of Aztecs fired some arrows and darts, and our allies destroyed them. Many canoes are being filled with people who appear to be of high rank, and they have begun paddling across the lake."

Everyone on the rooftop strained their eyes to look out on the lake, where several brigantines were engaged in running down canoes and overturning them. Malinali pointed to three very large canoes racing to get away. A brigantine under sail, aided by a good wind, was closing with them. The brigantine pulled alongside one of the canoes and, after some moments, it looked as if the Aztecs on the canoe boarded the ship.

A moment later, the ship's canon boomed in triumph.

"He is ours," concluded Cortez. "It is done."

This was confirmed when they saw the other canoes abandon their flight, turning so that canoes and brigantines alike were making their way back.

Cortez sent Francisco Verdugo and Luis Marin to bring Cuauhtémoc before him.

They returned sooner than expected. "Captain, we have a difficulty," they reported. "Cuauhtémoc has indeed been captured, by a brigantine commanded by Garci Holguin. Señor Holguin wished to bring his captive to you, but then Gonzalo de Sandoval, as commander of the entire fleet, demanded that Señor Holguin surrender the captive to him, wanting the honor of the capture to be his. What shall we do, Captain?"

Cortez shook his head with a weary smile, then held his hands up in mock despair. "Bring them all to me," he ordered.

The first to enter was Cuauhtémoc, erect, tall, and thin, in an elaborately embroidered cotton robe, wearing a large gold headband adorned with a crest of feathers. Malinali was surprised to see that he was so young, not much older than she[242]. Behind him came Sandoval and Garci Holguin.

---

242   Malinali was born in 1500, Cuauhtémoc in 1496.

"Doña Marina, please bid our guest a welcome while I talk briefly to my officers," Cortez requested. She did so, and the two of them stood aside as Cortez called out, "Gentlemen! Your dispute reminds me of a story. You know where I am from, Medellin in Extremadura[243]. It was founded before the time of Christ by a Roman General named Metellus, so my city was first called Metellium. His father was also a general, and was tasked to put down a rebellion against Rome in the kingdom of Numidia[244].

"The leader of this rebellion was a very dangerous man named Jugurtha[245]. The person who captured Jugurtha would be a great hero to Rome. Two commanders claimed the prize, Sulla[246] and Marius[247]. Metellus settled the dispute by asking the Roman Senate to decide. I shall settle the dispute between you - for I know what it is about - by asking His Majesty Emperor Don Carlos to decide which – or both – of you shall incorporate the capture of the great Aztec lord into your coat-of-arms. Both of you have done great deeds today, and both of you should be honored and memorialized. Please do not let your dispute soil this moment of history."

After a few stunned blinks of their eyes, Sandoval and Garci Holguin turned and bowed to each other. "Our dispute is over," they told Cortez.

Cortez turned to a puzzled Cuauhtémoc and a bemused Malinali. "Please convey my apologies, Doña Marina. Tell Lord Cuauhtémoc that he is my welcome guest."

When she did so, Cuauhtémoc replied, "Malinche! I have done all that I could to protect my country from you. But I have failed. So I ask that you end my life with the long knife you carry on your hip. I only ask, further, that you see that my wife and family come to no harm."

"Great Lord Cuauhtémoc," Cortez replied, "I do not wish to kill you and shall not. I wish to treat you with the respect and dignity you deserve. You defended your city with great courage. My regret is that you refused to make peace with me, as I so often begged you to do, before your great city was destroyed. Now I suggest that you rest. You should fear nothing among us. Your wife and family will be brought to you. Later, we shall discuss how the Aztec

---

243   See Chapter 23.
244   Roughly present-day northern Algeria along the Mediterranean coast.
245   160-104 B.C.
246   Lucius Cornelius Sulla 138-78 B.C
247   Gaius Marius 157-86 B.C.

people can best live in peace with their neighbors."

He turned to Verdugo and Marin. "Please see that Lord Cuauhtémoc and his family are placed in comfort and security, and are extended every courtesy," he instructed. He turned to Garci Holguin. "Señor Holguin, my warmest congratulations on your great feat. Today, Señor, your life has become a part of history." He then looked affectionately at Sandoval. "Gonzalo, my trusted friend. I entrust the Aztec ruler into your hands. See that he is respectfully cared for and, more importantly, very well guarded."

Then Cortez was alone with Malinali on the rooftop.

They gazed out upon the vast smoldering wreck of a once-great city. "This has been a horror, one which I did not want. Yet this is what a whirlwind does," Cortez said quietly, putting his arm around her. "Do you remember the day we first entered this city, the day I first met Montezuma?[248] That morning, we talked of the fear of the Aztecs that I was coming as the whirlwind of Quetzacoatl, a whirlwind that would bring 'the disembowelment of the world.' And I told you of the Bible story of the prophet Hosea, who lived thousands of years ago, but whose warning now seems directed at the Aztecs:

"For they have sown the wind, and they shall reap the whirlwind: the grain shall have no stalk; the bud shall yield no meal: and if it does, strangers shall swallow it up.[249]

"The Aztecs sowed this whirlwind with their evil. The One True God sent us as the whirlwind which the Aztecs must reap, for we are the strangers who must swallow up their evil. Now that evil is gone. Too many people have died horribly here. But they died less horribly than all the countless thousands, year after year after year for generations, whose hearts were cut out of their living bodies in sacrifice to Satan – and those countless thousands who would have been sacrificed had we not brought the whirlwind, and who now shall live for generations to come. The price for their lives, that which you see before you, had to be paid."

He looked into her eyes. "My dearest, just as God sent me here as this whirlwind, just as God entrusted your father's dream to him, so God sent you to me. Without you, I could not have succeeded. It is thanks to you that this land is liberated from Aztec evil and can now be free."

---

248   November 8, 1519. See Chapter 23.
249   Hosea 8:7.

Chapter Thirty Four

LA MALINCHE

alinali sat on the roof of her home, looking out serenely upon the sunlit waters of Lake Texcoco. Cortez had had the home built for her, here in Coyoacan, next to the palace of the former King of Coyoacan that he was using as his headquarters as he managed the growing empire of New Spain.

It was cool here, with the breeze coming off the lake, and the shade of the awnings and all the plants Cortez had brought up to the roof to make it a garden. It was peaceful and quiet - which was what she appreciated the most.

Almost a year had passed since the fall of Tenochtitlan, the capture of Cuauhtémoc, and the death of the Aztec Empire. As she looked back upon all that had happened since that day which the Spaniards called August 13[250], it seemed like just a day before, yet so long ago.

She remembered the riot of celebration that night at the palace in Tlatelolco, with all the Spaniard soldiers and Tlaxcalan warriors drinking quantities of wine and pulque, and Cortez stealing her away to their bedchamber, saying that it was with her alone that he wished to celebrate.

She remembered all the tears she had shed in the following days, tears of relief and tears of thanks to the Virgin Mary for being the instrument of Her will that her father's dream had come true. *"Tahtli! Tahtli!"* she had called out so many times, sure that his soul was watching over her with pride.

Pride. Was that what she felt for herself? She wasn't sure. The emotion she felt was gratitude, more than pride. She was overwhelmed by gratitude

---

250   1521. It is now mid-June, 1522.

that the Lord Jesus and His Mother had chosen her to be Their instrument in liberating her land from Aztec evil.

Why had she been chosen? She did not know. What she did know was that she should listen to the whispering voice in her head telling her not to be arrogant and boastful, not to feel superior to others, not to think that she ought to be worshipped - especially because she was. That voice was her father's.

She remembered hearing the voice so loudly when Chief Chichimecatecle and King Ixtlilxochitl, the great commanders of the Tlaxcalan and Texcocan armies, came to see her shortly after Tenochtitlan's fall. The look in their eyes had been far more than one of admiration - it was reverential.

She had been startled and speechless when they bowed deeply before her, reaching out to press the hem of her dress - the same simple cotton *huipil* she had always worn - against their foreheads in supplication.

"*La Malinche.*" That was how they addressed her, pronouncing the name as if it were a title of royalty. Her brow furrowed in puzzlement as she waited for an explanation.

"You do not know?" Chichimecatecle asked. "Surely you know that *El Capitán* has announced he no longer wishes to be addressed as 'Malinche,' but by his true name. He is Captain Hernando Cortez." He paused, smiling with satisfaction as he glanced at Ixtlilxochitl. "Although he has told us that, as friends and brothers, we should call him Don Hernando."

Of course she knew this - she had translated Cortez's words to them. She waited for them to continue. "And you know that *Malinche* means 'Master of Malina,' master of you, for we could only talk to him through you," said King Ixtlilxochitl.

She nodded, recalling the twists of her name. After her mother sold her into slavery, she was no longer Princess Malinali; she was only Malina, a slave girl sold to the Mayans. When she was given to the Spaniards, she was christened Doña Marina, as the Spaniards mistook the 'l' for an 'r'. When the Aztecs and other Nahuatl-speakers heard 'Marina,' they changed the 'r' back to the 'l'. Whenever they spoke to her directly by name, they would call her Doña Malina. But what was happening now?

Ixtlilxochitl continued. "This is why all the peoples of this land, the Tlaxcalans, the Texcocans, and all others now call Malinche *El Capitán*, having learned a word or two of Spanish. And it is why they are now calling you *La Malinche*, for it is you, now, who is 'Master of Malina.' You are *master of yourself*. It is their way of honoring you for achieving their liberation. All in this land know that El Capitán declared, '*After God, we owe this great victory to Doña Marina.*'[251] So it is that we have come to honor you... La Malinche."

Malinali felt faint. Her knees began to buckle, and her eyes lost their focus. *I must not do this,* she ordered herself, forcing her body to stand erect, forcing her mind to focus on Chief Chichimecatecle as he stepped forward.

"Soon they will be coming, La Malinche. In multitudes, people from every kingdom in this land will come to see for themselves the great lady, to kiss the hem of your *huipil* and ask for your blessing, to thank you for liberating them from the curse of the Aztecs. You must prepare yourself for this. Prepare yourself for their worship of you. In all of their names, we ask that you accept their worship, for it is truly sincere. Your blessing will mean the world to them."

She could stand no longer. "I... I must sit down," she told them, and they gently helped her to a couch.

"We shall leave you now," Chichimecatecle said quietly. "But please allow me to tell you one more thing. It is the greatest wish and prayer of our King Xicotencatl, that you come to Tlaxcala. It is the wish of all Tlaxcalans to see you in their land. Even now, Tlaxcalans no longer call the highest mountain in Tlaxcala by its ancient name, *Matlalcueye*[252]. They have given the mountain they worship a new name: *La Malinche*[253]."

"And the best way to Tlaxcala," King Ixtlilxochitl told her with a soft smile, "is by crossing the lake to Texcoco, where all our people wish to welcome you. The Texcocan women will perform for you a sacred dance of thanks and liberation which they call the *La Malinche Dance*."

They again bowed to her and left.

She did not know how long she had remained in a state of dazed confusion over what she had been told before she heard someone cough softly to announce his presence. It was Bernal. His smile spread sunshine into her heart. "So, you have been told what you have become," he said. "But don't

---

251 Cortez stated this in his Third Letter to Emperor Charles V, dated May 15, 1522.
252 The goddess who wears a jade skirt.
253 This 14,632' volcano with a ring of green forest around its lower slopes bears the name of La Malinche to this day.

expect me to touch the hem of your dress to my forehead."

They both laughed themselves silly. "Thank you, Bernal. It feels so good to laugh after... after learning..." Her voice trailed off.

"After learning who you are now?" he asked. His voice became serious. "Doña Marina, I have always known that you were a great lady. Now all of the people of New Spain know it also. You were born and raised to be a queen, a queen who became a slave, who as a slave liberated not only herself but everyone in this land. You have become much more than a queen, you are a *savior*. This is your destiny, Doña Marina. Please accept it. This is the destiny that God has willed for you."

She looked at him in wonder, and with a slight nod of her head acknowledged his words. "Thank you, Bernal. And thank you for being such a good friend."

"And so shall I always be," he replied. They talked for a while, reminiscing about what they had experienced. Then, flashing another broad smile, which she returned, he bowed and left.

The next day, just as she had been warned, supplicants came from every kingdom, near and far. She set aside a small room on the ground floor, where she would stand to greet them as they were ushered in, one by one. There were men and women, although more of the latter. Rarely did they speak, maintaining a reverential silence as they bowed almost to the ground and touched the hem of her *huipil* to their forehead.

Many of the women burst into deep tears at the sight of her, some repeatedly calling out "*La Malinche! La Malinche! La Malinche!*" None asked for anything, no prayer to be answered, no wish or favor to be granted. They simply came to be in her presence, to set their eyes upon her, to acknowledge what she had done for them.

Day after day, week after week, they came. When she had to restrict the time the worshippers could come to a few hours in the morning, they camped outside the home until the next day. Everywhere she went, she drew huge crowds. Cortez became concerned for her health and safety - and even more so when she told him a secret.

She had to be sure, and when she was, the time had to be special. She had seen little of Cortez in the three months since the fall of Tenochtitlan, as he was always riding off to inspect another corner of expanding New Spain. So when he came home on this night, she had everything prepared - a wonderful meal, good wine, a candlelit bedchamber.

She enjoyed listening to him regale her with stories about his travels during dinner, but he, being Cortez, noticed that she was looking at him differently. "You have something to tell me, my love," he said, not as a question but as an observation.

She stood up, walked around the table to him, placed his hand upon her abdomen, looked into his eyes, and said softly, "You are going to be a father."

Cortez stared down at where his hand rested, then bolted to his feet and embraced her. "You have given me an empire - and now you give me a son!" he exclaimed. "Oh, my Lady, my Lady - you are truly a gift from God."

She caressed his beard and whispered into his ear, "It could be a girl, you know."

He snapped his head back to look at her. "Yes... I suppose it could be. If so, I shall rejoice all the same!" The look in his eyes shifted. "Speaking of rejoicing..." They both glanced toward the bedchamber. Malinali took his hand and led him into it.

* * * * *

The months that followed were the most blissful of her life. Cortez ceased his constant exploration of the limits of the constantly growing New Spain. Instead, he focused on governing from his headquarters next to their home, and spent as much time with her as possible. He selected a young officer, Juan Jaramillo, the one whom he had assigned to guard her "with your life" during the horrific *La Noche Triste,* to be her personal bodyguard and to notify him if she needed anything at any time.

When she accepted invitations to visit Texcoco and Tlaxcala, she was rowed across Lake Texcoco in a canoe so elaborate that it was worthy of Montezuma, and greeted with delirious enthusiasm by thousands of Texcocans. King Ixtlilxochitl held her hand as they stood on the balcony of the king's palace and watched the central plaza below, filled with elaborately-costumed dancers performing La Malinche dances in her honor.

The king set aside a room in the palace where her worshippers could come to pay her homage. They came for days.

Then it was on to Tlaxcala, carried there on a litter festooned with quetzal feathers, and accompanied by Chief Chichimecatecle and hundreds of his warriors. Old King Xicotencatl was there to greet her upon her arrival, and her entrance into the city was a mass celebration. Yet it was very different from the one she received in Texcoco.

In Texcoco, it had been wildly tumultuous. In Tlaxcala, it was quietly reverential. The streets and rooftops of both were packed with people wanting to see her, but in Texcoco everyone was noisily cheering, blowing on conch shell trumpets, and pounding on drums - while in Tlaxcala, everyone was in a state of silent awe. Without a sound, she was showered with flower petals, the path strewn with them everywhere she went.

The old king brought her to stand with him in the middle of the central plaza, into which every Tlaxcalan in the city seemed to be squeezed. In a voice as loud as his age could muster, he addressed his people. "For generations, the Tlaxcalan people fought for their freedom and refused to submit to Aztec evil. We lived in poverty because we would rather be poor and free than be wealthy slaves. We thought this struggle would be endless, that we and our children and our children's children would have to suffer this poverty and fight forever, because the Aztec might was so enormous.

"The best we could hope for, we thought, was to continue to fight, endlessly, so that we might preserve our little island of Tlaxcalan freedom in a huge swamp of Aztec tyranny. None of us ever dreamed that the Aztecs themselves could be defeated, that their evil rule could be swept away with the wind, that the day would come when the Aztecs themselves would be no more.

"No one dared to have that dream - except the lady who stands before you. It is her dream that has brought us liberty. It is her dream that made it possible for El Capitán Cortez to rid this entire land of the Aztecs forever. We owe the freedom that we fought so long for and have today to this lady, to La Malinche."

Malinali looked at the old king and saw tears streaming down his face. She felt tears streaming down her face, as well. The huge crowd in front of her remained silent and motionless. Then one among them haltingly stepped forward to whisper "La Malinche," toss a flower at her feet and vanish back into the crowd. Then another, and another, one by one they came to whisper her new name and pay her homage with a flower.

She stood still as the flowers piled up front of her in the thousands. When the last flower was placed, she clutched the crucifix on her necklace, closed her eyes, and gave thanks to her father and the Virgin Mary for this moment. She opened her eyes to look with gratitude and love into the eyes of those before her. She bowed gently to them, then turned with King Xicotencatl to walk with him into the palace of Tlaxcala.

* * * * *

The memory of that moment was so vivid that it took a sudden pain to jolt her out of it – a sudden and sharply painful tightening in her abdomen that lasted for a few seconds, then stopped. She waited. When nothing more happened, she decided to not be alarmed, and continue enjoying the view of Lake Texcoco from her rooftop garden.

She had drifted off into a half-dozing reverie, looking out onto the sheet of cobalt blue, when she felt another jolt of tightening. She called for her guard, Juan Jaramillo. "Señor Jaramillo, please ask the doctor that Captain Cortez has provided for me to come," she requested. "Then please inform Captain Cortez that I think..." Before she could complete the sentence, he bowed and ran out of the room.

By the time the doctor and his assistants had arrived, the jolts were coming more frequently, every ten minutes or so. She was helped down to the bedchamber. By the time Cortez arrived, the jolts were every two minutes. Between jolts, Malinali could not help laughing at how nervous Cortez was. She called him *Capitán Confundido*[254], and everyone smiled - except El Capitán, who look even more bewildered. The doctor told him he must wait outside.

It was a boy, and perfectly healthy. After being assured by the doctor that Doña Marina was just as healthy as her baby, Cortez looked down upon her cradling her newborn and said, "I have never known such happiness."

"Nor have I," was Malinali's response.

"What shall be his name?" he asked her.

"Martín, after your father," she replied.

---

254 Captain Confused.

Cortez closed his eyes and said, "My happiness is now complete."

* * * * *

Their happiness lasted for little more than a month. It was the day of a big *fiesta* celebrating the patron saint of Spain, Santiago[255]. Malinali was nursing little Martín on her rooftop garden. Her guard, Juan Jaramillo, informed her that Cortez would soon be arriving. *I must get ready to attend the fiesta,* she thought.

But when Cortez appeared, she knew something was very wrong. His face was flushed as red as a tomato, his breathing was fast and shallow, and there was tragedy in his eyes.

He stood looking down upon her and Martín for a moment, then knelt beside her. "My love, I..." he began, then covered his eyes. When he took his hand away, she saw what she had never imagined she would see: Cortez was crying.

She held his hand. "Whatever is wrong, I am with you," she consoled. "Nothing can come between us."

He looked straight at her as his tears continued. "Something has."

She looked at him blankly.

"Years ago, in Cuba, I was forced to marry a young woman. Bernal, I believe, told you the circumstances."[256]

She nodded.

"Her name was Catalina. Her health was always frail. She almost died in childbirth - and the baby was stillborn. That broke her health and her spirit. She retreated from me and the world. I petitioned the Church for an annulment of marriage. But her family is very powerful in Cuba and Spain, and the annulment was denied. I had no more future in Cuba, which is why I came here for a new life."

He looked at her in torment. "That is what I have found with you. I was sure that, given what I have accomplished here, given my creation of New Spain, I would be granted the annulment and then we could... we could..." He could not complete the words.

---

255 St. James, Iago being James in Spanish. July 25, 1522.
256 Catalina Suarez in 1514. The story is told in Chapter 20, "The Legend in Cuba."

Malinali held Cortez's hand tightly. "My love, what has happened?"

Cortez turned his face toward the shimmering blue of Lake Texcoco, unable to look at her. "A ship from Cuba arrived a few days ago. I just learned of it. It carried Catalina, several members of her family, and numerous maids to attend to her. Gonzalo de Sandoval met her. She believes, he says, that I have established a new empire, that I am the King of New Spain, and she has come to rule it with me as a queen."

He turned to look at her. "It is just this arrogance – this treasonous arrogance towards our Emperor Don Carlos - that my enemies in Cuba and Spain accuse me of, so that they can convince the emperor to remove me, thereby enabling them to take all of New Spain for themselves. Yet Catalina believes it. She always was as foolish as she was frail.

"Yet I have no choice but to welcome her as my wife because, legally and in the eyes of the Church, that is what she is. Our chance for happiness is over, my love. Just as it has finally been granted to us, it is taken away. And I cannot even ask for your forgiveness, because I do not deserve any."

Malinali closed her eyes and wept. She held her new baby in one hand and Cortez's hand in the other, and cried her soul out, while Cortez remained unmoving and silent. Finally, she opened her eyes to look into his. With the weakest of smiles, she said, "I suppose, when God has given me so much, it was foolish of me to ask for more."

Cortez's gaze was steady. "I will always love you. I will ensure that you are cared for. I will always be a father to our son. This home is yours and always will be. Catalina will live in the old palace where I work – and where I must now live, as well. She will arrive in two or three days. I wish to spend those days with you, but... I am not sure I deserve to."

Malinali held his gaze. "Do I deserve to?"

He nodded, and kissed her. They spent the next three days with each other, in pain and in passion, for they knew that those days were the last they would ever have together.

* * * * *

She awoke at dawn to see Cortez pacing the floor. When he noticed that she was awake, he hurried to her and fell into her arms. Then, with a sigh, he stood. "I did not want to disturb you," he said. "I went outside to ask Señor Jaramillo what he had heard. He informs me that Catalina and her retinue will be arriving before noon."

Malinali sighed. "We knew this moment would come."

Cortez resumed his pacing. "Her presence here is a doom for me, my Lady. I will soon have to return to Spain to defend myself to His Majesty Don Carlos. The New Spain that I have created is too rich a prize not to be feasted upon by the parasites who infest his court - and I am in their way. They will use Catalina's coming to be Queen of New Spain to convince His Majesty that I am a traitor against him. But even if she hadn't come here, they would find some other excuse."

He stopped his pacing to look at her. "This is a struggle that is mine alone. You cannot be a part of it. I must know that you are safe, that you are protected and secure. My future now is not certain. I must be certain of yours."

"I am always safe when I am beside you, my Captain."

He looked at her with sad intensity. "No longer. What will keep you safe is the adoration the native people of this land have for you -- and Spanish law."

"Spanish law?"

"Yes. Spain is a culture that bows down to rules and legalities, as much as to the Church. Why do you think that I brought a Royal Notary - someone who keeps a legal record for the King - with me from Cuba, Diego de Godoy? Señor de Godoy maintains his record of the legality of my every action. I must make certain that you and what property I can provide you with are protected under Spanish law, as a Spanish citizen."

Malinali looked at him curiously. "But I am not a Spanish citizen."

"Then you must become one." Cortez began pacing again. Malinali had never seen him so nervous.

"What are you trying to tell me, my Captain?"

"This is something that I cannot command of you. Perhaps you will decide to reside among the Tlaxcalans, who worship you. Many peoples of this land do, but the Tlaxcalans above all. Perhaps there you would rule as Queen, for that is what you were raised to be. Perhaps you might return to your native land of Paynala and assume your rightful throne. But if you choose not to, then you must allow me to grant you an *encomienda*, an estate with a *hacienda* where you can live securely and in comfort, with property providing you with wealth. But... but... I cannot do this directly, as you are not a Spanish citizen, with the ownership of such *encomiendas* recognized by Spanish law."

Malinali rose out of the bed to stand next to Cortez. "I no longer wish to be a queen, to rule over a kingdom. It is a life of treachery and intrigue, where you can trust no one. How long do you think I would be worshipped by the Tlaxcalans, once I ruled over them? How long would it take for *faccións*[257] to form, plotting for power and against the foreigner? And how can I go back and seize power in Paynala without creating hatred and dissention? No, my love, what I have become is much more than a queen, and it is wise for me to have that be."

She took his hand. "So, yes, an *encomienda* where I can live quietly and peacefully is what I would prefer." She caressed his face. "And now you should tell me what you are afraid to."

Cortez looked directly at her. "You need a husband. A Spanish gentleman of at least minor nobility, a *hidalgo* like me. One whom I can trust always to take care of you, who would guard you and our son with his life. A courageous soldier who has always fought bravely in battle and has never once betrayed my trust, and who would always love you with honor and dignity."

Her eyes widened in shock but she held his gaze. She knew who he meant. "I have seen the look in his eyes," Cortez continued. "It is there every time he sees you. It is not a look of lust, but of respect, of adoration. He is a man of few words, but of great strength of heart. I would entrust you to him, my Lady."

At that, she felt as if she were falling into his gaze. "I shall always love only you," she whispered.

He kissed her with such passion that she knew it would be their last. Finally, he said, "Do I have your permission to discuss this with Señor Jaramillo? For I would never do so without it."

Malinali stood erect and tall before Cortez, and replied... "Yes."

Cortez raised her hand to gently press it to his lips, then bowed and left what would be their bedchamber no more.

---

257 Factions.

* * * * *

She looked at him for the first time. She had noticed him, and spoken to him, many times before, but now she was actually looking at him. He was tall, although not as tall as Cortez, and more slender, not as muscular. He stood erect, his dark beard closely trimmed, his large dark eyes avoiding hers.

She could see he was intensely nervous. "Please look at me, Señor Jaramillo," she requested. He did so hesitantly. As she studied his eyes, she could see he was nervous but not afraid. She saw strength, but also a deep gentleness. Cortez was an excellent judge of men, and now she understood why he had chosen this man to guard her. These were the eyes of a man she could truly trust.

They were in her roof-top garden, she sitting, he standing. She offered him a cup of water. "Señor Jaramillo, we have never really talked before." She made sure that her face had a pleasant expression. "I'd like to know something about you."

He took a sip of water and nodded in thanks for it. "Like many of Captain Cortez's soldiers, I am from that part of Castile called Extremadura, from a small town, Fregenal de la Sierra. It is near Badajoz, the city that is home to Pedro de Alvarado and his brothers. My father, Alonso Jaramillo de Salvatierra, is a *hidalgo* who owns property there and is the town's *alcalde*[258]."

"How did you come to leave there and join Captain Cortez?" she asked.

He took another sip of water. He was beginning to relax, and his eyes lit up at her question. "Ah, Doña Marina, I grew up in a world that was suddenly new, a world that had become incredibly exciting. We Spaniards had discovered a New World across the great ocean, a world that no one before us knew existed. Extremadura is an ancient land, filled with Roman ruins from over a thousand years ago. Our ways were ancient and seemed never-changing. Then, in a moment, our old world became filled with new discoveries and possibilities.

"I grew up hearing many stories of people from Extremadura who made these discoveries. They left to settle in the colony of *La Española*[259] founded by the Great Admiral, Cristobal Colón[260], then began colonies themselves.

---

258 Mayor.
259 Hispaniola.
260 Columbus.

As a little boy, I heard everyone talking about a man from our neighboring village, Jerez de los Caballeros, who boasted that he would begin a new colony himself and do great things. A few years later, we learned that he had done just that. He was Vasco Nuñez de Balboa, who founded the colony of Panama and discovered a new sea, the South Ocean on the other side of the New World.[261]

"I was determined to become one of these discoverers, myself. To do so, I had to become a *caballero hidalgo*, a knight. My father had me trained to ride a horse and fight with a sword from a very young age. But to become a true *caballero* required more training than he could provide. When I told him of my desire, he sent me to live in the household of his good friend, Don Diego Gomez de Alvarado, who was a very important nobleman in Badajoz. It was the Year of Our Lord 1510, and I was fourteen years old. Don Diego was happy to welcome me, for all six of his sons[262] had left for La Española that year.

"Don Diego had me trained well, and saw that I learned well also, for he had a fine library filled with books on many subjects. I was able to become a true *caballero* and, when I was ready, Don Diego and my father gifted me with horses and arms so that I could join the Alvarado brothers, who were then in Cuba. When I arrived there in the Year of Our Lord 1518, they told me about the expedition that Captain Cortez was forming. To be a part of such an expedition of discovery was my dream, so I did not hesitate to become a part of it. And that is how I came to be here."

Malinali found that she was staring at him as she heard these words. She bade him sit down. "There is no need to keep standing in my presence," she said with a slight smile. After a moment of uneasy silence, she added quietly, "You know, of course, why I asked you here… and what it is that we must talk about."

He blushed a deep crimson. "Doña Marina, I… I…." He stopped to compose himself. Then he sat erect and looked directly at her. "Doña Marina, I would be foolish in the extreme if I thought I could in any small way replace Captain Cortez in your heart. I will always respect your love for him, and his for you. All I can offer to you is my devotion, my word to you as a *caballero* that I will devote my life to your happiness, your well-being, and your safety."

She studied him carefully, then asked, "Why do you wish to do so?"

---

261   The Pacific Ocean, in 1513.
262   The Alvarado brothers, Pedro, Gonzalo, Jorge, Gomez, Hernando, and Juan.

He did not hesitate. "Because I never imagined there could be a woman such as you. Such women are the stuff of legends and myths, the creation of poets. For a woman to be so heroic, so noble, is from a dream, not reality. Yet you are real, and I have seen who you are with my own eyes. That I..."

She raised her hand. "Señor Jaramillo... I respect your emotions for I know they are genuine. But I need to be honest with you. Worship is not what I need. I already have that, from millions of people in this land, and it is a very humbling experience. I do not wish to feel humility with you. It feels as if I am some statue high on a pedestal your Romans once made - Bernal showed me drawings from a book he has. That makes you distant from me. I do not want that. You are a fine man, a man of good soul, a man I can trust. What I need for you to also be is a good friend. Someone I can laugh with and enjoy their company. Do you think this is possible?"

His eyes opened wide as he stared at her and stammered, "That would be... I would be..." He stopped, and simply said, "Yes, Doña Marina, it is." And for the first time, she saw him smile. It was a broad, cheerful smile and she returned it.

"Good. We shall be friends," she said. "And then... we shall see."

* * * * *

Their friendship grew. She enjoyed listening to him explain the history of his land, of how it once was a Roman province called Lusitania, then ruled by a people he called 'Visigoths' who were Christians, then conquered by an alien people he called 'Moors,' who believed in an evil god named 'Allah.'

She had heard Bernal talk of these Moors, but never in so much detail. She learned that the Moors established a kingdom called a 'Caliphate' in a city called Cordoba that ruled all Spain except in the north. From there, Christian knights fought a war they called the *Reconquista*[263] that lasted centuries, slowly recapturing their land until, finally, the last of the Moors were defeated in a place called Granada "when Captain Cortez was a young boy,"[264] and the Moors went back to the land they came from, called 'Africa.'

Juan - for she thought of him as Juan, by then - could talk of this, and

---

263   Recapturing.
264   1492; Cortez was born in 1485.

the other things he knew, for hours. She'd had no idea he was a man of such learning. There was a shyness about him that she found calming, in contrast with the huge, vibrant personality of Cortez.

"Juan, why did it take the Christians hundreds of years to defeat the Moors - and only two to defeat the Aztecs?" she asked.

She liked the way he smiled with joy when she asked a good question. "Ah, for that you would have to ask Santiago himself! The reason must be, I am sure, that he chose Cortez to lead us – and you to guide him. For without our great captain-general, and without you, without *La Malinche*, we would never have succeeded."

She made a face. "Juan, I am not La Malinche to you, remember? But why Santiago? I know he is a great saint, but why, every time there is a battle, do the Spaniards cry out 'Santiago, and at them!'?"

"Saint Iago[265] was the great disciple of our Lord Jesus, and he is the patron saint of Spain. He appeared with a sword, riding a white horse, at the Battle of Clavijo[266], enabling a great victory against the Moors which began the *Reconquista*. Because of this, we call Saint Iago *Santiago Matamoros* - St. James the Moor-Killer. He is buried in the cathedral at Santiago de Compostela. Many thousands of people from all over Europe make a pilgrimage there every year."[267]

He gave her a gentle look of awe. "All of the soldiers believe that Santiago Matamoros has guided our victory here. They also believe that the Virgin Mary guided you to help us, through him. After all, Mary was his aunt - Santiago's mother was Mary's sister."

A startled Malinali clutched her crucifix.

* * * * *

She realized, after a time, that she was growing genuinely fond of him.

---

265 St. James, son of Zebedee, a fisherman in Galilee, and Salome, sister of the Virgin Mary (cf. John 19:25 with Mark 15:40). He and his brother John were asked by their cousin Jesus to be one of the Twelve Apostles.

266 Supposedly at Clavijo in northern Spain in 844 AD between the Christian King of Asturias Romiro I and Moslems led by the Emir of Cordoba. The historical battle was at Monte Laturce in 859, where Romiro's son Ordoño I and his Asturians destroyed a large Moslem army with 12,000 Moslem cavalry dead.

267 And continue to do so by the tens of thousands every year to this day. Santiago de Compostela (Field of Stars) is in the far northwestern corner of Spain in the province of Galicia.

They walked and talked for hours along the shore of Lake Texcoco. He was always courteous and a gentleman, but slowly he was able to relax around her, even to joke with her and make her laugh. She truly needed that.

She had not seen Cortez since they kissed goodbye. Bernal told her that he was always gone exploring now – in large part to be away, or so Bernal suspected, from Catalina.

Malinali had reconciled herself to what she knew was a necessity. With patience and effort, she banished regret and resentment from her heart. She prayed to the Virgin not to let her soul be poisoned by such feelings, but rather to have them be replaced by the deepest gratitude for the many blessings showered upon her life.

A day arrived when she realized that her prayer had been granted. As she strolled through her roof top garden the beauty of the plants and flowers overwhelmed her, as did the sheet of shimmering blue that was Lake Texcoco. She felt that a great weight had been lifted off her heart, and in its place was nothing but a peaceful happiness at being alive.

She was glad to see Juan when he came, and when, as always, he bowed and kissed her hand, she gave him a joyous smile. He returned the smile, but hesitantly.

"Are you well?" she asked. "You seem very nervous about something." Then she noticed that he was perspiring, even on this cool autumn day.

"Doña Marina, I had the opportunity to speak with Captain Cortez today," he said in a voice that seemed more high-pitched than usual. "He has just returned from an exploration in a region called Xilotepec. He told me that a soldier named Juan Galindo had discovered a valley of extraordinary beauty some thirty leagues[268] north of here. It is called *Tequisquiatlapan* (*tay-qwees-kwee-at-la-pan*), the Place of Bubbling Waters. The Captain went to see for himself, and he found it to be like magic, with many springs of warm water that bubbles. The soil is good for growing everything. He said it was perfect."

"Perfect for what?" she asked.

"Perfect for..." He stopped and swallowed. "Captain Cortez told me that this valley of many square leagues would be his gift of an *encomienda* to you and me, if we..."

---

268   About 90 miles.

He stopped again. Then he drew himself to his full height, standing almost at attention, and looked directly at her. "Doña Marina, as a citizen of Spain and a *caballero hidalgo*, I ask for your hand in holy matrimony. I cannot think of a greater honor for my life than your acceptance."

Malinali took both of his hands into hers. She looked up at him and felt the peace in her soul. She replied, "Señor Juan Jaramillo de Salvatierra, I accept." For the very first time they embraced.

They immediately made arrangements to visit Tequisquiatlapan. Juan rode a horse, and she was carried in a litter by Tlaxcalans who vied for the honor, accompanied by a horde of her worshippers. The valley was as magical as Cortez had described. For such a huge valley with such fertile soil, she was surprised by how few people lived there - and they were Otomis, who wandered and never settled in one place for long. They too worshipped her, and held celebrations when they learned that this was to be her home.

She and Juan had a great deal of fun, bathing in the springs of warm water filled with bubbles. Then they chose a spot at the western end of the valley to build their *hacienda*. They decided that it would be called *Hacienda Galindo,* in honor of the soldier, Juan Galindo, who had found this beautiful place for them.

When they returned to Tenochtitlan, a message from Cortez awaited them. "Please come to Orizaba," was all it said. Malinali suppressed a smile. She had heard about Cortez founding a city at the base of the big mountain, Citlatepetl[269], with the funny Spanish pronunciation of the Aztec name for the area, *Ahuilizapan*[270].

Again, Tlaxcalans carried her litter, over the Paseo de Cortez, as it was now called – the pass that Cortez had used between the Smoking Mountain and the Sleeping Woman to reach Tenochtitlan[271], past Cholula, with its memories of the terrible battle there[272], to the slopes of the giant mountain that the Tlaxcalans insisted on calling La Malinche, where an elaborate "La Malinche Dance" was performed in her honor.

When they arrived at the entrance to Orizaba, Cortez was there to greet the couple. He escorted them to a newly-constructed church, where a distin-

---

269   Now called Pico de Orizaba, Mexico's highest mountain at 18,490 ft.
270   Shining waters.
271   See Chapter Twenty-Two, "Between the Smoking Mountain and the Sleeping Woman."
272   See Chapter Twenty-One, "The Trap of Cholula."

guished-looking priest in a beautiful red robe stood waiting for them.

"Señor Jaramillo, Doña Marina," Cortez announced, "I have the honor to present to you Father Juan de Tecto, professor of theology at the Sorbonne University in Paris, and the personal chaplain to His Majesty the Emperor Don Carlos. Upon my request, he has consented to perform your ceremony of marriage, which shall take place here tomorrow."

Malinali could tell how proud Cortez was of himself by how broadly he smiled.

He wore that same smile during the banquet he held for them, that evening. The men seated around the table, she noticed, were mostly new officers -- she recognized few faces. While Cortez and Juan were engaged in an intense conversation, she had a chance to talk with Father de Tecto. But it was with difficulty for he spoke in a strange accent.

"Forgive me, Doña Marina, but I am not from Spain," he explained. "I am from a place called Flanders, in the same city where His Majesty Don Carlos was born - Ghent - although many years before.[273] As a result, my native tongue is Flemish, like His Majesty's, and my born name is Johan Dekkers. When I went to Paris and learned French, my name changed to Jean de Toit. When His Majesty made me his chaplain and I joined the Spanish Court, my name changed again, this time to Juan de Tecto."

"How is it that you left your Emperor and came here?" she wanted to know.

With a warm smile, he replied, "Ah, Doña Marina, the life of a Royal Court is not for me. Even when he was only the King of Spain, the lands over which Don Carlos ruled were vast - all of Spain, the giant islands of Sardinia and Sicily in the Mediterranean Sea, and all of southern Italy which is called the Kingdom of Naples. As his Confessor, I had to advise him on all of it! But then, when he became Emperor and his lands expanded to include Austria and many Germanic states in the middle of Europe, I knew that I had to leave."[274]

His eyes lit up. "Doña Marina, if you only knew of all the stories told at the Court about Captain Cortez's discoveries, and of his heroic achievements

---

273 1468. Charles V was born in 1500, the same year as Malinali. Flanders is now part of Belgium, and was ruled by Charles's father, Philip.

274 Charles inherited Spain from his mother's parents, Ferdinand of Aragon and Isabella of Castile, in 1516. He inherited the Hapsburg Empire from his father's father, Maximilian, and became Holy Roman Emperor, in 1519.

in liberating this extraordinary new land. After the physical liberation of the people of this land from the Aztec agents of Satan, I knew they would hunger for their spiritual liberation. So I begged His Majesty to allow me to come here, to bring the mission of the Lord Jesus to these people. Don Carlos is like a son to me, and so, with much reluctance, he let me go."

His eyes studied her. "Yet I must tell you that the talk at the Court is not all of Cortez. There are many stories told of a beautiful, intelligent, courageous woman of this land who accepted Christ into her heart, and who guided Cortez so that he could achieve his great victory. Hearing these stories, I thought they were fanciful. Such women are found only in dreams or in songs sung by troubadours. In my letter to Captain Cortez, telling him of my coming, I asked if this woman did indeed exist. He replied that I would have to come and see for myself. Now that I have, I can say that these stories are indeed true."

Malinali blushed.

"Doña Marina, I am on my way to Texcoco, where my mission will be founded. Captain Cortez, who is on his way to the coast, asked me to meet him here, and inquired, as a personal favor to him, whether I, as the Emperor's Chaplain, would marry you and Señor Jaramillo. It will be the greatest privilege for me to do so."

Tears formed in Malinali's eyes. "What can I say but thank you, Father?" was all she could reply.

Just then, Cortez stood up, goblet in hand. "Tomorrow will see a blessed event," he announced. "Tonight, I wish to inform you that Señor Jaramillo has accepted my invitation for appointment as *Regidor*[275] of Tenochtitlan, which is to be the capital of New Spain. This is, as you know, a position of great prestige and responsibility, commensurate with the remuneration it receives. I have assured Señor Jaramillo, however, that it requires only his periodic presence in our capital city, so that he and Doña Marina may enjoy their *encomienda* of the Valley of Bubbling Waters - my wedding present to them."

He raised his goblet. All of the other men stood and raised theirs, as well, while Malinali remained seated.

"Gentlemen!" Cortez called out. "To the happiness and long life of this blessed couple!"

---

275 Chief Magistrate.

* * * * *

Malinali had brought little Martín, whom Cortez insisted on cradling in his arms during the wedding ceremony. As he gazed upon how resplendent she looked in a pure white *huipil*, he whispered, "You have never been more beautiful." The regret and longing in his eyes was painful for her to see.

The ceremony was performed with solemn dignity by Father de Tecto. When it was over, Cortez returned baby Martín to her arms, and said to her and her new husband, "May God bless you both. I have done what I can to assure you of prosperity. As for my son, during those times when I must be away, I know you will always be there for him, Señor Jaramillo, as you will be for Doña Marina."

A wistful smile crossed his face. "However, before you depart to share the joys of matrimony at your *encomienda*, I would like for you to indulge me in a favor - that you accompany me on my journey to Coatzacoalcos."

Malinali looked at Cortez in puzzled astonishment.

Cortez immediately continued, "In truth, it is not I who requests this. It is your friend Bernal - Señor Diaz del Castillo - to whom I have given an *encomienda* there, along with Gonzalo de Sandoval and others whom you know. It is his fondest wish that you visit him, so that he may hold a *fiesta grande* in your honor. I am going to view Gonzalo's management of the area, and Bernal begged me to persuade you to come."

With a smile of relief, and a nod from Juan, Malinali happily agreed.

* * * * *

When she and Juan arrived at Bernal's *hacienda*, everything was decorated for a huge celebration. Bernal raced out to greet them, followed by Francisco de Lugo, Diego de Godoy, Gonzalo de Mexia, then Sandoval and Jeronimo Aguilar. She was overjoyed to see them all. "So this is where you have been hiding?" she asked them playfully. "In Coatzacoalcos?"

"Yes, we are the ones who came here," replied Bernal. "The rest of us are scattered all over New Spain and beyond. Pedro de Alvarado is south in Guatemala, and Cristobal de Olid is even farther south, we hear, a place called

Honduras. We may never, all of us, gather together again. But those of us here, Doña Marina, have joined to celebrate your matrimony to one of our most esteemed colleagues, Señor Jaramillo, and to give thanks again for all that you have done for us."

She could not recall when she'd had so much fun. There was music and dancing and wine, of which she drank a bit too much. She noticed that Cortez left early. When she danced with Juan, the look in his eyes expressed great joy and pride in being her husband. *Yes*, she told herself, *my life is blessed.*

The next morning, Bernal asked her, "Doña Marina, the kingdom of your father, Paynala, is in this region, is it not? The kingdom of which you should have been the queen. Do you wish to visit it?"

She shook her head. "No, my friend," she answered. "I am dead to them. Let it remain so."

"Very well," responded Bernal. "I know that you and Señor Jaramillo are anxious to depart for your Valley of Bubbling Waters, which I hear is exquisitely beautiful - but could I ask for something, before you leave?"

She laughed. "You know you can, my friend. And you should also know that you and Aguilar and everyone else are very welcome to visit us on any occasion."

"The native people here have learned that La Malinche is among them. Would you receive them, Doña Marina? There is a plaza in the town of Coatzacoalcos where you could do so. It would mean the world to them."

She agreed.

Shortly after the sun rose the following morning, she and Juan discovered an escort waiting to accompany them to the town. There were her Tlaxcalan bearers with her litter; there was Bernal and Aguilar; there was Sandoval, Francisco de Lugo… and Cortez himself, in full polished armor mounted on horseback.

Bernal stepped forward to say quietly, "We are here in your honor, Doña Marina."

When they reached the town, Malinali was stunned by the vast multitude of people crammed into the plaza. There were thousands. "Your legend is greater than you know, Doña Marina," said Bernal. "I thought just the people from this town and nearby villages would come, but word spread quickly. Many of the thousands you see here ran through the night from far away, just to be in your presence."

Then she heard Cortez's booming voice addressing the crowd. Startled, she thought, *Am I expected to translate?* But Aguilar explained that it was for him to translate now, "not La Malinche." With Aguilar's assistance, Cortez gave a short yet inspiring talk about salvation through Christ. Then he said, "And now may I present to you a Great Lady whom we all thank for the liberation of this land from the cruelty of the Aztec - La Malinche!"

Malinali stood still in front of the massive crowd, while Cortez and the others Spaniards backed their horses or stepped behind her.

At first, the faces in the crowd stared at her. Then one woman fell to her knees, with her hands clutched in prayer and began weeping, followed by another, and another. An elderly woman stepped forward to bend low and rub dirt from the ground on her forehead. Soon, hundreds were coming forward to do the same in obeisance to her, while hundreds more dropped to their knees, silently praying and weeping. There was no sound except the shuffling of feet, the soft moans of the praying, and the occasional snort of the horses.

Suddenly, there was a shriek – an ear-splitting shriek of utter terror. Malinali had never heard anything like it. It sounded like a soul being tortured in hell. It was coming from a woman at some distance in the crowd, a woman who wore an expensive robe and many jewels. She fell to her knees, then flat on her stomach. Her shrieks from hell were unrelenting, never-ending.

Then Malinali recognized her. It was her mother.

Her mother who had sold her into slavery. Her mother who had stolen her kingdom away, who had turned her from a princess to a slave girl.

Malinali ran towards her. She knelt down to look into her mother's face smeared with dirt and tears. She realized what had happened, that her mother had come to see this legend called La Malinche having no idea that it would be her long-lost, long-forgotten slave-girl daughter. And she knew what her mother was terrified of – that in revenge La Malinche could order with a nod of her head or flick of her hand her mother's execution by the Spaniards, execution or torturous worse.

Her mother looked up at her in wide-eyed horror. "*You?? You* are *La Malinche?!?*" her mother screamed at the top of her voice. But before she could start shrieking again, Malinali pulled her to her feet and embraced her with all her might.

"Mother… Mother… Mother…" she whispered in her ear. "No harm is going to come to you, you need have no fear."

Her mother's stiff body slowly relaxed a bit. Malinali relaxed her tight embrace and took her mother's face in her hands, gazing into her still-frightened eyes. "Mother, you must understand," she said, "I am now a Christian. I love you and I forgive you."

Her mother looked back at her in complete bewilderment. "What do you mean? How is that possible?"

"Mother, the God of the Christians and His Son Jesus teach that only through forgiveness and love can our souls be at peace. I have embraced the Son of God and His Holy Mother, and my soul is truly at peace. I truly do forgive you, Mother. And, Mother! How stupid it would be of me to hate you for what you did to me! It is thanks to you that I met Captain Cortez! It is thanks to you that I became, through the grace of God, La Malinche! It is thanks to you that I was able to make my father's dream come true, the dream of liberating this land from the Aztecs."

She pushed down on her mother's shoulders so that they both sank to their knees. "Mother – do you think my father's dream coming true was an accident? Just as God guided me to Captain Cortez, God guided you as well. It is God's will that you did what you did – and look what you achieved, Mother. I am freed from the worship of evil gods and obedience to evil Aztecs – and so are all the people of this land. I have been given a son by Captain Cortez. I have been given a great gentleman as a husband. And know this, Mother – if I were to be made Queen of Paynala, if I were to be made Queen of all of New Spain, I would refuse, for I would rather serve my husband and Captain Cortez than anything else in the world. There is only one thing I would ask of you, Mother."

Her mother was breathing deeply. "What is that?" she gasped.

"That you accept the love of God, of Jesus and Mary, into your heart, and become a Christian with all your soul."

Her mother closed her eyes and nodded yes.

Malinali embraced her. "I love you, Mother," said her daughter.

And the mother replied, "I love you, too, Malinali."

EPILOGUE

I t was nighttime. Streetlamps spread a mist of light into the Jardin de la Conchita, where Tim and Cindy Jorgensen had been listening for hours to Maria Consuelo tell her story. Now she was finished, and Tim and Cindy were speechless. They sat in stunned silence, until Cindy finally stammered, "That... that is the most extraordinary story I have ever heard -- and it's true? It's real history? It all really happened?"

Maria smiled gently. "Yes, it's all true. There are witnesses who wrote it down, men like Bernal[276]. It is one of the greatest stories of heroism in the history of mankind - and it is the tragedy of Mexicans that they have spit on it."

"But how is that possible?" Tim protested. "Why isn't La Malinche worshipped as the great heroine of Mexico?"

"She is to us, the *mestizos* who are her descendants - but not to the *criollos*, and they have always controlled Mexico."

"What are cri..." Tom paused. "Maria Consuelo, you were kind enough to enchant us all afternoon, and it is now dark and dinnertime. May we invite you to join us for dinner tonight? Please?"

"That would be quite nice. Just one moment." She withdrew a cell phone -- Tom and Cindy glanced at each other, noticing it was a Blackberry -- made a call, then talked for a minute in voluble Spanish. When she was done, she said to them, "That was my husband. Most evenings I cook for him, but he said he could fend for himself, and for me to enjoy myself."

"Wonderful!" exclaimed Cindy. "Let's go someplace special. What would you suggest?"

Thinking for a second, Maria responded, "There's the *Jardin del Pulpo*. That's a short walk from here. It means the Octopus Garden. They have the best seafood in Coyoacan." Cindy noticed that Maria was keeping a smile to herself. She wondered if it was because they played Beatles music there.

---

276 Bernal Diaz del Castillo's *Historia Verdadera de la Conquista de la Nueva España*, The True History of the Conquest on New Spain, is considered the definitive eyewitness account. Cortez rewarded him for his services with an *encomienda* in Guatemala (larger than the one in Coatzacoalcos), where he spent the rest of his life. Born in 1492, he died in 1585 at age 93.

As they walked out of the Jardin de la Conchita, Maria said, "Cortez had this garden park made for La Malinche, you know. It was to be a place of beauty and privacy for her Daily Mass."

They walked up Higuera Street to the Plaza Hidalgo. On the other side of the small plaza, Maria pointed out a long, one-story building painted in bright colors. "It's called the 'Casa de Cortez.' It was built in the mid-1700s on the site where Cortez had his first headquarters in the palace of the King of Coyoacan. It's now Coyoacan's city hall."

As they walked up Allende Avenue, they passed a side street named 'Moctezuma.' "Yes, it's for Montezuma - it's just a silly way to spell it," Maria observed. Next was Cuautemoc Street, "for the last of the Aztecs," noted Maria. Then they came to the Jardin del Pulpo, on the corner of Allende and a street named 'Malintzin.'

Cindy stared at the street sign.

Maria nodded. "The street is named for her. It's her Aztec name." Seeing Cindy's puzzled frown, Maria explained further." '-tzin' is a title of respect and honor in the Nahuatl language, just as 'Doña' is in Spanish. That the Aztecs called her 'Malintzin' shows how much they respected her.[277] Thus they called Cortez 'Malintzin-é' – since the ending '-é' means possession or ownership - or 'Master of Malina.' The Spanish pronounced this 'Malinche.' This is why *La Malinche* means that she was her own master, she owned herself. It is a title of ultimate respect."

They were given a table to themselves on the small veranda. It was a lively diner-type place, with long chrome tables packed with local families. They ordered shrimp tacos, Modelo Especial beers, and the house specialty, *pulpo en su tinta*[278].

"Maria, I have so many questions," said Tim. "What happened to Cortez? For that matter, what happened to Malinali?"

Maria smiled sadly. "Cortez was never the same after Malinali was gone from him. He went off on a crazy expedition to Honduras which broke his health, and he started drinking. His wife Catalina died of a heart attack, and

---

277   The Florentine Codex - so called because it is housed in the Laurentian Library in Florence, Italy -- is the only eyewitness account of the Conquest written by Aztecs in Nahuatl. It was compiled by a Spanish priest, Bernardino de Sahagún between 1540 and 1585. It never fails to append the honorific '-tzin' to 'Malina' (how they pronounced Marina.) The only other person in the Codex to unfailingly receive the '-tzin' honorific is Cuauhtemoc, the last emperor - Montezuma only occasionally.

278   Octopus cooked in its own ink.

his enemies in Spain accused him of murdering her - when everyone around her knew she was always fainting and constantly ill, and that both of her sisters, Leonor and Francisca, back in Cuba, had also died of heart attacks."

She paused. "Still, he did many good things. He did not create his own kingdom, which he easily could have done, but always remained loyal to the Spanish crown – a loyalty that was not returned. He rebuilt Tenochtitlan into a great European-style city which he named *Ciudad de Misheeko*, now known as Mexico City. He spent years establishing peace between all of the native peoples, and gave them a religion of peace - Christianity - to unify them. No longer were they fighting and killing and eating each other. Cortez created the people of Mexico as Mexicans, and the nation of Mexico. Without Cortez, Mexico and the Mexican people would not exist. Cortes is the Father of Mexico, just as La Malinche is the Mother of Mexico."

She paused again for a bite of her shrimp taco and a sip of Modelo Especial. "As any student of history would not be surprised to learn, as soon as he had done this and given the Spanish crown this incredible present of *Nueva España*, New Spain, all the rich and powerful people around Charles V conspired to take it away from him. And they succeeded. He could not persuade Charles V otherwise. 'Everything is thorns,' he said of his last years. He died in Seville, Spain, of an infection in 1547. He was 62."

"And Malinali" asked Cindy.

"She and Juan had a daughter, Maria. They built a beautiful hacienda - their *Hacienda Galindo* - which still exists and has been made into a luxurious resort hotel. It's famous for weddings and honeymoons - you should go there! It's near the town of San Juan del Rio in the state of Queretaro, about two hours drive north of here.[279]"

Cindy grabbed Tom's hand. "Let's do it - we have the time!" She looked back at Maria. "What about Martín, her son with Cortez?"

For an instant, Maria gave them an intense look, then went on. "When he was six[280], Cortez took him to Spain, where he grew up to be a Knight of the Order of Santiago, a high honor. Malinali never saw him again, for she

---

279   The Hacienda Galindo website is http://www.fiestamericana.com/portal/p/es_MX/FA/GAL/1/0/
      descripcionhotel/GALdescripcionhotel.html
280   1528.

passed away before he returned to New Spain many years later.[281] When he got here, the Spanish colonial authorities accused him of plotting to overthrow them but, no matter how much they tortured him, he proclaimed his innocence. Eventually, they let him go. He returned to Europe, where his son Fernando was becoming a well-known military officer. In time, Fernando Cortez moved his family to Veracruz, where he was appointed Principal Judge. Fernando's son moved to Coyoacan and became mayor. His descendants live in Coyoacan to this day."

Cindy and Tim stopped in mid-bite and stared at Maria.

"Yes," she said with a gentle smile. "I am one of them."

Cindy finally stammered, "Maria, you are like royalty!"

Maria's smile was rueful. "I am far from that. We don't tell anybody about ourselves - or else we would be reviled as hated *Malinchistas.*"

"Malin-what?" asked Tim.

Maria sighed. "It is a term that exposes the black hole at the center of the Mexican's soul, the bleeding wound of self-hatred at the core of his identity, the civil war that wages within his heart. Mexico will never have a future until that wound is healed."

She paused and glanced at her watch. "It is getting late. To understand such things requires an education in the history of Mexico. I have studied it for many years, but let me put it into a few words for you, and then I must go. For three hundred years, Spain ruled *Nueva España* as a colony -- like England ruled your America. A completely racist caste society developed. At the top were the *peninsulares,* who came to govern from Spain. Next to them were the *criollos,* Spaniards born in the colony who kept their blood pure-white and never mixed with native people. Then came the *mestizos* of mixed Spanish-Indian blood who, over time, became the majority of the population. And at the bottom of the castes were people of all of the native Indian tribes, without any Spanish blood at all.

"The ones who ran everything, of course, were the *criollos,* for the *peninsulares* from the Iberian 'peninsula' of Spain were few, and content to let things be handled while they lived in idle luxury. The racist *criollos* treated the

---

281   Some believe Malinali died as early as 1529, but eyewitnesses saw her later, such as at Cholula in 1537. Letters retrieved in archives say she passed on in 1550. The most respected of all Mexican historians, Joaquim Garcia Icazbalceta (1824-1894) in his 1883 biography *Doña Marina,* says she died "rich and respected, the wealthiest woman in *Nueva España.*" Martin Cortez returned to New Spain in 1563.

mestizos as sub-human, and *Los Indios* as even worse. The resentment against them built up, until Napoleon gave it a chance to explode."

"Napoleon? In France?" Tim interjected. "What does he have to do with Mex..."

Maria's raised eyebrows told him to just listen. "Napoleon invaded Spain in 1808, and replaced Ferdinand VII with his brother, Joseph Bonaparte, as King. All of Spain disintegrated into chaos and rebellion, which meant that Spain really had no government to exercise authority over *Nueva España.* And so... Well, do you remember that we walked here through the Plaza Hidalgo?"

They nodded.

"That is named for a Catholic priest, Father Miguel Hidalgo. He was from a small town called Dolores in the state of Guanajuato, far to the north of here. Even though he was a *criollo,* he identified with the misery of the *mestizos* and Indians, and he organized a rebellion. He was joined by..." She pointed to the street sign on the corner that read *Avenida de Allende.* "...Ignacio Allende, a *criollo* captain in the Spanish Army. At midnight on September 15, 1810, Hidalgo had the church bells rung, and called upon the people who gathered in the Dolores plaza to revolt.

"That was Hidalgo's famous *Grito* - the Cry - for independence from Spain, and for freedom for *mestizos* and *Indios.* The next day, the revolt began, which is why September 16 is our Independence Day."

Cindy frowned. "I thought it was May 5ᵗʰ, *Cinco de Mayo...*"

Maria laughed out loud. "*Cinco de Mayo* is just an excuse for Americans to eat bad Mexican food, drink margaritas, and have a party. It has nothing to do with our independence, and it isn't a big celebration here. It commemorates the Mexican Army's victory over an invasion of French at the Battle of Puebla in 1862."

She wiped tears of mirth from her eyes. "I'm sorry. So... Hidalgo started the rebellion and soon had a vast army of poorly armed undisciplined peasants. But even 100,000 of them stood no chance against trained soldiers, so the rebellion was crushed, and Hidalgo, along with Allende, executed. When Napoleon was kicked out of Spain in 1814, Ferdinand VII became King again, and his colonial army was able to easily put down any pockets of rebels that emerged.

"The officer in charge of killing the rebels - which he did with incredible brutality - was a rich *criollo* named Agustin Iturbide. But in 1821, he made a deal with the rebels! If they joined him, he said, their joint forces could take Mexico City and declare *Nueva España* independent. It was a trick, of course. The joint forces did take the capital, and a new nation was declared on September 28, 1821, to be called *El Imperio Mexicano* - the Mexican Empire - and Iturbide crowned himself Emperor Agustin I! Yes, like Napoleon, at his coronation he placed the crown on his own head.

"The *criollos* had taken over the rebellion from the *mestizos,* and seized control of the country totally for themselves. It was a phony 'independence,' and the *mestizos* were of course left to live in the dirt, as always. The *criollos* began to fight amongst themselves for power, and a general, Antonio Lopez de Santa Anna, seized power from Iturbide, who fled to Europe. But the country, an uncontrollable mess, was falling apart. Santa Anna decided that he needed a *chivo expiatorio*, a *cabeza de turco*, what you call a 'scapegoat' or 'whipping boy' as an excuse to focus the blame for Mexico's problems away from himself and the *criollo* elite.

"He found it in a book written by a Cuban priest who knew nothing about Mexico and lived in Philadelphia - yes, your city in Pennsylvania. There was a publisher there who printed books in Spanish.[282] The priest, whose name was Felix Varela, hated the Spanish with an anti-Christian passion, and wanted Cuba to be independent, like Mexico. He never set foot in Mexico in his life and, against all of the historical evidence, he wrote a pervert's book of pornography that was invented out of his hate-filled imagination. It was called *Xicotencatl,* and Varela was too cowardly to put his name on it, so the author was listed only as 'Anonymous.'[283]

"For three hundred years, *La Malinche* was worshipped by the *mestizos* and *Indios* as their Liberator and Savior - but now, because the *criollos* needed a scapegoat, they stole her from us. And of course, because the *criollos* are so afraid of their manhood, the scapegoat had to be a woman, making her out to be the Eve who sinned against the Mexican nation - a nation that hadn't even

---

282   William Stavley Publishing.
283   Published in 1826. The plot was made up by Varela with no historical basis whatever - Xicotencatl the Younger noble and virginally pure, Cortez nothing but a monster, La Malinche an amoral traitorous villainess who sleeps with everybody. It is this image the *criollo* intellectual and political elite have striven to drive into the Mexican mind since the 1820s. The purpose of Varela's book was to demonize the Spanish and anyone who cooperated with them. It was set in Mexico and not Cuba only for deflecting attention away from Varela as a Cuban. Yet Santa Anna seized on the book's fictional story, pretending it was true as a political expedient.

existed until 300 years after she lived - the traitor who betrayed the Aztecs, a people of the most depraved cannibalistic evil imaginable, in favor of the hated Spanish, who brought Christianity to our land, who liberated us from the Aztecs!

"Santa Anna embraced the lies of this Cuban pervert, and claimed that all of the woes of the new country of Mexico were somehow the fault of a woman who lived centuries before. And it has been that way ever since. One of the most heroic, noble, and courageous women in history is called a whore by the *criollos*. They even call Mexicans *hijos de la chingada* - sons of the whore.[284]

"Well, maybe they deserve to despise themselves. They can hate themselves all they want. But the *criollos* demand that *we* hate ourselves, the *mestizos* who are the product of Cortez and La Malinche and wouldn't exist except for them. They dare to call us *Malinchistas*, a term of contempt meaning 'traitor to Mexico.' There is nothing more on this Earth that I am prouder to be than a *Malinchista*, an admirer and worshipper of La Malinche!"

At that, Maria burst into tears. Cindy held her hand and Tim gave her a napkin to dry her eyes.

"If you only knew the misery of this country," she said at last. "The source of Mexico's misery and poverty is the inability of its people to be proud of their country, to be proud of its history and of how it was founded by Christian heroes, by love and liberation from evil. Unhappily, in the moment of Mexico's birth as a free country, its rulers and elite spat on it. And now Mexico spits on itself. It is such a tragedy..."

When her sobs stopped, she sighed and said, "I must be going. I hope I have not troubled you with my story."

Tim grasped Maria's hand, along with Cindy. "Maria Consuelo, we will never forget your story as long as we live."

She nodded in thanks. "Perhaps, then, you would care to walk with me for a few blocks in the direction of my home. There is something I would like to show you."

"Of course," they said.

They walked along the street of Malintzin for a ways, then up to the next street above it, which Tim and Cindy noticed was named Xicotencatl. "Many people think it is named for the hero of Varela's book, the son of the King of

---

284   The famous insult to his countrymen by Mexican writer Octavio Paz in *Labyrinth of Solitude* (1950). Paz epitomized the profound misogynous fear of women that permeates *criollo* male society.

Tlaxcala, who tried in every way to prevent Cortez from liberating Tlaxcala from the Aztecs," said Maria. "A perfect example of how morality is turned upside down in Mexico – traitors are heroes and heroes are traitors, evil is good and good is evil, and liberation from human sacrifice is a bad thing."

"Sounds like George Orwell could have written a Mexican version of *1984*," Tim mused.

"But we prefer to think that this street is named for King Xicotencatl," Maria continued, "who realized that Cortez and La Malinche could save his country from the Aztecs. He became a devout Christian, remember, and his daughter married Pedro de Alvarado."

"What happened to him?" Cindy asked.

"Pedro de Alvarado founded the colony of Guatemala. The Mayans combined him with one of their deities and worship him as the god *Maximón* (*mah-shee-mohn*). There are shrines to Maximón in Mayan villages all over Guatemala to this day."

They walked along quietly until they came to a small wooded park, the *Jardin Xicotencatl*. "La Malinche is still worshipped all over this country, mostly in the small Indian and *mestizo* villages, where dances and ceremonies are performed in thanks to her and Cortez for bringing the True Faith to their land," Maria told them. "The villagers who live on the slopes of *Pico de la Malinche*[285] pray to her for rain and good harvests. All the local people who live in sight of the giant mountain Iztaccihuatl[286] think the Sleeping Woman is La Malinche, to whom they pray for protection."

One part of the park was brightly lit. As they walked toward it, Maria continued. "But such things would never be allowed in the cities, at least not publicly. Years ago, in the 1980s, our president then, Lopez Portillo, to win the favor of the *mestizos*, commissioned a statue in bronze by the famous sculptor Julian Martinez y Maldonado. It was of Cortez and La Malinche presenting their son, baby Martín, to the world as the First Mestizo. When it was placed in the Plaza de Hidalgo in front of the Casa de Cortez, there were riots and demonstrations, with thousands of people coming from all over Mexico City to protest for its removal. So it was taken away. Hardly anyone knows that it is hidden away here, in this unknown little park."

Suddenly they were in front of the monument. "Why, it's magnificent!"

---

285   14,435 feet high. It is located north of Puebla.
286   17,244 feet. East of Mexico City.

Tim exclaimed.

"It's so heroic, yet so... human," was Cindy's comment. "This is worthy of them."

"The day will come when Mexico itself will be worthy of them," Maria said firmly. "We cannot be proud of our country until we are proud of them. Can you imagine what it is like to be ashamed of your country's founders, instead of proud? You Americans have every right to be proud of your country's founders, like George Washington or Thomas Jefferson. Can you imagine how tortured you would be if all of the teachers and elite intellectuals insisted that your country was founded by a murdering invader and a traitorous whore?"

She looked into their eyes. "The founding myth of this country is a lie, a monstrous, evil, anti-Christian lie. At least now, the two of you know the truth. The Father and Mother of Mexico were heroic Christians. The founding of this country, its liberation from Aztec evil and receiving the salvation

of Christianity, is a saga worthy of an epic poet like Homer. I am no Homer, but still it is my dream to write a book of this saga, so that people will know the truth, so that Mexicans will be proud instead of ashamed of themselves, so that the civil war in Mexico's soul will end, so that this statue may come out of hiding and be placed in the sun of Plaza Hidalgo, where Mexicans can place flowers of gratitude upon it."

"Oh, Maria Consuelo! You must write that book! Please!" begged Cindy. Tim nodded vigorously in assent.

"I am trying, but I am afraid to come out of the shadows," Maria replied. "You have no idea how hatred for *Malinchistas* has warped the minds of Mexicans. It is why I go to *Casa Colorada*, where you first saw me, to pray to La Malinche for strength."

"Perhaps if your book were published in the United States first..." Tim mused. "I think I could help you there. I have contacts with publishers - even movie producers. Your book would make a fabulous Hollywood blockbuster movie."

Maria smiled grimly. "The movie would cause riots. There would be death threats, and theaters burned down. The truth about La Malinche would be too terrifying, too threatening - especially for all of those Mexican men who have to blame their inadequacies on a woman. It takes courage to face the truth."

Cindy took Maria's hand. "And it takes even more courage to write the truth. I know you have that courage, Maria. If there is anything we can do to help, we will do it. Maria..." Cindy brushed tears from her cheeks. "Maria, it has been such an honor to meet you." Cindy pointed to the statue of La Malinche. "She would be proud of you, Maria."

Tom asked, "What will your book be called? Do you have a title for your book - and for the movie?"

"Yes," Maria answered. "It will be called *The Jade Steps.*"

ABOUT THE AUTHOR

Jack Wheeler has led two careers for many years, one in the field of adventure and exploration, the other in philosophy and geopolitics.

At the age of 12 he was honored in the White House by President Eisenhower as the Youngest Eagle Scout. He climbed the Matterhorn in Switzerland at age 14, was adopted into a clan of Amazon headhunters and swam the Hellespont at age 16, killed a man-eating tiger in Vietnam at age 17, started his first international business (exporting cinnamon from South Viet Nam) at 19, is in the Guinness Book of World Records for the northern-most parachute jump (onto the North Pole), has led dozens of expeditions to the world's remotest regions including 21 times to the North Pole, taken elephants over the Alps retracing Hannibal's route, and has three first contacts with tribes never contacted by the outside world before (in New Guinea, the Amazon, and the Kalahari).

His book, *The Adventurer's Guide*, was described by Merv Griffin as "the definitive book for anyone wishing to lead a more adventurous life." He has been described by *The Wall Street Journal* as "the real-life Indiana Jones."

In the 1980s he conducted a series of extensive visits to anti-Soviet guerrilla insurgencies in Nicaragua, Angola, Mozambique, Ethiopia, Cambodia, Laos, and Afghanistan, and to democracy movements in Eastern Europe and the Soviet Union, as the unofficial liaison between them and the Reagan White House. Based on his experiences, he developed the strategy for dismantling the Soviet Empire adopted by the White House known as the "Reagan Doctrine." It worked.

Wheeler holds a Ph.D. in Philosophy from the University of Southern California with a specialty in Aristotelian Ethics. As the editor of *To The*

Point (www.tothepointnews.com), he has written over a thousand articles on geopolitics, world history, and the political and philosophical issues of our day. As the founder of *The Freedom Research Foundation*, he advises a number of Congressional offices in Washington and international corporations on geopolitical strategy.

The Jade Steps – written to help bring peace to the civil war waging within the soul of Mexico – is his first novel.